guilty pleasure

KEVIN DICKSON
& JACK KETSOYAN

[Imprint]
MAKE YOUR MARK

[Imprint]
MAKE YOUR MARK

A part of Macmillan Publishing Group, LLC
175 Fifth Avenue, New York, NY 10010

Library of Congress Control Number: 2017957955

ISBN 978-1-250-12227-8 (hardcover) / ISBN 978-1-250-12226-1 (ebook)

Our books may be purchased in bulk for promotional, educational, or business
use. Please contact your local bookseller or the Macmillan Corporate and
Premium Sales Department at (800) 221-7945 ext. 5442 or by e-mail at
MacmillanSpecialMarkets@macmillan.com.

Book design by Natalie C. Sousa

Imprint logo designed by Amanda Spielman

First Edition, 2018

1   3   5   7   9   10   8   6   4   2

Blinditembook.com

The scandals within
Like buried treasure
Remain hidden deep
Beyond any measure
But if knowing the truth
Is required for your leisure . . .
Ask, but remember:
A little white lie
Is the guiltiest pleasure

For Lindsey Kelk
(xo)

CHAPTER 1

THE WINDSHIELD WIPERS FOUGHT TO clear the blinding waves from the glass before the pouring rain immediately blurred Wilshire Boulevard back into a watery mosaic. Nicola slowed the Beemer down to twenty-five and moved to the right lane, sending a wave of dirty spray over a homeless woman sheltering from the storm at a bus stop.

"I'm sorry," Nicola mouthed, trying to make eye contact with the woman's blinking, scowling face as she flicked water off her soaked, dirty puffer with angry resignation. Nicola parked the car and opened her center console, digging under the stack of CDs in search of the emergency money she kept there. She closed her fingers around a bill that turned out to be a twenty and opened her passenger window, rain instantly spattering her passenger seat. She waved the woman over, extending the bill. The woman scampered quickly to the car and snatched the twenty from her fingers.

"I'm so sorry. Happy new year."

The woman flipped her off and tucked the bill into a pocket.

I asked for that.

Waze beeped at her from her phone, informing her that five minutes had been added to her trip. Nicola grimaced. She could not be late. Her movie-star client (and ex-boyfriend) Seamus O'Riordan was getting out of rehab in two days, and she was due to present her press plan to his agent and manager at two thirty. Waze now said she was going to arrive at 2:27. How could it possibly take her twenty-seven minutes to go three miles?

Even though her assistant, Alicia, and the rotating crew of interns at her publicity agency, Huerta Hernandez, had been given time off between Christmas and New Year's, her boss, Gaynor Huerta, had insisted that Nicola work every day, deflecting press inquiries about Seamus's dramatic and near-fatal overdose on a movie set in Ojai three months earlier and devising a meticulous step-by-step media cover-up for his return.

Miraculously, the media had accepted their fabricated story that Seamus's injury on the movie set had been more serious than doctors had realized. The trades had covered his departure from the movie in a businesslike way, and the tabloids hadn't suspected the cover-up. The current story line was that Seamus was recovering with family in Scotland—a risky lie, since Seamus didn't have much family left.

"The death of journalism makes our job a little easier," Gaynor had crowed after they were sure the media had swallowed the story. Even after an early slip up, where they'd switched from a torn ACL to a rotator cuff injury. Nobody had noticed.

With the news cycle at its usual fever pitch, the story had been digested and forgotten in just one stressful week. Nic occasionally wondered if Seamus had any idea how hard they'd worked on his behalf, and each time, she mentally chin-checked herself for thinking about him at all.

Seamus is a liar. Seamus is a junkie. Seamus is my client.

This litany had been her glue since the last time she had seen him, at his first rehab facility, in Malibu. She tried never to think, *Seamus broke my heart.*

She nervously twisted her fingers around the nylon bracelet he'd sent her for Christmas, from the second rehab place, this time in Seattle. She had decided that she would cut it off tonight, but she wanted to wear it to the meeting. *For luck.*

Two nights ago, after Gaynor had made her decline all New Year's Eve party invitations, she and Gaynor spent the night role-playing the upcoming meeting.

Gaynor had relished her chance to impersonate Seamus's English manager, Tobin Freundschaft, and his notoriously thorny agent, Jon Weatherman. Gaynor had dressed in a man's black suit, her thick black hair clipped to her head and hidden beneath a fedora. At times, Nicola had wondered if she was preparing for a meeting or a community theater production of *Chicago*.

For more than eight hours, they had sat in the Huerta Hernandez offices, snacking on a fruit plate and drinking champagne as Gaynor hurled increasingly bizarre questions and insults at Nicola, trying to ruffle her.

"Ay, malparida" was how most of the questions began. Nicola argued that Tobin and Weatherman wouldn't use language like that in a meeting. "You'll be lucky if they're that polite," Gaynor had cackled before launching into another round of preposterously rude test questions, like "Are you sure there's no sex tape of you and Seamus?" or "How the hell is a junior publicist from Buttfuck, Ohio, going to bail out one of the world's biggest movie stars?"

By the time they'd wrapped, the new year was five hours old, and Gaynor had finally permitted Nicola to check her phone. The long list of notifications had made her teary: texts from her mom and brother; multiple drunk texts from her BFF, Billy, and his new boyfriend, Seamus's former minder, Bluey; and finally, a long, heartfelt text from her roommate, Kara.

Hey Boo, I stayed in tonight hoping the dragon would send you home early. I even stole some Johnnie Walker Blue from Amber's so we could toast. I'll take a rain check on it, we can toast tonight. But I did a lot of thinking, Nico. I'm real sorry I let you down last year, I got out of my head and I really hurt you. Never again girl. I got your back. Thanks for standing by me and I promise to fuck up less this year. Promise! Love you.

Gaynor, who could sense drama a mile off, saw the tears spring into Nicola's eyes. She snatched her phone out of her hands.

"Careverga Seamus!" she cried, her glee visibly deflating when she saw that the text was from Kara. She still read the whole text.

"Seems like Miss Jones is still feeling *muy, muy* guilty for trying to sell you out," Gaynor teased.

Nicola's shoulders slumped. Forgiving Kara for trying to sell photos of Seamus and Nic to the tabloids had been one of the hardest things she'd ever had to do. As her mom had pointed out, if it weren't for Kara's meddling, Seamus would have continued lying and denying his drug habit to Nicola. Sometimes her mom was way too obsessed with the silver linings in situations, but this time, Nicola had clung to her words. Good had come out of Kara's selfishness. And she had been nothing but apologetic ever since. They'd arrived at a fragile peace that was getting easier day by day.

As the Global Talent Management offices appeared between swats of the wipers, Gaynor's voice swam into her head. "These people are the big time; they'll eat you alive." That was how she'd sent Nic off to this meeting, after losing the battle to accompany her. Nic was Seamus's publicist. It was time to put on her big-girl shoes and face his legendarily difficult team on her own.

Nicolita. Gaynor's voice echoed inside her skull. *These people are not human. They are wolves, and they will rip out your throat for sport. You need me there. They are scared of me. I will be your human shield.*

"Cállate, Gaynor!" she said aloud, and the voice in her head fell silent. She smiled. Even the fake Gaynor in her head responded better to Spanish, which she was learning slowly, through osmosis. She was currently fluent when it came to obscenities and fat shaming. *Thanks, boss.*

Reaching the Global Talent building, Nicola slowed, squinting to locate the entrance to the parking garage. Before she could find it, a gunmetal Tesla materialized out of the rain, nearly slammed into her, then skidded into a driveway beneath the building. Nicola followed suit, realizing too late that she had pulled into the employees' driveway and did not have a keycard. She began to reverse into the street when headlights filled her rearview mirror and she became trapped. The car behind her began to honk loudly. The security bar in front of Nicola went up. Frazzled, she threw the Beemer into drive and entered the parking garage, her wipers scraping loudly. She angrily turned them off. All of the available parking spots were marked RESERVED with a name plaque on the wall in front. She couldn't see any visitor parking. Ahead of her the driver of the Tesla, a generically handsome blond, got out of his car and pointed to a parking spot to her left. He then urgently mouthed, "Hurry up."

The driver of the other car started blasting his horn again, long, braying shots of sound that echoed around the small garage. Through her rain-speckled rear window, Nicola could make out maniacally flailing arms and anger. She followed Tesla guy's instructions and pulled into a solitary space that she finally saw was marked VISITOR.

Killing the engine, Nicola gathered the off-white Birkin satchel purse that Gaynor had forced her to bring. "Purses are power" was one of her favorite sayings. Standing slowly, she straightened the front of her black Calvin Klein jacket and pants and scoured the parking garage warily for angry car guy. She locked her car and looked for the elevator. Tesla guy appeared from behind a post and raised a hand, telling her to wait, his eyes widening for emphasis.

A car door slammed and Nicola saw the guy who'd been honking at her get out of his car and stalk toward an elevator bank. She slumped. It was Weatherman. He was talking loudly into a Bluetooth earpiece.

"I don't fucking care about the script," he barked. "I don't fucking care about story arcs. I want you to tell me about the back end, and I want you to guarantee two sequels, and I want you to tell me five fucking minutes ago. Now, quit wasting my time and get some fucking answers."

He vanished into the elevator lobby. When the door closed Tesla guy dropped his hand.

"Hey, I'm sorry," he called out across the garage. "But you did not want to get into that elevator."

Nicola walked toward him.

"Thanks, I think," she said, her brows knitting.

"That was me who buzzed you in."

"Huh?"

The guy stepped out from behind the pole. "I raised the security bar for you."

"Oh, then definitely thanks," Nicola said with a bigger smile. The guy stood there, as if he was waiting for something. "Anyway, I have to get inside fast. I'm here for a meeting."

"I'm Timothy," he said, extending his hand and still not moving. Nicola switched the heavy Birkin, filled with folders and her laptop, to her other hand and gave his a firm shake.

"I'm Nicola," she said casually. "Hey, do you know which floor the conference room is on?"

"You're Nicola Wallace, from Huerta Hernandez?"

She nodded.

"You're the ex-girlfriend, new publicist," he said slowly. "I'm in your meeting. I'm Weatherman's assistant agent for Seamus."

"I'm fine with just 'publicist,'" Nicola said quickly. "Let's get to the conference room."

In her almost two years in Los Angeles, Nicola had developed a mild, persistent irritation for elevators in three-story buildings. She reached for the door to the fire stairs.

"Fire stairs are always locked," Timothy said as her hand jiggled the handle. "Security precaution."

Nicola raised an eyebrow. "You're not supposed to lock fire doors," she said.

"You wouldn't believe how hard people try to get inside this building," Timothy said breezily, pushing the elevator call button.

"I'd probably find that easier to believe than locking a fire escape," Nicola said, stepping into the elevator, vowing to remain silent for the short ascent to the building's first floor.

The doors opened onto a hushed reception area. Nicola approached the brushed-metal-and-glass counter, where a model-looking young woman stared at her phone. As Nicola leaned in to announce herself, Timothy stepped between her and the desk.

"I have Nicola Wallace from Huerta Hernandez with me for the two thirty."

The receptionist didn't acknowledge him, either.

"Follow me," he instructed, taking long strides down a corridor flanked by glass walls revealing sparsely decorated offices, each containing a desk, a MacBook, and two visitors' chairs that she recognized from design catalogs. People sat at their desks, talking into headsets and staring at their screens. It reminded Nicola of a job she'd had at a call center for five hellacious months, in Dayton, Ohio, a lifetime ago.

As they neared the end of the hallway, Nicola saw a big glass wall with a small sign that read CONFERENCE ROOM 1. Weatherman sat at the head of the table. She could also see several other men, all in black suits with white shirts. Some wore ties. It looked like a Tarantino movie. Seamus's amiable manager, Tobin, waved as she walked in. They'd met once before, briefly, during happier times.

Nobody else moved. There was also one suited figure with their back to the door. Nicola did a double take at Crystal Connors's give-away severe, colorless ponytail. Crystal was the cutthroat veteran publicist whom Seamus had fired in favor of Nicola. Next to her was a stunning woman in an elegant strappy red Elie Saab mid-length dress, jet-black curls falling down her back. She was vaguely familiar, but Nicola couldn't place her.

Timothy opened the door and waved her inside before she had a chance to recalibrate. *Why is Crystal here?*

"Morning, everyone," Timothy said perkily. "I have Nicola Wallace from Huerta Hernandez with me. Are we all here?"

"What took you so long?" spat Weatherman.

"I'm sorry, Mr. Weatherman," Timothy said. "I was just making sure Miss Wallace found the meeting okay."

"I hope that Miss Wallace doesn't need your help to do her job," Weatherman said, his voice dripping with contempt as he eyed her up and down. "Miss Wallace, would you care to introduce yourself, or are you happy for Thompson here to be your assistant all day?"

Nicola groaned inside. The most powerful agent in Hollywood already hated her. *Great*. She blinked as slowly as she could and met Weatherman's gaze dead-on.

"Hello, Mr. Weatherman," she said coolly. "Hello, everyone. I'm Nicola Wallace from Huerta Hernandez PR. Tobin, it's good to see you again. Timothy I already met." Nicola stopped her gaze on the woman next to Crystal.

The woman opened her mouth to speak, and Crystal put a hand up, stopping her. Weatherman nodded at a seat at the opposite end of the table. Nicola slid into the mid-century leather chair as grace-fully as she could. The silence around the table was deafening. She locked eyes with the young man next to Timothy. After an awkward beat, he mumbled that he was Timothy's assistant. He didn't give a name.

"Thank you for coming, Nicola," said Tobin, a craggily handsome Viking with natural gray-blond hair and eyes like gravel. He gestured offhandedly at the bespectacled young man next to him. "This is my assistant."

Nicola moved her gaze around the table, past Jon Weatherman, until it rested upon Crystal, who was typing furiously into her phone and clearly making her wait for any kind of acknowledgment.

"Hi, Crystal," Nicola deadpanned. "I wasn't aware of any business that might require your presence here today."

Crystal stood, slowly, like a vampire after a long sleep, and extended her hand.

"Shake my damn hand, Wallace. Didn't that third-world madam teach you basic manners?"

Nicola stood and reached for Crystal's hand, but as their hands got close, Crystal suddenly sat down and left her hanging. Without skipping a beat, Nicola moved her hand to the woman seated next to Crystal. "And you are?"

The beautiful woman stood, surprising Nicola with her height. "I'm Bette Wu," she said. "I was on *Doombringers* on the CW."

Nicola didn't watch that show. She shrugged.

"I'm also an Olympic gold medalist? Martial artist?"

"Uh, nice to meet you." Nicola raised an eyebrow and looked from Jon to Tobin to Timothy. Nobody said anything.

Nicola counted to ten in the silence.

"Unlike everyone else at this table," Crystal finally said in a low snarl, "I have more than one client. Can we get this dog and pony show on the road? Are you waiting for Seamus to tell you what to do? Is the tail still wagging the dog around here?"

"Can it, Crystal," Weatherman snapped. "Nobody likes a sore loser."

"Listen, Weatherman," she said, her voice dripping with venom. "I wasn't the one who fired my agency. I wasn't the one who couldn't even control my client, my junked-out boozehound action star, long enough to get through a simple overdose."

"No, that would be me," said Tobin, pressing his palms flat against the glass tabletop. "I failed to see that problem on the horizon. And I'll ask you, kindly, to try to be professional when discussing our client."

"That *was* a professional assessment, and you know it," Crystal seethed.

"Okay, everybody." Timothy stood and opened his arms to include the table. "Enough of this. Let's acknowledge that this is a difficult time and a unique situation. Let's get started." He tapped his assistant on the shoulder. "My assistant is going to keep us on track. What's the first topic?"

The assistant nervously looked at a sheet of paper on the table in front of him and then began to speak, his voice cracking. "Meeting January second. Purpose of meeting. Seamus O'Riordan—"

"Get to the first fucking topic," Weatherman snapped.

"F-f-first topic is general roundup from Mr. Freundschaft."

Opening a leather folder on the desk, Tobin read from a neat printout. "Seamus has almost completed his stint in rehab," he began. "We have had very limited contact with him during this process. From talking to his doctors, it seems that he has been successful with his—"

"Get to the point, Tobin," Weatherman said. "I don't give a fuck about what his doctors are saying. Is he ready to work?"

Tobin shook his head slowly. "Yes and no, Jon. But we have to respect his recovery and not put too much pressure on him. He needs time."

"Don't give me that shit, Tobin. Don't even try it. That little overdose cost each of us over ten million dollars. We both wrote some pretty painful refund checks. What I need from you is Seamus's signature on a contract for a blockbuster before the end of the week."

"That's not how it is going to work this time, Jon," Tobin said, his British cadence very measured. "We both know that if Seamus feels like he's being forced to do something, he'll bolt."

Nicola hated how intrigued she'd become in this conversation.

Weatherman pushed his chair back from the desk and turned himself fully toward Freundschaft. "Tobin, we've talked. And you promised me that this time around, we'd be working with a new, improved Seamus. A Seamus who is happy to be a brand, who takes advice and lets his team do the decision-making. Is that no longer the case?"

"Hey, Jon," Tobin began, his tone threatening. "If you don't want to be in the Seamus business anymore, let me know right now."

Weatherman drilled his eyes into Tobin's, and Nicola watched his chest rise and fall slowly. He remained silent.

"I did talk to Seamus," Tobin said, breaking the tension. "I talked to him last night. And he will book a job, and it will be the right job. But he says he wants to read all the scripts before we attach him to anything."

Crystal laughed out loud. "That is the first sign that your client's career is about to implode," she said.

"That's the opposite of what we want, Tobin," Weatherman said, ignoring Crystal. "We have two blockbusters that we could put him on right now, one at Warner's, one at Disney, and the only thing he should be asking is which one has better back end. The answer to that is Disney. Say yes on his behalf, right now, and this meeting will be nice and short."

"That I cannot do, I'm afraid."

"Well, then you can tell Seamus this: Because he burned the studio so badly when he pulled that stunt on location . . ."

Nicola winced.

". . . he no longer has anywhere to live. He no longer has a car. He no longer has a wardrobe. And Crystal, has anyone at Huerta Hernandez asked you for the services of Donald Matson?"

Nicola's head whipped around at the mention of Bluey's real name.

"Donald Matson?" Crystal looked up from her phone. "Oh, you mean Bluey? Well, nobody has asked, but he's also not for sale. He works for me, and trust me, after I rescued Max Zetta from the incompetence of Gaynor Huerta, Bluey has been *very* busy."

Nicola grimaced as her mind flashed on Zetta's flameout scandal of last year. Gaynor had done her best to contain his fetish for religious icons until photos of Gaynor and Zetta together had nearly hit the Internet. Gaynor'd been lucky that Nicola's friend, Billy, had intercepted the story and killed it.

"I don't even want to think about that," Weatherman laughed humorlessly. "So, Tobin, have you told your client that without a movie, he will be returning to LA with nowhere to live, nothing to drive or wear, and without his winged monkey to wipe his ass?"

"He knows that, yes."

"And he still wants to read a fucking script?"

Tobin nodded and closed his leather binder.

Weatherman took his phone from a jacket pocket and typed for a minute.

"I've just e-mailed you the script for *Parallax*. It's easy money. A Disney trilogy, shooting back-to-back. Three paychecks for one job. Plus merchandising and theme park. It's a half-billion-dollar deal. I need him to read it within seven days."

"He doesn't get out of rehab for two days."

"Good. Then he'll have five days to read a script, which is four days and twenty-three hours longer than I get to read them. I want an answer on my desk by next Tuesday. And now let's clear up this publicist issue."

Nicola jerked upright. "I'm sorry, Mr. Weatherman, which issue are you talking about?"

"I'm talking about the ridiculous situation that we are in right now. I mean, congratulations, you got to bang a superstar and whatever the hell you did to convince him you could do this job, but, to be blunt, you can't. You can't do this, and we just need to make this go away as nicely as possible."

Nicola gazed rapidly around the table, suddenly grateful for Gaynor's brutal boot camp. Before she could speak, Crystal leaned forward slowly, like a spider over a fly.

"Thanks, Jon," she purred. "I'll be happy to resume service, and I have the press release ready to go out this afternoon. As we discussed, I will only charge crisis premiums through April. After that my rate will return to the usual ten thousand."

"Thank you for coming today, Miss Wallace," Weatherman said, almost politely. "I'm sorry we wasted your time and dragged you away from your office on such an awful day."

Nicola took a deep breath and counted to five. "I was hired by Seamus," she said, pleased by the strength of her voice. "And the fact that not a single outlet got close to the truth of the scandal is proof that I *can* do this job. I *have* done this job. There was no fallout from that incident."

"An incident that you caused," Crystal whispered.

"Yep." Nicola's anger flared. "I gave him the drugs. I shot him up."

"No, that was another Huerta Hernandez client," Crystal sneered, referring to former child star and current reality TV party girl Amber Bank, who'd visited Seamus in Ojai and given him the near-fatal overdose. "I'm not sure what Gaynor is up to, but your current client roster reads like the worst episode of *Celebrity Intervention* ever."

"Okay, that's enough," boomed Tobin. "This conversation is both embarrassing and pointless. Jon, why didn't you tell me you planned this? The one thing Seamus reiterated to me on the phone was that Miss Wallace is to continue as his publicist."

"But she's not," countered Crystal. "She's not. She's not a publicist. She was making coffee six months ago. She was opening mail. She got her claws into a drug addict and turned it into a career. She cannot do this job. She is nothing but a—"

Nicola slammed her palm loudly onto the glass tabletop, stopping Crystal in her tracks.

"Listen, you cracked-out Dementor," Nicola said in a forceful whisper, "the only skill you need to be a publicist is to lie and make eye contact at the same time, and trust me, Grandma, I've mastered that. There has not been one single story linking Seamus's incident to drug use, and having Amber Bank at our agency gave us leverage and ownership of the one loose cannon in the whole saga. I came to this meeting to present my press plan for Seamus. You are free to leave."

Crystal glanced at Jon. "Are you going to make the announcement, or shall I tell her?"

Timothy stood up and smiled. "Today we are welcoming Bette to

Seamus's team." He gestured at Wu, who was smiling widely. "She has agreed to be Seamus's new girlfriend."

Nicola felt panic and confusion rising in her chest. She fought to remain silent.

"We'll be the cutest couple," Bette crowed. "I mean, no offense, Nicola, but this is going to go totally viral."

"We're doing a showmance?" Nicola asked, her voice steady.

"Yes, Miss Wallace," Weatherman said. "Nothing like a new romance to distract the press."

"I see," Nicola continued, all business. "I wish you had told me earlier; we'll have to alter the media tour substantially. *People*, *Entertainment Tonight*, and *The Tonight Show* are all on board for first interview."

"Then they'll be thrilled to know they're getting the exclusive on his new girlfriend."

"Still, I'll have to make some calls."

Crystal rolled her eyes, which, due to Botox, was her only option for a facial response.

"Has Seamus been told?" Nicola said, staring at Tobin.

"He is aware," he replied cagily.

"Timothy," Weatherman interrupted, "what is the next topic for discussion?"

Thompson nudged his assistant.

"What is the current relationship between Miss Wallace and Mr. O'Riordan?" the assistant said, almost choking on his words.

"I'm sorry, what?" Nicola spluttered.

"Let me clarify," Weatherman said loudly. "Are you planning on continuing to fuck your client, or not?"

Nicola's fingers nervously reached for the small nylon bracelet, and she swallowed hard before answering. "My relationship with Seamus at this point and moving forward is purely professional, and he knows that." Nicola was again relieved that her voice remained steady.

"Good," said Weatherman with a smile at the edges of his mouth. "Then we can discuss the framework of Miss Wu's contract. After a successful six-month romance and its tasteful demise, Miss Wu will be cast as a lead in a Marvel franchise."

"See ya later, CW," Wu cackled. Crystal slapped her arm.

"So, let's get out of here," Weatherman said, pushing away from the table. "Tobin, I want that signature by Tuesday, and until then Seamus has no studio support. He can sleep on your couch, or, God forbid, pay for something himself. Bette, welcome aboard, thank you for agreeing to this mission, and Wallace, don't fuck this up. Let's reconvene with Seamus in three days. Happy faces all around."

He strode out without another word. Nicola grabbed her purse, stuffed her folder back inside, and tried to emulate Weatherman's exit. She wanted to ghost so badly. As she approached the elevator, she sensed someone standing behind her. She turned to see Timothy.

"I can find my own way, thanks, Timothy." Nicola forced a thin smile, then pressed the elevator call button once, as hard as she could.

"I wanted to apologize," he said.

"For?"

"For what happened in there. I'm sorry, I didn't know about the ambush."

The elevator dinged and the doors opened. Nicola stepped in, and Timothy followed.

"I can find my own car, Timothy."

"You're mad at me."

"I think you're lying."

"Why?"

"Because when I told you who I was, you reacted weirdly. You knew what I was walking into."

"No, that's not it," Timothy said slowly as the elevator reached the garage and the doors opened. "It's because I recognized you just as you said it, and you're even prettier in person than you are on TV."

Nicola felt a blush on her cheeks as she stepped out. "Well, that's nice of you to say, but I'm going to leave now."

"Wait—the reason I . . . would you let me take you out to dinner?"

Nicola turned to face him, dumbstruck. "You're asking me on a date after I just got burned at the stake in front of your entire squad?" she whispered. "Unbelievable."

"You think that went badly?" Timothy said, spreading his arms wide. "Do you have any idea how hard you just won that meeting? It was amazing."

"I did?"

"You kept your client and you kept your cool. You aced Crystal and you kept Weatherman on a short leash. You're a ballbuster. So yeah, of course I'd like to buy you dinner."

Nicola looked over to where her car was. She wanted to be out of this building so bad she could taste it. "Thanks, Timothy, but I don't think . . ."

"It's just dinner," he pleaded.

She touched the nylon bracelet again. She hadn't been asked out by anybody since Seamus went away.

Liar. Addict. Client.

She nodded. "Okay, fine. I'll have dinner with you."

CHAPTER 2

BILLY STARED OUT THE WINDOW of the minivan as it navigated the darkened switchbacks of the Hollywood Hills. Next to him Kara was plugging away at her cell phone, managing her "social media empire." Billy was slightly jealous, because he knew that if he looked at his phone for even a minute, he'd get carsick. He focused on the lights of the 101 below him, two distinct strips, red dots on one side, white dots on the other, two competing streams in opposite directions, neither side flowing terribly fast.

He glanced at Kara's phone and saw that it was 9:48. The gold-embossed Golden Globes preparty invite had promised a free phone and a punctual start time of nine p.m., with nobody admitted after eleven p.m. or when they reached capacity, whichever occurred first. Before they boarded the shuttle bus at Hollywood and Highland he had texted his friend Solstice, who was handling the check-in table.

Get here fast sweetheart, she'd texted back. *It's gonna be a beautiful disaster, and we're 3/4 full already.*

Billy marveled at the lure of a good gift bag. A free phone and some candles sure helped fill a party in forty-five minutes. He fussed with his cell phone in his pocket, hoping that Solstice was the only security he'd need to sneak it past. If half the celebrities on the tip sheet turned up tonight, it was going to be a busy night of gathering stories for *Spyglass*, the tabloid he worked at.

"You still have service?" he asked.

"I'm a personal hot spot," Kara smiled.

"You know you can't pull that out at the party or they'll make you check it."

"Amber says that only losers check their phone."

Billy pursed his lips at the mention of Amber's name. He hadn't heard from Bluey in an hour. He was on a stakeout with Max Zetta, making sure that the born-again alcoholic didn't get into any more trouble. Even though Billy was used to the weird hours they both kept, he couldn't help but wish they were at Bluey's watching *Downton Abbey* with Tojo the cat snuggled between them.

Dang, you got needy fast, Billy mused to himself. Once the weird animosity he'd felt for Bluey evaporated, sometime during their first night together, they'd quickly segued into coupledom. Bluey treated him like an adult, and Bluey listened to him—two things his previous dating partners had never done. The hardest thing to get used to was that Bluey made him feel safe, in a way that scared Billy. Until now, he'd never even realized that safety was a feeling he needed.

Over the course of only a few months, Billy had been spending less and less time at his small apartment behind the Gold Coast, and he found himself thinking in the plural "we." Dependency didn't sit well with him. The only person he'd ever depended on up until now was Nicola.

He had begged Nic to come along tonight, but she was wiped after the meeting with Weatherman. "All I'm doing tonight is a bubble bath and some records and a box of chocolates," Nic had said. He felt a pang of guilt over the brutal meeting she'd endured and wondered briefly if he'd made a mistake bringing her to LA from Ohio. He made a mental note to drag her out on a friend date tomorrow. He'd been devoting too much time to Bluey, and that was definitely a friend fail.

He was jolted out of his reverie as the minivan arrived at a nearly pitch-black cul-de-sac somewhere in the upper reaches of the Hills. The doors concertinaed open and people rushed the aisle and spilled out. Kara, blocking Billy from getting up, continued to post stories to her Snap and Insta.

"Come on." Billy nudged her.

"Wait. I need to make sure this post goes up. I can't post again until we find out what the privacy situation is."

Billy took out his own phone and saw a text each from Bluey and Nic. He smiled. Bluey wanted him to have a good night and promised to keep the bed warm. Nic was tired and cranky and wanted to know if Walmart was hiring. He smiled when her second text asked him to text her when he got home safely.

Kara stuffed her phone down the front of her pants and stood up, her 'fro bending against the roof of the van like a blaxploitation Marge Simpson. At the minibus's stairs, she slowed and turned.

"This will be easier if I go out backward," she laughed, gripping onto the driver's arm and slowly dropping one heel down at a time until she was out of the bus.

Before Billy followed her, he turned and handed the driver a twenty. "Something for your troubles."

"Thanks, man, but it weren't no trouble."

"What time do you finish tonight? When's the last bus back?"

"We go until it's done," the driver said wearily.

"Well, here's my business card," Billy said, pressing a card into the guy's hand. "If you see anything good, give me a call. I might be able to brighten up your night."

The driver saluted Billy and nodded. "Yessir, and thank you." He slid the money and the business card into his shirt pocket.

Billy stepped out into the darkness, instantly enveloped in a thick cloud of artificial fog. A blinking set of rope lights along the sidewalk guided him to the check-in table, where he spied Solstice putting wristbands on people and repeating "Just be quiet on your way down the drive, we don't want the neighbors to be mad" over and over.

She squealed when she saw him. "Hi, my favorite."

"Hi, lovergirl."

"You guys made it, excellent. Hi, Kara!" Solstice leaned over and hugged Kara.

"Here, let me give you the party wristband, and I also have the VIP bands for you guys. You can go anywhere, including the main mansion, but I'm going to warn you, if they see a phone in your hands inside the mansion, you don't know me. Capisce?"

"Yes, lover. Are you really gonna shut down the desk and come inside at eleven?"

"Sooner than that, baby," Solstice said firmly. "We are running two more shuttles and saving the rest of the space for the real A-list. And they don't need checkin' in."

Solstice glanced furtively at Kara and smirked. Kara didn't notice. Billy grinned. He gave Solstice a quick peck on the cheek and extended a hand to Kara. "Shall we?"

They locked arms and began to descend the driveway to the first house on the estate.

"Slow down, Bill," Kara said, jerking his arm. "This driveway ain't no cakewalk in these clogs."

"I told you that the driveway was long and steep."

"And I told you I have an image and a brand."

Billy gave her side-eye.

"Do you think Solstice can call for a golf cart or something?"

"It's not that far, K. We'll be seeing the party soon enough."

"I don't want to arrive sweaty, Billy. Please text Solstice."

Billy pulled out his phone and pretended to send a text. "Okay, let's keep walking until we hear back."

They walked slowly in silence for several minutes along a driveway flanked by towering hedges, following the trail of the rope light.

"We're gonna get attacked by a possum," Kara said, dragging Billy closer to the center of the drive.

"Why are you so nervous?" Billy said suddenly.

"I told you, possum attack, it's a very real possibility," Kara said, but Billy could tell she was lying.

"Out with it," he said, and Kara stopped suddenly, turning to face him in the near dark.

"I overheard Amber on the phone today," Kara whispered. "She said to someone that I was a basic hungry tiger and I shouldn't be on her show."

"Uh-oh. You've made the mistress jealous."

"Apparently," Kara said ruefully.

"Do you even want to be on her show?"

Kara sighed. "Do you mean, was it my dream to be cast as the sassy black friend on the worst reality show on TV? No. And do I like being that thing? No. But you know what? Everybody gotta start someplace. Look at Jessica Alba. Nobody even remembers that she had a crappy TV show."

"So let her fire you, then."

"Not yet," Kara said. "I need at least a full season. I've only been on the air for two months."

They rounded a corner and were confronted by a house, a garish combination of postmodern and Tudor, all glass and vaulted roofs with decorated eaves. A neon arrow by the front door pointed along a cobblestone path. They hadn't seen any people since they'd left Solstice.

"Is there anybody here?" Kara mumbled.

"Just you wait," Billy said. "This isn't even the main house."

Ahead, the path veered around a low brick wall atop which sat a black cube the size of a moving box. It was blasting deafening white noise.

"Oh, that's why we couldn't hear anything," Kara said, as if she'd solved a major problem. "The speakers are broke. They done blown their woofer."

"That's not a speaker, it's white noise; they're using it to drown out the sound so the neighbors won't complain. It's a huge deal; the city is trying to shut down all the party houses. You can't tell me this is the first time you're seeing one."

"Bitch, you know I don't pay attention." Kara laughed, her mood picking up noticeably as they cleared the path and the party appeared below them.

A rolling lawn was lit by LED spotlights that rotated rainbow colors across a crowd that Billy estimated was already close to a thousand people. The pool in the center of the garden was legendary for the nude women that the owners filled it with at parties, and even on a cold night like tonight, the nude women were delivering cocktails from a bar in the center to a crowd of eager, staring young men.

"None of those women will ever get a serious gig," Kara said with a dismissive wave of her arm.

"Says the reality TV star."

Kara ignored him. "There's Amber. I have to go say hi." She

instantly forgot that her platforms were hard to walk in, trotting grace-fully across the uneven grass in the direction of a group of women standing next to a life-size ice sculpture of a Lexus, one of the evening's sponsors. Billy watched as Kara crashed a circle that included SaraBeth Shields, Courtney Hauser, and Bette Wu. His brow furrowed. He'd watched as Bette had tried to crack the cool kids club for several years, and suddenly she was being welcomed warmly by Amber? Didn't make sense.

Keeping his head down, he began a quick lap of the party, not wanting to get stuck talking to someone he didn't like. He carefully threaded his way through the dimly lit forest of outstretched drinks and moving shadows. The compound grounds, roughly square in shape, flanked by the front mansion he'd just walked around and three similarly garish mansions on the other sides of the square, all of which faced the pool—it looked like public housing for rich people with no taste.

Sleek bars dotted the lawn around the pool, and a dance floor and lighting rig filled the space by the house at the rear of the property.

Farty electronica blasted from a wall of speakers beneath the raised DJ booth. Billy winced when he saw that the DJ was Primrose Golden from *Heiresses* on MTV. He wondered how much she was getting paid to plug her phone into the PA and show a lot of side boob.

"I'm in the wrong business," he said glumly, swiping a cocktail from a passing tray and continuing around the pool area. He stopped dead when he spied recently separated superstar Mason Dwyer forcing himself onto a young Latina. He moved closer to listen.

"Just take the key," Dwyer pleaded, pushing a hotel key card into her hand. "I told you, I'm in room twelve-ten; let yourself in later." He pushed his leg in between the woman's just for emphasis.

"I don't know," she said coyly. "I don't want to be all over TMZ tomorrow." She slipped the room key into the pocket of his denim blazer and patted his cheek. "Sorry, Mason, I would if I could," she smiled, deftly escaping his embrace and striding away.

Mason turned and saw Billy staring. "What?" he demanded.

"Oh, nothing," Billy said with a smile. "I wanted to push past but didn't want to interrupt, you know, the sealing of the deal."

"There's no deal to seal, friend," Mason said, even though they had never met before. He flashed his million-dollar smile and ran a hand through his disheveled blond hair. Billy noticed a lot more gray at his temples than there'd been in his last movie, and the crow's-feet around Mason's eyes had deepened, too. Separation had taken a toll.

"You got any weed?"

"No, sir," Billy said. "My name's Billy."

They shook hands while Mason scanned the crowd, looking for something. He did not volunteer his name, which irritated Billy. Stars always assumed that you knew who they were.

"Want my drink? I haven't touched it; I don't even know what it is."

"I can't touch a drink or I'll never see my kid again," Mason slurred.

"Huh?" Billy said, realizing that Mason was already drunk.

"Felicity has people watching me night and day. Her lawyers are breaking my nutsack on a daily basis. All I want to do is have a few drinks, get nice and high, and find a decent woman who I can spend the night with."

"So you came to a Golden Globes party? In Los Angeles?"

"I don't have a lot of options, man," Mason said with a half smile. "I'm presenting on Sunday, I have reshoots tomorrow, a custody court appearance, Globes rehearsals, and a press junket next week. Where would you recommend I go?"

"Good point." Billy punched him gently on the arm. "I feel your pain."

"Listen," Mason said softly, looking from side to side, "if you wanna be a pal, can you go to the bar and get me a triple vodka soda in a water bottle?"

Billy nodded and headed to the nearest bar. Thankfully the line was short and the waitress didn't bat an eyelid at his drink order, so he ordered one for himself, too. Mason smiled from ear to ear when he saw Billy returning with the drinks.

"Man, you done good," he laughed, reaching for both bottles.

Billy pulled one of them back. "This one's mine. I couldn't let you drink alone."

Mason's face fell for a second before he recovered and cheers'd his bottle against Billy's.

"Hope I can improve your night," Billy said.

"You wanna head inside VIP?" Mason said brightly. "Less chance of Felicity having a private eye in there."

From what Billy had heard of Felicity Storm, there was absolutely every chance that she had cameras on Mason at all times. This is what happened when one half of a Hollywood super couple got caught cheating with a new It girl. Hell hath no fury like an aging actress scorned.

Mason pointed to the mansion on their left, a smaller version of the main house. They walked up to the door and Mason pulled it open and walked inside. Billy tried to follow but felt a strong hand grip his upper arm before his eyes could adjust to the dim light inside the entryway. He turned and flashed his VIP wristband to the security guard, who immediately let go.

"Sorry, sir, just checking."

The first room was nearly empty. Three Disney Channel starlets lounged on a long, dark brown leather couch in front of the fireplace, a weed vape pen glowing brightly between them, coke residue on the tabletop. All three heads turned as Mason walked in, matching hopeful expressions on their faces.

"I saw that," Mason said quietly to Billy. "Let's explore."

Mason led the way through the house. Two bedrooms were locked. Either someone lived here, or people were inside doing whatever. Apart from the girls in the living area and roaming security guards, the house was empty. Mason led Billy to a sitting room at the back by the kitchen.

"Make sure the coast is clear," he instructed. Without waiting for Billy to reply, Mason took off his left shoe, lifted it to the coffee table, and peeled back the leather liner inside it, revealing a hollowed-out space in the heel that contained a vintage cocaine bullet. "See anybody?"

Billy shook his head. Mason twisted the bullet a few times, tilting it back and forth, then stuck it into his nose, snorting deeply. He repeated the action three more times before he offered it to Billy.

"Naw, man, I'm good," Billy said, turning quickly at a sound in the hallway. "Someone's coming."

In a flash, the coke was back in Mason's heel and the shoe was on his foot.

"Let's sit," Mason said with a sniff, gesturing at the couch built into the wall.

Billy did as he was told. This was perfect—he had lucked into next week's cover story, especially now, with the coke about to hit Mason's system and make him chattier.

"So what brings you to a party like this?" Mason asked, sniffing the coke back into his nose and failing. A large rock dropped out and landed on the pocket flap of his selvage denim jacket. Billy pointed at it.

"What? Did some fall out? I can't look down or the rest will drop out. Can you flick it off?"

Billy leaned across and flicked the little white rock off Mason's jacket.

"To answer your question, I came here with a friend."

"Oh, okay. Who's your friend?"

"You wouldn't know her. She's on a reality TV show."

"You'd be surprised. Since Felicity kicked me out, my nights are bad TV and good weed. I've watched a lot of shitty TV."

"She's on the Amber Bank show. She's Kara."

"I'm bad with names. But I watch that show. It's funny."

"She's the black girl."

"Oh shit, the one with the huge hair? She's really funny. That one where she had to get her driver's license was hilarious."

"You know that show's totally fake, right? Kara's been driving for a decade."

24

"Next thing you'll be telling me is that Amber's not that much of a bitch in real life."

"No, sadly, sometimes reality TV is reality."

"I figured." Mason laughed. "Amber is a lot of things, but a good actress isn't one of them. She gave my buddy a BJ in a bathroom at that Walgreens in West Hollywood, the one by La Cienega. He got herpes."

Billy let his face droop. "Look at my surprise," he joked.

"Yeah, I know. He asked for it. She's kind of the reason that I'm hiding out. She's always trying to get photographed with me. Right now, with Felicity trying to prove I'm a degenerate drug user and drunk, a photo with Amber counts as an awesome exhibit A."

Billy rolled his eyes at the lack of irony in this statement, considering Mason had just vacuumed up four huge bumps of coke and was currently almost through a triple vodka soda.

"Why'd you come to a party like this?"

"You sound like my agent. I'll tell you why. I am so. Fucking. Bored of my life right now. Bobby, you wouldn't believe."

"Billy. My name's Billy."

"Hey, man, sorry, my bad, Billy. You have no clue what it means to be part of a golden couple. I already couldn't do a damn thing I wanted for the last twelve years. That bitch had me on a short-ass leash. She says she hates the press but every month she had a calendar of things. I'd take the kid to the park, we'd go to Disneyland together, she and I would have date night. She had photographers on call. It was all a stunt."

"It worked."

"What the fuck does that mean, Billy?"

Billy took a deep breath. It looked like Mason was as angry a coke addict as Felicity was claiming in her court depositions.

"Sorry, dude, I just meant that it worked. It looked like you two were the happiest of couples."

"Yeah, so happy. I've been like a caged dog. The last time we had sex, that kid was two. She's eight now. And when I get caught cheating then I'm the worst person in the world. So mostly it's been me and online porn; we're a better couple than me and her."

He took a big swig of his drink.

Mason leaned against his seat, letting his head loll as the cocaine kicked in. A smile wreathed his lips as he closed his eyes and rubbed his palms on his thighs. He reminded Billy of the lion he used to see at the zoo in Cincinnati when he was a kid. It always bummed him out to see such a majestic animal looking so dusty and forlorn.

"Sorry to lay all this on you, man. I'm just blue-balled, and even at a shitty party like this I can't pick up. Before I met her, do you even realize what it was like at these parties? I had my pick of the women. I was never a douche about it—I'm a good Kentucky boy at heart—but you know what I'm sayin' is just that I got laid a lot. A *lot*. And after that, I was just a good husband . . . go do this movie, go do that movie, make us millions of dollars. You know what I heard?"

"No, man, what?" Billy knew this would be good.

"I heard she's a dyke, that's what I heard."

Mason finished his drink, tipping the plastic bottle upside down and catching the last few drops on his tongue. Billy handed his own untouched bottle to the actor, who swiped it from his hand and took another deep draft.

"I've never met your wife, so I don't know much," he began. "But wouldn't you know if your wife was a lesbian?"

"You don't know her at all, man. She's like an assassin that never gets caught. Nobody has any shit on her. Nobody. I hired a couple investigators—that's how I found out she had investigators on me; the best ones were like, uh, we can't work for you, sorry. So my guys found nothing. They followed her to hotels, they followed her for weeks, and she gave them the slip every time."

"So what makes you think she's gay?"

"I just know it," Mason said. Billy could hardly hide his disappointment.

"So why not just place that story, fight fire with fire?"

"She has a web of journalists that help her bury stories. She plants stories. She's destroyed so many careers. If she's up for a role she really wants, suddenly the actress she's up against will have her phone hacked and nudes will hit the Internet. Or she'll find their nanny, get the gossip, and leak it to the press. She's destroyed so many actresses. And nobody would ever suspect her. She's a fucking robot, and she's obsessed with her fame."

"Why didn't you leave earlier?"

"I love my kid, man. I love my little girl."

To Billy's horror, Mason started to cry.

"Dude, not here." Billy, panicked, looked up and down the hall that ran past the sitting area. There was nobody there.

"I'm sorry, man. You don't get it, I'm just so lonely, and take this the right way, but you're the first person who's even bothered to real-talk me since the breakup."

Billy picked up a napkin from a pile of them on the table and handed it to Mason. He took it and gently dabbed at his famous violet eyes, breathing deeply.

"Sorry, man, don't know where that came from."

"Hey, no worries, I can tell you're going through a lot."

"Yeah, and I can tell you're surprised that golden Felicity Storm is a heinous monster."

"Nothing surprises me anymore, especially when it comes to actors."

"Oh really," said Mason suspiciously. "You hang out with a lot of actors, then?"

Billy backtracked quickly, not wanting to have *that* discussion right now.

"No, dude, no, I just have some really pretty friends; they're always dating this actor or that actor."

"Yeah, right, like who exactly?"

Great. He's a paranoid cokehead. Billy decided the truth was the best defense.

"My best friend was dating Seamus O'Riordan."

"Oh shit, then you do know what's what," he laughed, his mood changing immediately. "That poor bastard, he's really fucked himself this time. If my next movie bombs, it won't be long before him and me are doing a buddy comedy for CBS. On-set injury, huh? That's code for painkiller addiction. That's what I heard."

"All I know is he's gonna be business as usual."

"Good luck with that," Mason said bitterly. "My new movie is tracking so bad with the test audiences, they are having me come and do a reshoot tomorrow. The damn thing's out in a month."

Billy stopped cold.

"You're *working* tomorrow?" Billy snatched the booze out of Mason's hand. "Listen, man, we just met and all, but trust me, you're going to feel a lot better if we get you out of here without any more of this shit." He pointed at the drink. Then he pointed at Mason's shoe. "Or any more of that shit."

"Great," he sighed. "I come to a party to get laid, and I end up getting high with a gay narc."

"Yeah, it's your lucky night, trust me."

"Why do you care so much, dude? Nobody cares. I ain't making you any money. That is the only reason anyone hangs around. And my reshoot is at night. I can sleep all day. Why are you even caring?"

"I just don't like seeing people make mistakes, not decent people. Look, I'll make you a deal. You agree to hang out with me and drink water, and I'll get a story into print about your wife. Anything at all that you want."

"How will you do that? She'll just shut it down. They'll call her and she'll give them something on me."

"It's Golden Globes; she'll be too busy to deal with a late-breaking story."

"God, where do I start?"

Billy was relieved that Mason was so excited by the chance to get something into print that he wasn't asking how. Yet.

"She's a germophobe. She pees standing up. She's anorexic. She's a cutter. She has depression. She goes to see her plastic surgeon every six months."

"You've just described every actress in Hollywood. There's got to be one thing that makes her unique."

"You'd never get it past a lawyer. No magazine would touch it."

"Try me."

"She used to turn tricks for old guys at Skybar."

"Uh, you're right, it's gonna be tough getting that past any lawyer in the US. Anything a bit softer?"

"Our marriage was arranged. Our studio set it up. I can see it all so clearly now, you know, looking backward with hindsight."

"Hindsight *is* looking back," Billy said, regretting it immediately.

"Huh? Whatever, our agents arranged our first date, and she was everything I wanted, she was perfect. And as soon as we had the baby, she was done. She actually offered me a contract last year; it specified how much time we had to spend together, and in return, I could see people behind her back. That's why I had that affair, and I think she set it up. I refused the contract, and the next week, my affair was in the magazines. Then she filed for divorce."

Billy looked at the pain on Mason's face. He decided to give *Spyglass* the Felicity angle instead of selling out Mason. "That'll work," he said. "Now how about we get you up off this couch and we do a few laps of the party and then I send you home so you can get some rest."

"Okay, man, and really, Brady, I can't thank you enough."

"One last thing—give me your coke. All of it."

Mason knew he had lost the battle. He took off his shoe and removed the bullet. He passed it to Billy, who unscrewed it and let the powder fall onto the rug, then pushed the empty bullet between the couch cushions.

"Fuck, man, you weren't kidding."

"I hate that shit," Billy said, rising to his feet and extending a hand to help Mason do the same.

"I need to pee, Brady," Mason said, wobbling slightly on his feet. Billy led him down the hallway to the bathroom and stood guard outside while Mason urinated noisily inside it.

"Hey, man, you really know that black girl from Amber's show?

You think she can keep a secret? Would she wanna maybe hang out with me later?"

Billy thought for a second. At the very least, Kara hooking up with Mason would drive Amber crazy with jealousy.

"Sure, let's go find her."

He pulled his phone out and texted Kara.

CHAPTER 3

AN HOUR LATER, A VERY different Kara was in an elevator headed for the twelfth floor of the Sunset Tower Hotel. She'd forced her Lyft driver to wait while she ran up to her apartment and toned down her look, and here she was: the 'fro barely contained by a vintage Courrèges scarf that Gaynor had given her for Christmas, her clothing choices—comfy jeans, a UCLA sweatshirt, and leather Gucci slides—so low-key that she felt as basic as Amber said she was. She nervously played with the enormous white plastic vintage sunglasses in her hand, unsure whether to put them on or not.

The elevator dinged as the doors opened onto the hush of the twelfth floor. She pulled the room key that Billy had given her from her jeans pocket and walked to 1210. Mason had texted her to let herself in, but it still felt weird. She took a deep breath and slid her key into the lock, which clicked open, and as the door opened, she was engulfed in the sickly petrol-and-skunk smell of weed vape.

"Mason," she called out, "it's me."

"Come on in," his instantly recognizable voice called back.

She pulled the door closed behind her and pushed against it twice to make sure it was locked. The scent of reefer led her to the living room, past a bedroom strewn with the clothes Mason had been wearing at the party. As she entered the room, Mason, now wearing workout shorts and a T-shirt promoting his new movie, stood up and extended his hand.

"We meet at last," he smiled. "I'm Mason. Thank you for coming."

Kara took his hand. "I'm Kara. You're so old-fashioned," she laughed.

Mason turned unsteadily and gestured to a selection of booze bottles, mixers, and food on a table by the window.

"I didn't know what you'd feel like, so I just had them bring a little bit of everything."

Kara's gaze moved from the booze buffet to the view of LA spreading out all the way to LAX from the window.

"Your blinds are open, Mason."

"Yeah, I love the view."

Kara walked over and pulled the blackout curtain across the window, then she pulled the patterned inner curtains across and turned to face him.

"You leave these open all the time?"

"Yeah, makes me feel less trapped."

Kara walked to Mason and rapped on the side of his head with her knuckle.

"Privacy. It's the most important thing in your world right now. Learn it."

"I'm twelve floors up; they'd have to be in a helicopter to get anything good."

"Or a drone, fool."

"Really?" Mason said with an exasperated face. "Sorry, Kara. Felicity took care of this shit so thoroughly when we were together. I just don't think about it. Last time I was single, there weren't any drones."

"And now there are." Kara went back to the table and set out two glasses. She scooped ice into them and, blocking Mason's view, poured vodka into only one, then topped them both with soda. She handed him the virgin drink, certain that the weed would make up for the lack of booze.

He walked across the room, plopped down on the bed, and patted the covers. Kara sat next to him, careful to not touch him. Now that she was here, she wasn't feeling it. There was nothing sexy about a forty-five-year-old drunk, even one this famous.

"I watch your show," Mason said, sipping on his drink.

"You do not," Kara said, turning to face him, a pleased smile on her face.

"Yes, ma'am, I do," Mason smiled back. "You make that show

great. At first I just left it on after *Heiresses*. Amber annoys me in a weird way; she always did. When she was a child star we were both on a talk show once, and I swear she hit on me. My agents got me out of there so fast. I was doing a lot of drugs at the time, but she looked about twenty. Turns out she was twelve."

"Wait, so you would've?"

Mason looked at the carpet and nervously swept one of his feet from left to right. "Before I got married and cleaned up I was a bit of a disaster. I would have shot first and asked questions later."

"Your analogies really need work," Kara said.

"Huh? What? I used to really like sex, and believe me, nothing about her said she was so young. I was pretty high, probably whiskey and bennies? Anyways, that's why I pay my team the big bucks, to keep me out of trouble."

"I got in here pretty easy."

"Did they ask you for ID in the lobby?"

"No, I walked straight in. If you act like you belong someplace, nobody questions you."

"That's bad though," Mason said, rubbing his head. "My manager has told them to check everyone out who comes up here."

"So maybe the guy just went to pee?"

"No." Mason stood suddenly. "Felicity probably got photos of you coming here. She's probably got someone on us right now."

"Well, I'm here now, so let's relax and I'll figure out our escape. Don't you have a guy?"

"A guy?" Mason sat back down, confused.

"Like a guy who makes it all work for you. A minder? A fixer?"

"I have no idea what you're talking about."

"Billy, who you met tonight, he's dating a guy who used to work for Seamus O'Riordan. Now he works for Max Zetta. He keeps people like you out of trouble."

"I thought your friend said he knew a girl who dated Seamus."

"That, too. That's how he met his boyfriend."

"So you know Seamus?"

"I've met him. . . ." Kara trailed off.

33

"Did you date him?"

Kara laughed out loud. "Oh, honey, if there's an opposite to that, that's what we did."

"Oh, I'm sorry, I just thought, you know, since you're here and all, that you dated white guys, too."

"Too?"

"Yeah, I googled you before you got here. Lots of rappers, no white guys. I'm sorry, I just assumed . . ."

"Assumed what?" Kara was enjoying Mason's clumsiness.

"I don't know, Kara." He laughed nervously. "I . . . uh, I haven't been in a position to make small talk for a long time. I'm failing pretty badly at it right now."

Kara reached over and picked up a joint off the bedside table and put it to her lips, waiting for him to light it. After a few seconds she took it out of her mouth. "Lighter?" she said.

Mason fished in the pockets of his workout shorts and pulled out a small red gas station lighter. He handed it to her.

"I guess chivalry is dead," Kara said, lighting the joint. "Listen, Mason, you need to relax. Nothing has to happen tonight, no pressure."

Mason took the joint and inhaled deeply. As he sent a plume of smoke skyward, Kara waved a finger in front of his face.

"I don't want to hear another word about your wife, your kid, or your situation. I didn't come here to be your therapist. I came here to throw down a little, or at least get a little head."

Mason's violet eyes sparkled and a slow smile parted his lips.

I knew it, Kara realized. *Of course. He married Felicity Storm. He likes strong women.*

"Do you accept my terms?" she asked, gently taking the joint from his fingers and putting it to her lips.

"Yes, ma'am, I sure do," Mason said, his voice cracking. His eyes glanced down to his shorts and back up. Kara followed his gaze and saw he was tenting.

"That's better." She closed her eyes and felt the pot start to relax her. She leaned her head against his and blew the smoke in a thin line at his mouth. He inhaled it slowly, and she felt his hands move up her sides. She expected them to rest on her butt or her chest, but they kept going until they reached the knot of her scarf.

"You sure you want to unleash that beast?" she whispered, her lips close to his. "Can you take it?"

"I wanna find out," he replied, his full lips brushing hers as he talked. His fingers deftly pulled the knot apart, and Kara felt her hair expand as the scarf slipped to the floor. Mason's hand moved around to the front of her shoulder, and he gently pushed her back.

"I just want to see you," he said. "You're so beautiful."

Now I know what Nicola was talking about, Kara thought. It was weird to be praised by a superstar.

"You're not so bad yourself," she said, dropping the joint into an ashtray and lifting her sweatshirt over her head.

"I have a full-time trainer," Mason said, pulling his shirt over his head and dropping it on the bed.

Kara nearly swooned at his body. "Dude, ain't you like forty or something?" she whispered. "You are fine."

"I'm forty-six in a couple months," Mason said, crestfallen. "Am I too old?"

Kara looked down at his chiseled abs and pecs. The truth was he was the same age as her dad, but her dad didn't look like this.

"Ain't you hairier?" she asked, not wanting to think about that.

"They waxed me for this movie," he said. "Is that okay?"

"You don't have to ask for my approval, dude."

"Sorry, sorry," he said. "Just making sure."

Kara leaned in and kissed him, mainly to shut him up. His lips froze against hers and she moved her hands up to his cheeks.

"Mason, kiss me like you mean it," she said into his face. His lips parted and he began to kiss her, a little too quickly and roughly. Kara pulled back.

"I want you to do something for me," she said. "I want you to pretend we are on a beach, I don't know, maybe in Greece, one of those white sand beaches. Blue water. Nobody else on earth. The sun's shining. And you want to kiss me, and you want to take your time."

Kara swung her legs across his lap and sat upright. Mason moved forward and slowly began to kiss her. *This is much better.* He threaded his hand through her hair at the back of her head and began to pull her in, kissing her with slowly increasing force. She moaned a little, and, encouraged, he ran his hand across her tummy and then trailed his finger across the side of her breast. She felt his tongue flick across hers. *Not bad for a white boy*, Kara thought, wondering if she was actually going to start getting into it or if this was going to be a washout.

Stop thinking and start playing.

She dropped her wrists onto his shoulders and began playing with his hair as the kissing continued. He wasn't rocking her world. The biggest movie star in the world was a mediocre kisser, or maybe she just couldn't focus. The fame thing was weird, it was messing with her, and the pot wasn't helping. Kara started to plan her escape, opening her eyes and looking to see where her Courrèges scarf had landed. She spied it under the chair beside the bed and made a mental note to not leave it behind. Lost in her thoughts of escape, her knee slipped off the bed, and she grabbed onto Mason's hair to steady herself, pulling it sharply.

"YES," he yelled into her ear before she could apologize. "Fucking YES."

Kara grabbed a firmer handful of Mason's hair and tugged it hard, pulling his head back. His eyes were closed and she felt him getting harder beneath her. Unsure of how far to push it, Kara drew her face alongside Mason's, her hand still pulling his hair.

"Tell me what you want me to do, Dwyer."

"Uuuunh," he groaned. "No . . . Kara . . . you tell me."

Kara rolled her eyes as the light went on in her head. This is why he stayed with Felicity Storm so long. He was a sub. Movie megastar was a bitch bottom.

She unstraddled him and stood beside the bed, never releasing her grip on his hair. She pulled him upright, even though he was a foot taller than her, and bit him on the chest, softly at first, increasing the pressure as he began to moan loudly.

"Okay, movie star," she whispered into his skin. "I'm going to let go of your hair for a second. We need to get these pants off both of us."

She released Mason's hair and he let his head hang forward, eyes on the floor, not meeting hers, his arms hanging limp at his sides. Kara stepped back and deftly wriggled out of her jeans and bra. When she looked up she saw him peeking at her.

"Did I tell you that you could look at me, old man?" she spat.

"No, ma'am. I'm sorry, I'm sorry," Mason said.

"Dwyer, I'm twenty-five years old. You call me *ma'am* again and this whole shitshow is over. Deal?"

"Deal."

Kara reached for the waistband of Mason's workout shorts, and as her hand brushed his skin, he began to tremble. She wondered if he was going to come from just standing there.

"You okay, actor?" she asked.

"Yes, m . . . mmm . . . mistress," Mason said furtively.

She whipped his shorts down and he kicked them away. She stepped back and looked him up and down. She'd already seen him naked—he'd gotten papped in the nineties—nothing new here.

"Not bad." She whistled, pushing him back onto the bed. As she began to guide him inside her, he stopped.

"Tie my wrists, please, mistress," Mason begged.

"I'm going to tell you to do one more thing," Kara said angrily, wrapping her hands around his wrists and pulling his arms over his head. "You're gonna fuck me right now, and you're gonna fuck me better than you've ever fucked a girl before. You got that?"

Below her, Mason's movie-star face spread into a grin.

"Will you tie my wrists first?" he said again meekly.

Kara suppressed a sigh and pulled the Courrèges scarf from the floor. She deftly tied Mason's wrists together with the same knot she used to tame her 'fro, then pushed him back onto the bed. Mason slid his hands behind his head and smiled at her.

"Okay, mistress, I'm ready to fuck you now."

Kara laughed huskily. "First things first, old man," she said, jumping up to the bed and lowering herself onto his face, her knees resting on his elbows and bending them back painfully. He groaned loudly and began to kiss her inner thighs.

This is more like it, Kara thought as warmth spread outward and Mason nibbled at one thigh, then the other. She could have stayed like that all night, but she remembered that he wanted her to be rough.

"Get to fucking work, pussy," she barked, settling her weight down and forcing him to eat her properly. She smiled as she felt him do as he was told and was surprised at his skill. He was much better at cunnilingus than kissing, and within minutes she felt an orgasm building.

"Not yet, buddy," she whispered, lifting herself slightly off his face and sliding her ass down along his taut body until she felt his dick prodding at her.

"You wanna show me what you got, actor?" she said harshly, trying to make eye contact with Mason. His eyes were cast down. Kara grabbed a handful of his hair and pulled it hard, making him yelp loudly. He pressed his penis against her and she slid back onto it and he began to fuck her tentatively. She relaxed her grip on his hair and slapped him across the face, shocking him.

"This is not the fuck of anyone's life, old man," she threatened. "Show me what you got."

Mason's arms strained against the Courrèges scarf and a loud moan escaped his lips as he picked up the pace and Kara smiled. She liked it up here.

✳ ✳ ✳

It wasn't bad at all, Kara texted Billy when they were finally done and Mason was snoring on the pillow beside her. *If this reality TV thing doesn't work out, maybe I can be a dominatrix.*

Stick with reality TV. I can't believe he managed to perform after all the booze and blow.

He got me off twice before he passed out. He's a trooper.

OK. I'm heading to bed.

Wait. Is Bluey there? I need help.

Yes. What?

He doesn't have a plan to get me out of here unseen.

Kara's phone dinged. Bluey.

Hey. You staying the night or leaving now?

Up to you.

We're in bed. I can pick you up around 8. Tell me your room number and I'll come up with a disguise. Does he need one too? Tell him for $1500 I'll do a security sweep.

Kara looked at Mason snoring loudly on the pillow, then went into the bathroom, digging around in the pockets of the jeans he'd worn to the party. She found a roll of hundreds and peeled off fifteen. She rolled the bills into a smaller roll and walked back to the bedroom, placing them in her jeans pocket.

Cash is in hand. Bring him a disguise. He needs all the help he can get, poor guy.

Poor guy my arse, love. OK, beddy bye time. See you at 8. Billy says you're in 1210. Be careful.

Kara leaned back and pulled the half-smoked joint from the ash-tray and lit it. While she waited for the lights to start dancing on the edge of her vision, Mason stirred, his eyes opening halfway.

"You're still here," he smiled. "That's great."

He threw a heavily muscled arm across Kara's belly and pulled her close.

"You gonna stay over?"

"Yes," Kara said. "You want me to, right? Sorry, this time I need to ask."

A sleepy grin lit up Mason's face. He reached up and took the joint from her and took a puff, then held it out to her. Kara shook her head and he stubbed it out in the ashtray.

"You like to spoon?" he asked. Kara nodded. Mason pulled her alongside him and killed the lamp. In the sudden darkness, she could feel his warm, rock-hard stomach against her butt and his sweet pot-tinged breath on her neck. He began to kiss her, gently, along her spine.

"Thanks for a really fun night," Mason said quietly. "And thanks for being cool with . . . you know . . . everything."

"What can I say?" Kara chuckled. "I'm a helper."

Mason squeezed her tightly. "Your friend was right, he said you're decent."

Kara pushed back against Mason and wrapped her arms around his, counting his breaths until he fell back asleep. Fourteen. With the weed beginning to cloud her thoughts, Kara took a deep breath and followed him into slumber.

CHAPTER 4

A TWO A.M. TEXT FROM Gaynor had instructed Nicola to be at work for a "multi-strategy meeting" at eight a.m. Luckily she had gotten up to pee in the middle of the night and seen the text. In her sleepy stupor, she had actually believed that Gaynor would be on time for an eight a.m. meeting.

The sky outside was an oppressive gray after overnight rain, and the offices were dark, gloomy, and unoccupied. Nicola unlocked her office door and carefully dumped her purse and her laptop bag on her desk, clutching her Venti skim latte for warmth. She looked at the clock on her wall: 7:48. She sipped her coffee, and her breath steamed. She hated the thermostat, an infuriatingly sleek blob with two buttons and no instructions. After stabbing at the buttons in random order, she resigned herself to waiting until the heat came on automatically at ten.

Shivering inside her coat, Nicola hit the light switch to the main bank of lights and illuminated the reception area and the hallway. The stage-door lights that spelled out HHPR on Gaynor's office wall were turned off. Since Max Zetta had fired her, Gaynor hadn't slept in her office, but an early morning meeting might have persuaded her.

Nicola trod quietly down the hall and knocked gently. Silence. Pulling her long camel H&M wool coat around her, she returned to her desk, plugged her laptop in to her workstation, and waited till it fired up. Her phone pinged. She expected an excuse from Gaynor, but it was from her mother.

Hey Peanut! Haven't heard from you in a few days. Just wanted to say I love you. Mom.

Nicola smiled and sipped her coffee. She loved the way her mom signed her texts. Looking out into the empty hallway, she decided to hit the call button.

"Oh, hi, Peanut," her mom said, answering before the phone even rang. "I didn't mean you had to call me. Did my text wake you up?"

"No, Mom. I'm at work."

"Already? Baby, is that woman working you too hard? Every time I try to call you you're at work."

"She's not working me too hard, Mom. It's the way this job is. It just doesn't stop at any given time. There's always something going wrong."

"Tell me about it, Peanut. I just got off a night shift, and my goodness, the things that people get up to at four a.m. at a Motel 6."

Nicola winced. She hated that her mom was still at the same place where she'd worked to put her and her brother through school after their dad had died.

"Mom, I thought you were the day manager!"

"I am, Peanut, I am. I'm supposed to be starting now. But Mae-Lin called in sick and nobody could cover, so I had to go in. I'm just going to go home and nap for two hours and come on back."

"Mom, no."

"It's okay, Nico. It's an awful day here; we got a storm. I'm happy to spend some of it in bed and the rest at work. Now, why are you at work so goddamn early?"

"Oh, you know, the usual. My ex-boyfriend gets out of rehab tomorrow, so I have to come up with a publicity plan for him."

"Better you than me," her mom clucked. "Are you sure you're going to be all right when you see him?"

"I don't know, Mom," Nicola replied, sounding fifteen all over again. "It doesn't matter. It's awards season—he'll be busy; I'll be busy. Hopefully it won't be too messy."

"Put yourself first, Peanut," her mom said, pausing for a yawn. "I know you're not good at it. I taught you well there. But *People* magazine says he's a successful millionaire, and you're just you. So put you first this time."

"You're right again, Mom. How's Biscuit?"

"All he cares about is that damn car you gave him, driving the fool thing all around Dayton like it's a sports car. He met a girl he kind of likes, but she's something called straight-edge."

"Oh, she doesn't drink or do drugs," Nicola said hopefully. "That's gotta be good, right?"

"I guess," her mom said in a way that let Nicola know she already didn't like this girl. "There's being sober and then there's being a complete downer about everything. She's a bit sullen, but he seems happy enough."

"For now, that's a really good thing, huh?"

"You know who else is happy? Billyboy. My goodness, I've never heard that boy talk like that about anyone ever."

"You should see them together, it's adorable," Nic said, smiling at a memory.

"Well, it seems like I need to get myself out there and meet this Bluey. And maybe this movie star, too, huh?"

"Mom, you can meet all of my clients if you want. That's fine. But oh, look at the time, I have to prep for a meeting. Go sleep, and I'll talk to you tomorrow."

"Nicola Wallace, I know when I'm getting railroaded."

"I love you, Mom. Bye."

Nicola busied herself in a mountain of e-mail requests to interview Seamus. She'd cut them down to a manageable handful when she heard a rustling sound from the front door and looked at the time. Almost eight thirty. The rustling continued but the door did not open. Nicola went to investigate.

Random huffing and scraping and some agitated whispered Spanish came through the door. She pulled it open, expecting to see Gaynor. Instead, she was nearly knocked over by Alicia, who'd been leaning against the door while she dug in her purse for her keys and now fell backward onto the floor of the office. As she landed, her black Forever 21 sheath dress rose up, her legs flew apart, and Nicola was horrified to see that she wasn't wearing underwear beneath her dark gray Spanx.

"You stupid bitch," Alicia growled, rubbing her wrist. "What the fuh?"

"What the what? I was trying to help you. Why are you here so early?"

"Gaynor told me I had to be here at eight for a meeting. I had to go an' get vodka and those marcona almonds she likes, and then I had to get all these coffees for her and you, and you know what, I got myself a peppermint latte, because I'm sick of always feeding you bitches, and nobody gives a fuck. Are you even going to help me up?"

Nicola looked at the various shopping bags from Ralphs, Whole Foods, and Starbucks. She turned and began walking back to her office.

"Please call Gaynor and find out when we can expect her. In the meantime, hold all my calls. And if I have to tell you one more time that you can't speak to me like that, I'll tattoo it above your eyebrows. Also, Alicia?"

"What?" the assistant grumbled, rolling over and beginning the long process of getting up onto her wedge heels.

"One: See-through Spanx are not underpants. Two: Ask Gaynor for the number of her waxer. Shag carpet went out in the seventies."

Nicola's patience for Alicia's Grumpy Cat entitlement had worn thin. Against all odds, Gaynor had not fired her, mainly because her now thirteen-year-old twins, Patrick and Sylvester, loved her. They treated Alicia like a surly pet, training her to be classier and dressing her up in fashions they created for her. Her work performance had worsened since she'd traded Pinterest for Snapchat, spending most of her day putting digital dog ears and snouts on herself or posting makeup advice for "cholas," as she called her peers.

Somehow, Gaynor saw potential in Alicia, as an influencer and as a plus-size model. Her son Sylvester was moving forward with his plans to design a runway collection around her, and her other son, Patrick, was taking her to CrossFit and dictating her diet. But right now, the future model's noisy snorting and huffing was both irritating and distracting. Nicola got up and closed her door.

I'm surrounded by children.

In the single minute she'd been out of her office she had received nearly seventy new e-mails. She scanned through the subject headers for anything that didn't say Seamus or Kara, stopping cold at one that said, simply, DINNER TONIGHT!

It was from Timothy. She'd been waiting for him to cancel, and here it was. *Ugh.* Not only was he not canceling, he had made a reservation at Fig & Olive for eight p.m. and wanted to know if he could pick her up.

Nicola had never been a fan of the pre-date pickup, preferring to have her own transportation when the date most likely went to shit. She replied that she was excited for the date, too, but she'd meet him there since it was just around the corner from the office and she'd be working late.

She paused. She would have to go straight from work to the date. She texted Kara.

Hey! Can't come home between work and date. Can you please pull and bring me an outfit?

Not sure. I'm not home yet. You're not going to believe where I am. You have a date?

Nicola groaned. She'd have to call in clothes from a designer. And she didn't care where her roommate was.

I'm with Mason Dwyer. Sleepover. I have a story.

Mason Dwyer? For once, Kara wasn't exaggerating.

One hitter or repeat performance?

He's talking repeat. You're not gonna believe it. We spooned all night.

Wait up for me tonight

No way. You need to hook up with your date.

Possibly the last thing I need. Wait up.

Gotta go. He just flushed.

"*Mi Cola!* I'm in the conference room; don't keep me waiting."

Nicola froze. Gaynor, the most naturally noisy person she'd ever met, could also be the most stealthy. Gaynor was usually surrounded by a minor maelstrom, most of it of her own making. She wore noisy clothes, she muttered constantly in Spanish, her jewelry chattered and chimed, and she seemed to exist in a small whirlwind. Unless she wanted to sneak up on you.

Nicola snatched her phone off her desk and headed to the conference room. Gaynor, in a fuchsia velvet pantsuit with a ruffled white tuxedo shirt beneath it, smiled broadly at her. She picked up one of the three large black coffees that Alicia had gotten for her and took a sip.

"*Mija*," she said perkily. "Today, the gloves come off. Today, you are a publicist."

"I was a publicist yesterday," Nicola said quietly, taking her seat without breaking eye contact with Gaynor. "This outfit is new. You look like Strawberry Shortcake's pimp."

"*Ay, coño.*" Gaynor kept smiling. "I hope you look this fresh at forty-five."

"You're forty-five?" Nicola smirked. Gaynor's age was a national secret.

"I'm talking about the pantsuit, *monita*. You have no right to be in such a good mood today. Please don't tell me you're excited like a little schoolgirl to see your pill-popping ex again?"

"I'm in a good mood because it's nine a.m. and all my e-mail is answered, I've had my coffee, and I have a date tonight."

Gaynor set her coffee down and gave Nicola's simple Ann Taylor suit a disapproving look.

"So you're finally accepting it and going for women?"

"A date with a man."

"How could you meet a man? You've been here every minute you've been awake. It doesn't matter, we'll be here late. You'll have to call and let her down gently."

Nicola had sworn she wouldn't tell Gaynor whom the date was with.

"It's with Timothy Thompson from Global Talent," she spat a little too proudly.

"Nicolita, I've told you. Agents are worse than actors. Here, let's go through your Bumble; I'll get you a nice unemployed millennial."

"Calm down, Gaynor. It's a date, not a commitment ceremony."

"Let me give you the number of a nice young dyke . . . what about Kari Fox?"

"She's gay?" Nicola said quickly, immediately hating herself for still being so naïve.

"In time, my young apprentice, you will learn to spot the following things on first glance: addiction, homosexuality, evil, and lies. And you will learn to sign those people quickly. They will make you rich."

"Did you know Seamus was an addict?"

"Are you asking as an *amiga* or an apprentice?"

Both answers were dangerous.

"A friend."

"Okay, no. I figured he was just a run-of-the-mill drinker, bit too much whiskey at parties, but he is better at hiding his truth than most."

"That's not good news."

"I know, Nicolita, and you know that better than I do. But right now, let's hustle so you can go on your bad-move date tonight. What do you know about this Bette Wu bidniss?"

"Did you just say *bidniss*?"

"I learned it from Alicia."

Nicola groaned loudly.

I am surrounded by children.

"I stayed up all night reconfiguring the press plan to incorporate Bette. They want us to dress her—I suggest we tell Crystal to suck it. Until Seamus signs a movie, he's cash poor, so the less out-of-pocket for us, the better."

Gaynor sank a straw into her coffee and sipped.

"*Bueno, bueno. Más fuerte.* I like it. Okay, supergirl, show me your press plan."

Nicola nodded and opened the folder she had brought with her. She spread out a sheaf of papers on the desk: TV, PRINT, RADIO, AWARDS SHOWS, RED CARPETS.

"I can't focus on so many words. This looks like something my kids would show me. I meant just tell me what we are being offered, and we'll take it from there."

"TV is easy. It has to be *Kimmel*, and we are going to push for it to be the Oscars after-show."

"That's nearly two months away. And Seamus won't want to do the Oscars."

"Seamus's days of doing what he wants are over," Nicola said. "You should have heard how they talked about him. He's a trained monkey at this point. In two months his fans will be invested in the Bette story line. *Kimmel* will be the payoff."

"Get him on *Kimmel* two days before the Oscars and you will win."

"You know who really wants him? Dr. Phil."

Gaynor pinched her nose and started waving the air around her face as if she were banishing a bad smell.

"*Guácala!*" she spat. "Never mention that hillbilly's name again in this office. He is for people who can't afford a publicist. Unless we start working with those *brujas* from Bravo, God forbid, we never take his calls."

"The official story," Nicola said, ignoring Gaynor and trying to get somewhere with the meeting, "is that Seamus's injury on set was much worse than we at first thought. I've talked to the doctor you recommended, and he wants to be a part of the story. He's happy to go on TV and talk about the injury that Seamus suffered when he fell during sword training. We're going to take Seamus to that sports rehab doctor in Relondo Beach, the one that's always on MSNBC, and set up some photos."

"Who gets those photos?"

"*People* magazine, der."

Gaynor beamed with pride. "Do they know it's fake?"

"*Fake* is such a strong word."

"Does Seamus know he's doing this?"

Nicola paused before answering. She quietly pushed the papers back into a neat pile and closed the folder. "Not yet," she said quietly.

"And you think he'll cooperate?"

"He has to, or he'll be doing *Sharknado Nineteen* by the end of the year."

Gaynor brayed her hyena laugh. "Who's picking him up tomorrow?"

"Bluey is gonna do it," Nicola said softly. "It really sucks. He doesn't know it yet, but he doesn't have anywhere to live. He doesn't have a car. He doesn't have any friends. The studio put his clothes into storage when he went to rehab. Bluey is trying to get them today, but Crystal is watching him like a hawk, and she says he's not allowed to help Seamus anymore. It's not his job. When Seamus books a movie, we need to poach Bluey."

"The most shocking thing is that their friendship appears to be real."

"It's real. He's going to live at Bluey's in Highland Park until he finds something else."

"I don't even know where that is." Gaynor made a flicking motion with her hot-pink nails. "But it sounds disgusting. Why is a movie star living in *la olla*?"

"Literally every show on HBO, Netflix, and Amazon films there. Anyway, that's where he will be until he books something else or decides to rent his own place."

"Remember, Nicola, there's nothing tighter than a Scotsman's purse strings."

❋ ❋ ❋

The girl in the mirror of the HHPR office bathroom did not look as tired as Nicola felt. She also looked way sluttier than Nicola felt, and she regretted involving Gaynor in her wardrobe selection. She was clad in a black Gemma halter lace sheath dress that was too low on top and too lacy on the bottom for her liking. Even with sheer makeup, she felt like a bartender at Bootsy's. She fought down an urge to cancel.

"Only cowards cancel," she told the girl in the mirror. Her plans to walk the four blocks to Fig & Olive had been derailed by the spiked Gucci heels that stole her heart in the stylist suite. She called a car, said good night to Gaynor, and went down to the street to wait.

Two minutes later, she was getting out of the car at Fig & Olive. As she straightened up and closed the door, movement at the corner of her eye caused her to spin around, prepared to whack someone with her Fendi purse. It was Timothy.

"Nicola, hey, so good to see you," he said, wrapping her in a hug that lasted two beats too long.

"Oh, hi, I guess we're hugging. Hi, Timothy."

He kept one hand on her back as he ushered her through the front door of the restaurant.

"Our table is ready," he said. "I already checked." Nicola wondered just how early he had gotten there.

Bypassing the maître d' station, he led her to a table in the far corner of the main room. He pulled her chair out for her and gently pushed it toward the table when she sat. *Billy is going to die when I tell him I've found the last gentleman in Hollywood.*

"So, how was your day?" he said enthusiastically, taking his seat.

"Oh, you know, the usual. We derailed a few scandals, issued a few 'no comments,' and united Israel and Palestine."

Timothy laughed, and Nicola noticed his teeth for the first time, alabaster white and improbably perfect.

"Same here. I organized production insurance for Seamus and cured cancer."

"Ooof," Nicola laughed. "Which was harder?"

It was Timothy's turn to laugh.

"In comparison, the cancer was a breeze. I don't want to talk business all night, but as a team, we really have our work cut out for us if we want to keep our percentages high."

"I'm not on a percentage."

"You know what I mean," Timothy said brusquely. "Anyway, I think that our boy is up for some good stuff. If he books Parallax, it's new houses for all of us."

Nicola looked around the room. Even though Gaynor had given her a sizable raise, buying a house anywhere in LA was something she couldn't even dream of. A sea of servers clad in black tended tables around them, but nobody had come to them yet, and there were no menus on the table. She wanted a drink. Now.

"So, why don't you tell me a little about yourself." Timothy gave her another dizzying smile. "You appeared on my radar suddenly, shall we say?"

"Not much to tell," Nicola said uneasily, wishing a waiter would interrupt. "I'm from Ohio, I've been in LA awhile, you know where I work."

"That's an oversimplification. You're this year's publicist success story. What's your secret?"

"Luck," she said simply.

"Well, I hope some of that luck can rub off on me."

Nicola searched his face for hints that he was being flirty. "I'm sorry . . ."

"Oh, I'm so ready to be a senior agent. I've been doing all the footwork at Global for seven years; I'm ready for the big time."

"What will it take to get you there?"

"One. Great. Client." Timothy slapped the table three times for emphasis. "Same as what happened to you, basically. I have a bunch of C-listers; I just need one A-lister to believe in me, and I'll be in the stratosphere."

A waiter appeared at the table, set a drink in front of each of them, and disappeared without a word.

"What's going on?" Nicola asked.

"Oh, I took the liberty of calling your assistant today and finding out what you like. I wanted to treat you to a nice surprise. No need for menus tonight. You're in my capable hands."

Nicola bit her tongue to stop herself from answering. She counted to ten in her head. Alicia had left to take care of the twins before lunch and hadn't returned. Who had Timothy talked to? She lifted her drink to her mouth, and the pungent aroma of Campari and orange peel filled her nose. It was a Negroni. He'd talked to Gaynor. She sipped and tried to conceal her anger.

The waiter reappeared with a platter covered in ice and raw oysters. He placed the platter in the center of the table and once again vanished without a word. Nicola surveyed the wreckage of shells, ice, and shriveled gray meat and fought down an urge to gag.

"Would you like lemon on your oysters?"

Nicola smiled invitingly and nodded. She'd never eaten an oyster; she'd never felt the need. They looked like bat scrotums and they smelled like low tide. Timothy took a tiny spoon and sprinkled an oyster with grated horseradish and some tomato garnish.

"It's the only way to eat these things," he smiled, picking up the oyster shell in his fingers.

Fuck you, Gaynor, Nicola thought as she reached out, grabbed an oyster, and lifted it to her lips. Timothy watched her eyes as he did the same and noisily slurped the oyster into his mouth. Nicola took a deep breath and willed her mouth to transport the oyster from her lips to the back of her throat before she could taste it, gulping quickly to make sure it went down instead of coming back out.

"You don't chew them?" Timothy asked, licking his lips.

"No." Nicola smiled as tears stung her eyes. "Why would I?"

She took a swig of her Negroni, swapping one taste she didn't like for another.

"Who's on your roster aside from Seamus?" Timothy asked, heaping condiments onto another oyster.

"Brian Gregory, Kara Jones, and Seamus are my principals, and I work with Gaynor on all of her other clients, like Paul Stroud and Amber Bank. Why?"

"Reality stars and superstars. Kind of a weird cross section, huh? You're probably doing it right, actually. A diversified portfolio."

Nicola wondered if he'd notice if she didn't eat another oyster.

"What do you mean?"

"Well, if you're gonna do movie stars, do men. You'll have a longer relationship. Men have careers for decades. You line up a few good men, no pun intended, and you'll have clients for years. For reality stars, do the women; they get that white heat for a year or two and then vanish. You probably just need two more of each and you'll be set."

"Or I could try to find some great actresses and help guide them into long and lucrative careers."

"Won't happen." Timothy lifted another oyster to his face, shaking it for emphasis. "Every It girl in Hollywood vanishes when she hits thirty-two. I'm not kidding. They'll start with the big movie, follow with a few more big movies, they'll rack up a Golden Globe and an Oscar nom, and then they turn thirty-two and they vanish. They'll resurface in several years on a high-profile premium cable network, HBO or Netflix. But they won't need a publicist because they won't get any press. In their forties, they'll come back as either head detective on a CBS procedural, or even worse, as a mom on the CW."

"So jaded," Nicola said, deciding not to eat any more oysters.

"Wait till you've been in the business as long as I have."

"And how long is that?"

"Seven years. I told you."

"That doesn't seem long enough for you to become completely sexist."

"Oh, here we go again." Timothy rolled his eyes and put his oyster shell back onto its icy tray. "I'd love to be able to find some actress that I could represent for twenty years."

"Then why don't you?"

"Hey, I don't want to fight, and I also don't want to be held responsible for the industry. I work within it; I don't define it, and I don't tell the public when to fall out of love with an actress."

Nicola remained silent for a few seconds and then defiantly took an oyster shell, brought it to her lips, and tipped its contents onto her tongue. She made eye contact with Timothy as she chewed the oyster into a slimy paste and swallowed it.

"Delicious," she said as soon as it was past the point of making her gag.

"Are you single?" Timothy asked suddenly.

Nicola nodded cautiously. "You?"

Timothy nodded. They simultaneously reached for the last two oysters, eating them in silence, Nicola wincing at the zinc-flavored sliminess.

"What happened with you and Seamus?" Timothy asked deliberately.

She flinched slightly. "Nothing, really," she said, moving her knife slowly back and forth across the tablecloth. "We went on a couple dates, but it became clear early on that it wouldn't ever amount to much more than that, and then he went away to . . ." Nicola paused, scanning the room.

"Clean up his act?"

"Yeah, that."

The waiter refreshed their drinks and spirited the tray of empty shells and ice away. Nicola picked up her knife and nervously tapped it on the table. Timothy placed his hand over hers, stopping the nervous knife movement.

"Well, I'm glad to have you on the team. That meeting was stressful, and Weatherman was hard on you, but you have to see it from his side."

"I have to, do I?"

"Until you've had to pay back a ten-million-dollar commission because your client messed up his drug intake, you won't understand."

"I dunno." Nicola pulled her hand away from his. "If I'd already made quite a few ten-million-dollar commissions out of a client, I'd be more concerned about their well-being."

"Oh, Wallace, you have a lot to learn."

Nicola fought down an urge to get up and leave. She was about to respond when the waiter returned with a sprawling, rare steak resting in a pool of blood.

"Madame, monsieur, your chateaubriand," he said, setting the carnage on the table.

Nicola felt her anger rising. *Gaynor would never eat food like this.* The waiter returned with two sides, potatoes and brussels sprouts. Nicola glared at the plates. She'd be stopping at In-N-Out on the way home.

The waiter began to slice the steak, placing several chunks onto Nicola's plate. Her stomach froze at the bright pink meat. She was a well-done girl. After the waiter slid another few hunks of bleeding steak onto Timothy's plate, he vanished. Timothy automatically picked up the potatoes and swept four of them onto Nicola's plate, then did the same with the brussels sprouts, their moldy odor rising into her nostrils.

"Everything okay?" he asked with a smile.

"Yes," she lied. "It looks great." To her horror, Timothy reached across the table and began to cut her steak into even smaller pieces, raising one to her face.

"What the hell are you doing, Timothy?"

He appeared dumbstruck. "I'm sorry . . . ," he began. "Some women like it when I do this. . . ."

Nicola sighed angrily. "Most of your dates want you to feed them?"

Timothy nodded, still looking confused.

"Well, I'm not like them, I guess," Nicola said with a wan smile. "I'm okay to feed myself, but thank you, it's a nice gesture. I guess."

"That sure went weird." Timothy took the steak and put it in his own mouth, chewing sullenly. "She said you were tough."

"Wanting to feed myself doesn't make me tough. . . . Wait, who said I was tough?"

"Nobody," Timothy mumbled. "Oh, okay, Gaynor said you were tough."

Nicola raised one eyebrow. "So, did you talk to my assistant, or did you talk to Gaynor?"

Timothy set his cutlery down. "Nicola, I'll level with you. I talked to Gaynor. She told me what to expect, and how to win you over."

"How's that working out for you? You've served me a drink I don't like and a plate of food I wouldn't eat with *your* mouth, and you've managed to insult me, several times over."

"Jesus, I see why Seamus went for you; he likes a straight talker."

Nicola bit down a logjam of responses. "Look, Timothy, this probably wasn't a great idea. I don't know if you brought me here for a business meeting or to get on Seamus's good side or what . . ."

"I brought you here on a date," he whined like a spoiled kid. "There was something about you at the meeting that told me I wanted to know more about you. And sue me—I wanted to make a good impression, so I called the only person I know who knows you! I mean, the only one who isn't in rehab."

He offered her a slight smile and made a face that would have been irresistible to a five-year-old. "How can we save the night?" he asked earnestly.

"Can we send half the steak back and get it up to a nice well done, and get some beer in a chilled glass? And those baby cabbages need to get sent back to whatever hell they came from. I'd love a side of fresh spinach."

Without another word, Timothy raised his hand and summoned the waiter.

✳ ✳ ✳

An hour later, both of them were laughing. Something had definitely shifted after Nicola's little outburst. Four beers each hadn't hurt, either. Timothy had told her about growing up in Kansas and they had bonded over small-town stories. Nicola noticed that she was finally having a good time, despite herself. She'd eaten more of the steak than she had expected to and was pleased when the waiter came and asked if she wanted any dessert instead of just springing some upon her. She declined, and Timothy caught her eye.

"Would it be okay if I ordered us some drinks instead of dessert?"

Nicola smiled and nodded. Timothy spoke fluent French to the waiter, who nodded neatly and took off.

"So, did it get any better?" he asked, looking into her eyes.

"Yes, Timothy. Thanks. Sorry about my freak-out earlier. I still can't get my head around people being comfortable being spoon-fed on a date. I'd like to save that till I'm eighty. And then I'd still rather struggle on my own."

"Totally copacetic," Timothy said, sounding like a grandpa trying to be hip. "And we haven't even talked shop that much."

"Why would we talk shop on a date?" she teased.

"I want to help you," he said simply. "And as I've been warned, you're not one to accept help. But I still think we should talk work a little."

"I'm intrigued," Nicola lied. The waiter returned and set a goblet in front of each of them, and Nicola could smell the oaky notes floating from the glasses.

"Whiskey?"

"Armagnac," Timothy said, raising his glass. "It's seventy-five years old." He sniffed at his glass. "It smells so amazing, it's almost a shame to drink it. Cheers, to you and to us and to smooth sailing."

She nodded and fought down a memory of her first date with Seamus, on the yacht. Taking a sip of her Armagnac, she kept it in her mouth, enjoying the dull pain.

"Perfect, huh?" Timothy said.

"It is," she agreed. "Now, what is this work matter? Let's get it over and done with."

"Okay. Keep this in your back pocket, and remember, this is up to you to bring off. Weatherman was nervous about telling you this. We don't have an NDA with you, and we can't afford for you to get poached and sell us out."

"Timothy, if I wanted to get rich selling Seamus out, I wouldn't be sitting here with you."

"Well, here goes," he said, drinking the rest of his Armagnac obscenely fast. "We need help to make the Bette thing work."

"That sounds like a Tobin job."

"Seamus doesn't listen to Tobin. Or anyone, actually. The art of managing Seamus is to let him think he makes his own decisions."

"He doesn't?"

"No successful celebrity does."

"So you think that he'll listen when his ex-girlfriend asks him to pretend to date someone else?"

"Tobin thinks that Seamus would do anything, if *you* asked him."

Nicola's heart made an odd, painful twinge. "I'm not comfortable with this one, Timothy," she said softly. "I think you should talk to Bluey."

"I will talk to Bluey when he's part of our team again."

"And until then?"

"You're our de facto Bluey. And Seamus must never know."

Nicola slumped visibly.

"I know, I know, but this deal with Bette is costing us a lot."

"Of money?"

"No, favors. It's not easy to get a studio to agree to giving someone like her a lead role in a franchise."

"Because she's a TV actor."

"Precisely, but with the right relationship and, you know, the plastic surgery that they all get—"

"*They*?" Nicola was shocked. "Asians? That's racist as fuck."

"Christ, calm down, no. Actresses. Don't tell me you haven't ever noticed that every actress's face changes after her third movie. Did you think it was contouring? A flattering haircut?" He laughed. "Padawan, it's facial lipo, cheekbone resculpting, eye lifts, and brow smoothing. For women *and* men. It's boob jobs and ass lipo and implants and lasers and anything else that sounds invasive and painful. And we've agreed to pay for that for Bette, too."

Nicola shook her head. Bette was naturally breathtakingly beautiful.

"So how do you feel about setting your ex up with a fake girlfriend?"

"I feel fake jealousy and real relieved. I also feel like an asshole. And I'm telling you now, he won't like hearing it from me."

"You know why he'll do it? He'll do it when we tell him that until he books another movie, we've frozen his assets due to outstanding debt. If he does what you ask, he gets a black Amex with no daily limit."

The waiter delivered another round of Armagnac. Nicola drained hers in one long, fiery gulp.

"Thanks for your help, Timothy. I need to get myself home. Tomorrow's going to be a long day."

CHAPTER 5

KARA HAD BEEN SITTING AT the empty table in the deserted dining room at Fred Segal for nearly twenty minutes. A camera assistant measured the light on her face for the fourth time and nodded at a cameraman huddled behind a camera a few feet in front of her. Someone's walkie crackled.

"We are ready for Amber. Repeat. Ready for Amber."

Kara blew a kiss at the cameraman and rubbed her upper arms for warmth. Amber had already insisted that they move seating locations from the outdoor patio to the center of the room, and now, to the corner. "This place looks too empty; I only eat in crowded restaurants," she had instructed before vanishing once more into the production van.

Kara had seen Amber's hair person, Bobo, wandering around the parking lot under an umbrella, talking on the phone, so she knew Amber wasn't getting her hair done. She could see Amber's Starwaggon parked in a far corner of the lot. If Amber was inside, she was getting high.

"Hey, Kara." She looked up to see Melanie, the sexy senior producer for *Bank on This*, approaching, her jet-black hair pulled into two long ponytails. "We're gonna need your help with this scene."

Kara looked at her phone. It wasn't even quarter past eleven yet, and they were an hour behind schedule. Amber was being Amber. And Kara was getting tired of being her wrangler.

"Anything, sister," she said, grinning slowly.

Melanie sat in the chair that Amber should have been sitting in and leaned in close. "Look, girl, you and I both know what's going on. Amber doesn't want to film in an empty restaurant, but we can only shoot till noon. Then they want paying customers in here. I'm not gonna do twenty TV releases. We have to flip the script."

Kara groaned. She had come to hate that saying in just a few months. Reality TV flipped the script daily.

"I know, I know, and I'm sorry." Melanie rubbed Kara's bare shoulder. "The story line for today is that Amber is going to find out that she's doing a photo shoot for *Vanity Fair*."

"Yeah, I have my lines, I know."

"Well, they're changing. She's going to be too high to get the reaction we need, so we are just going to spring a bunch of surprises on her, via you."

Melanie pulled a rolled-up script out of her pocket and tried to flatten it on the table.

Kara looked it over and shook her head. "You want me to tell her that SaraBeth Shields is talking behind her back? And that Paul Stroud is dating someone new?"

"Sorry, I know it won't be easy, but we have spent so much on this location, we need to get something salvageable or my ass is toast."

Kara reached over and took one of Melanie's ponytails in each hand and pulled them gently.

"Anything for you, mama," she joked in a raspy voice.

"If I thought you meant that, I'd be canceling today and taking you home," Melanie said with a wink.

"If I ever go for girls, there's nobody else for me."

Melanie stood up, grabbing at her heart and pretending to swoon. "Promises, promises," she laughed. "I'll be back with crankypants in a second. You good with the paper script, or you want me to hide an earpiece inside that hair of yours and feed you the questions?"

"I got this," Kara said. She watched as Melanie walked out to the parking lot, her ass swaying in her skintight stretch jeans. *Dating her wouldn't be the worst idea*, Kara mused. *Probably smarter than whatever I'm doing with Mason.*

Since she'd left his hotel room yesterday morning, unrecognizable in men's overalls and her hair squeezed into a hard hat, Bluey by her side, Mason had texted her constantly. Bluey had swept his hotel room, finding two audio bugs and a micro-camcorder. Mason had been furious yet grateful. He'd wrapped his reshoots at three forty-five a.m. and begged her to come back to his room. She had politely declined. He replied with a sad-face emoji and a dick pic.

She had a live one on the line. But Bluey warned her not to see him again until after the Globes.

In the corner of her eye she saw the door of Amber's Starwaggon fly open, and a mushroom cloud of weed smoke drifted into the drab, rainy sky. Two production assistants with golf umbrellas waited for Amber to stagger down the two steps. They grabbed her by one arm each and led her en masse to the back door of Fred Segal. As soon as they were under cover, Amber broke free of them and picked up her pace. She slouched toward Kara and dropped into her seat.

"Did you sit there the whole time, bitch?"

"What else am I gonna do, cracker?" Kara pointed at her Afro, then out to the rain.

"What the fuck do I know about n . . . urban hair?" Amber said, glancing at Kara with fake horror, the way she always did when she almost used the N-word.

Kara refused to bite. This was Amber 101—she was in a bad mood, she didn't want to film today, and, if possible, she would sabotage it and make it someone else's fault.

The sound guy moved in and lowered his boom over the table, meaning that Amber had refused to wear a mic again.

Melanie clapped her hands and shushed everyone in the room. "Okay, we're gonna go until we get this. We have less than thirty minutes before they let the public in, and we have a lot of ground to cover."

A lot of ground? thought Kara. She only had two things to mention.

Silence fell over the room, and a waiter brought two identical salads and set them in front of the girls.

"I can't eat this," Amber said, pushing it back.

"You're not going to eat it, just pretend."

"Can you please make some small talk?" Melanie yelled.

Amber was so high, she could barely hold her head up. Her eyes were puffy and red, and if Kara liked her a little more she would have said something.

"Did you have fun at the Globes party?" Kara began, lifting a piece of chicken to her mouth with a fork, then replacing it on the plate.

"I don't even remember," Amber replied, pushing her food around slowly. "Was I there? Was it so lame that I don't even remember? I should have thrown my own party."

"Whatever. If you don't want to talk about what happened, that's fine."

"Why?" Amber was suddenly alert. "What happened?"

"Your fight with SaraBeth? Does that ring any bells?"

"I wouldn't call it a fight. She showed up in that Calle Del Mar dress I made famous, waving a crack pipe all over the place. Whatever happened to manners?"

Kara bit her tongue, choosing to not mention that Amber's crack pipe had fallen out of her purse in the kitchen last week and shattered all across the floor. In front of her parents.

"I sure don't know. Anyways, SaraBeth was talking shit about you all night."

"Like I said, I don't care. I brought that desperate beast up from the gutter, and I can kick her right back. She's like a rescue-dog celebrity. I can take her back to the rescue and switch her out for a loyal pet, not some angry dog that's been chained up all its life."

Out of the corner of her eye, Kara saw a broad smile spread across Melanie's face.

"Why do you keep her around?" Kara asked, knowing that Amber would never tell the truth—that she'd refriended SaraBeth to stay in touch with Seamus while he was in the Malibu rehab.

"She was funny for a while, like in a sad clown kind of way." Amber actually shoved a large piece of chicken into her mouth and began chewing while she talked. "I love charity work, but you can't help everyone. Let's face it, she isn't ever going to be famous again."

"She's still kind of famous . . . ," Kara began.

"She couldn't get a paid appearance in Poland! The meth has destroyed her voice, everyone knows she lip-synchs. Jesus—why did you even bring her up?" She spat the remaining chicken back onto her plate. "I've lost my appetite."

"Sorry," Kara said. "Did you read Perez today?"

"I don't read Perez, he calls me and tells me the news I need to hear."

"So did he call you and tell you that Paul Stroud is dating Kiri Anderson?"

Amber threw her fork into her salad. Perez had *not* called her on this one.

"Why would I even care? He's not my boyfriend, and why are we even talking about Kiri? Maybe all that coke burned out her sense of smell? They belong together. It won't help her career."

"What do you mean? He's fucking huge."

"Can you guys stop swearing so much," Melanie yelled.

"Fuck off!" they both yelled back, flipping her the bird.

"Thanks, bitches," Melanie said absently. "Keep rolling."

"You really don't care?"

"No, bitch, no, I've told you. No, he's literally just a friend."

"Have you talked to him lately?"

"Yeah, he's just wrapping on that movie, the one with Tom Kendall."

Kara's head jerked up involuntarily. She hadn't spoken to on-the-rise megastar Kendall since they'd hooked up on the set of the same movie nearly three months ago, when Seamus was still the movie's star.

"You guys are still talking?"

"Not really; I have other people who keep me up to date on everything that's going on in this town."

Kara nodded and moved the piece of chicken up to her mouth, then back to the plate.

"Like I heard that someone is trying to sell a sex tape of you and a mystery man. . . ."

Kara froze. Amber had her chin resting on her hands, her blue eyes open wide in false innocence. Kara gulped. She looked over at Melanie, but Melanie was fussing with the front of her shirt. Nobody on the crew was making eye contact with her.

I'm being set up. I'm being set up. Fuuuuuuck.

"Has mama been making naughty movies?" Amber said in a baby-girl voice. Kara fought down panic.

"I ain't that stupid, girl," she said, trying to sound light. "Who you getting your news from? *In Touch?*"

"As if, Jonesy."

Kara wanted to hit Amber so hard.

"Who has the highest selling sex tape of all time? That's right. Me. And my sex tape agent called me for your number."

Kara knew she'd been totally set up. She looked at the two cameras. There was no way this discussion was going to happen in front of them.

"Well, I don't think your sales record has anything to worry about." Kara's mind was racing. Was it her rapper ex, Jimmy J? Everyone knew that a sex tape needed two celebrities to sell. Had Jimmy J secretly saved their Skype sex sessions? She hadn't filmed anything since. . . . She stopped breathing. Tom Kendall. She had set up her old Flip camcorder in her purse and let it run when they hooked up. And she had left it on the counter in the panic after Seamus's overdose. Nicola had checked after, and nobody had found it. She needed to call her paparazzo contact Gino. His agency had been on-site during that whole disaster.

Continuing to fight down panic, Kara needed to end the scene as quickly as possible.

"No, I know that," Amber said tersely. "As if millions of people would want to watch *your* sex tape. I was just wondering if you knew."

"I'm an old-fashioned girl. I ain't never made no sex tape," Kara laughed, and reached for a bread roll, knocking a full glass of iced tea into Amber's lap.

All the yelling was a small price to pay for ending the scene.

✳ ✳ ✳

In the chaos that followed, Kara ran to her car and sat hyperventilating in the driver's seat. Melanie texted that they had lost the location and she was due at Amber's in two hours. Kara moved to the back-seat and curled up in a ball, her mind racing.

She pulled her phone out of her pocket and frantically dialed Gino the paparazzo. They hadn't talked since she'd decided not to sell out Nic and Seamus on the movie set in Ojai.

"Hey, Gino."

There was a long pause.

"Gino? It's me."

"New phone, who dis?"

"Gino, don't be a dick, you know who it is."

"Oh, wait, it's the stupid bitch who probably cost me a million dollars. Amiright?"

"Christ, Gino, yes, it's Kara. Look, I need to ask you something."

"Kara, yep, that's the name of the stupid bitch who cost me a million dollars. Do you have any idea how much money we could have made for those stupid photos? You and I would have been sitting pretty."

Kara felt her panic turn to anger and her breathing sped up. She fought to keep her anxiety under control.

"Gino, I need to ask you something."

"You know what's funny? Every one of you bitches is nice to me when you need something. It's been three months—did you even call to say sorry?"

"No," Kara said, surprised. It hadn't actually occurred to her to call and apologize to the man who tried to blackmail her into selling out her friend. "I went to the Hallmark store and they didn't have a card for that occasion. Gino, can I just ask you a question?"

"You're going to anyway."

"Gino, did your guy find a camcorder up in Ojai?"

"Don't know what you're talking about, darlin'."

"Are you telling me the truth?"

"Why? Do you suddenly trust me?"

Kara was silent.

Gino continued. "Right. What does it even matter? I'm a liar, you're a celebrity. But I'll tell you one thing. If I did find your camcorder, I wouldn't have a problem selling whatever was on it. You know. As karma."

Kara hung up, then went to Gino's contact in her phone and blocked his number. She inhaled deeply and held her breath. That hadn't gone too badly, she reasoned. He didn't appear to know about the camcorder. She ran a fingernail around the screen of her phone. She'd have to text her ex-boyfriend Jimmy J, the boy-band rapper she'd dumped via a meme that went viral, then sold out to *Spyglass* magazine.

Hey stud it's Kara. You shoppin a sex tape of us? Hearin' rumors. <3

Her phone dinged almost immediately.

Burn in hell traitor bitch ho U fuck me up goooood

Then another ding:

We made a sex tape?

Kara exhaled with a smile. It wasn't J.

No daddy talk l8er

Girl where u at right now? We could make 1

Chuckling, Kara blocked his number, too.

A loud rapping at her window made her jump in shock. SaraBeth Shields and Courtney Hauser were peering into her car. Kara felt her teeth clench when she noticed that SaraBeth was wearing an expensive blue Lily Ashwell dress, dirt smudges along the hem. She'd called that in for Amber to wear. SaraBeth must have stolen it from Amber's trailer. It was ruined now.

"Hey, skank," SaraBeth said. "Production said Amber was out here."

Kara fought down a snicker. Amber had told everyone on production to never tell SaraBeth where she was. SaraBeth had still never figured that out, despite being sent on a wild-goose chase every time she turned up on set.

"Do you see her?" Kara said. "She ain't here."

Courtney Hauser, her arm in its usual filthy cast, struggled to light a cigarette in the rainy wind. She was clad in a hot-pink Juicy puffer and too-short denim cutoffs, her painfully thin freckled legs disappearing into a pair of trashed brown Uggs.

After flicking at her lighter unsuccessfully, she hunkered down in the gutter, vanishing out of Kara's view. When she stood back up, she exhaled a cloud of acrid smoke into Kara's just-opened window.

"Hey, Jones," she said in her sandpapery voice.

"Hi," Kara said, waving the smoke away from her face, surprised that Courtney even remembered her. She'd never called Kara by name before.

"I hear Seamus is coming back to town this week," Courtney said.

"Are you telling me or asking me?" Kara said gruffly, pushing the door open and standing beside them.

"Neither, I guess," Courtney said. "But that's why we came to find Amber. She told us to tell her the second we found out anything about him."

"She says your friend is still in love with him," SaraBeth added.

"Are we eight years old?" Kara said, looking up at the rain. She was going to have to wrap the 'fro for the next scene.

"No need to be defensive," Courtney continued. "Don't shoot up the messenger."

"Isn't it 'don't shoot the messenger'?"

"Depends who you ask." Courtney pinched the cigarette between her fingers and took a deep drag. "So what have you heard about Seamus coming back to LA? Is he still gonna be living up by Soho House?"

"So you're asking?" Kara said.

"I told you she was a bitch," SaraBeth said.

They were fishing. Amber had sent them.

"You guys, I'm not a bitch," Kara said with a false smile. "It's just sensitive. The house that he's rented, he don't want everyone to turn up at once."

Both girls turned to face Kara.

"Do you have the address?" SaraBeth asked eagerly.

"You gotta call him to get it," Kara said, fluffing at her hair. "You got his digits?"

"Yeah, of course," SaraBeth said, obviously lying.

Courtney tossed her cigarette onto the rainy parking lot and started digging in the pocket of her cutoffs, producing a business card. She handed it to Kara.

It read HOUSE OF HAUSER and featured a 310 number.

"Give this to Seamus, and I'll give you five hundred bucks," she said. "If you tell your roommate, a sex tape will be the least of your problems."

Courtney spun clumsily and walked off without looking back. SaraBeth tottered behind, raindrops soaking her already-ruined dress.

Kara flicked the business card up into the pearly sky and watched as it landed in a dirty puddle.

She texted Melanie that she had really bad cramps and needed to go home and lie down. She'd be at Amber's house by three. Then she called Nicola, who answered on the first ring.

"Are you okay?" she said. "A voice call is always bad news."

"Can I come to the office?"

"Yes, Kara, what's wrong?"

Kara scoured the parking lot to make sure she was alone.

"Code red, Wallace. Coffee Bean by your office. No Gaynor. Five minutes."

"Okay, Kara, I'm leaving now. Are you okay? What's going on?"

"Absolute dramurgency."

CHAPTER 6

NICOLA WAS HALFWAY THROUGH HER iced Americano when Kara finally arrived at Coffee Bean.

"I nearly broke my neck getting here in five minutes. Where the hell were you shooting?"

"Fred Segal."

"You could have walked here in three minutes."

Kara pointed at her hair, then at the rain, then at a well-known paparazzo sitting at a table near the window.

"This city is a land mine. That for me?" Kara pointed at a second iced coffee on the table. Nicola nodded. "It's a little cold for an iced drink, wouldn't you say?"

Nicola shrugged. "You get what you're given. If you don't want it, I'll take it back to the office for later."

"You're my publicist; you're supposed to know my drank."

Nicola laughed. "I'm your seven-hundred-and-fifty-dollar-a-month publicist, so you can get your own drank. Drink. Whatever."

"We don't have time for this right now." Kara slid into the chair opposite and swiped the coffee. "We have our very first scandal."

"So Felicity Storm found out you banged her husband?"

"He likes it when I treat him mean," Kara whispered with her hand over her mouth. "And it's fuuuun."

"That's kind of amazing," Nic said. "What else?"

"Nicola, not right now," Kara continued, her mouth still covered. "*Yo. Tengo. Uno.* Sex tape."

"Using a language I don't speak, in a city where most people do speak it, is probably not your best strategy."

"*I have a sex tape,*" Kara hissed.

Nicola pushed back in her chair and sighed. She should have seen this one coming. "Are you sure?"

"Well, no, but Amber says it's true."

"The obvious question is, have you filmed, or been filmed, with anyone?"

Kara dropped her eyes and took a long, slow sip of her coffee, then swiped her phone on and tapped out a text.

Nicola's phone dinged, and as she read the two-word text, her eyes bugged out.

"Grab your coffee," she said, standing noisily and gesturing for Kara to move. "It's time to break out the big guns. This is a Gaynor matter."

✳ ✳ ✳

"Karita, *mi fufurufa*, I always knew you were a little bit loca, but even for you, Jones, this is impressive and terrifying," Gaynor said, pacing around the HHPR boardroom. "This isn't a scandal, it's a civil war."

Kara rolled her eyes at Gaynor's theatrics. Gaynor saw her, and Nicola watched her boss's eyes narrow in anger.

"Firstly, we need to find out if it's true, or just a rumor," Nicola said, stepping in.

"*Ay, no,*" Gaynor said. "The facts don't lie. She filmed it. The camcorder went missing on a hot set. It's never been found. And now, a few months later, people are talking about a sex tape between two people that nobody knew had sex. The next step is obvious."

"Yeah, mama gets rich and famous," Kara said, reclining in her chair and putting her feet onto the chair next to her.

"Kara," Nicola said angrily. "You don't have the tape. Someone else is angling to get rich, and you won't get famous, you'll destroy your career, and your poor parents, and what about your sister? She's still in college."

"Yeah, you're right." Kara looked suddenly crestfallen. Nicola was right as usual. Her parents were already worried about their eldest daughter in Hollywood. A sex tape would break their hearts. "So is there any way we can leverage it into something without it ever being released?"

Gaynor pressed her fingers against her temple.

"Nicola, please call Billy immediately. Ask him to help us. For this, we will pay him, but this is not a *Spyglass* story."

Nicola grabbed her phone and dialed.

"Babycakes," she said seriously. "Code red. Can you come here? Kara made a sex tape. Amber says it's circulating. Not for publication . . . sorry, B . . . Okay, see you soon."

"He's coming here?" Kara said. "Scandal gets all you bitches moving."

With lizard speed, Gaynor moved to Kara's side, kicked her feet off the chair, and turned her so they were face-to-face.

"If one single person ever mentions this tape, if news ever breaks, even one outlet, even a"—she paused for dramatic effect—"*podcast . . .* you will be finished. You will lose this tiny amount of fame and this pathetic attempt at a Hollywood life. You will be working at an Old Navy . . . *outlet* . . . and even then, they won't stop coming after you."

"Gaynor, I'm the client here. You can't talk to me like that."

"Nicola, please tell Señorita Jones that we no longer represent her." Gaynor walked through the door. "Charity cases shouldn't be this much work."

"Okay, okay, o-motherfuckin'-kay," Kara said, slapping her hand on the table. "Tell me what the big deal is?"

Gaynor turned back to her, keeping her hand on the door handle. "Tom Kendall is going to be a superstar. He is squeaky-clean. His team has laid the groundwork for a ten-year run of blockbusters. Do you know how much money that means? If they can keep him away from drugs and"—she glared at Kara—"*fufas*, they will all make millions upon millions of dollars. So, please, tell me, do you think that anyone is going to let a sex tape turn their golden goose into a laughingstock?"

"You act like I did this on purpose," Kara said. "Can't we try to sell it and then accept a nice five-million-dollar buyout to not release it?"

"It's charming that you think the choice is yours," Gaynor said.

"And it's also adorable that you're so naïve. Have you ever met his publicist, Meredith Cox?"

Kara shook her head.

"She is a psychopath. She doesn't issue denials; she scorches the earth. She is everyone's worst enemy. She will plant drugs on you, or set up a DUI. You'll end up in jail. She's like a Colombian gangster in head-to-toe Ann Taylor."

Kara looked at Nicola.

"She's not exaggerating," Nicola said softly. She'd been able to steer clear of Cox so far, but she had heard the horror stories.

"So, what do we do?" Kara said.

Nicola stood up and raised a hand to pause Gaynor.

"We wait for Billy to get here, and we find out if this is even true. If anyone comes to us, we deny. Actively deny. This tape does not exist. This tape was never made. Kara, are there any photos of you together from Ojai?"

"I took some on my phone; he didn't take any. The only people who saw us that night were at the dinner."

"And the riggers and gaffers who were still working."

"They're all covered by the movie NDA," Gaynor interjected. "But there was a pap on set that night."

"He doesn't have anything; I called him."

"*Madre mía.*" Gaynor stormed back into the conference room. "That is the last independent action you make. Now he's alert. From this second, you can make your stupid show, and then you can go home. No clubs. No restaurants. Low profile till this blows over."

"I'm going to the Golden Globes, and you can't stop me." Kara stood up and looked at her phone. "I have to get up to Amber's house to continue shooting."

"Tell them you're sick. We need you here," Gaynor said.

"No, Kara, you should go," Nicola said firmly. "Don't give Amber any ammo. Just be as happy and natural as you can, and act like there's no sex tape."

"She's right," Gaynor conceded. "And it isn't acting. There's no tape."

The daylight through the conference room window faded to gray. A small army of empty coffee cups had taken over the center of the table.

"I can't find any evidence; nobody has heard anything," Billy said. "And if I drink one more mouthful of coffee the top of my head is going to blow off."

Gaynor silently rose from the table and walked out of the room.

"Do you think there's a chance Amber made it up?" Nicola said, exhaustion in her voice.

"I don't," Billy said, reaching over and taking her hand. "But hey, at least it's not a sex tape of you and Seamus."

Nicola's head snapped up. "As if—" she began.

"No, no, I know," Billy said quickly, giving her hand a squeeze. "Like Gaynor says, you're not getting paid enough to care this much. At the end of the day, you don't have a dog in this fight. It's Kara's issue. If she's clever, she'll be fine, and if not, well, you tried."

"I'm not good at distancing myself from this stuff yet, B. It feels like it's my job. Kara ultimately never hurt me; she just considered it. We're all guilty of that. She just wants to be famous so badly, it makes her do dumb things."

"You can't unmake someone's bad decisions for them."

"You've been telling me that for a long time now."

"Maybe one day it will sink in."

"Maybe."

They smiled at each other in silence for a minute until the peace was broken by Gaynor returning with a drink tray. She placed it on the table and gestured at the bottles of Bombay Sapphire and vermouth and the jar of Spanish olives.

"Billy, don't tell me *un cacorro* like yourself doesn't know how to make the perfect martini after all those summers as a pool boy or whatever."

"Or you could just ask me to make some drinks."

"Where's the fun in that?"

Gaynor sat beside Nicola. The three of them had been making very cautious phone calls to their contacts all afternoon, unable to say too much. Asking about a sex tape without naming names was exhausting.

Billy got up and started fixing the martinis. His phone buzzed on the table and he glanced at it, smiled, and added a fourth glass to the line.

"Bluey is on his way here; he says he has something for us," he said, unable to contain his grin.

"Do you know how much Crystal pays him?" Gaynor said bluntly. "He's the best secret weapon in Hollywood."

"These days, it's Max Zetta who's paying most of his salary, and not that you heard it from me, but Max is not afraid to drop some extra cash on top to get what he wants."

Gaynor grimaced.

"I'm familiar with Señor Zetta's financial generosity in exchange for secrecy."

Billy and Nicola let the awkward silence ring out while Billy shook the martinis.

"How far away is he?"

"He's not far," Billy said, deftly pouring four drinks. He put down the shaker and began to spear the olives. They heard the door to reception open. "In fact, that should be him now."

Like a fifties housewife, Billy delicately stirred a martini with the olives and then stood upright by the door. As the craggily handsome Australian appeared, Billy kicked one of his heels back, kissed Bluey on the lips, and then presented his martini.

"Hard day at work, honey?" he asked brightly.

Bluey's face broke into a smile so wide his eyes became little green slits. Nicola shook her head at the change in Bluey: he'd terrified her at first, but his gruff, enigmatic exterior had melted away once he started dating Billy.

Bluey planted another kiss on Billy's lips, swiped the martini, and threw it back like a shot.

"Does that answer it? I'll take another; reuse the olives."

"Ahem," Gaynor coughed, waving her nails at the other martinis that Billy hadn't finished garnishing yet.

"Sorry, my queen," Billy said, dropping a spear of olives into the other three drinks, then quickly shaking up another for Bluey, who walked around the table, kissing Nicola on the top of the head and then blowing a kiss at Gaynor.

"Gaynor," he said. "I don't know how you put up with that disgusting Zetta bastard for so long. I've done a lot of weird shit in this town, but he manages to shock and appall me daily."

Gaynor crossed herself, then pretended to puke on the desk.

"Did you find something?" Nicola said hopefully. Bluey nodded and slowly took the seat opposite Gaynor.

"It's legit. It's out there. But whoever owns it knows what they're doing. They know it'll get shut down fast, so they're insisting on a ten-million-dollar contract on the table for the privilege of watching it. If you have the contract ready, they'll come to your office and show it. They want it to go to Vivid, but there's money on the table from Russia, which would be the worst-case scenario."

Billy handed the fresh drink to Bluey.

"And it's definitely Kara and Kendall?" Nicola asked.

"Confirmation is shaky, but likely. Amber must still be on very good terms with the company that released her tape, although I talked to that guy and he hasn't been asked to make a bid on it."

"But why tell Amber?" asked Nicola.

"A little bit of buzz never hurt a sex tape's reputation," Bluey said. "And you said that Courtney Hauser knows, too? It'll be all over town by the Globes. But there's no evidence. Nobody has seen it; nobody has even a still image on their phone. It'll just be idle chatter until the tape is sold."

"But how can they sell it without Kara or Tom signing off on it?"

"You put it online at fifty bucks a download and wait for the cease and desist. If you own the footage, you release it in other countries. It's a rolling ball and the lawyers will keep shutting it down, but the money will start pouring in. At that point, Tom and Kara may as well make some of that money."

"His people will never let that happen," Gaynor said.

"I know," Bluey laughed. "I saw Meredith Cox at Spago today, in the distance. She didn't look happy."

"She never does," scoffed Gaynor. "She has the face of an abused spaniel."

They all sipped at their drinks and looked at their phones.

"So that's it for today, huh?" Nicola said. "We just sit and wait for something to happen?"

Gaynor nodded. She looked at Bluey. "So what did Max have you doing for him today?"

Bluey rolled his eyes. "You know I can't tell you exactly, but I *can* tell you that he had me shopping for holy water and religious stuff over at the Crossroads of the World chapel on Sunset, and I got you something."

Bluey rummaged in his jacket pocket and pulled out a glow-in-the-dark rosary He slid it across the table to Gaynor.

"Something to light your times of darkness."

Gaynor smiled and picked it up, clutching it against her bosom.

"*Madre mía*, I'm so glad he's your problem now, not mine."

"Speaking of problems, I need to get out of here or traffic is going to become one for me." Bluey stood and walked over to Billy. He leaned and gave him a smooch on the lips.

"Hey, Nic," he said. "Why don't you two go out and have a nice night at the Peppermint Club tonight? On me."

"Sure, I guess," Nicola smiled. "Why? You working tonight?"

"Not exactly. Did you forget? I have to go pick up Seamus at the airport."

CHAPTER 7

THE GENTLE BUMP OF THE wheels touching the tarmac woke Seamus from his reverie. He was back in Los Angeles. *Well, Van Nuys.* Wherever that was. Seamus nervously tried to remember how many times he'd flown in and out of Van Nuys. It was easily a hundred times, and there was still no way he could find it on a map.

The wheels screeched as they hit the ground and the brakes gripped. He pulled forward in his seat, his hands clutching the armrests, his knuckles white, the backs of his hands bloodred. He forced himself to breathe deeply and willed his hands to relax, hoping that the rest of him would follow suit.

He brought his hands to his lap, rubbing them together purposefully. Gazing out the small window, he saw the usual pinpricks of white and blue lights dotting the darkness, each light circled by a sphere of winter haze. *It's going to be cold out there*, he thought. LA cold. Which was a lot more pleasant than the Seattle cold that he'd endured for the past ten weeks in rehab. Even though his rehab suite was heated, he never felt warm enough. It had felt like he was frozen inside.

The lights came on in the small cabin, and the only other occupant, a pleasantly jovial flight attendant named Dee, smiled at him from her jump seat.

"Welcome to LA, Mr. O'Riordan."

He nodded in her direction and smiled back. His brow furrowed. Had he fallen asleep right before landing? Or was he just that lost in thought? He didn't know.

The jet taxied briefly before stopping some distance away from the small terminal and squat air-control tower. The sight of the vintage buildings made him smile. Van Nuys Airport was basically an aerial Greyhound bus terminal for celebrities. Pushing himself upright in his chair, he patted his pocket to make sure his phone was there. He toyed with the idea of turning it on, and decided against it. Bluey had assured him that he would be there to meet him. Bluey! He'd be seeing him any second. His chest tightened with an unexpected nervousness.

I failed him.

Bluey had been on his mind almost as much as Nicola during the therapy sessions in rehab. Whether Bluey was actually a friend, or an employee, or an enabler, or a combination of all three had been a large part of his therapy. Bluey's offer of a place to stay had given Seamus the answer he wanted. Bluey's voice had cracked as he made the offer, and in the emotion, Seamus knew that Bluey was a friend. After that, his anxiety was able to focus on the person who'd occupied most of his therapy: Nicola.

Deep in thought again, Seamus hadn't noticed the flight attendant approach him, and he jumped when she brushed his arm.

"Sorry, sir, I didn't mean to startle you," she said with a laugh. "We're about to open the door, and your car will be waiting right there. As far as we know, the coast is clear, but it's a clear, windy night, so visibility is high. Probably a good idea to pop your hood up and draw the strings a little."

"Thank you, Dee," Seamus said earnestly, flashing her a smile as he pulled his hood over his recently shorn head. "Thank you also for everything on the flight. That was great."

"You're so welcome," she said as she walked over to the door and unlocked it. He wondered if she was expecting a tip, and felt bad since he had no cash in his pockets. As the door opened, extending its small staircase down to the tarmac, Seamus inhaled deeply, enjoying that strange bouquet of manzanita, smog, and earth that was uniquely Los Angeles. He stood and grabbed his small rolling suitcase from behind his seat and carried it to the door. This little bag contained all of his current earthly belongings. *Snap out of it, you maudlin fool.*

He ducked to clear the doorjamb, and as he stood upright at the top of the stairs, he saw a grin break across Bluey's broad face through the windshield of a new hybrid Escalade. He attempted a smile back, but tears rushed his eyes. *Rehab has turned you into a pussy,* he scolded himself as he descended the stairs in three bounds, threw his bag into the backseat of the SUV, then opened the front door.

"You can't even get out and hug me?" he laughed.

"Mate, I want to squeeze the goddamn life out of you, but I'm pretty sure I got followed, so get your arse into the seat and let's get the hell out of here."

Seamus clambered up into the passenger seat and threw back his hood.

"Mate, where's your sexiest man alive curls?" Bluey laughed, rubbing his knuckles across the stubble on top of Seamus's head.

"I did it meself," Seamus said proudly.

"No kidding," Bluey laughed. "You missed some bits. We'll fix you up when we get home."

"How long will it take us to get back to your place?"

"Depends," Bluey said, turning serious. "We're going to go out a service entrance and hopefully I can get across to the 405 without being seen. Then it's just a quick shot across on the 118 to the 210 to the 2."

"They don't teach you how to speak freeway in rehab, Blue."

"Roughly twenty-five minutes. We should be at my place before eight. You hungry?"

"I'm hungry for a good keg beer."

"It's okay for you to drink?"

"I was in rehab for opiates, Blue, not for being Scottish. They wanted total sobriety, but I met them halfway. Just gotta keep it in check."

✳ ✳ ✳

The drive to Bluey's house in Highland Park was uneventful. No chase, no paparazzi to evade. Bluey pulled the Escalade into the parking space below the converted garage/guesthouse he had called home for nearly a decade. Seamus had spent many a night crashed out in the spare room, and as he trudged up the stairs to the front door,

Seamus realized that this was the closest he'd come to having a home of his own in LA, and that he'd been homesick for it. Once more, he blinked away the sting of tears.

Bluey unlocked the four deadbolts and one keypunch lock and pushed the door open. Immediately Seamus's ankles were swarmed by Tojo, Bluey's stocky black cat.

"Someone's pleased to see you," Bluey said, taking Seamus's bag from his hand and carrying it into the spare room, turning on lights as he went.

Seamus kneeled down and gave the top of Tojo's head a solid scruffing, and was rewarded by the roar of Tojo's purring. The cat purred louder than anything Seamus had ever heard before. During one particularly blurry morning after crashing at Bluey's, Seamus had been convinced an earthquake was starting, only to discover it was Tojo purring on the pillow beside his head.

While Bluey put his bag in the spare room, Seamus surveyed the living room, the designer couch, the aboriginal painting on the wall, the succulents nestled in bright pottery bowls on top of the mid-century credenza. It really did feel like he had come home.

Tojo, tired of being ignored, unleashed a long, low meow as Bluey came back into the room.

"I wish he'd let me pick him up," Seamus said, suddenly needing a hug from anything.

Bluey grabbed Seamus's hoodie, lifting him up to standing.

"Hey, you're choking me," Seamus protested.

"I don't care; it's my turn for a hug," Bluey said, wrapping his strong arms around Seamus and holding him so tightly Seamus couldn't breathe. He felt the tears coming again and broke from the hug.

"Relax, mate, I ain't hittin' on ya," Bluey smiled, until he saw the tears sparkling in Seamus's eyes. He sighed deeply and sat on the couch, patting the seat beside him. "I know, mate. I know. Come sit."

Seamus sat beside him, and Tojo jumped up and sprawled across their laps.

"There's one thing I want you to know, O'Riordan. And it's that I'm so proud of you. I'm so proud."

"It's not like I had a choice," Seamus said, dragging his fingers through Tojo's thick fur.

"We both know that's not true," Bluey said bluntly. "You've been avoiding rehab for as long as I've known you, which is what? Six years now?"

"I don't know what I was so afraid of, to be honest." Seamus looked him in the eye. "It wasn't bad at all. After I realized that the first place was not going to work, I just knew I wanted to be done with the pills. I don't know what shifted, but something did."

"It's going to be rough, Seamus, don't pretend it's not. We know why the pills were there. You were bored. You aren't good with boredom. You never wanted a pill when you were out drinking beer with me. You never took a pill when you were with Nic—" Bluey stopped short, wishing he hadn't said her name. Tojo's purring filled the room.

"Where's that beer you promised?"

"Do you want to go down to Figueroa or over to York?" he asked, grateful for the change of subject.

"Let's go to York; it's a bit more low-key."

Bluey slid out from under Tojo and stood up.

"Do you want to shower or change or hang your clothes up? I haven't had a chance to get over to where they stored your other stuff yet. We can go on the weekend."

"I'm pretty good to go, old friend."

"Give me two minutes," Bluey said. "I'll call ahead and get a corner table cleared."

"Oh, wait." Seamus felt suddenly embarrassed. "Did they give you any cash for me?"

"No, mate, but we're good."

✳ ✳ ✳

Ten minutes later, they were ensconced at a table in the back corner of a dark pub called the York. Seamus was sitting facing the back wall. The activity of the bar, not too busy for a weeknight, took place behind him. He wanted to lower his hood but had to wait until Bluey finished scoping the place out.

His finger nervously traced the outline of his phone through the denim of his jeans. He still hadn't turned it on since landing. He wasn't sure who knew he was returning to LA tonight, but the thought of turning it on filled him with anxiety. He pulled it out of his pocket, flipping it like the useless brick it currently was. He wanted to see if Nicola had texted but worried that she hadn't. Frustrated, he set it facedown on the table as Bluey returned with two pints of beer.

Bluey slid into his banquette and raised one of the beers. "Cheers, mate. It's good to have you back."

Seamus raised his glass and clinked it against Bluey's. He pulled it to his lips and drank deeply, his first drink since he'd left Ojai. In an ambulance.

"I wasn't sure if they let you drink in rehab, so I just got beer since that's what you said you wanted. Are you off hard liquor? I also took the liberty of ordering us some food. I got you a steak and I got myself the chicken. We can swap if you like the sound of mine better, and then—"

"Bluey," Seamus interrupted. "There's something I need to tell you, and I'd like to do it now before there's a chance you can say it's the booze talking."

Bluey nodded. "Go ahead."

"I just spent ten weeks staring at my belly button, mate. I did nothing but think. And what I want to tell you is, I was stuck on a couple of things, and one of them was you."

Bluey sat upright, a look of confusion on his face.

"I had to identify the negative influences in my life," Seamus continued. "And my counselors really had me drilling down on you. Were you an employee? My dealer? Or were you an actual friend? They really did a number on me. It felt so fuckin' awful to think of you as anything but a friend, and it wasn't until I saw you tonight, till you hugged me at your house, that I knew I was right when I argued that you were my friend. I stood up to them and insisted that you were the only real friend I had in LA. And I'm really, really glad that I was right."

"I don't know what to say," Bluey said slowly. "I mean, I can see your angle, but from my point of view, I was getting paid to hang out with my friend. I had the best job in the world."

"And that job is gone now."

"And here we are."

Seamus downed the rest of his beer.

"Shay," Bluey began, "thank you for saying that. And also, thank you for realizing it. I have to tell you something. I've been thinking, too. I shouldn't have been so afraid of the boss dynamic, I should have kicked your arse off those pills years ago. But I got caught up in it, too. They take the edge off, I'll give 'em that. But I had no idea you were shooting up. When I heard that, I knew I had screwed up, as a friend and an employee. But mainly as a friend."

"That was all Amber," Seamus said, with sudden bitterness. "She kept giving me pills and the next thing you know she's tying me off and shooting me up."

"And you didn't stop her?"

Seamus shook his head. "I told my counselors that I was too high, but I could have if I really wanted to. I had just lost Nicola. I just felt so pathetic—I had literally betrayed the first girl I really cared about since my mum died, and I let that toxic, jealous bitch shoot me up. I didn't feel like I was any better than her."

"Ah, but you are. You're a good man. You're a good friend."

"Thanks. Have you seen Amber at all?"

Bluey laughed. "Mate, you wouldn't believe my life. Crystal's got me on Max Zetta patrol mostly. I'm still doing general duties with her roster, like bailing out Ethan Carpenter and his new beard, but most days, I head out to Malibu and make sure that that born-again nutcase isn't getting into any new scandals."

"I'm sorry, Blue."

"It's okay, boss—Sorry, not boss," Bluey laughed. "Crystal upped my pay a stupid amount. She's billing Zetta directly for double what I was getting when I took care of you."

"Well, at least some good came out of it."

"She wasn't too happy to hear that you were moving in to my place. She said that if she catches me helping you during work hours, I'm instantly fired."

"She's bluffing. She knows how much trouble Zetta can get into. And if it happens, you can work for me."

"Crystal is my employment sponsor so I can work legally. I'm stuck with her. Let's just have fun as friends."

Seamus smiled so wide it was contagious. Bluey grinned at him and darted back to the bar to get more beers. Seamus turned his phone over. This time he pressed the power button and punched in his ten-digit security code. He watched impatiently as it searched for service, then began buzzing as messages appeared on the screen, filling it with green and blue bubbles of text. Weatherman, Gaynor, Timothy, and Tobin welcoming him back to LA, details of a meeting with them two days from now at ten a.m., and one from Amber.

A little bird tells me you're back in town. I'm hosting after-hours tonight. Come!

He grimaced as he read it. Bluey slid back into the seat opposite with a tray of four beers.

"I figured it's easier to buy in bulk if you're gonna suck them down like the last one, champ," he laughed. His expression changed when he caught a glimpse of Seamus's face.

"What happened?" he asked.

"I checked my texts."

"Something bad?"

"Not exactly," Seamus said slowly. "The usual. Jon. Tobin. Timothy. Gaynor. And one from Amber inviting me to an after-hours at hers tonight."

"We'll get you a new phone number tomorrow." Bluey handed him a beer. "Don't answer her. She's the enemy now. I'm so glad you never slept with her."

"She tried so hard," Seamus laughed. "But that's not it. I was hoping to hear from Nic."

"Aaaaah," Bluey said enigmatically, taking a swig from his beer.

"Have you seen her, Blue?"

"I'm dating her best friend, Seamus."

"You're kidding me," Seamus laughed.

"O'Riordan, the first rule of being friends is that you have to start asking about me," Bluey said. "I've been dating him since, oh wait, the night before you overdosed."

"I'm really sorry, Blue. I knew you hooked up, but I just see you as a lone wolf."

"That's fine. Or at least that *was* fine. That was fine for then; I had you to take care of. But while you were gone, I took care of someone else, and I let him take care of me. I don't want to curse it, but I'm pretty happy."

"Well, I'm happy for you, and I promise to get better about asking about your life. Now that you have one, I mean."

They both laughed and sipped their beers in silence, Bluey tapping his fingers along to the music on the jukebox.

"It's okay, Seamus." Bluey punched him in the arm. "I'm just breaking your balls. You can ask about Nicola."

"So you've seen her, then?"

"Yeah, I was over at her place the other night."

"How's she doing?"

"Do you think she'd show me?"

"You're right. Dumb question. What about Billy? Does he tell you anything she says?"

"Do you think I'd tell you?"

"Bluey. I've thought of nothing but her since I went away. Why the hell couldn't I ruin it with someone I didn't care about so much?"

"I'm sorry," Bluey said. "I'll tell you what I can. She's buried herself in her work. She's never home. She and Billy have to pencil in time to hang out, and half the time one of them cancels. They're both working long hours. We all are."

"But she seems okay?"

"Nicola will always show the world that she's okay," Bluey said softly. "I've never met a girl with walls so high."

Seamus hung his head down. A familiar ache spread across his chest.

"Drink up, mate," Bluey said, touching his arm tenderly. "I can tell you one thing."

Seamus looked up at him hopefully.

"She hasn't taken off that bracelet you made her. I saw it on her wrist the other night."

Seamus polished off his beer and reached for another off the tray.

"That's the best news I've had in months."

CHAPTER 8

BILLY WAVED AT NICOLA FROM a table in the front window of Kings Road Café, and she threaded her way between the tables to get to him. He could tell by the set of her jaw that she wasn't in a good mood.

"Morning, Peanut," he said cheerily.

"Yes, it is morning," she responded sourly, dropping into the seat opposite him.

"You were happy when we left the Peppermint Club. What's changed? I already ordered your coffee. . . ." He pushed a steaming cup of black espresso at her.

"I'm not sulking," Nicola said, picking up the hot cup. "Well, not exactly. I'm PMSing a little. Maybe a lot. I just want today to be over."

"You're the one who's always telling me that every day has something good in it."

"That's just shit my dad used to say. Today's gonna prove him wrong." She raised her coffee to the ceiling. "Sorry, Dad."

"Peanut, the sun is out, sort of, and we are actually at breakfast together, and it's just the two of us. You've already had a good thing for today."

"Great," Nicola said unenthusiastically. "So in forty-five minutes my day goes to shit."

"I'm ordering pancakes for you."

"Go ahead. I'm already bloated enough, I'll eat the crap out of them. It's not like I'm about to be naked for anybody anytime soon."

"Jesus, Nico, what is the matter?"

"Are you about to spend the day masterminding your ex-lover's reentry to Hollywood?"

"Fair, and are you sure there's none of this I can use?"

"Not this week. After this we can give Sandy some scoop."

"The only scoop I want to give Sandy is a scoop of rat poison,"

Billy said drily, wrinkling his nose at the thought of his clueless executive editor, a horse-faced woman with a voice like a crow. "The worst day of Gaynor is better than the best day with her. It's like working on a high school paper with a dethroned homecoming queen."

"I know, B. I'm sorry. I'm just too on edge to rationally strategize and/or exploit my ex-boyfriend's new fake relationship with you. Because it's totally normal."

"Will he like Bette?"

"Is that more important than how I feel about this?"

"Not at all, but I know how you feel about it. And it's your job, so you'll do it. Do you want to talk about your feelings here?"

Nicola grimaced and finally smiled. "You're right. What was I thinking? No, I don't want to talk about my feelings. It's just stupid. He'll like Bette fine. It could be any actress. He's a stubborn mule and he'll hate the whole process."

"Which is how long?"

"Depends. Six months. Or she doesn't get the movie lead. And it's a cool role; they're gonna use an Asian actor for a white character for a change."

"Who gets the first look at the couple?"

"*People* magazine will somehow obtain shots of the secret dinner; that's Friday. It will be an online exclusive in exchange for first quotes together in the issue on stands next week, around Golden Globes coverage."

"That reminds me, are we going to the Globes together?"

"I have you down as my plus-one for parties, but we will be with Seamus and Bette."

"What about Kara?"

"She's on Amber's list. If she needs someone to walk the carpet with her, she can have Alicia. Gaynor is walking Amber. You could walk Kara if you wanted to."

"Seamus is doing the carpet?"

Nicola gently cuffed Billy across the back of the head. "*Por pendejo*," she laughed. "As if. Where are my pancakes?"

Billy flagged down their server and ordered fresh coffees, two short stacks, and sides of bacon and fried eggs.

"Seamus and Bluey hung out last night."

"Yes." Nicola bowed her head. "I know. Did you . . . uh . . . hear anything?"

"Not really; I stayed at my place. There will be two very hungover dudes in Highland Park this morning."

"He's drinking?"

"He didn't go to rehab for a drinking problem."

"That's the last time you say anything about rehab in a public place," she admonished him with a stern look.

"Yes, Nicola. Please forgive me. Now, do you want to talk about your feelings around Seamus being back in town?"

"There's nothing to discuss, B. Not really. I have to keep it professional. If his team gets its way, our professional relationship will be as doomed as our IRL one."

"So book another date with Timothy."

"I told you why not last night."

"Yeah, like, ten words."

"Okay, here's ten more. He's handsome, bland, bad at listening, condescending, and he's Seamus's agent. I'm done getting my meat at the same place I get my bread."

"Not even a kiss?"

"I considered it. I mean, anywhere else, it would have been a no-brainer one-nighter. But in LA, it would have been a disaster."

"It is a small town."

"It's a crappy double standard," Nicola snapped. "You banged half of LA and nobody gave a rat's ass. I'm two missteps from being shipped back to Dayton with a huge red *S* on my shirt."

"An *S*? For *spinster*?"

Nicola threw a sugar packet at Billy. "For *slut*."

"Ugh, I hate that word."

"I hate the concept. But whatever. It's not like I have time for a boyfriend anyway."

"Keep telling yourself that," Billy said, pointing at the bracelet on her wrist.

"Oh, do go fuck yourself. Where are these pancakes? Gaynor just texted. She's already at the office and she's asking where we are for the Kara meeting."

✳ ✳ ✳

Twenty minutes later, Billy and Nicola walked into the reception of HHPR with a bag of takeout pancakes. Nicola had eaten one in the car downstairs. At the sight of Alicia with her foot up on her desk, painting her toenails bright red, she was glad she hadn't eaten the other one.

"Oh, hi, Alicia, don't mind us," Billy chirped, placing his takeout bag on her desk by her foot. "Would you like some breakfast?"

"Oh, hai, Billy," Alicia responded without looking up. "And no. I can't eat no breakfast. Patrick has me on a juice cleanse."

Billy looked around the office. All the other desks were empty; there was nobody else to give the pancakes to.

"This place is a ghost town today."

"The current interns don't believe in starting work before eleven," Nicola said, shoving her key into her office door and pushing it open. She paused and waited for a bellow from Gaynor, but all she could hear were the grunting sounds that Alicia was making as she painted her toes.

"Come in here until we're summoned," she said, motioning urgently to Billy. "Let's try to eat before she catches us."

"You could just eat and tell her to fuck off with her opinions."

"Tell who to fuck off, Billy?" said a creaky voice behind him. Billy jumped.

"Gaynor, do you float? Are you a ghost? And seriously, you need to let Nicola eat at work, she's PMSing like crazy." He paused, registering Gaynor's outfit for the day, which was a crocheted earth-tone poncho over a black bodysuit. With red slingback heels. "Also, the eighties called. They want their blanky back."

She ignored him.

"*Mi cola*, you know what's better than calories for cramps? A good stiff *pinga*. If you go get laid, you will feel better about life."

"Let me just make a note of that, boss," Nicola said, eyeing her foam container. She could smell the maple syrup. "Nope. Too hard. I'll eat the pancake. It's easier."

"We have a lot to do today, Nico. Whether you're eating for depression or a hangover, I don't think you're going to want to be feeling fat when Bette Wu arrives. Hand it over."

Nicola glared at Gaynor with a flash of such unbridled anger that Gaynor stepped back.

"Okay, *mija*, eat your damn sugar breakfast. I don't understand how the uterus has more power over women than the *chocha*. It's upsetting. Meet me in the conference room." She turned and strode off. Billy faced Nicola, about to open his food, and was dismayed to see Nicola gathering a notepad, her phone, and a pen and heading for the door.

"What? I've lost my appetite."

＊　＊　＊

Gaynor sat at the head of the conference table, her arms extending from the sides of the poncho, her burgundy nails fussing with her explosion of blue-black hair.

"That was quick," she smirked as Nicola and Billy took their seats at the table.

"Speaking of quick," he said, "let's get this over and done with. I have a magazine to put out."

"That works for me." Gaynor faked a yawn. "How about you tell me what you want in terms of stories, and I just say no?"

"The sex-tape rumblings are getting louder. We have a deal with Kara. If the story breaks, it's ours exclusively."

"Has Sandy said anything?" Gaynor was all business. It always tickled Nicola to hear her accent vanish as soon as the going got tough.

"She heard a rumor," Billy began. "But I told her it was with Jimmy J, so she isn't interested. You know, because he's black."

"This story will never happen, on record," Gaynor said firmly. "Even if they show it on CBS."

"We have a deal," Billy said sternly.

"Do you remember what happened when you nearly got caught balls-deep in Ethan Carpenter? Multiply that by a million. His last movie made a quarter of a billion dollars. He wasn't even the star. A lot of people are very invested in making him pay off. Some *pobrecita* bitch from a basic cable reality show won't be allowed to derail this."

"Kara isn't that easy to control," Billy said. "And every story has a price."

"Some stories can kill people."

"And the Oscar for best dramatic performance goes to . . ." Billy smiled. "Fine, fine. There's no story."

"I'm glad you agree, Señor Kaye. I like it when you have common sense."

"Thanks, I think."

"*De nada*. Before you go, I have to ask you a favor."

"Anything, mama," he said with a grin.

"I'm having some client issues," Gaynor said slowly. "Today, I've been informed that four of my long-term clients no longer require my services. Can you keep your ear to the ground and listen for any chatter? Something doesn't feel right here."

Billy began to make a joke, but as he spoke, he noticed that Gaynor's hand was shaking. She covered it up by reaching for a bejeweled vape box. She put it to her lips and inhaled deeply. Billy and Nicola exchanged glances as Gaynor slowly exhaled an impenetrable cloud of white vapor that rose through her thick hair, obscuring her face.

"*Gracias*, Billy. I will call you tomorrow," the cloud said. "I have also heard some rumors about SaraBeth Shields that might interest you."

"No dice—we're a SaraBeth-free zone. Sandy hates her. What can you get me on Adrian Zuma?"

"That's easy." Gaynor exhaled a long, thin stream of smoke from her red lips. "TV's most popular sitcom dad is Hollywood's hottest bachelor, no?"

"Exactly," Billy said enthusiastically.

"He isn't single; he's fucking his TV daughter. Has been for years."

"She just turned seventeen," Billy said.

"Exactly. So you can expect an announcement of sudden love in a year, when it's legal. But I can double source for you that they started when she was twelve."

"My lawyers will be calling you this afternoon," Billy smiled, dashing around the table and wrapping Gaynor in a hug.

※ ※ ※

The mood at HHPR was completely different two hours later. Every desk was filled by an intern, and Gaynor's twin sons had overhauled Alicia, squeezing her into a sleek black dress that they'd tailored for her. With her hair swept up in an elegant chignon, she looked more like a TV host, and Nicola had to admit, the change was impressive.

Gaynor had switched into a vintage steel-gray Miyake pleat dress that hung and bounced around her as she walked, concertina-style, showing flashes of red between the gray pleats. Nicola had been forced into a near-black drop-waisted Prada dress and simple black buckle flats. Gaynor had attended to Nicola's hair and makeup herself, straightening her curls with an iron and adding some individual lashes at the outer edges of her eyes.

When Bette Wu walked into the conference room, Nicola was grateful for the makeover. Bette, her muscles rippling, wore a tight McQueen sheath dress that showed off her pert booty and smooshed her small, natural boobs together at the cutout keyhole. Nicola almost swooned. *Damn, I'm getting a girl crush.*

All good feelings were banished as Crystal Connors appeared behind her client, in her trademark tailored black man's suit and a matching fedora. *She looks like the Babadook*, Nicola thought, almost laughing.

Alicia, who'd been placing coffees on the conference table, actually spun around and bowed at her.

"Miss Connors, welcome to Huerta Hernandez," Alicia said confidently. "You must be Miss Wu. Please, take your seats."

"Nicola," Crystal said cheerily, her mouth almost smiling. "It's good to see you. Bette, say hi to Wallace."

"Hi, Wallace," Bette deadpanned, rolling her eyes.

As Crystal folded her mantis frame into one of the chairs, she spoke. "Does Ms. Huerta plan on joining us?"

As if on cue, at that moment Gaynor sailed in, her Miyake dress shimmering around her like a cloud and still managing to draw attention to her flawless legs. Nicola could tell that Crystal's eyes were rolling behind her black sunglasses.

"Mujeres, bienvenidos." She blew kisses to both of them. "Bette, you're even more beautiful than I expected."

"Thanks, I guess," Bette said, taking her seat.

"Gaynor, you look marvelous; is that the Miyake that you bought when we were together?"

"Yes, my dearest, it's the one I bought fresh from the runway."

"Bought is a strange choice of words, but you've kept it in wonderful condition."

Nicola saw Gaynor's lips thin slightly, but she recovered immediately.

"I would like to welcome you all here, and once again remind you that this meeting is top secret. If anyone breaks the secrets of this discussion, who am I gonna call?"

"The cartel," Alicia and Nicola said in unison.

"My god, you're ridiculous," Bette said, opening her small purse. She took out a stick of gum. She ripped off the paper, leaving it on the table, inserted the gum between her perfect pink lips, and began chewing noisily.

Gaynor and Crystal exchanged glances, and Crystal slowly placed her hand under Bette's mouth.

"Spit," she said.

Bette began to argue, then changed her mind. She pushed the gum out of her mouth and it fell into Crystal's waiting hand. Crystal deftly wrapped it back in its wrapper and dropped it into Bette's purse.

"*Gracias, paisa,*" Gaynor smiled. "Now let's get to the business. Bette, you are our chosen one; you are the new girlfriend of Seamus O'Riordan. There's no need for us to discuss any of the finer points of your contract with Global Talent. Today, we are only concerned with the public side of your relationship. The magic."

"Look, Gaynor, I think I got this. This isn't my first celebrity relationship, you know."

"Technically," Gaynor said with a raised eyebrow, "it is. The other guys you've dated—let me see if I have this right—two supporting actors from Netflix? They don't count. The Thai Leonardo DiCaprio. Nope. Two YouTubers and some Hamptons heirs. None of these helped you crack the A-list. This is your finishing school, young lady. However, if you're determined to continue being a millennial disaster who knows better than me, please say so and we can end the meeting now."

Bette looked to Crystal for support.

"I told you she was worse than me," Crystal said.

"Bette, if you're obedient, I'm pleasant. This is an unusual pairing, with clients from two competing agencies entering into a fictional relationship. As you've heard, it's more common to have it all handled in-house."

"Except the only eligible females that Gaynor represents are reality TV whores," Crystal said. "Or at death's door."

"Not today, my old friend," Gaynor cautioned, splaying a palm in Crystal's direction. "This is a meet and greet. We play nice. And then we can leave the girls to get acquainted."

Nicola's uterus spasmed at the thought of spending the rest of the afternoon with Bette. The actress didn't look too pleased about it either.

"Well, Miss Wallace does know Mr. O'Riordan the best of all of us," Crystal said coldly.

"I will be guiding him through this process as professionally as you would," Nicola said, eyeing Crystal.

"How has his return to Los Angeles gone so far?" Crystal asked.

Gaynor looked at Nicola, who shrugged.

"Are you telling me that he hasn't contacted his publicity firm since his return to Los Angeles?" Crystal almost smiled again.

"I exchanged texts with him last night," Gaynor said. "He is doing well."

"But our first date is tomorrow," Bette said plaintively. "He and I need alone time before the day."

"Incorrect," Nicola said. "You will meet at the Global offices tomorrow, but your date will be like any first date. Get to know each other then. You're going to the Nice Guy. There will be a *People* photographer inside, hiding in the kitchen. The shots will be on People.com by midnight, with insider quotes that we are just waiting on approval for from Weatherman's team. Bette, we will expect you here for your fittings and makeup at two p.m. Crystal, as agreed, we will be handling our own invoices—hair, makeup, stylist—you pay for Bette; we handle Seamus. Same with transport."

"I want to go to Golden Globes parties," Bette said.

"It's a free country," Gaynor said brusquely. "If you learn one thing: What do you say to anybody who asks you about Seamus?"

"I say 'no comment,' der."

"No. You do not speak," Gaynor commanded. "'No comment' is a quote. Say nothing. You look at them like they're made of rotten meat, and you keep on walking. You say absolutely nothing to anyone. You don't talk to a soul about him."

"When do we do TV? I can talk about him then, right?"

"You'll never do TV as a couple. You're a couple only in public. In interviews, which can only ever happen when this team is present, we will step in and say that we don't permit personal questions."

"This is so lame," Bette protested.

"This is the girl you picked for this?" Gaynor asked.

"Yes, Gaynor," Crystal sneered. "Celebrities willing to be a fake girlfriend to a junkie star aren't exactly a dime a dozen."

"You guys, I'm right here," Bette said in a kittenish voice.

"Sorry, Bette, you're right," said Nicola, trying to save the situation. "This seems weird, because it *is* weird. We have to work together, but we all have a vested interest. We want our client to skate through awards season and hopefully a new movie over the summer without any undue interest. And you come out the other side a movie star in your own right. We won't tell you how to do martial arts; you won't question us when it comes to publicity. Right?"

"Fine," Bette said, crossing her legs and sitting like a child. "But you gotta admit, it's weird to pretend the boyfriend-girlfriend thing."

"You're an actor. You pretend to be a brain surgeon; you'll get over it," Gaynor spat.

"I like that one better," Bette said to Crystal, pointing at Nicola.

"Not for long," laughed Gaynor. "She didn't used to *pretend* to be his girlfriend."

Nicola kicked Gaynor under the table.

"Don't listen to her. Sometimes she mixes up her meds," Nicola said. Crystal reached across the table and high-fived her.

What the fuck is happening here? Nicola wondered. Why was Crystal being nice to her? Until two minutes ago, Nicola had never even considered that Crystal knew how to be nice.

Her phone, facedown on the table, played a single wooden chime as a text came in. As Gaynor and Crystal continued bickering, Nicola fought down the urge to grab the phone and flip it over. It was the alert sound she had assigned to Seamus. She saw Bette turn toward her.

"What the fuck is wrong with you? You look like you saw a ghost."

"Oh, I'm sorry, I have to take this; it's the reporter from *People* setting up your coverage for tomorrow night."

Gaynor gave her a quizzical look as she stood and snatched her phone from the table. As Nicola pulled the conference room door closed behind her she heard Bette squawk, "What aren't you telling me?" at Crystal.

Nicola didn't dare look at her phone until she got to her office. She felt her pulse in her ears as she turned her phone upward.

Hey Ohio! Guess who's back in town? Could use a friend. You free tonight?

Nicola took a deep breath. A panicky cluster of feelings rocketed around her brain. She had fought the instinct to contact Seamus since last night, and she had been fighting a losing battle all day. She was disappointed that he hadn't texted her sooner. He wanted to see her. But she had to go back into a meeting and set the scene with a woman who would be his pretend public girlfriend. She toyed with the idea of not responding for an hour or two.

Nicola Wallace, what the fuck is wrong with you?

She realized she was still breathing fast. She pinched the skin on her inner wrist. "Snap out of it," she whispered to herself. "This is not happening. This is never happening again."

She took ten deep breaths in a row and went back to the meeting. Bette was talking.

"So, I just need to maybe spend some time with Seamus before the Friday date. We need to get our stories straight. Maybe we can spend the afternoon together?"

Nicola saw Gaynor's face shift from boredom to annoyance. Bette was about to cop it. Even Crystal looked away.

"Listen, *chinita*," Gaynor said, her voice gravelly. "This is not a relationship with anyone but the public. This thing that you are doing is acting. This is the role that you are playing until you land your next role. We are your directors. We are your dressers. We pull your strings."

"The fuck did you just call me?" Bette stood up, her cheeks turning red.

"Was I racist? Did I offend you? Crystal? Why didn't you tell me your client was a sugar-puff pussy-ass baby?"

"Crystal, are you going to let this old bitch talk to me this way?"

Crystal raised one hand and slid her pitch-black sunglasses down her nose just enough to reveal one of her blue-gray eyes.

"Listen to me, now," Bette said, her voice suddenly steely and deep. "I won my first gold medal for tae kwon do in 2008. I was sixteen. I had been training for ten years. You guys treat me like I'm some actor who did a two-month 'learn to act' course and got a TV show. That's bullshit. I'm disciplined and I'm driven. I know what I signed up for and I know how to deliver it. Now start fucking treating me like I'm the talent and not just some whore from the street."

Nicola fought the urge to give her own high five to Bette.

"Sit the fuck down," Crystal said curtly. "You want a career? Learn to be obedient. I told you coming in here not to shit talk Miss Huerta. Don't make an enemy that you can't defeat, and honey, trust me, you'll be in tears before she breaks a nail."

Bette wasn't having it. "I'm your client, Connors. I pay you. Because I am the star."

Crystal placed both of her palms flat on the table. "Bette, there are no stars in this room. If you can reign your bullshit in long enough to listen to what we tell you to do, in time, you might be a star. Hey, Gaynor?"

"Yes, *mija*," Gaynor said.

"How many starlets have sat at this very table and told you that you need to listen to them because they're a star?"

"Ay, Crystalita, I lost count in the nineties—do you remember? Every six months there was a new plague of actors with shows on networks. Every six months, a new bunch of interchangeable white people. Crystal, where are they now?"

"They're all back in their small towns. They're all flipping burgers and raising kids and acting in local productions of *Wicked* and telling anyone who'll listen about that time they were on a TV show on the WB."

"I'm not white. I'm different," Bette said defiantly.

"You know what will make you different?" Nicola said coldly. "Listening to us. Now can we all stop bickering and just get on with it?"

Gaynor picked up her phone and started punching at the screen. Nicola's phone pinged. She turned it over.

WHERE DID YOU GO?

"Are you two texting each other?" Bette said incredulously. *She is sharp*, Nicola thought.

"No," Nicola said quickly, silencing her phone and placing it face-down on the table.

"I have a question, if I'm allowed to even ask a fucking question."

"Yes, Bette?" Nicola allowed condescendingly.

"Can I post on Snap or Insta from the date?"

"Please, ladies, allow me," Nicola said when she saw their Botoxed foreheads attempt to move. "Do you understand what a *People* exclusive means? It means you do nothing without approval from all three of us."

Bette looked crestfallen. "I post all the time," she whined. "I can't let my fans down."

"I think we're good," Crystal said, rising to her feet. "Bette, go wait in reception. I've changed my mind; I need to discuss some things with you this afternoon."

Bette began to protest, thought the better of it, and let herself out of the conference room. Nicola heaved a sigh of relief that Bette apparently wasn't spending the afternoon there any longer.

"Really, Crystal?" Gaynor made a gagging face. "That was the best you could come up with? Or did you do it to twist my titties because you lost Seamus?"

"Sadly, that is the best I can do. These millennials are hard to work with. Nobody wanted this gig. Nobody. Everyone thinks they're gonna be a star forever."

"*Dios mío*," Gaynor said as she walked to Crystal and gave her a hug. "Actually, Nicola, can you excuse us? We have some private business."

Nicola shot Gaynor a quizzical glance. Gaynor nodded slowly and mouthed "It's okay."

Stepping into the corridor, Nicola pulled the door closed behind her and flipped her phone on.

She texted Seamus.

Runyon Canyon. Fuller Gate. 8pm.

CHAPTER 9

KARA RUBBED HER TUMMY AND eyed the bag of Takis on Alicia's desk.

"Hey, sister, wanna hook me up with a snack? I'm starving."

"How you stay so skinny, *puta*?" Alicia snarled, angrily tossing the Takis across the office. "And how dafuq do I get your metabolism? You ate a cheeseburger like half an hour ago."

Kara froze, about to open the Takis. Alicia was right. She had just eaten. And the feeling in her stomach wasn't hunger. It was butterflies. She tossed the bag back to Alicia.

"I forgot I ate." Kara smiled. "I . . . uh . . . I have a date."

"*Sí*, Kara. You've been talking about it with Miss Huerta since you got here. Your date with Errol Flynn."

"It's so hard to tell when you're paying attention," Kara said, pacing across the reception carpet. Nicola's door was closed—she'd been on a conference call with Seamus's people for hours, according to Alicia. Prior to the meeting, Nicola had texted that Bette was a bigger nightmare than she'd expected. Kara wanted to sneak a candy bar to her.

She checked her phone for the umpteenth time. It was 3:27. She was supposed to meet Mason at the Four Seasons at four thirty. She'd changed her mind and her outfit five times since she arrived at Huerta Hernandez an hour ago. If she didn't distract herself, her current dark brown Nasty Gal A-line coat would be on the dressing room floor alongside the previous outfits.

"I always pay attention, when I feel like it," Alicia said. "And I googled it, and Errol Flynn is super dead, so I know you're using a code name."

"You had to google that?"

"Bitch, I'm twenty-two." Alicia snapped her fingers in Kara's direction. "You could have called him Heath Ledger and I'd still have to google it to be sure."

Gaynor materialized at Kara's side, startling her.

"*Mamacita*, so nervous," she purred. "American girls act like movie-star dates are something special. It's Thursday. You're just the Thursday girl."

"I dunno," Kara said, flipping the bird at Gaynor. "He said that he's been super lonely and nobody will go near him."

"Yes, and I'm sure that little fable works very well for him with all the other girls of the week."

"Does it ever get boring to be so cynical?"

"Not really, no."

"Wouldn't you love to be knocked off your feet by someone and have romance and all that goes with it, even at your age?"

"Don't be beastly, *mija*," Gaynor said, unruffled. "At my age, as you put it, I don't give a fuck. I am approaching my give-a-fuck meno- pause, and there are only a few fucks left in my ovaries. I'm fuck- barren. I'll waste them on someone worthwhile or not at all."

Kara stopped pacing and stared at the carpet, then at the wall. Gaynor had a habit of throwing a dart right into whichever Achilles' heel was weakest. In the days since she'd seen Mason he had texted her so frequently that it had gotten *almost* annoying. If he weren't famous, it would have been too much. But the idea that half of Hollywood's most golden couple was thinking of her was oddly re- warding. Amber had noticed a distinct change in Kara's mood and was exhaustively trying to coax the reason for the mood swing out of her—so that the producers could exploit it on the show.

"Okay, yes, it's exciting," Kara said. "Go ahead. Make another joke."

"Uh-oh, she's being honest," Gaynor said to Alicia. "Trusting an actor. We all just watched this story end badly for Nicolita."

"Oh, honey, I don't do heartbreak, and I don't do trust," Kara laughed. "Not in grade school, not in high school, and definitely not in Hollywood."

Gaynor gave her a pitying look. "Heartbreak is better for you than new shoes, a day off, and cunnilingus all put together," she said. "Heartbreak keeps you young. Getting hurt means you're still alive. I miss a broken heart more than I miss any man."

"Bitch, you trippin'," Alicia grumbled from her desk.

"*Cochinita*," Gaynor said, steel in her voice. "If you call me bitch one more time, I'll beat you like it's the eighties. Also." Gaynor stalked to the front of Alicia's desk, plucked the bag of Takis, and ripped them open. Then she tipped them into the trash can beside Alicia's desk. "Heartbreak will probably be the only exercise your poor heart gets. You're supposed to be on a juice cleanse."

Alicia crossed her arms and glared back.

"So where is this man taking you for your midweek one-night stand?"

"We've already had one night, so this is a repeat performance."

"That's not an answer."

"We're spending our time at the Presidential Suite at the Four Seasons."

Gaynor's face remained perfectly still, but Kara knew that she thought she was raising an eyebrow.

"So you approve?" she asked.

"Eh, it's a nice place for a rendezvous. East or West Presidential Suite? You don't want to be flashing your titties at the wrong peephole."

"Oh shit, no; he didn't say. Let me ask."

Kara pulled out her phone and fired off a quick text. Her phone dinged back almost immediately.

"He says there's only one Presidential Suite," she said, perplexed.

"Honey, you tell him that you're with Gaynor and she's been turned north and south in both the East and the West."

Another text came in, and Kara's face fell.

"Oh no, no, no," she said, reaching for her pink Fendi peekaboo shearling purse, her eyes widening. "Gaynor, is there another Four Seasons?"

Gaynor started laughing, low at first, and then her hyena cackle kicked in.

"Oh *mija*, no, no," she gasped. "He's taking you to the four-thousand-dollar no-tell-motel Four Seasons?"

Kara looked at her phone, horrified. "There's a Four Seasons in Westlake Village?" She scowled. "How the fuck am I going to get clear across the Valley at three thirty?"

"Take Laurel Canyon and pray, mama," Gaynor laughed, high-fiving Alicia. Kara grabbed her purse and keys and slammed the door behind her.

✳ ✳ ✳

Ninety minutes and thirty miles later, a traffic-weary Kara punched the button for the seventh floor of the Four Seasons Westlake Village. As the doors closed behind her, drowning out the lobby noise, Kara looked at her reflection in the brushed-metal interior.

"Girl, you need to pep it up," she said, pinching her cheeks and fussing with her 'fro. She felt tired and her eyes hurt after driving into the sun for so long. It felt like she'd been chasing the horizon all day. She looked at her phone as the elevator deposited her at her destination. A screenful of texts. Mason. Amber. Gaynor. Nic. Billy. They'd all have to wait.

She stepped into the hallway and followed the sign to the door of the Presidential Suite. As she raised her fist to knock, the door opened, and Mason, in loafers, ripped jeans, and a pressed plaid shirt, grinned. This time he looked like a movie star at least. She slipped into his arms, kicking the door closed behind her.

"That took you forever," he said, pressing his cheek against her ear. "But thank you for coming, and sorry I wasn't clear. Are you mad at me?"

"I ain't mad exactly, but that 101 put a knot the size of Oklahoma between my shoulders."

Kara broke the embrace and turned her back to him, waiting for him to start rubbing her shoulders. When nothing happened, she leaned back against Mason.

"That was me asking for a back rub!"

"Oh right, sorry. Of course," he said, and she felt his strong hands grasp her shoulders and start to knead them, his thumbs digging into the tension around her spine. She melted back against his chest.

"I'm really glad you came. I thought that you'd flake."

"When I found out you were clear across the Valley?"

"No, just in general, I've, uh . . ."

"Oh, don't worry, dude," Kara said gently. "I know I'm not the first girl you've brought here."

"You're the first one who's showed up," Mason replied, his hands slowing slightly. "I'm not even kidding."

Kara rested her cloud of hair against his neck and sighed.

"Well, they're all stupid."

"I just forget that it's far for people," Mason said. "It's not far for me."

"You live in the Valley? That's where I grew up."

"No, I live in Malibu—it's a straight shot across the canyon."

"You still live in the same place you had with Felicity?"

"No, she's living in that house." Mason paused. "I . . . well, we owned . . . it sounds not cool to say."

"Just say it; I'll decide if it's not cool."

"Well, Felicity wanted to buy a lot of Malibu, so we own seven houses in Malibu. Some on the beach, some up Temescal."

"You're right. Borderline uncool."

"I've always bought houses," Mason continued earnestly. "Even with my first TV show, the first thing my dad made me do was buy a house. I was seventeen, living in a big empty house on Mulholland with no furniture. I just had like some outdoor furniture and a mattress in this mansion."

"Not gonna lie." Kara turned to face him. "That's kinda adorable."

"You think? Felicity always made fun of that story."

"She sounds like a real snatchatorium." Kara laughed. "Also, not sure if anyone's ever told you, but it's still not great to talk about your ex on a booty call."

"This is a booty call?"

"You tell me."

"Nah, it's a date. Lemme show you around our mansion for the night."

Mason took Kara's heavy purse from where she'd dropped it on the floor and slung it over his shoulder. "Follow me."

Kara whistled as they entered a dining room straight out of the *Titanic*, embroidery and woodwork and heavy, dark furniture cluttering a room twice the size of her living room in Hollywood.

"This is some old-lady bullshit right here," she said.

Mason turned and took her hand. "It's a Four Seasons, what did you expect?"

"Something from late last century? I feel like I'm on a detective show on A&E."

"If my wife keeps up her reign of terror, my next gig will be A&E."

"And there she is again."

"Sorry, Kara. I'm not super good with having an inside voice."

"I get it." Kara squeezed his hand. "You just need to know it's a boner-killer."

"Imagine being married to it."

Kara felt her frustration start to flare. She let go of Mason's hand and grabbed the front of his shirt. "That was the last mention of you even having a wife, okay?"

Mason licked his lips and smiled. "Yes, mistress."

"How about Miss Jones?"

Kara dropped her hand and it was instantly enveloped in Mason again. He led her into a bedroom that was again disappointingly chintzy and pointed out the window.

"We have a view of the waterfall," Mason said with a smile.

"But it's fake."

"But it's a waterfall, technically. Water is falling over rocks."

"You've spent too much time on movie sets."

Kara walked him to an east-facing window and pointed. "I grew up just over there," she said. "Right by the Budweiser factory. The smell of beer brewing makes me feel like I'm five again."

Mason laughed. "I grew up near a cigarette factory," he said, nuzzling her ear. "I hate smoking, but if I smell an unlit cigarette, I'm back there, instantly, that funny sweet smell on those long, boring days."

"I miss being a kid," Kara said, kissing him quickly on the lips. "Sometimes I get so jacked of all this crap, I wanna just go to the skate park and hang with the BMX kids and steal some beer."

"Now that," Mason said, kissing her back, "can be our third date, if you'd be so kind as to say yes."

Kara closed her eyes and began to kiss Mason slowly, gently. He hugged her and started to run his hands up under her shirt. Just as he began to work on her bra, he stopped suddenly.

"What's wrong?"

"Shoot." He kissed the top of her head. "We're right by an open window. I need to keep this shit clear in my head. Your friend Bluey gave me a list of things to watch. It's exhausting remembering all of it."

He disengaged from Kara's arms and walked around the room, pulling all the blinds closed, plunging the room into total darkness.

"Great, now where's the light switch?"

Kara laughed. He really was useless. She pulled one of the blinds back to let some light in. Mason blew her a kiss as he flicked a switch beside the bed, illuminating the room. Then he sat on the bed and patted the coverlet. "C'mere, Miss Jones."

Kara walked slowly to him, swaying her hips as she went.

When she was toe to toe, Mason lifted her shirt to just below her breasts and began to kiss her stomach with a feather-light touch that sent shudders across her shoulders. She reached around and gently cupped the back of his head. She remembered the last time and grasped a chunk of his hair, pulling lightly. He moaned as if on cue. She pulled harder and his moan turned into a growl and he broke the kiss.

"You're into this stuff?"

"I dunno," Kara said. "I like seeing you get so turned on, and honey, last time I pushed your buttons, you more than pushed mine back."

"I was wondering if we could try something?"

"Something like what?"

Mason got up and went to the wardrobe. He returned with a small overnight bag emblazoned with the logo from one of his movies. He unzipped it and turned it upside down, dumping a cluster of leather-and-fur restraints and some rope onto the bed.

"Miss Jones, I'd like you to tie my wrists together, just for a while, tell me what to do, pull my hair the way you do, make me yours."

Kara raised an eyebrow and looked from Mason's pleading eyes to the tangle on the bed and back again.

"Black folks generally aren't too fond of shackles," she said with a husky laugh.

"But I'm white," Mason said hoarsely. "Flip the script."

"Don't make me overthink this," Kara said, pulling Mason's shirt over his head and forcing him down onto the bed. "You already sound like the producer on my show."

CHAPTER 10

NICOLA STEPPED THROUGH THE SECURITY door of her building and looked up into the darkness of Runyon Canyon, the wrought-iron of the gates barely visible in the night mist. She tightened the collar of her Zara overcoat and walked a few steps toward the gates. As she drew near, a figure emerged into the pool of light from a streetlamp, making her gasp, frozen in her tracks, until its arms opened and she heard a familiar voice.

"Nicola, it's me, Seamus. Sorry, I really didn't mean to scare you."

And there he was, walking up to her and wrapping her in a hug that was comfortable yet reunion-appropriate. She hugged him back, then pushed him away gently.

"Let me look at you, you big oaf," she smiled. Seamus stepped back and scuffed the ground with the toe of his work boot, looking around nervously.

"You look like you're about to rob a bank in the Andes," she said, surveying his all-black ensemble of jeans, thermal jacket, and knit cap. "Your beard got really long."

"And I buzzed my head," Seamus grinned, whipping his cap off to reveal a quarter inch of dark fuzz.

"You've become a hipster," she exclaimed.

"Junkie hipster is all the rage in Seattle these days," he said, regretting it instantly when he saw her face darken. "Too soon?"

"Way too soon, O'Riordan." She motioned him through the gate and into the darkness of the park. "Let's go for a walk."

They headed onto the path between the oaks without speaking, the sound of their crunching footsteps and the occasional siren wafting up from Hollywood Boulevard breaking the silence.

"I brought some water in my backpack in case you want some," Nicola said, patting at the shoulder straps of her Herschel pack.

Seamus stopped walking and produced a surprisingly large thermos from inside his jacket pocket.

"And I have whiskey."

"Is that a good thing, or do we need to call your sponsor? Do you have a sponsor? I'm sorry, Seamus, I don't know how to react, except for knowing that for Biscuit's rehab, he's not allowed anything, he's not even allowed to have cough medicine or kombucha because of alcohol."

Seamus turned and put a warm hand on her cold cheek. "It's okay. I won't drink if it makes you nervous. That's why I wanted to see you tonight, before we get into all the business of what's coming up ahead. Let's find somewhere to sit and talk."

"There's a bench if we take the steep trail off to the right," she said quietly, wondering why she always felt the need to be above Los Angeles. Maybe it seemed more manageable when it was seen from a distance. "How do you feel about night hiking?"

"Is that a new hipster thing? Does it go well with my new image?"

"Yes, you're very cutting-edge." Nicola pointed to a steep, narrow trail heading off from the main path. "Want me to go first?"

"Yeah, I think it's safer than having me fall backward onto you."

"I'm stronger than you think, action hero."

"Didn't you carry me down the stairs in Ojai?"

Nicola froze. "Seamus, we're going to have to figure out a way to talk where you don't drop painful stuff into the middle of innocuous conversation."

"Remember that time I told you that I use humor to deal with difficult situations, and you said that was a good thing?"

"Touché, but humor by definition is funny."

"I'll try, Nico," he said. She winced at the use of her nickname but let it slide as she scrambled up a steep part of the incline. He clambered up behind her, and as the ground leveled out, he touched her arm.

"I don't know what happened that night, Nico. Bluey said you did carry me down the stairs, and that you drove like a maniac to save me."

"All of that is true."

"I'm so sorry. And I heard that Kara brought the paparazzi on set. But you guys are still friends."

"*Ay.*" Nicola exhaled. Why couldn't Bluey have explained this part to Seamus, so she didn't have to? "Kara got railroaded into selling us out, except we'll never know if she would have actually done it. Your overdose derailed her plans. She says she'd already decided not to. I think I believe her. It was so hectic after you went away. We had to move, and it was just easier to do it together. She apologizes constantly, and we have both been working a lot, so we don't see each other."

"So, you're not exactly friends."

"I'm not sure we exactly ever were, and that's okay," Nicola said, thinking aloud. "Billy says that she and I are Hollywood friends. I'm all right with that. She's decent."

"I'm happy to see that you are as good at putting walls up against friends as you are against boyfriends."

"Everybody's got their own survival skills."

"How about Amber?"

"We've avoided each other as much as possible. She knows that I want to rip her weave out and break a few of her teeth, so she insists on meeting Gaynor away from the office."

"You're scrappy."

"She fucked me over; therefore she must die."

Seamus chuckled in the dark, and Nicola resumed walking along the trail.

They ascended the rest of the short path to the bench in silence. Seamus stood until Nicola had sat down as was his gentlemanly way, and then he carefully sat close to her, but they did not touch.

"I want to start by saying thank you for agreeing to see me tonight," he said, his palms open in front of him. "I actually didn't expect you to say yes."

"Full disclosure? I wasn't going to," she said, noticing that he pressed his hands together suddenly, as if he was going to reach for her hand and then thought better of it. "I really wasn't going to say yes."

"What changed your mind?"

"You have a lot of hard work ahead of you, and today I had a meeting that showed me how hard it's going to be. For us both. I didn't want our reunion to be one more thing that's difficult, in a room with agents and studio folks and actors. That's not fair to you. It's not even fair to me."

"Do I want to hear about the meeting?"

"Do you want your friend or your publicist to answer?"

"Can't you just be my friendicist?"

"They're giving you a set-up girlfriend to help deflect bad press."

"Yeah, I heard."

"And you're okay with it?"

"No, personally I'm the opposite of okay with it."

"But you're doing it because . . ."

"Because I cost a lot of people a lot of money. It was my mistake, so I need to fix it. I'd rather talk about a fake relationship than have to tell the story about how drugs ruined my real one."

"I had a meeting with Bette today."

"And?"

"And she's going to require you to be a very good actor."

Seamus laughed. "Actually, can we not talk about that just yet? It's work, and I have some things I want to talk about that we can't discuss in front of Weatherman."

Nicola swallowed hard. She hadn't expected this reunion to be so effortlessly comfortable.

"Sure," she said with false enthusiasm.

"I want to share some stuff with you," Seamus began. Nicola looked at him. *Share* wasn't a word that pre-rehab Seamus would have used. "I want to walk you through my rehab process and my breakthroughs. Nico, I know I ruined us. Whatever relationship we can have now, it's important to me."

"You hurt me, O'Riordan, and I haven't had time to get to a therapist, so yes, you can talk, but please don't end tonight with a plea for a reunion. Okay? We have a crazy few months ahead, and we are better off as friends."

"Nico, I'm honored you'll even consider still being my friend. I've told you that."

"So let me have it. I've been in the dark about your past couple months."

"I asked Bluey to keep it quiet from you, in case, you know, in case I failed."

"He's a good secret keeper."

"That he is. In a nutshell, the Malibu rehab was basically an after-hours club. If you wanted drugs, you could get them. If you wanted anything, you could get it. And at the end, you got the equivalent of a doctor's note for the studios so you could get insurance to make a movie."

"Did you use in rehab?"

"No, Nico. Please believe me. But there's rehab and there's rehab when the patients are offering you drugs every day. I needed to get the hell out of there, so I asked around and heard about a place in Seattle. On Yelp it said it was a ballbuster but it had a great reputation for success and staying clean. I went up there and I completed their program. It worked in a really strange way. They do aversion detox and behavioral stuff, but the main thing that helped me was the therapy. I learned something, and I'm just going to say it. I'm an adult baby. I'm pathetic. I wasn't even much of an addict. I apparently hate what I do for a job."

"You hate acting?"

"I hate the person I am when I'm acting. I stand in front of an entire film crew, hundreds of people, and I do these odd things, and I get paid millions of dollars. Then I leave and I'm this hollow, useless human who can't just pop down the market and buy ice cream. I need a bodyguard to hit In-N-Out. I'm in a fishbowl, and every word, every movement is analyzed."

"And there are people dying in Syria . . . ," Nicola said tersely. "I'm sorry, but it's hard to accept that your good looks and good fortune have driven you to get high to deal with misery."

"I was lonely," Seamus said, and in the near dark, she could see the desperate nakedness on his face. "I *am* lonely. There. That's what I learned. I don't give a fuck about being a hypocrite, or a stereotypical misunderstood actor. I was just lonely. Do you think I'd hang around Amber Bank if I had a chance of spending a single night at home with you"—he paused, then corrected himself—"or a girl like you?"

Nicola shrugged.

"That's the thing," he continued. "There aren't girls like you. Not here. Not even at home. People see the fake stuff first. They see the billboards, they see reports of huge paydays. They see bragging rights. I know you've heard this before, but the hard fact is that I was just a sad, alone guy struggling to connect with anyone. Nico, it wasn't until last night that I was certain that Bluey was a friend and not an employee."

"Is that why you wanted to meet tonight? To find out the same thing about me?"

Seamus nodded and wiped at his eyes. Nicola's heart cracked as she realized that he was starting to cry. She gently put an arm around his shoulder and pulled him to her.

"You wouldn't have come if you weren't my friend," he said into her jacket.

"I didn't agree to this job to make the money," she said. "If we're going to be stupid honest, the most appealing thing about this job is that I get to take care of you. Does that make me a friend? I'm not here because I am an employee."

"I'm sorry," Seamus said, almost sobbing. "I became a crybaby in rehab. I literally had to tear all my walls down to get to the bottom of this bullshit, of why I was popping pills to avoid shit."

"I think I found the walls you pulled down and I used them to make mine double thick."

"Yeah, Bluey told me that you'd tried to close off."

"Oh, so it was okay for him to come into my house and refuse to talk about you, but he was able to talk about me?"

"It wasn't like that. He didn't sell you out. I think I pestered him into submission, and he didn't really submit too much."

"So how do we keep you from being lonely?"

"That's the million-dollar question. I can't do anything I did before. I can't go to crappy parties full of strangers; I can't surround myself with yes-men . . . people. I'm scared of taking a job that turns out to be three months in a strange city living in a sterile hotel room."

"Seamus?"

"Nico?"

"Are you afraid of being lonely, or are you afraid of being alone?"

"What's the difference?"

"A lot. I love being alone; I love having time to read a book and play records and not have to talk. Being alone is a gift. Being lonely is another thing altogether."

"Do you get lonely?"

"I've been lonely," Nicola said slowly. "At various stages in my life. Even though my dad was in and out of my life, I felt lonely when he died. And I was so lucky to have Billy around. Then he moved out here, and I guess I filled that void with Antony. Hindsight is an amazing lens. I can see I was lonely while I was with him. I filled my time, I did indoor rock climbing, a lot of group activities. I was in Facebook groups for every local hiking group. Charity work. My mom was so proud; she thought I was going to run for mayor or something. But yeah, I was lonely. And it's not the same thing; you can't read a book or play a record to feel less lonely."

"Are you lonely now?"

"I haven't really focused on it. I don't think so. I was hurt and a bit Alice in Wonderland when I met you, and I was hurt when you went away, but I was also thrown into a whole new level of career bullshit, so I've been too busy to do much self-reflection."

She watched Seamus process what she said, his face serious, his thick eyebrows dancing as he listened.

"And you're still hurt, I can tell that much."

"You stung me good." She paused. "But before we go on, can you explain to me how it's okay that you have a thermos of whiskey two days after getting out of rehab?"

"Drinking's never been a problem for me, and I chose to focus on the drug that could kill me. I don't get drunk too often. I'm a social drinker, and my counselors agreed that I could continue to drink, but if my sponsor thinks I'm swapping one addiction for another, they'll call me back. Why do you ask?"

"Because I could use a sip," she said with a smile. "I didn't realize you wanted to drag me up here to talk about feelings."

He pulled the thermos out of his pocket and unscrewed the lid. He handed it to her, and as she raised it to her mouth, her head swirled with the aroma of cinnamon and cloves.

"What is this? It smells like Christmas. I thought you said it was whiskey."

"It is, but I made you what my dad used to make us for Christmas, even when we were kids. It's whiskey, apple cider, and spices. I mulled it this afternoon. And just the smell of it was enough to calm me down and get me here."

Nicola raised the thermos to her lips, and the warm liquid made her lips tingle and filled her mouth with a complex bouquet. It did taste like Christmas. She tipped her whole head back and felt the drink spread warmth out through her body as it went down. She closed her eyes at the absurdity of her situation, that this movie star whose strange life had intimidated her at first was now meekly seeking her approval. Then it occurred to her that she was doing exactly what he was talking about: she was taking his fame and using it to see him as something other than what he was.

He's an actor, her brain reminded her. She passed the thermos back to him and he took a long, slow draft. She took her arm from his shoulders and pointed to their right, in the dark.

"See that tree over there?"

"Mmmmhmmm," Seamus said, wiping his lip and handing the thermos back to her.

"On Christmas Eve, I was all alone. Everyone took off, and it was the first time I'd ever been alone on Christmas Eve."

"Oh, Nico, I'm sorry."

"Don't be. I recommend it to everyone. There's an owl that goes to that tree, and it was there on Christmas Eve. I listened to it hoot every now and then, and I fell asleep waiting for it to hoot. I fell asleep feeling like everything was going to be okay. I woke up in the morning and made myself breakfast, I called home for a chat, and then I came up here and walked around before it got too busy. I didn't feel lonely."

"Maybe I need a Christmas Eve alone to show me the way."

"Well, that's nearly a year away. Ideally you'll find the key a bit faster than that."

"Do you think my new fake girlfriend will help?"

"Not in the slightest," Nicola said. "She's really into this whole fame concept. She wants it badly."

"I don't know if it's worth it," Seamus said bitterly. "There's another option, Wallace. There's always another option."

"I'll bite. What's behind door number two?"

"I stop being an actor."

"Because you've really just always wanted to direct?"

He laughed, long and hard. She smiled. It was the first time he'd seemed happy all night.

"No, it would be a sheep farm in northern Scotland."

"And the sheep would banish your loneliness?"

"No, but that would be my home. I'd be forced to settle in and make something of myself instead of just jumping around the world and never having any roots."

"Why don't you set down roots here? Buy a house? Get a dog?"

"I would have to make another movie to do that."

"I'm confused."

"All my money is tied up. When I make a movie, I sign all the money over to my accountant, and he hides it from me. They pay the bills, and they pay me a small salary. I have a corporate card, but I don't know the PIN. Have you ever seen Harrison Ford at an ATM? Stars send people to the bank for them. For the most part you and I probably earn around the same, in terms of cash on hand. I didn't want to come out the other side of this with nothing. I've met some actors who've been doing this for forty years, and they tell me about the money they've spent on cocaine or hookers, and it's just alien to me. Oh, hey, I snorted four million dollars' worth of coke. I spent a million on hookers. Now they're all desperate to play the grandpa on an NBC sitcom so they've got some retirement income. As bad as I got, I rarely spent money on pills. People just give them to me. So as long as I stay here, I can't have the life I had, and I don't know what life I *can* have. It's tricky."

Before she could hide it, Nicola smiled at Seamus's rambling answer. "Did you rideshare here?" she asked.

"I did."

"And where are you headed after?"

"Back to Bluey's. Why?"

"I don't want you to be alone, but I don't know what to do with you."

"Don't do anything with me. I want to head back soon and do some thinking. He's out tonight with Billy, so I can actually be alone."

"Is that a good thing?"

"I want to find out."

She smiled and took his hand and tried to look for stars in the gray night sky.

"Can I keep the whiskey?" she asked.

CHAPTER 11

PALE WINTER SUNLIGHT FLOODED THE conference room of Global Talent Management as Nicola let herself in. She was the first to arrive, according to the receptionist, who hadn't even looked at her, but had at least spoken this time. Nicola walked to the window to take it in. The view out over Rodeo Drive and up to the hills of Bel Air had been hidden by the rain last time. She breathed deeply, then turned and looked at the long, black enamel top of the table. Eight seats lined one side, with just one seat on the other side, and one seat at the end of the table. Name cards sat in front of most of the chairs, as well as some printed forms and bottles of Fiji Water.

She saw Weatherman's name at the head of the table closest to the window and breathed a sigh of relief that she wasn't sitting next to him. Her name was between Tobin and Bette, and not next to Timothy, who she realized she'd forgotten to text back last night. She quickly moved to her seat and fired off a text.

Timothy! Busy day yesterday, see you in a minute.

She opened a bottle of water and looked at the sheet of paper that was in front of her. It was headed, in bold, NONDISCLOSURE AGREE-MENT. She picked it up and looked it over. It was a legal document that swore all the participants of the meeting to secrecy or they would "incur a fine of ten million dollars," among other penalties. She picked up a pen and signed the paper, then pushed it into the center of the table. She saw that Seamus would be sitting across from her and noticed with surprise that there was an NDA in front of his vacant seat, too. She pulled her phone out of her purse. It was 8:50. The meeting wasn't due to start for ten more minutes. She should have stopped at Coffee Bean.

Glancing around the table again, she noticed a place card for a Brad Reinstein. She wondered who that was. Either way, for Seamus to have to sit facing eight people like some hellacious job interview didn't feel right. Nobody wanted to face a panel of people who were going to tell you how to live your life for the next year, complete with a companion. As she was thinking, the door opened, and she looked up to see Crystal usher Bette into the room.

"Nicola, how lovely to see you," Crystal said with what seemed to be genuine positivity.

"Yeah, hi," Bette said, with considerably less enthusiasm.

"What is this? A fucking wife-swapping party?" Crystal flicked one of her mannishly short fingernails at the row of name cards on the table.

"You're over here, by me," Nicola said.

"We're all on that side of the table, and he's facing us?" Bette said with strange excitement.

"Yeah, like a job interview," Nicola said.

"Or a firing squad," Crystal said, guiding Bette to her chair.

Nicola waited for them to sit down before asking the question that had been bugging her since Bette had been evasive so far.

"So, Bette, have you actually met Seamus before, or will today be your first time?"

"As if," Bette said, plonking into her seat. "We've met, like, so many times."

"Oh, really?" Nicola was trying to not sound like a bitch and failing. "*Like*, where?"

"Parties, red carpets . . . places. I dunno."

"Nicola, I assumed that Gaynor was joining us; her car is downstairs."

"Yeah, it is, but she's here for something else."

Crystal leaned forward and looked at Nicola, her frozen face conveying nothing. "I don't know why she's here, Crystal. Honest."

Crystal pulled out her phone and started texting, presumably to Gaynor. Bette pulled out her own phone and began taking selfies. Without saying a word, Crystal snatched the phone and deleted the photos.

"What the hell do you think you're doing, Crystal?" she wailed.

"See that paper in front of you? It's an NDA, you moron. You sign it and then you forget you were ever here. You don't post photos of it to your two million followers on Snapchat."

"It's an Instagram Story. And I have four million Snap followers."

"Sign the paper and remember one thing. You were never here. This meeting never happened."

Bette hunched in her chair like a scolded child. Crystal put Bette's phone back on the table, and Nicola started counting Mississippis until she picked it up again. She almost made it to three Mississippis.

A shuffling sound at the door startled her, and an army of black-suited white men filed into the conference room. Timothy caught her eye and gave her a small wave. Weatherman took his seat in silence, his assistant taking the seat nearest him on the long side of the table, then Timothy, then another assistant, then Tobin, who turned to Nicola as he took his seat.

"Nicola, it's a pleasure to see you again. I trust you're well."

His friendliness took her by surprise.

"Hello, Tobin. I'm doing great, thanks. How are you?"

"What is Seamus's ETA?" Weatherman interrupted.

Tobin pulled out his phone and swiped it on. He pushed a few buttons, and Nicola saw a dot marked SEAMUS moving along Wilshire. *They've got the bastard chipped like a dog.*

"They just crossed La Cienega. We have five minutes or so."

"They?" Nicola asked.

"He's with Brad Reinstein, his sober coach."

Nicola was perplexed. "I didn't know he was getting a sober coach."

"Neither did he," said Weatherman coldly. "Until today. Trust us, Miss Wallace. It's better this way. And while we can speak freely, I'd like to remind everyone that today's meeting will be run by myself and Mr. Freundschaft. Miss Wallace, please present your press plan, but don't ask for his opinion. Miss Wu, you'll be introduced to Mr. O'Riordan—"

"We've already met. Like twenty times."

"Miss Wu, if you interrupt me again, I'll ask you to leave. Crystal, please muzzle your client. All I want from you is a 'nice to meet you' and a smile."

Bette began to protest, and Crystal literally put a hand to her client's mouth. "You got it, Jon," she said with a smile that didn't touch her eyes.

"Timothy," he continued, "I'll leave you to deliver the good news."

"Thank you, Jon. I'm glad we were able to get it locked in."

Nicola wondered what they were talking about.

"Now, one last piece of business: if we could all sign the NDA that's on the desk in front of you. Do it now, please, and Daniel"—he spoke to his assistant to his right—"will pick them up and take them out of here." He took a pen from a pocket inside his jacket and signed his own form, passing it to Daniel. Everyone else finished signing the forms and shuffled them down to the end of the table. Daniel checked all the forms, signed his own, shook them into a neat pile, and quickly left the room.

"Before we get started, one last thing. Mr. O'Riordan has expressed distaste for the serious side of the business, so let's all remember to make this meeting . . ." He paused and smiled a slimy grin. ". . . fun."

The elevator bell dinged down the corridor and Nicola grimaced as the usually inanimate receptionist greeted Seamus warmly by name. She looked expectantly at the door, and within seconds Seamus appeared, accompanied by the receptionist and a handsomely weather-beaten man who looked vaguely familiar.

Seamus, in work boots, blue jeans, a vintage REM T-shirt, and a plaid Pendleton jacket, waved his arms widely.

"Hello, everyone," he said cheerily enough, his eyes scanning the room. A chorus of greetings sailed back to him, and Weatherman got up and wrapped him in a strong hug that Seamus took a second to reciprocate. As they pulled apart, Seamus pointed to his name card on the table.

"So that's where I'm sitting? It feels like this is the principal's office and I did something really naughty."

"Don't be silly, Seamus," Weatherman said with an awkward

laugh. "Happy new year! We're just glad to have you back, and we've assembled the team to update you so we can all get back to doing what we all do best, and that is making you the biggest movie actor in the world."

Nicola noticed that Weatherman did not say *star*.

Seamus turned toward his chair. For a second Nicola saw him roll his eyes, then he looked directly at her briefly before he sat down.

"Hey, everybody, this is Brad Reinstein, my sober coach. Brad, this is everyone. You can see their names on these adorable little nameplates. And what, pray tell, is this NDA doing in front of me?"

Tobin stood up and reached across the table, extending his hand. Seamus followed suit, and they shook hands.

"It's really good to see you, Seamus," Tobin said warmly. "Ignore that; it wasn't supposed to be for you. We just have a lot of new people here today, and we need to make sure that we are able to continue the good work done by Miss Wallace in terms of keeping recent events away from the hounds of the press."

Seamus smiled broadly at Nicola. "Miss Wallace did good, huh?"

"Zero press pickup," Tobin said. "Which, if you'd ever bother to set up a Google alert for yourself, you'd know."

"Tobin, I just spent ten weeks without a phone, and you'd be shocked at how life-changing it is."

"I'm sure you're right, old friend," he laughed. "I hope to never find out."

"Seamus," Weatherman stood, opening his arms as if he were about to give a wedding toast. "We are all so happy to have you back, and to see you looking so damn healthy. Except the hair. What happened to the hair?"

"It'll grow back, boss," he laughed.

"That it will, that it will. And we seem to have come through this as little more than a hiccup. From what we hear, the movie that you left in the fall has had nothing but problems and reshoots, so perhaps it was a blessing in disguise. Let's begin with Miss Wallace, as she's going to outline your press strategy. Also, Miss Wallace, if you'd be so kind, could you please introduce Miss Wu to Mr. O'Riordan?"

Nicola froze inside. Was Weatherman trying to make this whole stunt seem like her idea? She was suddenly jealous of Crystal's Botoxed, immobile face as she gathered her notes and raised her eyes to meet Seamus's.

"Seamus, hi, it's good to see you again," she began. He nodded to her. "First things first: it's been our experience that the easiest way to distract the press is to give them a new relationship. So, we have taken the liberty of securing the services of Bette Wu to be your . . ." She paused. ". . . press companion, through awards season at least. After that, it will depend on what direction coverage takes. Seamus, this is Bette. Bette, meet Seamus."

Nicola saw a dark cloud pass across Seamus's face as he stood and extended a hand. Bette stood, but instead of offering her hand, she walked around the table and gave Seamus a hug.

"You big silly," she said, still hugging him. "We've met like twenty times."

"Of course we have," Seamus said, not hugging her back. "Bette, it's good to see you."

Nicola looked at Bette and cleared her throat. Bette ignored her.

"Yeah, last time I saw you was at that party in the Hills; you were there with—"

"Bette," Crystal barked. "Sit down."

"Whatever, Jesus." Bette slunk back to her chair. Seamus sat down.

"Anyway," Nicola began. "We are confident that with the right series of media placements we will be able to avoid any coverage of your departure from the film. The official story is that the injury was severe, requiring a long recuperation in Scotland and at home here in Los Angeles."

"Should I be taking notes, Nicola?" Seamus said, picking up his pen. Nicola couldn't tell if he was joking or not.

"No, Seamus. I'll be e-mailing you an outline of our talking points, and you and I will do some media training at Huerta Hernandez this evening, before your first event with Bette."

"Event?" Bette crowed, glaring at Crystal. "You said it was a date!"

"Technically, yes," Nicola continued. "It will be a date. Due to the Golden Globes this weekend, we are on an expedited schedule, and therefore the first public date is today. We will have exclusive coverage on People.com by morning, and they will have the exclusive story, with on-record quotes from Bette, on stands next week. Both of you have clothing selections pulled and ready. Brad, will you be Seamus's driver going forward?"

"I can drive myself," Seamus said flatly.

"Noted. We will arrange a car immediately. So, for the next week, your only answer to questions about the relationship is no answer at all. The only places you will encounter press will be leaving the restaurant tonight and then at the Globes on Sunday. Seamus, they want you to do the press room."

Seamus groaned. "I didn't win an award. Do I still have to suck up to them?"

Tobin jumped in. "Man, you know this is the easiest crowd you'll ever face. Charm them, flirt with them, show them how well-healed your injury is by picking up one of those old bitches in the front row. Nobody will even think to do any real reporting."

"And in the event of any untoward questions," Nicola continued, "I step in and say we have to leave for another engagement."

"Am I doing the press room, too?" Bette said hopefully.

"No," Nicola said to her face. "You will wait with Crystal until it's time for us to go to the parties. We will attend both the Foreign Press party and the HBO party, both for under a half hour, and then we will leave."

"But when do I give my quotes to *People*?"

"You already have," snarled Crystal. "I e-mailed them to the reporter yesterday."

"But that's not . . ." Bette grabbed Crystal's arm.

Nicola began talking over her. "We are still working out the TV exclusive. It's probably going to be *The Late Show*, around the Oscars. There's no point in doing it now; there's nothing to promote. It gives us nearly two months to let the news cycle eat its own tail."

"Sounds good, thanks," Seamus muttered.

"Thank you, Miss Wallace. And now let's hear from our man Timothy Thompson, who has some very good news."

Timothy opened a zippered leather-bound folder on the table in front of him. He pulled out a novel and passed it across the table to Seamus, who barely looked at it. It was *Parallax: Quest 3*, the conclusion to the bestselling book series.

"Heard of this book?" Timothy said proudly. Seamus shook his head. "Well, you will. Because as of earlier today, you're the lucky bastard who gets to play Sibelius, the mysterious and sexy leading man who leads our plucky heroine through the geometrically impossible minefield of a postapocalyptic world."

There were gasps around the table, then Bette squealed and started clapping. "Oh my God," she said. "That movie is the summer tentpole of next year. That's amazing."

"She's right," Timothy said with a smile. "And the good news is, no audition, and no fallout from Ojai. We were able to build upon your pre-Ojai rate, and in fact we were able to boost your back end. So, my friend, if you'd like to sign here, we can all be back in business as if nothing ever happened."

Tobin reached over and took the contract from Timothy's hand.

"Seamus and I will be going out for lunch after this. I'll handle the contracts then, if that's okay. Signing them right now feels a bit . . . I don't know . . . improper."

"Whatever works for you guys, of course," Timothy said, not skipping a beat. "And more good news: we've got a month before shooting starts, and even better, principal photography is happening all at once, with pickups as the effects nerds need them. Various locations."

"Please don't tell me it's in Romania or Iceland," Seamus said with a wan laugh.

"I wouldn't do that to you, buddy," Timothy said. "It's shooting partially here and partially in Rosarito, Mexico. Just four hours' drive, or a quick flight."

"Mexico?" Seamus said. "I shot there a few years ago. It's . . . it's . . . okay. It's fine."

Nicola watched Weatherman, Tobin, and Timothy all exchange glances.

"Seamus," Timothy continued. "This is the dream gig. It's three big paydays for one long job, and then you'll have blockbusters out three summers in a row. This is the holy grail of making movies. We have the script; we have all read it. Tobin has a copy for you. There are a few changes already, but for the most part, we're good to go. Technically, we can book you on another movie late this summer, since the initial shoot is February until June."

"Thank you all," Seamus said, looking around. "I didn't really expect any good news today. That's amazing. Crystal, Bette, thank you for coming. I'll see you tonight."

Crystal appeared surprised by their sudden dismissal, but she recovered quickly, standing and hooking a hand into Bette's armpit on her way up.

"Where are we going?" Bette squawked. She pointed at Nicola. "Why isn't she leaving?"

"Bette," Seamus jumped in. "I have some unfinished business with Miss Wallace."

"Yeah, that's what I hear," Bette snapped.

Weatherman tapped Daniel on the shoulder, and he sprang into action.

"Miss Connors, Miss Wu, please come with me; I'll validate your parking." He rounded them up like a sheepdog and herded them out through the door. Nicola was most shocked that Crystal did not make a sound. As the door closed behind them, Timothy made to continue speaking, and Seamus raised a pointed finger at him, signaling him to wait. They sat in suspended silence until they heard the ding of the elevator that was taking them back to their cars.

"What the actual fuck are you guys doing setting me up with her?" Seamus demanded, anger boiling into his voice. "Bette says we met before, right? You know where? Every shitty Hollywood Hills drug party I've ever been to. She's tight with that whole crew; she knows Kiri and Amber and Courtney and SaraBeth."

"This is not cool," Brad said. "We will need to distance Seamus from anyone who can be branded as an enabler, so if you can find him a new companion . . ."

Weatherman's face began to redden, and Tobin spoke before Weatherman could explode.

"Thank you for your concern, Mr. Reinstein, but trust us, Seamus, we've done a thorough backgrounder on Bette, and she's clean. She tested negative for drugs, and as far as we can tell, she's hanging around that crowd for the same reason she's agreeing to play this part in your press campaign: simply to get ahead. She's a climber."

"And if she's good she gets a movie role. I know all that," Seamus said bitterly. "I just don't want to give Amber a foot in the door of my life. If she senses that Bette could be useful, she'll turn her into a puppet in no time."

Nicola looked at her nails, her phone, anything to avoid seeing the desperate hurt in Seamus's eyes.

"Seamus, your recovery is the most important thing to us, and we wouldn't do anything to endanger you," Tobin said, his voice warm with compassion. "We've vetted her thoroughly, and she's the best vehicle we can find."

"And what's up with signing me up for a movie without asking me? I don't know if I want to do this. This isn't how we do business. Tobin? You think this kind of shit is okay?" Seamus was getting riled up. Nicola wished she'd left with Crystal.

"Let me handle this, Tobin," Weatherman said, his smile gone. "Do you know how much your little overdose cost this agency, O'Riordan? Do you know how much it cost you? You probably lost out on fifty to eighty million dollars. Which means that I for one lost out on seven to twelve million dollars. Tobin here lost the same. Even if you don't care, even if you have enough money, that one hit of smack nearly undid all the good work we've done with you for the past eight years. So you're taking this fucking job even if it's worse than *Divergent*. You're going to play the game, and you'll play by our rules, and we will all. Get. Rich!" He smacked the table for emphasis.

Seamus looked angrily from Weatherman to Timothy and back again. Then he looked at Nicola. "I'm sorry you had to see that," he said.

Christ, he's going to cry again. Nicola panicked.

Then he looked at Tobin.

"Let's go, Freundschaft." Seamus got up from the table. "Brad, I'll call you when I need to get picked up." He turned and let himself out of the room, and Tobin scrambled to catch up to him. Nicola was waiting for the elevator ding but heard a door open.

"He's taken the fire stairs," Weatherman said. "Timothy, follow him and unlock them. You two can leave." He gestured at Nicola and Brad. "Thank you for coming."

Before they could answer, Weatherman got up and walked out, with Timothy close behind him. Before the door closed, Timothy turned and mouthed "I'll call you" to Nicola. Then she was alone with Brad.

"Welcome to Hollywood," she said wearily as she gathered up her papers and shoved them into her Birkin.

"It's okay, honey," he said. "This ain't my first time at the rodeo."

"Oh, you do a lot of sober coaching?"

"I'm not talking about that," he said, reaching into his pocket and pulling out a business card. "I had a TV show in the nineties. I used to be known as Brad Rainer."

A light went on inside Nicola's head. That's where she knew him from.

"Oh, I'm so sorry, I thought I recognized you. You were on *Bel Air*; you were the sexy pool boy, the runaway."

"Aren't you a little young to remember that show?"

"My mom had a crush on you," Nicola said with a smile.

"All the moms had a crush on me," Brad said wistfully. "And I had a crush on pills, and before long, nobody had a crush on me anymore."

"Well, at least you're sober now."

"Yes, ma'am. And I'm talking to agents about getting the come-back going."

"Oh, great. Good luck," Nicola said, preparing to leave.

"Before you go, here's my card. Please make sure they use my stage name in any stories, and if we get photographed together, it's in my contract that you'll say that I'm a friend that Seamus met in acting class."

"Oh, I see."

"So, I don't know how you'd feel about it—I don't have much money at the moment—but if this show gets off the ground, this could be good for you."

"Good for me?"

"Yeah, if you wanna be my publicist, too."

Nicola's phone rang. It was Seamus.

"Sorry, Brad, I have to take this." Nicola pushed past Brad and headed the wrong way down the hall.

"What is it, Seamus?"

"I'm sick to my stomach that you saw that," he said.

"Are you okay?"

"I'm humiliated. They treated me like a dog."

"Nah, you just have a shitty job."

Seamus laughed his best throaty chuckle. "You still at Global?"

"Yeah."

"Do something for me, yeah?"

"Uh, sure."

"Pop your head into Weatherman's office and tell him to fire my sober coach immediately, then tell him I'll do his movie if he makes the studio pay for Bluey as my helper, and move him to Huerta Hernandez. For two hundred and fifty thousand bucks."

"My pleasure," Nicola grinned.

Something was finally going right.

CHAPTER 12

SEAMUS PULLED THE LOANER TESLA into the parking lot of Huerta Hernandez just as Bette emerged from the elevator doors. He swung the car in her direction and pulled to a halt close enough to her feet that she jumped back. The silence of the car unnerved him.

"Jesus, what's wrong with you?" she yelled.

He leaned across the front seat and opened her door, pushing it wide. "Fine, thanks, how are you?" he said.

"You nearly hit me," Bette fussed, getting into the passenger seat.

"I didn't nearly hit you," Seamus said, waiting for her to fasten her seat belt. "I got this car half an hour ago. I'm still learning the brakes."

"I can't believe they gave you a Tesla; it's so substandard." Bette flicked her fingernails at the lights and screen on the dashboard. "You should totally have a Bentley."

"Maybe next time," Seamus said sarcastically as he pulled out of the driveway and waited to make a left on Beverly. He glanced at Bette. According to Nicola, she'd been in hair and makeup since two p.m., and it showed. Her long black hair was tousled around her head, and even though she was probably wearing a lot of makeup, it didn't look like it. Her broad face and high cheekbones looked bare, and her lips were pale pink in the dark light of the car.

"You look amazing," he ventured.

"Thanks," she said with sudden enthusiasm. "I wanted to go for something a bit more dramatic, but I lost that battle."

Seamus wondered if that battle had been with Gaynor or Nicola but refrained from asking. He'd heard from Gaynor that Bette had wanted to wear something revealing but they'd nixed that in favor of a dramatic red silk Carolina Herrera gown.

"I think you look perfect the way you are," he said, regretting it instantly. He hated small talk. It was going to be a very long night. "That's such an award show gown for dinner, but you look amazing."

"Are you just saying that?" Bette said in a little-girl voice that was too close to Amber's for comfort.

"No, Bette." Seamus leaned forward to make sure he could make the left turn. "I meant it."

"I'm so excited," she purred. "I love going to the Nice Guy. Isn't it the best?"

"I wouldn't know, Bette; this'll be my first time."

As they headed west on Beverly with Bette prattling on about her previous visits to the Nice Guy, Seamus ran through the instructions that Nicola had drilled into his head: Use the valet on La Cienega for their arrival. No talking to any lurking paparazzi on their way in. The place was small and he would feel like everyone was staring, and that was because they would be. They were to stay at the restaurant for a minimum of ninety minutes before using the rear exit. A retractable canopy would be extended all the way from the restaurant to the passenger door of the car. Sorry, Nic had told him, there was no way to guarantee privacy for the driver.

After turning right on La Cienega, Seamus started scouring the street for his destination.

"Oh my God, you just totally drove right past it," Bette said, pointing to a nondescript building next door to a Persian carpet joint on the other side of the road. Glancing quickly over his shoulder, Seamus made a U-turn and swung into the valet line.

"Okay, you know what to do, right?"

"Der, O'Riordan," Bette smiled. "I'll get out and stand there, let them get some photos, and you'll come around and escort me in. So simple."

"I don't see any photographers." Seamus was suddenly nervous.

"Oh, baby, you will."

Seamus exited the car as the valet came around the front. Out of the corner of his eye, he saw Bette emerge from her side and stand upright on the sidewalk. Out of nowhere, a barrage of flash pops blinded him. Seamus looked down at his feet and walked around to Bette. Keeping his head down, he guided her to the wooden door, smiling at the ironic NO PHOTOS PLEASE sign on the door. They stepped inside a tiny vestibule, a heavy black velvet curtain obscuring the rest of the room. As the flash ghosts faded from his eyes, he and Bette were greeted by a lithe blond woman holding an iPad like a clipboard.

"Mr. O'Riordan, Ms. Wu, welcome to the Nice Guy. We have your table ready."

The woman consulted her touchscreen for their table location and then used her other arm to pull back the curtain.

I don't know how she'd have found our table without that iPad, Seamus thought as he surveyed the tiny restaurant dining room. Nicola had warned him that it was small, but this was ridiculous. Six U-shaped booths flanked three walls, and two dining tables filled the center of the room. An old-timey bar occupied the entire fourth wall. He could see people at every table except one booth. Just as Nic had predicted, when he and Bette stepped from behind the curtain, every person turned to stare.

The hostess consulted her iPad again and nodded for them to follow her to the empty table. As they made their way, Seamus felt Bette's hand seek his and fought an instinct to push it away. Instead he folded his big, rough fingers around her tiny, tough ones, the calluses reminding him that she was a trained martial artist who could snap his neck. When they reached the table, Seamus stood and waited until she slid into the circular bench.

"Crystal told me you are a gentleman," Bette said, nodding. "That's kind of hard to believe."

"What's hard to believe about being polite?" Seamus slid into the other side of the table, noticing an upright piano and a microphone on a tiny stage.

"You're funny," Bette said without laughing. "Nobody is polite anymore."

"They have live music in here?" Seamus changed the subject.

"Oh, dude, so many huge stars just get up and play, you never know. Sometimes, you might get Nick Jonas or Justin Bieber or John Mayer."

Seamus pasted a fake smile on his face and nodded, hoping that none of those people would turn up tonight.

The bartender left the bar and walked over to them.

"Good evening, Mr. O'Riordan, Ms. Wu. My name is Errol; I'm your mixologist. Would you care to order something, or would you like me to custom-craft something based on your tastes?"

"I'll take your best scotch. Neat. Make it a double. And some water, please."

"I'll take a custom, please," Bette added.

"Of course, madam. Tell me your three favorite types of alcohol."

"I love Midori, Southern Comfort, and Absolut Mandrin."

"Got it," Errol said, bowing and heading back to the bar.

"I hate that fuck-boy haircut," Bette hissed as he left.

"The what now?"

"Oh my God, don't you even know?" She pulled out her phone and typed, then turned it to him. "Look. If you google 'fuck-boy hair-cut' you get that haircut."

Seamus saw she was right.

"Well, I've learned something today. At least today's not a waste."

"Yeah, you should never sleep with a guy with that haircut. He'll just break your heart."

"Thanks for the warning."

"Wait, are you bi?"

"No, Bette. I'm Scottish. We use humor. Almost constantly. I was joking."

Seemingly unable to process that statement, Bette scanned the room. "Ugh," she whined. "There's literally nobody here except us. They've sent us here on a loser night."

"Sorry to disappoint you. Also, it's ten past eight. I'm sure some-body more interesting than me will turn up soon."

"You know what I mean," she said, reaching across the table and taking his hand. "Everyone's looking. Let's give them something to talk about."

"Another thing—I'm not really into PDAs even when I'm really dating someone. It's just too . . . scrutinized. I don't know. We don't need to overdo it."

Bette left her hand encircling his. Errol returned with a tray. He set a glass of water in front of each of them and put Seamus's scotch in front of him, then turned to Bette.

"Ms. Wu, I present to you a drink originally served at Raffles over a century ago."

He handed her a tall, frosted glass containing a murky lavender liquid. Bette took the glass and passed it straight to her lips, taking a sip.

"Oh my God, this is delicious," she squealed.

"Uh, cheers, I guess," Seamus said, picking up his snifter and draining half of it in one gulp. He didn't know how he was going to tolerate this for another eighty minutes.

"Are you drinking that for real or just to throw people off the story?"

"Which story are you talking about?"

"You can be so dumb," Bette laughed. "The rehab thing. You're not allowed to drink if you just got out of rehab."

"I'm allowed to drink, Bette," Seamus said as if he were talking to a child. "I'm having a drink because I want one, not to do it for any effect or because people are watching."

"Well, you should have had him make you one of these custom cocktails; they're delicious."

"Maybe next time," Seamus said, downing the rest of his scotch.

Their waitress appeared and gave them menus.

"Can we start with a dozen oysters and the meatballs?" Bette, suddenly businesslike, raised her palm, declining her menu. "Thanks. Seamus, you really should try the rib eye."

"You must have read my mind." Seamus smiled at her.

Bette took over their order, from memory, ordering his steak medium rare, a chicken parm for herself, and sides of truffle fries and baby broccoli. As the waitress went to repeat the order back to her, Bette waved her nails at her and dismissed her.

"I think you got it, honey," she said as the waitress turned away.

"This place is so tiny," Seamus said, making more small talk.

"Every place in Hollywood is tiny. I'm surprised that you're surprised, actually."

"I hope the food is good."

"It's better than cooking at home. My mother hates it that I can't even cook."

"Tell me about your family, Bette."

"What's to tell? I know that they gave you my bio and a bunch of stuff to read. Didn't they?"

He nodded.

"Yeah, they gave me one about you. At least I read mine."

"I read yours. I just wanted to hear it in your words. We're going to be spending a lot of time together over the next few months; we may as well see what we have in common."

"You are so old-fashioned," she said with a fake laugh. "Okay. I was born in Arcadia, just east of LA. I competed in martial arts tournaments since I was, like, eight. I have three brothers and I got sick of them kicking my ass. It's been a long time since they've been able to. One day at a tournament, an agent asked me to audition for *Survivor*. They're always looking for Asians, but Asians are too smart to do shit like *Survivor*. I said I wasn't interested, but I took his number. My mom made me start acting lessons immediately. After six months, I called him back and went in and he got me an audition for my first show, on Disney Channel. I train seven days a week, even though I'm retired from competition. I want to be a movie star. The rest is history."

"That wasn't exactly what I meant. I knew all that stuff from the info packet that Gaynor gave me."

"So what do you want to know, big boy?"

"What do you do in your spare time? Do you date? Who are your friends?"

"I train. I fight. I do martial arts for four hours every morning.

I'm learning Mandarin right now. I like going to clubs and parties. I'm not sure what you're looking for."

"Common ground, I guess," Seamus said, wishing he could check his phone.

"Look, I'll be straight up with you. Yes, I'm dating someone. Have been for a while. But he's not right for getting me to the next level."

"So he's not famous?"

"He's not white," Bette stated without any ire. "He's like me, Chinese American. He's an engineer. We've been dating for six years."

"And you've never been photographed together?"

"Sure. By my mom."

"You know what I mean."

"Right. He's kind of boring; he hates fame and going out."

"So why do you keep him around?"

"Oh, I love him. I'll marry him when I'm thirty."

"You're twenty-five."

"Right."

"So until then, you're going to do these setup things?"

"If that's what it takes," she said coldly. "You know what I'm talking about."

"Sorry, Bette, I don't. And I know that reeks of white male privilege. But I never did anything for this. It just happened."

"Well then, you're lucky. Don't feel bad. You got there. I'll get there. We're helping each other."

She pulled her phone from her purse and studied it. Seamus wondered if he'd upset her.

"Oh fun," she said. "Crystal wants us to take photos in the photo booth. I was going to say we should do it anyway."

Seamus craned his neck and looked around the room, not seeing any photo booth.

"It's out back by the bathrooms," Bette explained. "We'll take some pics when we go outside to smoke."

Seamus sighed. He hated smoking.

"I don't smoke," he said.

"I didn't mean cigarettes." Bette began rummaging in her purse. Seamus fought down an urge to panic, fearing that she was about to pull out a joint. Instead, she produced a vape box. "Nobody smokes anymore. We can vape. I have raspberry-vanilla in there at the moment."

"Like I said, I don't smoke. Actually, Bette, where are the bathrooms? I may as well go before the food comes."

Bette produced a black glasses case from her purse, opened it, and put the glasses on. "Listen, I know we can't post, but I'm just going to Snap the drinks menu. Don't worry, I won't show your face."

She pressed a finger to her right temple, and a white circle of lights began spinning in the corner of the frame. When she was done she put them back in the case and looked at him.

"What?"

"What the hell was that?"

"Don't tell me you don't even know what Snap Spectacles are."

"Okay, I won't tell you."

"I can show the world everything from my point of view; it's totally a thing. Everyone does it."

"I'm allergic to social media," Seamus said. "I don't think it's good for the human race."

"Ugh, you're so old. The bathrooms are down there."

She thumbed backward over her shoulder, indicating a hallway that he hadn't even noticed, and, without looking up, continued texting on her phone.

So this is what a fake girlfriend is like, Seamus thought as he walked away.

✳   ✳   ✳

Glancing around the empty bathroom, Seamus considered using the urinal, but it, like so many other things in his life, had been rendered off-limits by his fame. It was too easy to sneak photography. As it was, he had to carefully inspect the air vents in the stall before he peed.

Once he was done, he washed his hands in the main bathroom

area, then paused and returned to the stall. He pulled out his phone. There was a screenful of texts, most of them from Nicola. He pushed through to a voice call without even reading them. She answered before he heard it ring.

"Are you okay?"

"Nico, she's awful." He laughed.

"Not as awful as talking about an overdose with Kelly Ripa," Nicola said.

"Fair point. I just wanted to check in real quick. And maybe waste a few minutes of time chatting to you."

"Are you in the bathroom?"

"I am."

"Then you need to go back. Last thing we need is someone saying you spent five minutes doing bathroom blow when the *Enquirer* reporter stops them outside the club."

"Ouch."

"I'm sorry, Seamus. I really am. But you have to get back out there. You have one hour to go. It's going well; I've already had a landslide of e-mails and phone calls asking about you and your new girlfriend. Also, two blogs have already posted trend stories on your cropped head, so you're a fashion plate, too."

"Fook me." He shook his head. "Okay, Nico. Wish me luck."

✳ ✳ ✳

"Everything okay?" Bette asked as Seamus slid back into his seat.

"Yeah, why?"

"You were gone awhile."

"I was gone three minutes; I had to answer some texts."

"Word to the wise: answer your texts at the table."

"You sound just like Nicola," he laughed, noticing two fresh cocktails on the table. "What's this?"

"You said next time you'd try one."

Seamus picked up a tumbler of fragrant brown liquid. He tasted it and furrowed his brow.

"You don't like it?"

"It's okay," he said, licking his lips. "It's just kind of weird." He took another big sip.

"Mine's really good. This time it's got absinthe and strawberries. Want a taste?"

Seamus grimaced, shook his head, and drank more from his cup. The liquor relaxed him slightly.

Their waiter appeared with the oysters and the meatballs and placed them on the table. Bette picked up a little oyster fork and speared one of the meaty gray blobs. She moved it in the direction of Seamus's face.

"Bette, no, I can feed myself."

"Gaynor told me that I had to do it."

Seamus rolled his eyes and opened his mouth, letting her plop the oyster on his tongue. He closed his mouth around it and enjoyed the salty slipperiness.

"Are you a chewer or a swallower?" Bette asked suggestively. He chuckled and bit down into the oyster.

"Does that answer your question?"

"I can't chew them," Bette said, popping one in her mouth and swallowing it instantly. "The taste is nice, but I'd rather have a dirty martini."

"Then why did you order them?"

"Gaynor, der." She speared another one and presented it to him. This time he surprised her by leaning forward and biting it with his teeth.

"Do you want to try the meatballs?" She began cutting into one of the two meatballs with a knife.

"Bette, I can cut my own food." He reached across the table and touched her hand. "I appreciate it, but you really don't have to do everything that Gaynor says."

"No," she corrected him. "*You* don't have to do what anyone says. *I* have to do every little thing that they tell me to do. Jump, bitch, jump."

"Bette." He leaned forward conspiratorially. "You are golden. We're in this together. I'll report back that you were perfect, and everyone will be happy. Please. Don't feel like you have to act like their servant."

She slumped her shoulders dramatically. "Does that mean we can actually just have fun?"

"This whole thing will work better if we do, right?"

Bette clicked her fingers in Errol's direction and signaled for more drinks.

"I have to drive," Seamus protested. "I'm already feeling a bit fuzzy."

"Do you want to go to the photo booth before our food comes? I need to go smoke."

❋ ❋ ❋

An hour later, Seamus was more than ready to leave. The late-night scene had begun to trickle in. Every seat at the bar was taken, the two outdoor smoking areas were overcrowded, and a guy was tuning the piano and checking the PA system.

"What's the matter?" Bette asked. "You look nervous."

"It's getting a bit intense in here," Seamus said, making a pained face.

"Do you think enough people have seen us?"

"I don't give a fuck, my dear," Seamus said with a laugh. "And I have to tell you, this was a lot easier and nicer than I anticipated."

"You probably thought I was a total bitch," Bette said seriously.

"Not exactly," Seamus said, noticing a tiny slur. "I just wondered why anyone would take this kind of a gig."

"Captain Obvious. How many people in this town are in relationships with people they love?"

"I suppose." Seamus rested his head on his hand. He realized he was drunker than he should be. "Damn, those drinks were strong."

"Do you need me to drive?"

"You've had as much to drink as I have, young lady."

"You sound like my dad. Except the accent. I am totally fine. I'll drive."

"No, I'll do it. We're going out the back way; there shouldn't be a problem. Let's get the check and we can head out."

"There's no check." Bette crossed her eyes. "Did you not even read the instructions for tonight? Your team put your Amex through already."

"Oh, I paid for this?"

"I don't know how you guys handle that kind of stuff. Probably, if my team are anything to go by."

"You know, I really don't pay attention to the money stuff. I have a guy."

"O'Riordan, you need to pay attention to your money. You'll get ripped off."

Seamus watched her talking as if from a distance. The drinks had hit him harder than he expected. Therapy had turned him into a lightweight. He chugged the water in his glass and then reached over and took Bette's untouched water glass.

"You're all business all of a sudden," he said. He relaxed against the soft back of the booth and looked around the room. Bette pulled out her phone and took a selfie that she began doodling on with her finger.

"I thought you couldn't do that in here."

"I'm with you, Seamus," she said, her finger poised mid-doodle on her phone. "I can do anything at all. I could shit on that table over there, and it would be their problem."

"You know what's not attractive? That."

"Are you always such a buzzkill?"

"I just try to not be an asshole," he said with a smile to soften the blow. "Just because we can get away with something doesn't mean we should do it."

Bette tapped at her phone and then stared at it as she waited for her photo to upload to Snap.

"I'm sorry, I missed that," she said with a broad smile.

"Let's get the car, then," Seamus said, motioning to their waitress. "I'm good to drive."

The waitress arrived at their table. "Can I help you?"

"Yes, please," Seamus said with his best movie-star smile. "We're ready to leave. Can you arrange to have my car brought to the back entrance?"

"Of course, sir. Please give me a few minutes. I'll come back when we have it all set up for you."

Seamus nodded, and when he looked back at the table, Bette had the photo strips from the photo booth laid out on the table in front of her and was taking a photo of them.

"No, Bette, you're not posting them."

"Der, stupid. I'm sending them to Gaynor. They're going to go up on People.com."

"The fuck they are," Seamus said, reaching for them. Bette beat him to them and carefully folded them into her purse.

"They are," Bette said. "It's out of my hands. They're going to say that we left them there and someone found them and gave them to *People*."

Seamus groaned out loud.

"What? This is exactly what your last two girlfriends did."

Seamus paused for a moment. *No, it's not*, he thought. *The last one never did anything like this.*

The waitress reappeared at his elbow. "Your car is ready," she said. "Please follow me."

As they walked to the rear of the restaurant, Seamus was aware once again of every head turning to watch them. He took a deep breath to stem a tide of anger in his throat. He was so up and down tonight, he thought sourly.

They reached the back door quickly. The waitress pushed open a heavy security grille, leading into a black fabric tunnel, at the end of which was their Tesla.

"This is such bullshit," Bette complained as they stepped into the tunnel. "This tunnel thing draws more attention than if we just walked to the car. It's so lame. It's on wheels. As soon as the paparazzi see them drag it out, they come and wait. And you're gonna get photographed anyway. It only hides the person getting into the passenger seat."

Seamus suddenly understood Bette's offer to drive. It would mean she'd get photographed.

"Them's the breaks, m'dear," he laughed as they reached the car. He opened the passenger door for her, then stood to wait for her to get in. She didn't.

"Are you okay?" he asked.

Bette was grabbing the end of the concertina tunnel, testing it here and there.

Suddenly she gave the edges of the tunnel a push and it rolled back, revealing her and Seamus to a horde of photographers. So many flashes exploded that it became one long explosion of white light. Blinded, Seamus tried to cover his eyes with one hand while feeling his way around the car with the other. A valet opened his door and he fell inside, pulling the door closed. Bette was standing upright at her door, looking slowly from left to right, a pout on her face. He considered leaving her there.

"Bette, please get in the car," he yelled over the din of the photographers, all the while making sure his anger did not show on his face. One angry photo could sink this charade.

As if in slow motion, Bette folded herself into the passenger seat and, looking straight ahead, gingerly pulled her seat belt across her lap and fastened it. Seamus waited as security from the club moved to the front of the car and tried to clear the photographers who had jumped in front of the hood, barring their escape. Seamus gently tapped his foot on the accelerator, and the car shot forward. A photographer in front of Bette screamed as the car rolled over his foot. The security guards waved their hands at Seamus to stop, but he tried again, this time making the car roll glacially forward as flashes continued to come at them from all sides. Eventually security cleared the paps from the front of the car and Seamus was able to peel out into a tight U-turn, then a right onto La Cienega without looking to see if he was clear.

They both flinched as they heard a car screech close behind them. Seamus looked in the mirror and saw that it had nearly hit them. An elderly woman driver flipped him off as she mouthed obscenities. He looked in his side mirrors and moved to the left lane, then sped across oncoming traffic onto Melrose.

"Where the fuck did you learn to drive like that?" Bette smiled. "That's so hot."

"On a movie set," Seamus said through gritted teeth. He remained silent as they headed back to the Huerta Hernandez building.

"I thought you were driving me home," Bette said when she realized their destination.

"I can't risk the DUI," Seamus said tersely.

"I can drive us," Bette said, and once again Seamus wondered if she was flirting.

"No, just call a car. I'll wait with you, then I'll call one for myself." Seamus lied. He had no idea how to call a car. Bluey was up in Malibu on business, and he didn't want to be drunk in front of Nicola. It looked like he'd be sleeping in the car underneath his publicist's office, like any other megastar on a string of bad luck.

CHAPTER 13

"IS THIS THE ROOM THAT Whitney Houston died in?" Kara rolled over on the bed of the Beverly Hilton suite that Huerta Hernandez had booked for the Golden Globes.

Gaynor looked up from her ad hoc media station—three laptops crowded around a desk in front of the glass windows.

"*Mija*, don't be so ghastly," she said, crossing herself. "That poor woman."

The bathroom door burst open and Alicia stepped out. "Kara, I heard that. Don't say that, I couldn't even finish wiping."

"But you did . . . right?" Nicola said from her perch, cross-legged on the bed with her laptop on her knees.

"I had to rush. What if Whitney Houston's ghost was watching me pee?"

"Hang on, I'm googling it." Kara whipped out her phone.

"You guys don't understand, we are gonna have to move rooms if this is where it happened." Alicia made the sign of the cross, then the sign of the evil eye. She glared at the closed bathroom door as if it were breathing.

Gaynor looked up from the e-mail she was writing. "This hotel is packed more solid than your Spanx, Alicia. There are no rooms for us to move to. Now get over here and start answering these *gonorrea* e-mails."

"I was gonna do my hair; I got a keratin treatment. And Sylvester is coming by with my outfit for later."

A smile spread across Gaynor's face. "Yes, he is, and he has made you something truly great." She paused. "And if you want to wear it, you will get over here and start telling all these *coños* no comment on this whole Seamus and Bette story. Cut and paste. 'I'm sorry, we are unable to comment.' Next."

Alicia plopped herself down into a chair at the desk and began to methodically respond to the e-mails on Gaynor's computer. Gaynor walked to the minifridge and pulled out a glass pitcher of Negronis that she had brought from home.

"Nicolita, it looks like our little story has worked perfectly," she said proudly. "All the press care about right now is Bette. Nobody has bothered to ask where Seamus has been. What time will he be here?"

"He's in the limo now, but there's traffic. He should be here in like thirty minutes."

"I wonder if he'll remember me?" said Alicia absently.

"He was in rehab, not brain surgery," Gaynor laughed, cuffing the back of Alicia's head with the back of her hand. *"Por pendeja."*

"You can't hit me, you know," Alicia sniffed.

"I can slide my boot up your ass till the heel stops it, and you'll still turn up for work on Monday," Gaynor said, amusing herself. "And please stop telling my sons about the things I say. The last thing I need is sensitivity training from a thirteen-year-old."

"Seamus told me to say hi to you already," Nicola said, looking up from her laptop. "Sorry, I forgot to tell you. We've been so busy."

Alicia gave Gaynor the bird and turned her attention back to the laptop.

"I think this *is* the room she died in," Kara announced, sitting bolt upright on the bed. "According to celebritydeathscene.com, they renovated the room and installed a new bathtub, and then they changed the numbers around so nobody will know if they're in the room or not. Alicia, go up a floor and see if we are beneath 534. Judging from photos, this is the room. End of the hallway, no rooms next door."

"Alicia is too busy, you morbid thing," Gaynor said. "Isn't it time you started getting ready?"

"My face is done, and all I have to do is tease out the 'fro and we're good to go," Kara smiled.

"Do you want to put the preshow on the TV?" Nicola asked.

"God no." Gaynor shuddered. "I don't even want to see the awards. Why watch a bunch of white celebrities drunk and on coke if none of them are paying me?"

"Do I really have to go to the parties an hour before you guys?" Kara whined. "Can't I just be part of Seamus's entourage?"

Gaynor drained her drink. "Nicola, talk to your client."

Nicola didn't look away from her computer.

"Fine, whatever." Kara got up from the bed and went into the bathroom and locked the door behind her. Almost immediately, the sound of a phone camera clicking came through the door.

"She's taking selfies," Alicia said.

"In the bath," Nicola said.

"The shocking thing is that she waited," said Gaynor, pacing the room with a drink in her hand. "It must have been killing her to wait five minutes to Snap the fuck out of that bathtub. Alicia?"

"Yes, señora Huerta?"

"Run down to the gift store and get ten packs of Altoids and ten packs of mint gum. Use the corporate card."

"Can I get some Cheetos?"

"Did my son design your gown to match red-stained fingertips?"

"But I'm hungry."

"Yes, a new feeling for you, but trust me, you'll get addicted to it any minute now."

Alicia slowly rose to her feet and sulked out of the room.

Gaynor glanced nervously at the door behind her. "Nicolita, I have to ask you something. In confidence."

Nicola sat up and pushed her computer off her lap. "Shoot."

"Have you heard anything about people leaving our agency?"

Nicola shook her head. "No. Why?"

Gaynor pulled her boxy vape out of her purse and held it to her lips. She closed her eyes and emitted jets of white vapor from her nostrils.

"Not cool," Nicola exclaimed, waving the cloud away from herself.

"What?" Gaynor barked inside the cloud. "All the crack that's been smoked in this room and you complain about a little nicotine?"

"So what's going on?"

"I don't know, Nicolita. Maybe it's just a feeling. But two more old-timers are late with their retainer payment this month. Ava and Lucinda. They still owe for last month. And I called their manager yesterday and he hasn't returned my call."

"Maybe it's just cash flow," she offered.

"No, no, no, you'll learn. It's shorthand in the publicity world. When a client leaves you, they go quiet, they don't pay, and the last thing is the letter from the lawyer. And an updated NDA to be signed before you get your final check."

"But you've been with both of them for years. I thought you were all friends."

"My sons are my friends," Gaynor said with a trace of bitterness. "Everything else in this town is business."

"Thanks . . ."

"*Mi Nicolita*, do you think you're the first one to come along? The first one I helped? You will betray me." Gaynor raised her palm to stop any protest. "And it's fine. It's the business."

"Is that what you did to Crystal?"

Gaynor polished off her drink with a flourish.

"I hate it that you're so smart. Why can't you be like all the other young girls, fixated only upon yourself? You remember things. It's a curse, for both of us."

Nicola couldn't tell if Gaynor's gloomy outlook was a passing mood or a sign of something more serious. As Gaynor raided the mini-fridge, Nicola turned her attention to her laptop. The fake relationship was a strategic success, but the sheer volume of media response was overwhelming her. Bluey had taken Seamus to his Globes rehearsal yesterday afternoon, then Bette had initiated a second date at some bar in Hollywood after he was done, and nobody had seen Seamus since. Every press outlet on the planet wanted her comment on the relationship. She wondered if they'd slept together, and her stomach clenched in response.

"Gaynor, how capable do you think Alicia is? Can she take over my e-mails, too? I still have over five hundred to answer, and I need to start getting ready."

"Sure, if she wasn't doing mine," Gaynor said, not looking up from her phone. "*Mija,* make a list of the ten important people and delete everyone else. They'll figure it out. Confirm it to TMZ and let God sort out the rest."

"I can't," Nicola said. "My mom told me to be nice to everyone on your way up, so that they're nice to you on your way down."

"I'm sure that works great at the Holiday Inn, but this is publicity, the business of lies. It's better for your soul to lie less, so only lie to a few and let the ripples spread. You'll sleep better, and at the end of the day, you will have lied to less people. Hit that delete button, Nicolita. It's more addictive than cocaine."

"Am I on your shit list today, mama?"

Gaynor exhaled loudly. "My psychic told me that someone was going to betray me; I assumed it was you. Who else do I trust? Something feels uncomfortable against my skin, like a dress from Kohl's."

Nicola got up and went over to Gaynor. She reached out to touch her shoulder, and hesitated. Had they ever touched before? She wasn't sure. Her fingers tentatively touched the satin-and-jewel-encrusted shoulder pad, and she was surprised that Gaynor didn't pull away. She let her hand rest there.

"Gaynor, I owe you so much, and I'm loyal like a wolf. You can worry about anything you want, but worrying about me is a waste of your time."

Gaynor reached up and rested her hand on top of Nicola's. "Thank you, *mija,*" she said. "Now go pour that bullshit into your e-mails. The world will love you."

Nicola rolled her eyes and went back to the bed. She looked at the time. Seamus was late and ran the risk of getting stuck in a crush of photographers. She kicked herself for not insisting on picking him up. The sound of water rushing into the bathtub drowned out the constant click of Kara's phone taking photos. Nicola rolled her eyes as she imagined the photos that Kara was about to take.

The door to the outside hall swung open.

"Altoid delivery for Ms. Wallace."

She looked up to see Seamus in a midnight blue Armani tuxedo, his eyes sparkling below his close-cropped scalp. He'd trimmed his hipster beard. He looked amazing. He was smiling broadly and holding a stack of Altoids tins in his upturned palm. Behind him, Alicia was bouncing up and down with excitement.

"Look who I found wandering the lobby!" she squawked. "Gaynor, I think that we got photographed when Seamus gave me a hug."

"Great," said Nicola sarcastically. "Another relationship for the world to e-mail me about."

"Tell them it's all true, boss." Seamus walked over and sat on the bed by Nicola. "Who doesn't love Alicia?"

"Me?" clucked Gaynor as a smile engulfed Alicia's face.

"Hey, ladyboss, what's the plan?" He leaned over and kissed Nicola on the cheek.

"Well, I need to get changed at some point, then we can go down to the viewing party for a short appearance."

"Did Whitney really die in this room?"

"Sorry, I told him already."

"Signs point to yes," Nicola said. "But I need to change into my dress."

"It's not like he hasn't seen you naked before," Gaynor said. "You Americans are ridiculous sometimes with the prudishness."

"I'll cover my eyes, Nico. Promise."

"Fuck you all," Nicola said, standing and beginning to pull her T-shirt over her head. "And if you sneak a peek, O'Riordan, I'll be explaining a black eye to the tabloids tomorrow."

⁂ ⁂ ⁂

When Nic was dressed, Kara, Seamus, and Nicola headed downstairs to the viewing party at Circa 55. The Globes were about to start, literally above them in the ballroom. The jewels in the back of Nicola's loaner Diane von Furstenberg black-and-navy sequined gown kept catching on the fabric of her chair.

"I'm really worried that I'm going to wreck this dress," she said, breaking an awkward silence as they all pretended to watch the feed on the TVs around the room.

"You got photographed in it as we walked in," Kara said. "You'll be okay. You'll probably get to keep it."

"How long do we have to stay?" Seamus asked for the fifth time.

"We don't have to do anything. We've been seen. Our next stop is for you to present, which takes five minutes. We have to be backstage in about forty-five minutes. Press room after that, and then we can hit the parties," Nicola recapped.

Seamus inhaled deeply. "It's too late to back out, huh?"

"Boo-hoo, Seamus," Kara snarked, rubbing her fists in front of her eyes. "Come on, you two, this is a party, not a funeral."

Nicola and Seamus exchanged glances but remained silent.

"Do I have to sit with you guys?"

"I never said you did, K," Nicola replied. "Go explore."

"I wanna join Mason; he's been texting me nonstop. But I'm not even allowed to stand near him tonight."

Seamus shot Nicola a strange look.

"I'll explain later," she said.

Kara looked at all the other tables in Circa 55, each one occupied by a group of bored, sullen actors and their teams. She saw Grace Davis, this year's ingenue, and her team, mingling with Richard Ford Price and his entourage. She wondered if there'd be a showmance by the end of the night. She heard an announcer say the awards were beginning. Nobody in the bar looked up at the televisions. Most people had their heads down in deep discussion; the rest were on their phones.

"Go out and do a lap of the pool," Seamus said. "Go pretend-smoke. You might meet some fun people that way. That's what I did the first time I came to this."

Kara acted like she'd been told the secret of life. "Hey, thanks, Seamus." She hugged him around the shoulders. "Thanks for hooking a sister up." And she was gone.

"That was easy," Nicola laughed.

"Should have done it when we got here," Seamus smiled. "Is it just me, or do you feel like we're her parents, making her sit at the adult table when she wants to go outside and play?"

"That's how I feel about her every day," Nicola said. "Do you want to hear the Mason Dwyer story?"

Seamus shook his head. "Not really; it's not my business."

Nicola turned her shoulders to face him. "Hey, while we're alone, how are you doing?"

Seamus paused and took a sip of his mineral water.

"It's been a rough landing," he said eventually. She waited for him to continue, but he didn't. He kept his eyes on the table. Nicola watched him, certain that he was about to tell her that he had slept with Bette yesterday.

"I heard about you and Timothy," he said.

"Oh," Nicola spluttered. "Uh, we did go to dinner, yep. That did happen."

"He says you guys went on a date," Seamus said bluntly, still not looking up. "Why didn't you tell me, Nico?"

"You have enough to deal with."

"It's okay. You can date; I'm in no position to blame anyone for anything, but I thought I could count on you for honesty."

"Seamus, I'm sorry. I don't know how to navigate this."

Seamus raised his head, and his green eyes bored into hers. "With honesty. Like a friend."

"Ouch," she said. "You're right. I'm sorry. I just didn't know how fragile you'd be."

"That's a fair question. I figured that rehab was my time to be fragile, but this week has been one long kick in the nuts. Fragile is going to be my state for a while."

"If it's any consolation, it wasn't much of a date. At first I thought it was a pity date, after Weatherman ripped me a new one. But no, in his mind, that was a date."

"So are you going out with him again?"

"I'll be honest. I don't know. Have you ever had a date that left you totally neutral? Like zero opinion? That's how I felt. I haven't thought about it or agonized over dumb things I said or worried about when I'd hear from him again."

"So you didn't sleep with him?"

"No, Seamus, I didn't sleep with him."

"Why not?"

"Seamus!"

"Did he try?"

"Kind of, maybe. It was like a textbook date, and in that textbook, after you hit the prescribed bases at dinner, you have the option of sex that would also hit the necessary bases. Like playing sex Monopoly. Pass Go and collect two hundred dollars."

Seamus laughed, but Nicola was starting to get angry.

"You slept with Bette last night," she said, surprised to feel tears stinging her eyes. "So much for fake girlfriend. I forgot you are an actor. Everything's fake with you."

He reached over and touched her hand. "Nico, I didn't sleep with her, I promise," he said. "I gotta tell you, though, lass. Rehab's made me a lightweight. Two drinks and I'm out. I slept under Huerta Hernandez on Friday, and crashed at Bette's tiny Hollywood apartment last night, on the couch."

Nicola softened. Being jealous of a fake girlfriend was almost too complicated for her to deal with. "I thought she lived out east?"

"That's her parents' place. She has a studio on Poinsettia."

"I'm sorry, O'Riordan. Don't quite know where that came from."

"Yeah, you do," he said softly. "Yeah, you do. And it's okay." He squeezed her hand. "We'll get through this."

"Oh my God, there you guys are," squealed a voice from outside by the pool. They looked up and saw Bette, Crystal, and—Nicola's stomach dropped—Timothy walking toward them.

"Our night just went to shit," she whispered as they approached. They quickly pulled their hands apart.

Bette leapt into the chair beside Seamus and slid her hand into his. Timothy took the seat next to Nicola and planted a quick peck on her cheek. Crystal remained standing.

"Where's Gaynor?" she asked brusquely.

"She's not coming down until the after-party starts," Nicola explained.

"I need to talk to her," Crystal said. She pulled out her phone and began texting as she walked away.

"Good to see you, too, Crystal," Seamus called out after her. She flipped him off without turning around.

"So how's you guys' night been so far?" Bette asked way too enthusiastically.

"Boring," said Seamus.

"Busy," said Nicola.

"This party kind of sucks," Bette agreed.

"You sound like Kara," Nicola said.

"Yeah, she texted me it was loser lodge," Bette said. "Listen, I'm gonna get us all drinks." She got up and headed for the bar.

"Hey, Seamus," said Timothy. "Sorry, we didn't know she was so damn perky."

"She's all right," Seamus said. "She's just got her eyes on the prize."

Nicola wondered if Seamus realized that he was the prize.

"Either way, it's just temporary," Timothy said. "And once you start this trilogy, you'll be working a lot; you won't see her. It's just a lot of up-front face time. We'll get through it."

"Like I said, man, I'm fine. I don't care," Seamus said, his voice getting stronger. "But you need to quit pretending like it's not your fault. You guys forced me into this, so stop apologizing. It's fucked up and it's weird, but, hey, that's what I'm paying you twenty percent for."

Nicola considered stepping in but decided to sit back and let this one play out.

"Now, now, Seamus," Timothy said cautiously. "We're all on the same side. I talked to Weatherman, and it doesn't look like we'll need the smokescreen to continue for the whole time. The news moves so fast these days. You'll get time off for good behavior."

"I should have robbed a bank," Seamus said gloomily.

Bette returned with a tray of drinks. She placed one in front of each of them and sat down.

"Cheers, motherfuckers. Let's at least pretend to be having fun."

Nicola saw Seamus's shoulders droop. "Seamus, it's time to do a quick carpet and get you backstage."

"I thought you said forty-five minutes."

"I lied," she said, standing up.

He shook his head and picked up his drink, finishing it in one gulp.

CHAPTER 14

PEERING FROM THE LOBBY AT the deserted red carpet, Nicola had to admit that Gaynor was a genius. When she first told Nicola to wait until the awards started before taking Seamus down the infamous press gauntlet, Nicola had been dumbfounded.

"Doesn't everyone pack up and leave once the awards start?"

"Ding ding ding," Gaynor had said joyously. "But there'll be a few photographers still smoking and hanging around. You'll still get your shots without having to talk to a single . . . whatever they're called these days."

"Reporter? Blogger? Vlogger?"

"*Sí*. That."

A huddle of photographers still occupied the photo pit on the side of the carpet, but the rest of the press area was deserted, the majority of the press having decamped to the actual press room to watch the awards.

"You ready, O'Riordan?" she whispered, grabbing him just above the elbow and leading him through the glass doors.

"Yes, boss."

As they drew near the start of the red carpet, a live-wire panic spread through the photographers.

"Hey, Seamus, you doing the carpet?" one of them yelled.

"We have thirty seconds for some photos," Nicola called back. "We have to make it quick; he's presenting shortly."

As the clamor of voices shouting Seamus's name grew louder and more intense, they both put their heads down and began to walk quickly along the carpet. The clamor grew louder and louder until, gratefully, it turned into an even blast of white noise that Nicola could ignore.

Nicola let go of Seamus's arm just before he reached the photo pit, and he walked the last ten feet by himself, his face smiling as he slowly turned his head from side to side, giving good coverage to everyone. In the distance, she could see TV crews scrambling to get set up. She needed to get him out of here before they started rolling.

"He's wearing Armani," Nicola yelled into the noise before quickly pulling her phone out and staring at the blank screen while she counted to twenty.

"Thanks, everyone. We need to get inside," she yelled, stepping forward and grabbing onto Seamus's upper arm. They moved rapidly along the rest of the carpet, ignoring the pleas from the TV crews—pleas that turned into obscenities as the cameramen realized that Seamus wouldn't be stopping for them.

At the end of the carpet, Nicola approached a security guard and flashed Seamus's backstage laminate. As the guard radioed for instructions, she noticed that every single person around them was filming or photographing Seamus with their phone. He was standing patiently, a pleasantly dull expression on his face. She didn't know how he could stand it.

"Thank you for your patience," the guard said after a minute. "Please follow me. Because you're a little late, we have to go in through the ballroom."

Nicola saw Seamus's shoulders slump.

"What's wrong?"

"Have you been to the Globes? It's like an Illuminati party for successful white actors on coke. Everything I hate about this business will be in that room."

"Walk quickly, keep your head down."

"That is the thing." Seamus smiled at her. "I can't. I have to be on. Eyes sparkling, big smile."

"Seamus, that isn't the hardest thing you've had to do lately. Still walk quickly."

Nicola nodded to the guard and they set off in the direction of the ballroom doors. A pack of guards parted magically and let them pass, and another guard pulled the door open for them, immediately drowning them in the deafening noise of applause and laughter. The room was relatively dark, and a clip from a movie was playing on the screens that flanked the stage. The guard made sure they were following, then darted to the right, around the top edge of the auditorium. They had nearly made it to the backstage entrance when the clip ended and the house lights came up. Without raising her head, Nicola knew that every eye in the room had spotted them, and the final twenty steps to the safety of the backstage area turned to molasses.

"Keep moving, Ohio," Seamus said through a gritted-teeth smile, and finally they were backstage. A producer in a headset immediately descended upon them.

"Mr. O'Riordan, we're glad you could make it. Are you his publicist?"

Nicola nodded, and a piece of paper was shoved into her hands.

"We have had a last-minute rewrite of Mr. O'Riordan's script, and I need you to approve it."

Nicola glanced at the paper in horror. She had been firm with the Globes that Seamus would only present solo, and he wouldn't do any humor. The new script referenced the on-set accident and had Seamus joking about how he'd been off work so long because he'd damaged his "pickup arm."

"We aren't doing this," she said bluntly. "Please go back to the script that we approved on Friday."

"What's the problem?" Seamus asked, an edge of panic in his voice.

"They want you to do a skit," Nicola said. "Don't worry, we're not going to do it."

The producer leaned in close to Nicola's ear and put a hand over his headset microphone.

"We can't change anything now."

Nicola started to argue, but Seamus took the paper from her hand and looked it over.

"This is fine, I can do this," he said to the producer, who looked like he was about to implode.

"Thanks, Mr. O'Riordan," the producer said curtly. "Please come over here and we'll walk you through your marks. You are live at the top of the next segment when we come back from break. Approximately twelve minutes away."

The producer walked Seamus to the other side of a bank of screens showing various cameras inside the ballroom, and Nicola watched as the producer acted out what Seamus was supposed to do while Seamus pretended to pay attention. After several run-throughs, the producer darted off into the darkness, and Nicola rejoined her client.

"Did they mention this at rehearsal?" she said under her breath.

"I blew it off. This ain't the Oscars."

She glared at him. He was impossible.

"And are you really fine with that stupid script?"

"Oh, not at all. I'll go out there and wing it," Seamus said with a laugh. "This thing's been going for an hour; everybody is drunk and high. The Golden Globes is like doing karaoke with your peers. Nobody cares if you mess up."

"I care."

"And I love you for that," Seamus said, chucking her chin gently with his knuckles. "Don't ever stop."

They stood in silence, watching as an eight-year-old girl was named Miss Golden Globe. Nicola nudged Seamus during her curtsy.

"This is creepy."

The producer reappeared and walked Seamus to the little green tape squares on the floor at the side of the stage. The commercial break began, and the hubbub of conversation from the ballroom filled their ears. Nic looked out over the crowd. She'd never seen so many famous people crammed into such a small space. She watched them preen and fawn over each other, visiting other tables, patting each other on the back. It looked like any wedding, anywhere. A voice came over the PA, informing the audience that they were coming back from commercial and could everyone please take their seats, then a voice started counting down from ten. As the voice said "two," the producer nudged Seamus, and Nicola watched as her ex-boyfriend turned his star wattage to eleven, sauntering confidently onto the stage and up to the microphone to a thunderous round of applause and not a few catcalls.

"Anybody wanna arm wrestle?"

The room went crazy. Nicola looked at the monitors and saw a bunch of arms shoot up as actors volunteered.

"Nah, just kidding," Seamus said. "But thank you all for your get-well cards that your agents wrote and signed for you and posted all the way to Scotland. It meant a lot. I'm here tonight to present Best Supporting Actress but before we get to that, can I just point out that this is Hollywood, I'm foreign, and I get press. So where's my award? Who is the Scottish rep on the Hollywood Foreign Press? Lemme buy you a beer, buddy. I want one of these things."

The room erupted into laughter. Nicola felt her heart burst with pride. He was handling this like a pro. She looked at the producer—his face was pale. Seamus had gone off script. He was making a dramatic throat-cutting gesture at another producer. She wondered if Seamus was going to get canned.

"Anyways, enough about me," Seamus said into the mic as he pulled an envelope out of his jacket. "Let's put these poor lassies out of their suffering."

He theatrically tore the envelope in half, and the crowd gasped.

"Talk about arm strength." He mugged into the camera while his fingers struggled to pull the two halves of the envelope back together so that he could read the name inside.

"And the Golden Globe goes to Imogen Umberly for *Doubt Proof Double Down*."

As the crowd rose to its feet and Imogen began her long, histrionic walk to the podium, Seamus slowly stepped backward to stand next to Miss Golden Globe, who was delivering the actual award. When Imogen eventually reached the stage, she snatched the award from the model and, without even acknowledging Seamus, began her teary acceptance speech.

Seamus immediately began to slowly walk off stage. The producer waved his arms frantically, telling Seamus to wait there, but Seamus ignored him.

"Quick," he said to Nicola, "let's hit the press room before Imogen. We can do two questions and then get bumped when she gets there."

As they entered the press room, Nicola spotted Billy and waved as Seamus walked directly up to the microphone.

"Hey, everybody," he said affably. "We have to keep this quick, we have a very excited Imogen Umberly headed our way. I just wanted to say a quick hi and answer a couple of questions."

"Tell us about you and Bette!" yelled a haggard old woman in the front row.

"That's not a question," Seamus said, grinning at her. "Next."

A barrage of voices asking about Bette followed, and Nicola stepped up to the microphone.

"No personal questions, sorry," she said, and a chorus of boos filled the room.

"How is your arm healing?" asked another elderly woman in the front row in heavily accented English.

Seamus recognized her from previous Foreign Press events. She was the Swedish representative. He bounded off the podium and snatched her up in his arms, lifted her above his head, and then set her gently back on her seat before stepping back to the microphone.

"Seems like it's better, eh?" he said to the blushing woman. "I've been exercising by lifting good Scottish beers. That always does the trick."

A portly man in a mustard sports jacket stood and yelled, "Why won't you talk about Bette?"

Before Nicola could step in, a jumble of noise came down the hallway.

"And here comes the woman of the hour," Seamus said into the mic. "Ladies and gentlemen, please welcome Imogen Umberly."

Seamus turned to Nicola and nodded in Billy's direction. The two of them walked back alongside the press. Seamus grabbed Billy by the arm and hauled him out of his chair.

"Party. Now," he said.

✳ ✳ ✳

Ten minutes later, they were all ensconced at the same table that they'd left barely an hour earlier. This time, Gaynor, Alicia, and the twins, Patrick and Sylvester, were waiting for them.

"Nicola, will you be my publicist?" Sylvester said as they approached, blowing Nicola a kiss.

"You know it, Sylvester. Just tell me when you can afford me."

"Mom says you have to do it for free."

Gaynor pulled her phone out and pretended to check e-mail.

"I got paparazzied!" Alicia bellowed, brandishing her phone, a Getty Images–branded portrait of her on the screen. Nicola and Seamus each took a second to drink in her outfit. Patrick and Sylvester had designed it with Alicia in mind, and the transformation was incredible. The high-necked formal dress was black silk shot with silver thread, skintight without seeming it, amplifying her curves while somehow hiding her flaws. Deft pleating across the hips somehow forced attention up to Alicia's boobs, which were pushed up and out. She looked like a forties pinup.

"I'm not surprised," Seamus said. "You look amazing."

"Oooh, look at her." Alicia pointed at Nicola. "She gettin' jelly."

"Just when I was about to give you a compliment, too," Nicola said, taking a seat next to Gaynor.

"*Women's Wear Daily* is going to do a profile of my boys," her boss said proudly, pointing to a leather-bound portfolio on the table. "They couldn't believe the sketchbook."

Nicola looked at the two thirteen-year-olds destined to be featured in a reputable fashion blog. They were engaged in an ice-throwing war. At a Golden Globes party.

"That's great, but first you better hope that they don't hit Nicole Kidman with an ice cube."

"She's a mother; she'll understand," Gaynor said with a smile as she gazed at the boys.

"Have you seen Kara?"

Gaynor smiled admiringly. "*Mija*, that crazy *puta* is working this party hard. I told her, walk it like you're Angelina Jolie, and *madre mía*, she's been slipping into every A-list clique as if she belongs there. She's had photographers snapping her all night. And you know what else?"

"Surprise me."

"She's been avoiding Amber, or anyone who can link her to reality TV. She's acting like a movie star. You'd be proud."

"You're right, I like the sound of her as a movie star better than as a betraying paparazzo."

"Nicolita, you forgive even slower than I do."

"I keep her on a short leash," Nicola said bluntly. "She learned her lesson, but it's Hollywood. She'll screw up again."

As if they'd summoned her, Kara appeared in front of them, pushing her way through a cluster of black-suited execs. Gaynor was right. In a simple, sheer blue-gray Vera Wang gown with sprays of jewels at the hem and shoulders, her 'fro at full volume, she looked like a movie star.

"Nicola," she squealed. "You're here. You won't believe who I've been talking to."

"It's the Globes. I'll believe it."

"I've literally talked to everyone. I made Donald Glover call my sister! He said I should audition for him. He didn't say what for, but OMG. And best of all, you're definitely not going to believe this. I talked to Tom."

"Hanks?"

"Kendall, silly," Kara said, beaming. She lifted a glass from the bottle service tray and splashed some vodka into it. "Cheers to me, right?"

Nicola and Gaynor exchanged sudden, knowing glances.

"Kara," Nicola barked. "Off switch. Now. Real talk. Ladies' room."

Nicola leaned in close to Seamus and whispered "Be right back" in his ear. Before he could respond, she and Gaynor stood, and, grabbing Kara's wrist, Nicola lead them through the crowd to the ladies' room. She groaned aloud as they drew nearer to the bathrooms, where long lines extended out from both the men's and the women's.

"To the room," Gaynor said, pointing up the stairs as if she were orchestrating a getaway.

They hurried up the stairs and across the crowded lobby, where another large, noisy crowd was waiting for the elevators.

"Fucking cocaine," Gaynor hissed. "In my day, people were civilized. They'd just pass a bullet right at the table. These days, everyone's a narc. Look at this bullshit. Everyone trying to sneak upstairs for a toot."

"We're on the fourth floor," Nicola said, heading for the fire stairs. "We're walking."

"You guys, I need to get back to the party," Kara whined. "Do not make me break a sweat, a nail, or a heel."

"I said off switch, Jones," Nicola said, an edge of fury in her voice. Kara went quiet.

As the door opened into the stairwell, they disturbed a group of young actors doing coke off the backs of their hands, the air thick with pot smoke. They didn't even look around as Gaynor led the way up the stairs.

When they reached the door, Gaynor stood expectantly. Nicola gave her a confused look.

"*Tienes una llave?*" Gaynor said.

"In *inglés, por favor?*"

"A key. Do you have a key? Alicia has mine."

Kara reached inside her bra and pulled out a keycard, letting them into the room.

"You guys are so overreacting," she began as they filed in behind her. Gaynor held up a single, silencing finger as she walked to the bar area and poured them each a Negroni from her pitcher.

"No need to be uncivilized," she muttered as she handed a drink to each girl. "*Salud.*"

"Can you bitches please explain this cloak-and-dagger bullshit? I just said I talked to him."

"Was his publicist with him?" Gaynor asked.

"No, he was with his dude crew," Kara said. "He was happy to see me, and we chatted for a while. He wants us to meet for lunch tomorrow."

Once again, Nicola and Gaynor exchanged worried glances.

"Don't you think this is all a bit weird?" Nicola said. "You don't hear from him for months, but suddenly, as news of a sex tape leaks, he wants to meet up?"

"He didn't mention a tape," Kara said. "There's probably no tape."

"There's a tape," Gaynor said. "I've been in this business long enough to know that in celebrity land, where there's smoke, there's a scandal."

"Well, I'll go meet him tomorrow and find out."

"No," Gaynor said firmly. "You will not go. You will not be seen with him, photographed with him, or linked to him in any way."

Kara started to protest, but Nicola cut her off. "She's right. If there's a tape, and you guys get seen together, this whole thing will blow up. It'll push the tape to market, there'll be a bidding war, and it'll come out. I thought you said you didn't want it to come out."

"Of course I don't want it to come out," Kara said. "I've thought about it. It would crush my folks. And my sister is in college; it would be so embarrassing for her. And I don't want to be that girl. I don't want to be the black Amber."

"Then it's settled. No visit."

Kara slumped, realizing she wasn't going to win this one. "Fine," she sighed. "Whatever. Can I go now?"

Her phone dinged and her eyes widened as she read the text.

Kara! So lovely to see you tonight. Can you come to my room at the Peninsula tomorrow at noon? See you then, regards, Tom

She handed her phone to Nicola, who showed it to Gaynor, who made a face like she'd smelled something bad.

"He didn't write that text," she said. "Someone is setting you up."

"I dunno," Kara began. "He's kind of awkward and old-fashioned. He talks a bit like that."

"Maybe Kara should go," Nicola said suddenly. "What if this is the best way to end this mystery once and for all? I can go with her."

"You're not coming on a date with me," Kara said. "And I'm going."

"It's not a date," Gaynor said brusquely.

Nicola handed an empty glass to Gaynor, who poured herself another Negroni, then filled Nic's glass and handed it back to her.

"I really miss the eighties," Gaynor said wistfully. "All that coke and fucking and sneaking around seems so innocent now. Nobody filmed anything."

CHAPTER 15

KARA BANGED ON NICOLA'S DOOR.

"Hello? I know you're still here! Your car is downstairs. I'm going to let myself in in three, two . . ."

The door pulled open and a bleary-eyed Nicola stared ruefully out from under a messy mop of brown hair.

"Kara, I was up till five a.m. This better be good."

"Girl, we came home together. I know you were asleep at two."

"I started answering e-mails at two. I fell asleep with my laptop on my chest after five. I've slept for four hours."

"Cool story, Nic." Kara pushed past her and sat on the edge of her bed. "If things go well at the Peninsula, maybe you'll be up all night answering e-mails about me."

"Somebody already liked your look last night. They've added you to Amber's *Vanity Fair* photo shoot this Saturday."

Kara blew on her knuckles and then dusted them on her chest.

"And in the other corner, newcomer Kara Jones . . . ," she said. "Really? *Vanity Fair*?"

"I'm making a monster," Nicola laughed. "But it's weird. There are plenty of solo shots of you but none with Tom. Weren't you photographed with him?"

"Yeah, I'm pretty sure. I had a photographer tailing me most of the night. That's weird, huh?"

"It's not weird; it means that his team managed to shut down any photos of you together. I don't think you should meet him."

"Please. It takes two signatures to release a sex tape. I ain't gonna sign; he ain't gonna sign. Maybe he just wants a rematch?"

"He's had three months to ask for a booty call."

"Well, whatever, he wants to see me, so I just need to bounce a few fashion ideas off you."

"You're the stylist," Nicola yawned.

"And you're the friend-slash-publicist, so it's your job on at least two fronts."

"I talked to Gaynor. She wants to set up a meeting with Meredith, his publicist. Can we talk you out of this?"

"You were a lot more fun before you started dating Seamus." Kara fussed with her hair. "For real. You weren't there last night; Tom was so friendly, like totally asking about me and what I'd been up to."

"He was probably high."

"Oh, girl, he was high AF, but what if he's really into me?"

"Two days ago you were wondering if you were developing feelings for Mason."

"I talked to Bette last night. It's hard for minorities to get ahead. Dating Tom would be amazing for me, even if it's short term. Mason isn't going public with me anytime soon. I'm his little black secret."

"Seamus is so miserable with Bette. And Bette was on a good trajectory already. She's just impatient. Don't listen to her; she's not a real girlfriend."

"Then he shouldn't date her, or are you now speaking for yourself?"

"As your friend, I strongly suggest that you don't go to see Tom."

"And as my publicist?"

"If you get photographed together, my rate goes up. Substantially."

✳ ✳ ✳

The hallways of the Peninsula were deathly quiet as Kara made her way from the elevator, following the signs on the walls that led her to the door of the California Suite. She took out her phone and texted Nic, who was still trying to talk her out of it.

Going in. Wish me luck.

She glanced left and right one last time before she knocked.

She heard footsteps approaching, and the door opened. Tom, his sandy-blond hair a mess, leaned out and looked up and down the hallway, then ushered her inside. He pulled the door closed behind her and locked it.

"Criminy crickets." Kara whistled as she surveyed the expansive suite. "This is bigger than my apartment, and honey, my apartment is big."

"Uh, hey, Kara." Tom shifted from one foot to the other. He reached out for a hug, then reconsidered. Kara stepped in and hugged him. She felt his arms encircle her waist and his hands patted her back.

"What time did you finish up last night?" she asked, stepping into the ornate living area. She slipped onto the large white couch and pulled one of the overstuffed pink cushions into her lap.

"I didn't," Tom sighed, slumping into the opposite end of the couch. "I haven't been to sleep yet. I mean, I tried, but you know . . ."

He looked so awful that Kara was pleased to hear he hadn't slept. It explained the wreck of a man she saw. This barefoot jorts-and-polo-wearing frat boy was not the leading man she'd hooked up with in Ojai. And he certainly lacked the wattage of Mason Dwyer. She made up her mind that she wasn't going to sleep with Tom. No matter how hard he tried.

"Did you want to order some food? I need to order a couple drinks; that might be the only thing that helps."

"Drinks sound great," Kara said, noticing that the soles of his feet were cracked and dirty.

Tom slowly pushed himself off the couch and wandered over to the house phone. He called downstairs and ordered four Bloody Marys and four shots of Jägermeister.

"What is this?" Kara was visibly outraged. "Spring break?"

"What?" Tom rubbed his head as he returned to his perch on the opposite end of the couch. "Hair of the dog. All those Jäger bombs last night, never a good idea."

"Especially not when you're thirty-whatever."

"I'm twenty-eight," Tom said, as if that explained everything.

"Well, it's good to see you again," Kara said brightly, pushing the cushion off her lap and onto the floor. "I didn't get a chance to give you my number in Ojai."

"That's fine; I can get someone's number. I just didn't try yet."

"Oh . . ."

"I mean, we only wrapped principal photography last week. Seamus really fucked us up. They did a complete rewrite, and I don't even know if it will work. I've been pretty depressed; this was supposed to be my big break, and now, like, it still could be, but who knows?" Tom sat and pouted. "It went from an awesome A-list buddy movie to being me and some washed-up TV actor."

"Like I said, it's good to see you again," Kara smiled, wondering why everyone in this town was such a goddamn crybaby.

"Yeah, you look great," Tom said, looking around the room.

"Tom, I don't understand what's going on . . . ?"

"Don't you, Kara?" Tom's voice rose, and he winced and grabbed at his temples. He repeated it, more quietly this time.

"I'm not sure, Tom. Am I here for lunch or a rematch?"

"Why? So you could film it again?"

Kara shook her head. "No. I learned my lesson."

"You needed to learn that it's not okay to film someone fucking you without their permission?"

"Tom, I promise you that footage wasn't for anyone. It was for us. I was documenting my entire trip to Ojai."

"For what us? For who? Your paparazzi boyfriend?"

"Huh? I don't have a boyfriend, paparazzi or otherwise."

"So it's okay that you tricked me into fucking you because you needed some footage for a documentary?"

Kara sighed. She didn't know whether to get up and leave or try to keep the conversation going. Nicola had been right.

"I didn't come all the way here so you could humiliate me," she said evenly.

"How are *you* humiliated? You're not the one who comes in like a minute flat, you're not the one with a zit on your ass, you're not the one who literally rolls over and falls asleep with the rubber on almost as soon as he's finished."

Kara felt sick. Tom had seen the tape.

"Wait, Tom, have you seen it? Is it real?"

"The bitch who sold the tape asks if it's real. I don't believe this."

"I heard the rumors. Yes, I'm on the trail of someone who claims to have seen it."

"Oh, please shut your lying mouth." Tom slapped the couch angrily. "Don't act like you're so innocent. You think this is going to make you famous!"

He reached for two remotes on the coffee table and turned on the TV. He pushed the other remote, and Tom's bedroom in Ojai filled the screen. A rumpled bed occupied the top corner of the television screen. Kara's voice filled the room.

"Nice dirty talk," Tom said angrily.

"Tom, turn it off," Kara said, reaching for the remote. He snatched it away from her.

The doorbell rang.

"Our drinks are here," Tom said, pushing off the couch with a burst of angry energy. "Enjoy the show. I'll be right back."

He shoved both remotes into the rear pocket of his jorts.

Kara turned her attention back to the television. In the dim lighting of two bedside lamps, she watched herself strip seductively, dancing around and beckoning an unseen Tom into the frame. *I don't look bad at all.* After a few seconds, a very naked Tom walked into the scene, and Kara fell to her knees and started blowing him theatrically. Her Afro bobbed back and forth like black cotton candy.

Tom returned with a tray of drinks, handing her a shot of Jäger. She took it and threw it back without waiting. He followed suit.

"You can turn it off," she pleaded.

"Why? It's about to get to the good stuff," he whined, drinking a second shot of Jäger. "You're about to see my dick, then watch me jackrabbit you for about ten seconds and then fall asleep drunk and start snoring. You push me off you like you're disgusted with me."

"It was more than ten seconds," Kara corrected him, still watching the action onscreen. "At least it's kind of dark. You can't see too much."

"Jones, you can see enough to wreck my entire career."

She reached over and took a Bloody Mary.

"I never meant to hurt you," she said, stirring her drink with a celery spear. "What can we do to save this?"

"I need you to sign a contract; I have it here. It will mean that you've agreed that this is private material, that it's not for sale, never will be, never can be."

"Isn't it too late for that? The cat is already out of the bag."

"Kara, please sign the contract." Tom moved across the couch toward her. He rested his palm on her knee. "You don't know who you're dealing with. Just sign it. Sign it and leave and we can hopefully forget this ever happened."

He got up and went over to a sideboard. Opening the top drawer, he pulled out a two-inch-thick contract.

"Holy shit, that's what I have to sign?"

"That's one of them," he said, pulling out two more. He returned to the couch and set the contracts on the coffee table. He pulled a pen from beside the lamp at the end of the couch.

"It's three copies of the same contract. It just says that you agree that our private property has been stolen and you do not authorize its sale. It's invasion of privacy."

"And what if I don't sign it?"

"Why wouldn't you sign it? Come on, man, this is awful." Tom pointed at the screen, where Kara was now lying on her back, playing with herself while he struggled to get a condom onto his penis. Kara saw his point.

"Can you turn it off, please?" she asked softly.

He fished the remote out of his back pocket and switched the TV off. Silence filled the room.

"Thank you."

"Do you think I want to watch that shit?" he said angrily. "But you know how many fucking people would?"

"I filmed it for me. I film everything. Everyone does these days."

"My team have cameras on us both now, in case you try anything, so at least you understand."

"Cameras? Where?"

"Listen, Kara, you made a dumb mistake. Don't make another one. Please just sign it."

"I can't," Kara said simply. "This thing's the size of a *Vanity Fair*.

173

Did I tell you I'm shooting for them on Saturday? Let me read it and I'll sign it and get it back to you."

"Is this the first contract you've ever seen, you dumb bitch?" Tom started stalking around the couch. "Do they even pay you to be on that piece-of-shit TV show?"

"No need to be a dick about it, Kendall," Kara said, standing up. "I'll take them with me and I will bring them back, signed, later today."

Kara jumped in shock as the double doors to the suite's bedroom opened with a click. She turned and gasped as she immediately recognized the gaunt, drawn-faced brunette in her trademark black suit and blue shirt. It was Meredith Cox, Tom's publicist.

"Thank you, Tom," Meredith said, her harsh voice bouncing off the walls. "I will take it from here. Take your drinks into the bedroom. Get some sleep. Everything will be okay."

※ ※ ※

Tom pushed the bedroom doors closed and set the tray of drinks on the bed. He heard the sound of a slap, and Kara shrieked. He quickly turned on the TV and held the volume-up button to try to drown out the noises from the other room. As the random movie went to ad break, he heard both women yelling over the top of each other until the cacophony ended in a long, agonized scream from Kara.

Tom winced at sounds of muffled thumps and groans. He drained the Bloody Mary, followed by the last shot of Jäger. Another painful scream over an ad for some high blood pressure medicine. Tom climbed onto the bed and pulled a pillow over his head in an attempt to drown out the horrible sounds. Meredith had told him that this was part of her job, and he was paying her to do that job. He just didn't want to hear it.

※ ※ ※

Nicola flung the door to their apartment open, looking frantically from side to side to locate her roommate. Splashing sounds were coming from Nic's bathroom, so Nic rushed in.

"Jones, what the . . . ," she began, her voice trailing off as she saw the blood splattered across the white porcelain. "Oh my God, Kara . . ."

Kara took a deep, shaky breath and tried to talk. She got half a word out before a wrenching sob shook her chest and she collapsed onto the counter.

Nicola, panicked by the blood and the sound of Kara's crying, pulled her phone out of her jeans pocket.

"Did he hit you? Kara, tell me now, because I'm gonna call nine-one-one on that asshole, right now."

Without raising her head, Kara's hand reached for Nic, pulling her close.

"No," she managed to say in between heaving sobs. "It wasn't him."

Confused, Nicola set her phone on the countertop, moving to stand behind her friend. Gently, she rested her hands on Kara's shoulders and drew her into an upright position. As Kara turned to face her, Nicola gasped. One of Kara's eyes was swollen shut, blood poured freely from a wide split in her bottom lip, and her shirt was torn and scuffed with dirt.

"How did you get home?"

"Lyft," Kara sobbed. "I said I'd fallen down some stairs."

"Do you need an ambulance?"

Kara groaned loudly and gripped her stomach. "No, I need to get in your bath and wash this off. I just can't be alone."

Nicola drew Kara into a hug, causing her to flinch.

"My ribs, Nic. She kicked the shit out of my ribs."

"She? Kara, who did this to you?"

"You can't tell a soul," Kara sobbed. "It was Meredith."

Nicola's mind was racing. "We have to call the police; you've been assaulted."

"Do you think I stand a chance against her? Please. I need to suck this up and move on. This shit happens all the time, and I ain't got a leg to stand on. Please stay with me, let me take a bath, and then can you sit with me while I sleep?"

Nicola took Kara's hand and led her across the living room and into her bathroom. She started the water in the tub and motioned for Kara to sit on the edge so that she could take her platforms off.

When the water was deep enough, she added some bubble bath and Kara slowly stripped and got in. In between sobs, she told Nic about the scene at the Peninsula.

"We have to call Gaynor," Nicola said. "And Bluey. We have to fight fire with fire."

"No, Nic. That's the thing. She said she's still going to destroy me, and then she's gonna go for Gaynor."

Nicola groaned as a light went on in her head.

"Shit. She's the reason our clients are defecting. She's known about this tape for a while."

"She probably thinks we all set it up together. How can we stop her?"

Nicola sat in silence, searching for a solution.

"Gaynor is already stressed to the breaking point. Did you get a sense of timing from Meredith?"

"No. It wasn't something that came up, what with the punching and the kicking."

"We need some time. Let's see if Billy can distract her while we figure out the next steps."

CHAPTER 16

EVERY SEAT AT THE *SPYGLASS* conference room table was taken when Billy arrived at the Wednesday morning staff meeting. His cluelessly self-absorbed executive editor, Sandy Sandstein, was shuffling the daily pile of new photos from the pap agencies, her vapid brown eyes flicking from one photo to the next. She was wearing an embroidered peasant blouse with the top buttons undone, revealing her freckly chest and a neon blue bra. Billy shuddered. She looked up from her task and surveyed the room.

"Why are interns sitting at this table?"

Two young girls apologized profusely, got up, and stood with the other interns against the back wall. Billy took one of their vacated seats and set his notepad, pen, and iced Venti skinny caramel macchiato on the glass tabletop.

"Is that everyone?" Sandy asked Christine, the office manager, whom Billy called his favorite and his savior. She was the only person at *Spyglass* he liked.

"Yes, Ms. Sandstein, everyone is here."

Sandy laid the photos flat on the table and pointed to a stack of magazines, the week's new issues.

"Did everyone have a chance to see the competition?" she said frostily. "We missed out on a lot of stories this week. A lot." She turned and glared at Billy.

"Hi, Sandy, how are you?" he said cheerily.

"I'd be a lot better if we had some quotes on the new Seamus/Bette relationship, like *People* does. Or if we had the exclusive photo booth strip, like *People* does."

"I told you, we don't have the money to do the deals that *Us* and *People* can do."

"And I've told you that we don't need the money when we have the leverage. I will see you in my office after this meeting to discuss our next steps."

"Yes, fearless leader," Billy said, still smiling broadly because he knew it drove Sandy crazy. She dramatically turned away from him and began interrogating Debra, the fashion editor, a harried bottle blonde in her late forties.

"How did we get the Globes best dressed list so wrong?"

"It's wrong?" Debra deadpanned. "It's a list. It's opinions. How can it be wrong?"

"It's so different from everybody else's," Sandy whined. Sandy hated it when *Spyglass* wasn't magically the same as *People* magazine. "Everyone in the fashion community is laughing at us."

"I'm in the fashion community, Sandra," Deb said, as if she were talking to a pet. "And I can assure you, our list is the one that the fashionistas are agreeing with. We're the only list that isn't a bunch of advertiser and publicist favors. We are the gold standard at the designer level."

Billy knew that Debra was lying to Sandy, and she was doing it brilliantly.

"Oh, okay," Sandy said tentatively. "If you say so."

Debra winked at Billy.

Sandy rapped one of her large acrylic rings on the tabletop and then picked up a pen. "Okay, it's ideas time. I want five good story ideas from all senior editors. Let's start with you, Billy."

"First off, we have Kara shooting for *Vanity Fair* this weekend—"

"Pass. She needs something interesting. Is she even working with us anymore? I feel like she's gotten dull."

Billy paused. "They asked Courtney Hauser to audition for *Big Brother*."

"Is that show still on? Next."

"Stella Nazarian might be pregnant."

"Get the photo department on bump watch. Don't mention it again until you can prove it."

"And I have one more. Mason Dwyer divorce shocker, his side of the story."

"You're full of shit; you don't have that."

"Thanks for your confidence, Sandy. I *do* have it. I have more scandal than you'd be willing to print. I'm working on my file and you'll have it by tomorrow. I think it could be our cover for next week."

"Oh, so you're picking the cover stories now? Amazing. I'll expect that file on my desk before you leave *tonight*."

"I have plans tonight, Sandy."

"And now you don't."

✳ ✳ ✳

After the meeting, Billy lingered in the staff lunchroom, talking to Debra until Sandy had texted him three times asking him why he wasn't in her office. He let himself through the security doors and very slowly walked toward her office, aware that she was watching through the glass walls.

"Where were you?" she whined as he pulled the door shut behind him.

"Nature called," he said.

"I told you that you should go lacto-ovo-vegan. Or paleo."

"Those are opposites. It's so hard to pick."

"Billy, why didn't we have anything on Seamus? You are his friend, aren't you?"

"No, Sandy. He's my friend's *client*. It's the same reason we didn't have any stories from your friends' clients. Every week I have to tell you that we can't have everything."

"And every week you tell me that because we missed out on a story that you should have gotten."

He paused, and for a second he wondered if she'd called him in to fire him. He didn't want to get his hopes up.

"Billy, we need to talk. Kara isn't working out for us. She's just not doing anything interesting. I didn't say anything in the meeting, but you did say she'd have a big story this week."

Billy sucked his lip. He never should have hinted at the sex tape. Luckily, he'd been vague enough. He nodded at Sandy to continue.

"What? I thought we had a sex-tape shocker cover?"

"Well, we don't. There's no tape."

"So she lied to us."

"I never said that. I just said there's no tape."

Double negatives often confused Sandy, and Billy was pleased to see her sit back and try to ponder what he was saying.

"Sandy, look at today's issue. Thanks to Kara we got killer insider reporting at the Lexus party last week—you got photos of nearly every celeb there, you got the tip that SaraBeth is going to go do burlesque in Vegas, you got confirmation that Amber and Paul Stroud are hooking up again even though he has a new girlfriend, and we're the first magazine to print that Perry is making another season of his show with his ex-wife *and* the name of Ethan Carpenter's new beard . . . uh . . . girlfriend."

"I wanted the sex tape." Sandy pouted. "Just tell me what happened."

"Are we firing Kara or not?"

"Can we pay her less?"

"Would you take a pay cut for doing your job well?"

"I'm not talking about me, and some of this comes from upstairs."

"I don't understand how she's not working out."

"Remember when we asked you to find a certain kind of celebrity?"

Billy furrowed his brow. He hoped Sandy wasn't going to say anything racist.

"Yes, a celebrity who'd work with us."

"No, silly, a white one. I mean, come on, Billy, we've tried for three months now. She can't even lock down a good boyfriend."

Billy wished he could tell her about Mason, then checked himself for falling into her racist logic.

"You know you can get into trouble for what you're saying?"

"Not really. She's a freelancer, she has no contract, and I can let her go at any time. California is an at-will state."

"Can we give her a warning? See if it makes her get better stories?"

"Maybe," she wheedled. "What's in it for meeee?"

"Who do you need to hold your book this time?"

"I wrote a new one," Sandy said perkily. "It's about a magazine editor who steals the heart of a presidential candidate. Her name is Xandi White. It's called *The White House*. I'm self-publishing in a month. I need some celebrity endorsements."

"How about Bette Wu? I can get her."

"You're so dense. I can't have a yellow person saying they love a book called *The White House*."

He sighed. "I'll get you Zina."

"By tomorrow."

"And Kara keeps her job?"

"For now."

He left her office, cursing himself for not recording her on his phone and sending it to the HR department.

✳ ✳ ✳

Billy lied to Sandy that he had to go meet a source for the Mason Dwyer file and left early. As his car inched through Hollywood, Billy called Bluey. He got voice mail. A light drizzle began, turning his windshield to a shattered crystal of red lights and passing shards of white. The rain soured his mood—he knew it meant an extra half an hour in traffic. He just needed to get to Bluey's, shower, crawl into bed, and wait for Bluey to hold him.

As his car moved slowly along the wet street, he realized he hadn't talked to Nicola all day. He dialed her, and she answered before it rang.

"I was just about to call you," his best friend said.

"Where you at?"

"Where else?" she said. "The boys are here. Alicia is melting down. I don't know where Gaynor is. Like ten people are here doing makeup tests on Kara for the *Vanity Fair* shoot, and get this: Gaynor was too scared to tell Amber about Kara being added to the shoot. So she made me do it."

Billy burst out laughing into his phone.

"I'm glad you think it's funny. Billy, you should have heard the shit that came out of Amber's mouth."

"I'm good with imagining it, thanks," he said, still smiling.

"Do you think Sandy is going to run the anti-Felicity angle from Mason?"

"She's into it. Why do you want to piss off Meredith Cox again?"

"I said I'd tell you as soon as I can. Please, just make sure you print whatever he gives you. Kara said it's going to be juicy."

"Sandy's not exactly reliable, but I'll do my best."

"When can I see you?"

"When can you get Seamus a place of his own?"

"Are you blackmailing me? His people are negotiating with the studio. As soon as the check clears, I guess."

"Does a studio pay for your apartment?"

"Good point," she said.

"I might call your mom after I talk to you," Billy said. "Have you talked to her?"

"Not for a couple days," Nicola said. "I can't deal with the questions. She's totally Team Seamus."

"Tell her you're seeing Timothy?"

"*Seeing* might be a bit strong. *Deflecting* is probably a better word."

"Oh, he's finished, then. If you're deflecting, even a Bullet Bill wouldn't stand a chance of getting through."

"Pretty much. Listen, I have to go. I still have about two hundred e-mails to answer before I can leave, and I have a hot date with my pajamas, some pinot noir, and a movie."

"Which movie?"

"I'm not telling you."

"If you watch *My Life as a Dog* without me, there'll be trouble."

"I can smell something burning, gotta go."

She hung up.

He looked around and saw to his dismay that in the whole time he'd been talking to Nicola he'd only traveled to Ivar. Four blocks. He needed to get his ass off Sunset. He turned onto Ivar into dead-stopped traffic, immediately regretting his decision not to wait for the 101. He was in for it now.

His phone rang, startling him. A Dayton number he didn't recognize. He answered.

"Hello, William, is that you?" His heart sank. It was his bio mom; they hadn't talked in a decade. She sounded like an old lady. He took a deep breath.

"Yes, Mom. It is."

"I was wondering if you're coming back to Ohio anytime soon."

"I don't have any plans to."

"That's too bad, William. Father Alan said we should mend our fences while Poppa still has the time. He's sick, William."

"How sick, Mom?"

"It's stomach cancer, William. It's hard to tell. We have the whole church praying for a miracle."

"Well, that and a shitload of chemo might do the trick."

"Still a smart aleck, I see."

"I'm still a lot of things, Mom."

"Well, I just thought you'd want to know that Poppa is sick."

"Thanks for letting me know."

"Will you send him a card, William?"

"Yes, Mom," he lied, knowing he never would. "I'm driving, and I don't want to get a ticket for talking on my phone. Take care and tell Dad hi."

He didn't wait for her to respond before he ended the call.

＊ ＊ ＊

An hour and twelve miles later, he found a parking spot in front of Bluey's. He trudged up the driveway past the main house and smiled when he saw a light on inside. Bluey's car wasn't there, but he'd left a light on for Billy. A weak smile crossed his face and he slid his key into the lock, opened the door, and walked up the short flight of stairs to the apartment.

Turning the corner, his heart fell. Seamus was asleep on the couch, fully dressed and snoring loudly. Billy kicked off his shoes and tiptoed past him into Bluey's bedroom, pulling the door closed behind him. Tojo raised his sleepy head and gave Billy a small welcome meow. He sat on the bed and ran a hand through the cat's dense fur.

He texted Bluey.

How far out are you babe?

Cutting across to the 134. Waze says 10 minutes. Can't wait to see you.

Billy sighed with relief.

I thought you said Seamus was busy tonight.

He is. Wait. Is he there?

Sleeping on the couch.

Sorry. See you in a minute. Don't be angry. We will still have a date night.

Billy lay back on the bed and closed his eyes and fell immediately asleep. He woke with a start what felt like a second later with Bluey leaning over him, kissing him on the lips.

"Oh, hey, baby."

"Hey, mate," Bluey said softly. "Do you wanna keep on sleeping for a little while?"

"No, I'll be up all night."

Bluey lay alongside him and rubbed his rough hand over Billy's shoulder.

"You mad, mate?"

"Not at you," Billy said, rubbing his eyes. "I just thought we'd have the place to ourselves."

Bluey nodded, then pulled Billy's head onto his chest.

"I've been so busy with shit, I forgot that Seamus's birthday is tomorrow. He's usually pretty needy around his birthday. I should have seen it coming. This is my fault."

"No, it's really not. He's an adult. He can sort out a cake and some candles."

"You have a lot to learn. Listen, let me go out and get rid of him."

"I'll come with you. Strength in numbers and all that."

They got up and went into the living room. Seamus stirred on the couch and his eyes fluttered open.

"Hey, guys," he said affably, pushing himself into an upright position.

"Hi," Bluey began. "I thought you were out with Bette tonight?"

"Yeah, me too," Seamus said groggily. "We had to go to this thing this afternoon and do the whole grip-and-grin and get some photos. It was weird. We had a few drinks, and as soon as the photographers cleared out, she took off."

"I thought you guys were getting along," Billy said.

"Me too." Seamus seemed genuinely confused. "Guess it's just a business deal after all."

"Of course it is," Bluey said, going into the kitchen and pulling three beers out of the fridge. "And don't you forget it."

"So what's the plan for tonight?"

"Well, Billy and I had planned on going to dinner."

"You don't mind if I crash, yeah? I'm buying!"

Bluey and Billy exchanged resigned glances.

"With what, O'Riordan?" Bluey clinked his bottle against Billy's but left Seamus hanging. "Did your team sort out your lack of cash?"

"They're working on it." Seamus rustled in his jeans pocket and pulled out a thick roll of hundreds. "They gave me this to tide me over till I can get an ATM card."

"How the fuck did you sleep with that in your pocket?"

"I'm just happy to see you," Seamus cracked. Bluey high-fived him.

Billy rolled his eyes. He hated how bro-some they were when they were together.

"So where are we going? The sky is the limit."

"Somewhere local," Billy said. "Traffic is terrifying. Your choice."

Seamus scratched his head. "I dunno, you guys. I normally let Bluey take control."

"Me too," said Billy lasciviously. Bluey cuffed him across the back of the head.

"Seamus, I haven't called around for this; our options are super limited. I didn't think we'd be seeing you till tomorrow."

"Tomorrow? Why would you be seeing me tomorrow?"

"Your birthday, duh. Your annual happiest-day-of-the-year crap."

"Oh, I'm busy. Nicola is taking me out."

"She is?" Billy said.

"You bet. She just doesn't know it yet."

CHAPTER 17

"I'M NOT REALLY DRESSED FOR anything fancy," Nicola protested twenty-four hours later as their chauffeured black-windowed SUV limo crept south on the 5.

"You look perfectly fine to me, lass," Seamus grinned in the near-darkness. Nicola looked out the window. The 5 looked identical from Valencia to San Diego. She had no idea where they were.

"Listen, O'Riordan, I know it's your birthday, but you can't tell me that absolutely everybody except me was busy. Where's Bette?"

"She only does dinners in public. Which is understandable, since we're a human window display at Neiman Marcus. If they ever open a celebrity zoo, she and I can sit in a cage right in front."

"Still not so sold on the idea, huh?"

"Depends on the day," he said, still smiling. "When I'm making a movie, and there's a love scene, I do it. It's obviously strange to have someone's tongue in your mouth as part of your job, but in the grand scheme of things, it's easier than most crossword puzzles. This thing with Bette is like that."

"You're a one-man *Inside the Actor's Studio*. Now, how about you tell me something to make me feel less like I'm being railroaded into a date."

"This ain't a date, I can promise you that. However, Ohio, I can also promise that this will be fun. I love my little traditions. This is one of them. I thought you found them charming?"

"It was charming when we were dating. Now it feels like a client thing, and while we're celebrating your birth, my e-mail inbox will explode and I'll be up until four in the morning answering them. Again."

Seamus didn't say anything, and Nicola felt him staring at her in the darkness. She turned to look at him but didn't say anything.

"I'm sorry, Nico. Good news, though—I had Tobin sort out the payments to Huerta Hernandez, so Gaynor will be getting a very big check tomorrow."

"Well, that will definitely make her happy. Won't really affect me, though."

"How can I make you smile? It's my birthday, and I want you to have fun."

"When are you going to tell me where we are going? Please tell me we're not going to San Diego. I have one day left to iron out the details for the *Vanity Fair* shoot with Kara and Amber. And it's been an absolute dumpster fire of a week."

She hadn't told anyone about Meredith's attack on Kara, but it played on her conscience every time she said Kara's name. They would get revenge, but so far, her anger was making it hard to serve it cold.

"Please take this the right way, lass, but *Vanity Fair*'s standards must be slipping," Seamus said with a laugh.

"Yeah, I have a funny feeling that this story will end up being burned off as a single spread in six months. If it runs at all. No." She paused. "I take that back; I think it's actually advertorial and they're not telling Amber. They'll get paid a fortune by the designers, and the girls will model it for free."

"That was a Nicola answer. I'd missed those."

"What? That's what's going on."

"You could have also just laughed or flipped me off. I love it when you ramble."

"And I don't love it when you're evasive. Why do you have a coat? I'm wearing an outfit that was barely acceptable for work. I'm wearing ballet flats and a hoodie my mother gave me for my birthday. With kittens on it, Seamus. If I get photographed next to you, people will think you're out with a recent escapee from a cult."

Nicola couldn't shake the feeling that she was being railroaded. Weatherman had called and informed her that his team were all at something in Cupertino and that it was Seamus's birthday and they'd appreciate it if Nicola could take him out. Gaynor had been indifferent. "Either take the loser out or let him cry himself to sleep on someone else's couch. I really don't care; I have enough to worry about," she'd said before turning and locking herself in her office, adding that she'd care more after he paid his bills.

Kara had been understandably needy since Monday. They'd told Amber that she'd fallen at the Globes because of her platforms and couldn't film all week. Nicola hired the show's transgender hair and makeup artist, Bobo, to come in and work their magic. It had been hard to watch her friend, normally so vivacious and funny, turned into a beaten dog, flinching at loud noises and bursting into tears whenever she recalled the events at the Peninsula, which she'd done every night.

Nicola had mainly agreed to Seamus's birthday outing since Billy deserved a night without a hairy Scot on his couch. Billy had been so excited to hear that they were getting a night to themselves, he hadn't even given her a pep talk about what not to do.

"I didn't get you a present," Nicola said glumly. "I'm just about the worst ex-girlfriend in the world."

"Not really, Ohio. I have several of those, and you're way better."

"Oh, yeah, sorry."

"Your presence is presents enough."

The limo lurched as it sped up and took a ramp to the left. Nicola was confused, not sure how a freeway could have an exit on the left, but she saw the lights of the cars swoop below them and suddenly they were deposited on a street with motels on both sides. She pressed her hand against the glass to make vision easier. They pulled up at a security gate, its bright fluorescent glare barely penetrating the backseat. The limo moved again, and Seamus began to pull his coat on.

"Are we going to be outside or inside?"

"Yes," he laughed. "First one, then the other, and then the first one. Rinse and repeat."

"If you'd like an ass kicking for your birthday, you're going the right way about it."

The door opened and a cold gust of night air blew in.

"After you, my sweet," Seamus said with a dramatic wave of his hand. Nicola crawled across the floor of the limo on her knees and then clumsily extended one leg down to the ground. A mystery hand appeared from the darkness.

"Good evening, Miss Wallace," said an altogether too perky male voice. "May I help you out of your limousine?"

Nicola gripped his hand and attempted a graceful dismount, ending up looking like a flamingo getting out of a Fiat. When she was able to straighten up, she was staring at a young blond man with braces on his broad smile. His name badge said ANDREW. Then she noticed the twin orbs at the top of his name tag.

"Welcome to the happiest place on earth," he trilled, turning to help Seamus out of the limo.

Seamus, I'm going to kill you.

They were at Disneyland.

Seamus scrambled out of the limo without Andrew's help. He stepped in close to Nicola and whispered in her ear, "You said you'd always wanted to come here."

"Yeah, like a normal person," she said, rolling her eyes. "You know, like going on rides and stuff without a zillion people taking my photo."

"Watch," he whispered. "And learn. You're at Seamus O'Riordan's annual Disneyland birthday party."

Andrew stood motionless during their exchange, but as soon as they turned to face him again, he came back to life.

"Mr. O'Riordan, Miss Wallace, my name is Andrew, and I'll be your personal guide tonight at the Magic Kingdom of Disneyland."

"Call me Seamus, Andrew." Seamus extended his hand and they shook. Nicola followed suit.

"Yes, please, Andrew, call me Nicola."

"I must say," Andrew said, his southern accent extending his vowels, "Nico-la isn't a name you hear all that often. It's a very pretty name."

"Thanks, but it's pronounced *Nickel-uh*. I hope you still like it as much." She smiled.

"Well, yes, I sure do," he said enthusiastically. "So a little birdy tells me that tonight, we have a birthday, and we have a first-timer. Was the little birdy telling the truth?"

Seamus nodded, and Andrew reached inside a pocket of his plaid vest (*which did not go with his terracotta pants at all,* thought Nicola) and produced two round buttons. He pinned the one that said IT'S MY BIRTHDAY on Seamus, and the FIRST-TIME VISITOR pin on Nicola.

"So, are we ready to have some fun tonight?" he said, clapping his hands. "Let me see. I have you down for dinner at Club 33 in the private dining room, and we will do a little shopping, but the rest of the night is up to you. Wish upon a star, and I'll do my best to make your wishes come true."

"Is the park open tonight?" Nicola asked hesitantly.

"Well, yes, Miss Wall . . . I mean Nicola. But that won't be a problem. And Seamus, sir, I understand that not only is it your birthday, but you're going to be a cast member, too! I love the Parallax books. That's just wunnerful news. Tonight's going to be a celebration you'll both remember for the rest of your lives."

"Well, that is definitely some exciting news, Andrew. Isn't it, Nicola?"

"Yes, Seamus," she said through gritted teeth. "Especially if you're a cast member of something."

"The new movie is Disney."

"It is?" Nicola scrunched up her nose.

"At least I'm not the only one on my team who doesn't read their e-mails."

Andrew motioned them toward a small golf cart with Disney logos. They got in and it hummed as it sped them through the dark parking lot. Nicola wondered what the large warehouses they passed were, so she asked Andrew.

"Well, I'd hate to spoil the magic, Nicola," he said with the same irritating smile.

"They're the rides," Seamus said. "It's genius. You never get to see that you're just on a ride inside a warehouse."

"Unless you're me and this is your first time and you're showing me that this is basically the Dayton county fair in Disney drag."

"And Miss Wallace is right," Andrew said, still smiling. "My goal as your guide is to let you wunnerful folks experience Disneyland just like anyone else. Unfortunately, we have a big crowd at the main entrance right now, so we are going to have to use the entrance via Pirates of the Caribbean, but the good news is, if you are hungry, that entrance just so happens to drop us right by the elevator to Club 33. If that works for you two, I think that's what we should do."

Nicola shrugged, since she didn't know what any of that meant. Seamus pointed at his birthday button. "Let's get this party started."

Andrew parked the golf cart next to a beige wall that looked like the side of a Toys R Us. He led them to a security door, swiped a key card, and let them inside a bland, utilitarian corridor. They followed him along the hall, then up a flight of stairs and along another hallway.

"We're inside Pirates of the Caribbean now," Seamus said.

"You're just the naughtiest," Andrew scolded Seamus. "When we get down this next flight of stairs, I'm going to go ahead and make sure that the lobby of Club 33 is empty."

At the bottom of the stairs, Andrew slipped through a door, leaving them alone.

Seamus turned to make a joke and froze at Nicola's angry expression. "What?"

"You think that Disneyland is a small private birthday destination? Seamus! Are you joking right now?"

He reached up and rubbed her chin with his thumb.

"You'll see. This is one of the safest places for us to go out in all of Los Angeles. This is literally my favorite night of the year."

"Are we even still in Los Angeles?"

"Listen, Ohio," he said in a deep whisper. "Relax. Nobody will know we are here."

"Is this another one of your secret places?"

Seamus nodded. "Well, kinda. But anyone can walk through the main entrance. Nobody can do it like this. You'll like it."

The door opened, and Andrew's grinning head popped back in.

"Good news, guys. The coast is clear. Come on in."

He pushed the door wide open and Nicola stepped from a dull utility corridor back in time to an overwrought 1850s hotel lobby. A middle-aged woman sat at a desk on a dais.

"Welcome, Mr. O'Riordan, a very happy birthday to you. And Miss Wallace, I hope your first visit to the park is as magical as you've dreamed. Your table is ready. Andrew, please take them up."

Andrew sprang up three steps to an antique elevator and theatrically pulled the metal grille door open.

"Madam, monsieur," he said, ushering them inside. Seamus and Nicola squeezed in beside Andrew. He slid the grille closed and cranked the handle to the up position. The elevator ground to life with a quiet clanking sound, and they began to go up. For three seconds. Then it stopped. Nicola thought it had broken down.

"And here we are." Andrew seemed inordinately excited that they had reached their destination. He pulled the door open and led them out into what looked like a larger version of Nicola's super-gay theater teacher's family home. Mismatched antiques and paintings lined the walls and filled glass cabinets. There was no evidence that they were in Disneyland at all. It was almost too surreal.

Andrew led them through a heavy wooden door into a small dining room with forest green wallpaper and more bland antique paintings.

"I'm going to get you two settled and then I'm going to leave you to have a wunnerful dinner," he said, pulling out a chair for Nicola. "Your server will let me know when you're done, and I'll be back to give you your VIP tour of the park."

And then he was gone.

"That was intense," Nicola said as Seamus sat down opposite her.

"You get used to it. All cast members talk the same way. That's how they talk in studio meetings, too. It's like a weird cult."

"That's the second mention of cults tonight. I think we're cursed."

"I think we're blessed. I really just wanted a place where we could be alone, and we can catch up."

"Because none of those things sound date-like."

"Of course it's not a date; I have Bette and you have Timothy."

"Oh, that's right. Lucky us."

"Can I ask? Are you actually dating Timothy?"

"Depends how literal you want to be," Nicola said, noticing the intense gaze Seamus was giving her. "We went on a date, we've been texting, and he keeps mentioning another one. In high school, the answer would be yes. It's LA dating. You just talk about it and never do it."

"He's not good enough for you," Seamus said, scratching at his arm. "He just doesn't have the right stuff."

"He'd die if he heard you say that."

"Yes, yes, he would."

A young black woman in the ugliest teal-and-brown patterned vest Nicola had ever seen came into their dining room.

"Good evening, folks," she said amiably. "My name is Jessie Leann and I'll be your server tonight." She paused and opened menus, handing one to each of them. "We've opened a very special bottle of Kosta Browne pinot noir for you tonight, to welcome you to the Disney family. We'll have that up real quick. I'll be back in a minute to take your order. Is there anything else I can help you with?"

"Yes, Jessie Leann," Nicola said with a sly smile. "Your vest. How on earth do you deal?"

Seamus laughed out loud. Jessie Leann gave a knowing smile. "It's okay. And I'll never be tempted to steal it."

She stepped aside as their drinks waiter came in with the bottle of pinot noir. He poured for Seamus, who sniffed and nodded, then completed the pour and left.

"Cheers, O'Riordan, and the happiest of birthdays to you."

He clinked his glass against hers and took a sip. "Nico, I really want to thank you for coming."

"Stop. Stop it right there. Can it. Put a lid on it. Can I say something before the night goes any further?"

Seamus set his glass down. He nodded.

"Tonight, can you forget about post-rehab apology guy? Can you just be you? Can you give me shit and make me laugh? No mention of Ojai!"

"I can try," he said. "You know, I'd really like that. I wonder if I can pull it off?"

"Kara has a word for it; she coined it for Amber."

"What is it?"

"*Dramnesia*," she laughed. "It's when you just forget something dramatic happened. Which, for Amber, is pretty much every day."

Seamus raised his glass. "To dramnesia," he smiled. "And if I'm taking off the gloves, I'm gonna just say it, lassie: if you keep on seeing Timothy, I'm gonna have to break both his fooking legs."

"I didn't say replace the sorrow with jealousy. Also, stay in your box, O'Riordan. No telling me what to do, please."

"Listen, you think dating an actor was a mistake? You won't know what hit you dating an agent. You may have managed to find the one profession that's more emotionally bereft. Don't do it."

"That's telling me what to do. Maybe I preferred you as a super-sorry twelve-stepper."

"And I prefer you exactly like this, you sassy bitch."

"You've been hanging around Billy too much," she laughed.

"Yaaaas kwaaaaan." Seamus laughed back. "Get it, girl."

"You should be on *Broad City*."

"God, I love that show. I'd do it for free."

"Now, that I'd love to see." Nicola felt herself relaxing. "Did you get lots of birthday texts?"

"Yeah, everyone was texting and e-mailing last night, you know with the time difference and all. It's not such a big deal to be thirty-six, is it now?"

"It's better than the alternative." She sipped her wine. "This wine is phenomenal. Is this place actually foodie? We're still in a theme park."

"This is just a private club in Orange County. It's the privacy that brings me back. Before the food comes, I have something to ask you."

"Shoot."

"I have to go down to the location in Mexico next week, and they're talking about having me do some on-location interviews, for the Blu-ray and maybe also *Entertainment Tonight*. You should come with me."

"You can't do *ET*," she said, all business. "Unless they guarantee in writing to hold it until the movie is coming out."

"Fuck it, Nico, can't we just give the first interview to *ET* and be done with it all?"

"You sell that to Weatherman, and I'm totally okay with it."

"So *ET* can wait," he laughed.

⁂ ⁂ ⁂

The first bottle of pinot soothed Nicola, and the second one eased the memories of the past week. Over dessert, Seamus did a series of impressions of the other people in the Seattle rehab, which had Nicola in stitches, laughing so hard that her abdominals ached and she begged him to stop. As soon as their dessert plates were cleared, Andrew had reappeared and ushered them back to the golf cart. Nicola found herself completely adrift, traveling in an electric cart around the perimeter of a glorified county fair, wishing that she could just walk through the main gates and see it all like a regular person.

Those feelings evaporated at their first stop, a roller coaster in pitch darkness. Andrew gave them matching black hoodies to wear, and Seamus put his hood up over his head without being told to. As they walked along a deserted corridor to the loading area, Andrew told them that the lines were always over an hour wait. Stepping out into a clattering, clanging space that looked like a sci-fi movie set in the eighties, Nic saw thousands of people in line, waiting, and she felt a guilty twinge that she didn't have to wait like them.

After conferring with the kids working the ride, Andrew hustled them into a waiting car. They were spirited into a cloud of dry-ice fog and lasers.

"So you have no idea what this is going to be like?" Seamus yelled over the pulsing music that was coming from their seat backs.

"Nope," Nicola laughed. "It's a roller coaster, I guess. Andrew said it's wunnerful."

"Aye, lassie, that it is."

The car began lurching up an incline, spinning planets and stars flying past them. Seamus struggled to raise his hands in the air and urged her to copy him. "C'mon, Ohio, don't be a chicken. Holding on is for chickens."

Nicola smirked as she remembered how reluctant Seamus had been to jump off a yacht not even a year ago, and she raised her hands. She flinched slightly when Seamus grabbed her hand and forced it higher in the darkness, and resisted pulling it away. The car crested the incline, plunging them into pitch-black, then sending them ricocheting blindly through a field of stars. Seamus hooted and hollered almost in sync with the ride, and the sheer joy in his laughter made Nicola smile broadly. She hadn't heard him sound this happy in a long time.

After they exited the ride, Andrew explained that the easiest option for them was to visit all the rides on the perimeter of the park.

"Does that include the castle?" Nicola asked.

"Why, nosirree, ma'am," Andrew said with a misleading smile. "The castle is in the dead center of the park. If we want to go in there, I need to call for a security detail. You just let me know."

Seamus took one look at Nicola's disappointed face and replied, "Looks like we're gonna need a security detail."

Twenty minutes later, after pushing through the crowded, darkened park with their hoodies tight around their faces, Nicola and Seamus were standing on top of the castle, as cast members bustled around them setting up for a fireworks show.

"This is a fairy-tale castle?" Nicola whispered. "It's smaller than Amber's house."

Seamus laughed and spread his arms wide, gazing out over Main Street.

"But this is our kingdom, lass. And they're gonna set off fireworks for my birthday. All hail King Seamus of Tinker Bell Land."

"Wait—are you turning thirty-six or six?"

Seamus's reply was drowned out by the fireworks exploding in the sky above them, countless falling embers twinkling and sparking around them. Nicola fought an urge to lean back against Seamus.

"This is the most romantic non-date I've ever been tricked into," she said loudly over the noise.

"This ain't a date," Seamus said, pushing his hood back from his face. "It's me fookin' birthday, and it's grand as hell, I'd say. Look at this bullshit!"

Seamus gently gripped Nicola's shoulders and slowly rotated her in a circle so she could take in what he was seeing. All around them, not terribly far below, Disneyland spread out in a blur of trees, flashing lights, and strange shapes. The fireworks threw irregular, random shadows and shards of light across the park. A flock of panicked ducks flew past, quacking loudly at the annoyance.

"Nobody gets to come up here, Nico. Nobody. Right, Andrew?"

Andrew, who'd been loitering quietly nearby, sprang back into his normal, overly eager state.

"Why, yes, Mr. O'Riordan, it's certainly not normal for us to come up here."

"You're not going to lose your job, are you?" Nicola said, her voice full of worry.

"No, Miss Wallace. I'm just going to have to say that Mr. O'Riordan insisted, and who am I to refuse?"

Nicola pulled a business card out of her purse and handed it to Andrew.

"If you get in trouble, have your boss call me. I'll tell them that you were bullied into it by a selfish, entitled movie star."

"Between you and me, Miss Wallace"—Andrew leaned in conspiratorially—"there isn't any other type of movie star."

They both burst out laughing.

"What? What's so funny? It's my birthday. You can't have secret jokes on someone's birthday!"

"Is that another one of your weird Scottish traditions?"

"No, but we do have a tradition where it's okay to push an annoying person off a castle parapet on your birthday." Seamus jokingly nudged Nicola toward the edge of the castle, then pulled her back.

"Damn," she laughed. "If I'd have known that, I would have invited Alicia, Gaynor, and Amber."

"I have one last special birthday gift, you guys," Andrew

interrupted. "Since we're out in the park, we can swing by any of the gift shops, and you two can have anything you want."

"Shut up," said Nicola, still laughing.

This was definitely better than going to Disneyland the regular way.

✳ ✳ ✳

The nighttime winter air bit into Nicola's face from the slightly open window as their limo sped homeward on the 5. Across the bench seat, Seamus was asleep, his head lolling back every time the car sped up or slowed down for traffic. Occasionally, it fell forward, startling him enough to make him jerk backward, but not enough to wake him.

He must be exhausted, she thought as she watched the parade of passing lights send patterns across his peaceful face.

She pulled out her phone. It was 11:47. The screen was a jumble of texts, Facebook messages, and various app notifications. Gaynor had been trying to convince her to get a second phone just to use for work, and she finally admitted to herself that now was the time, even though the thought of carrying two phones made her uneasy. She unlocked the phone and scrolled through all the texts, most of them from numbers that weren't in her address book, all of them asking for a comment on Seamus and Bette's relationship. Was Alicia giving out her cell number to everybody who called?

The ones from actual names weren't much different, mostly asking about interviews or photo shoots. There was one from Timothy. She checked that Seamus was asleep before she slid it open.

Hey beautiful! How'd you like to end the week on a high note? Dinner, Friday?

She looked at Seamus again and felt a pain in her heart. What was she doing? This lovable-yet-broken man-child could barely take care of himself, and the remainder of their evening at Disneyland hadn't done much to convince her otherwise.

They had walked along another hidden hallway, emerging into a massive gift store filled with toys, clothes, and souvenir crap. Seamus had hung back in the corridor, telling Nicola to go out and get them some swag. Feeling entitled and guilty, she walked out with their security guard, handing him things that she knew she could send to her mom and brother. Bluey's decor did not lend itself to Disney, and he would kick her ass if Seamus came home with too much of it. When they returned holding just a few plush toys and some sweaters, Andrew looked concerned.

"Miss Wallace, please, take as much as you want."

"Yep, this is as much as we want, thank you," she had said firmly, noticing Seamus smiling as she said it. They rode a few more rides, then Andrew said he thought it was time to head over to California Adventure.

Seamus pulled Nicola aside and asked her if he could rain check. He suddenly wasn't feeling well. Nicola had Andrew call their limo instead. Seamus apologized profusely as they drove back to the freeway, and then fell asleep almost immediately.

She watched his chest rise with each deep breath and smiled as he began to snore quietly. She hadn't seen him look this relaxed since their night together in Ojai. Overcome by a wave of exhaustion, Nicola considered resting her head on his chest and trying to sleep. *Snap out of it*, she chided herself. *Keep it professional.*

Liar. Client. Junkie.

She pursed her lips and swiped her phone open, then tapped out a text to Timothy.

As long as it involves mezcal, laughing and not-work, I'm in. Pick me up tomorrow at 8 at la oficina.

CHAPTER 18

GAYNOR'S EL DORADO WAS ALREADY parked when Nicola arrived at eight a.m. She found herself longing for the days when that meant that Gaynor hadn't gone home yet. Lately it meant Gaynor had been in for at least an hour already and she'd be crazed on caffeine. Quiet mornings to herself were a thing of the past. She looked and saw Alicia's beater Sentra parked in a guest spot and rolled her eyes. It wasn't going to be a good day.

Kara rustling around the kitchen at five thirty had been her first alarm clock. Nicola had heard pills rattling around in their bottles as Kara self-medicated with diuretics and handfuls of dietary supplements all designed to help her lose the maximum amount of weight before the *Vanity Fair* shoot tomorrow. She had been gone when Nicola finally got up at seven, explaining via text that she'd gone to a double session of cardio barre and would be at the office by ten to run through the clothing. With Amber.

By the time the limo had dropped sleepy, unwell Seamus in Highland Park last night and then taken her to her apartment it had been after twelve thirty. Nicola had masturbated quickly and furiously in an attempt to drive the tension out of her shoulders and let herself get to sleep quicker, but then she'd just lain in bed for another hour, wondering about everything.

Seamus. Timothy. Work. Life.

She'd toyed with the idea of texting Billy, but remembered that late-night Billy was now Billy-with-a-boyfriend and was most likely asleep in Bluey's muscular arms. Even in this age of social media and cell phones, there was nothing lonelier than one thirty a.m. on the West Coast.

She'd barely slept four hours before Kara woke her, and as she drank her morning espresso out on the chilly balcony, she considered canceling on Timothy. She bargained with herself that she would decide at noon.

She got out of her car and walked across to the elevator, and once again her mind flashed back to the sight of Seamus sleeping peacefully in the limo, and her heart gave another one of those annoying pang things. She stabbed at the elevator button so hard her nail bent back, making her wince.

"See what you get for being stupid?" she said in the empty elevator.

The elevator remained silent.

The office door opened halfway and stopped, blocked again. Nicola tried to squeeze in between the opening and the guest couch that was blocking it. She pushed through into a jumble of rolling racks packed with clothing, shipping boxes, boxes of shoes and boots. There was no clear path to the hallway to her office. It looked like someone had erected a fashionable barricade against zombies. She wondered if she could use it to barricade herself inside her office.

A crowd of voices emanated from the hallway and she began stepping between and over boxes to get to her office and see what was going on.

Holding on to the corner of the wall for support, she swung her legs over the last shipping box and stepped into the hallway by the conference room door, gasping loudly at the sight of Alicia in head-to-toe Spanx with Sylvester draping a heavy sash of black raw silk across her shoulders. Neither of them acknowledged Nicola.

"What's going on in here, you guys?" she said as innocently as she could.

"Good morning, Miss Nicola," Sylvester said brightly. "I'm doing some concepts for my upcoming collection."

"I'm just the pincushion," Alicia said, raising her arms in mock despair. She'd lost probably thirty pounds in three months and toned up with cardio barre. With her new, softer makeup, the receptionist had transformed into a brassy seductress.

"Does this mean I'm going to have to go get my own coffee?"

Alicia's job performance had not improved alongside her appearance. She nodded. Nicola unlocked her office and set her purse and laptop on her desk and prepared to walk over to Starbucks when she heard Gaynor call out.

"Nicolita, *mija*, come in here."

"I'm just going to go get us coffees, Gaynor. I'll be five minutes."

"There's a lot of forgetting who is *el jefe* in this office. How about you get your white ass into my office now."

Nicola stomped into Gaynor's office, where two coffees waited on the desk. Gaynor, wearing a teal Lycra bodysuit with a black-and-white shag fur vest, motioned her to take a seat.

"You already sent Alicia to Starbucks?"

"I went and got them. I didn't want to interrupt Sylvester."

"Before we start," Nicola said, taking a long sip of her iced Americano, "we need to talk about that vest. Please tell me it's fake."

"Darling, the only thing I fake is interest in my clients. This is genuine monkey fur." Gaynor pulled a packet of Misty cigarettes out of her drawer and lit one. "This is vintage, if it helps you to know that the monkeys died a long time ago."

"You're wearing a monkey fur vest? Gross."

"People eat monkeys. In Colombia when I was a girl, a monkey fur coat was the same as wearing a McDonalds wrapper. So save your PETA bullshit. Here"—she tugged on the long black-and-white fur—"feel it; it's surprisingly soft."

Nicola didn't want to touch it. Fur freaked her out.

"You're smoking actual cigarettes."

"Vaping is bad for you. I saw it on the news."

Nicola put her coffee down and drew a breath to answer.

"Eating is disgusting," Gaynor interrupted before Nicola could speak. "I bet you gained five pounds when Seamus went to Seattle."

"Four," Nicola lied. It had been eight. "Why are we stressed?"

"I was right. Now Gloria Pasternak and Hayley Turner are terminating us, and they're not going to pay us for December. And Paul Stroud is coming in this afternoon, and I think it's for bad news."

Gaynor sat back and blew a smoke ring at the ceiling. Nicola jumped as Gaynor's dog Fuchi popped its head out of her vest.

"I knew your boobs looked kind of big in that hideous vest," she said.

"I don't want her to go chew on any of the shoot clothing."

"Which is why you should have left her at home."

"What time is Kara coming?"

"She'll be here in about an hour."

"Amber is coming at the same time. Do you want to deal with them together or separate?"

"I don't care," Nicola said absently, trying not to breathe the smoke that Gaynor was sending her way. She fanned the smoke away and looked up to see Gaynor sitting back in her chair, her crimson lips pursed.

"What?"

"Are you going to tell me how your dinner date was with Seamus?"

"It was professional."

"So you didn't have an emotional reconnection?"

"I jerked off when I got home."

"*Ay, mija.* So that's a yes, then." Gaynor leaned forward, pushing Fuchi back inside her vest. "Nicolita, you need to step back. You're going to be great in this town. You don't need to spend yourself on an actor. Especially not this quickly."

"Great in this town? As what? All I do is answer e-mails and sit there during someone else's interview. Is this what being a publicist is?"

"Less existential, but yes," Gaynor said. "*Mija,* you really need to get laid."

"I have a date with Timothy tonight," she said, hating how defensive she sounded.

Gaynor scowled. Her phone buzzed as a text came in. She picked it up, and a look of consternation came over her face.

"Amber won't be coming in today; something has come up apparently."

"Right, because she has *Vanity Fair* shoots every week."

Gaynor kept reading as additional texts came in.

"She's sending someone to pick up her clothes later today. She is now telling me what Kara is and is not allowed to wear in the shoot.

Hmmmmm. She can wear purple . . . blue . . . yellow . . . nothing too sexy . . . *Dios mío*, we're gonna have to send her out there dressed as a burro piñata with this color scheme. Miss Bank is not going to be upstaged."

"Yeah, I knew it was going to be a delicate balance-slash-miracle. Maybe it's better that she's not coming in."

"A brain-dead *puta* like her should be bringing us champagne for getting her into *Vanity Fair*. She will be getting a taste of my boot in her bruised asshole tomorrow if she keeps this shit up. Whatever happened to single-word texting? This *perra* is texting me fashion rules when she should be texting me compliments. Screw her." Gaynor dramatically set her phone facedown on the table.

"Gaynor," Nicola began tentatively. "Are we in trouble?"

"*Sí*, it's not great; we are losing our core clients, the ones who pay us five thousand dollars a month to do nothing. But it's okay. That time has passed; there are no stars anymore. It is the old way: get famous, sign up with a publicist. Nobody ever wanted to fire their publicist, because firing your publicist is an acknowledgment that your career is finished. These days, it's easy to stay in the public eye with Instagram and Twitter. Nobody needs to pay sixty thousand dollars a year to someone in the hope that they'll get one story in *Closer*."

"That sounds grim. Seamus told me last night that a very big check is headed your way."

"Yes, I talked to Tobin earlier. That will help. But I want to talk to you about a change of direction here at Huerta Hernandez. We are going to do something I've always wanted to do. We are going to make our own stars. These days it's easy. Anybody with small talent, no shame, and a big ego can be a YouTube celebrity lifestyle blogger."

"So you want to be a publicity agency for the non-famous?"

"You sound like my financial advisor," Gaynor spat. "You're the oldest twenty-nine-year-old I've ever met. Ask my boys, ask anyone under twenty-five, and they'll tell you all about these bloggers and vloggers. They're stars—no, *mija*, they're more than stars; they're brands. Once they get a million hits daily on their blogs, the money starts pouring in."

"Does an online celebrity need a publicist?"

"Not exactly, but they need a marketer, and let's face it. A good publicist is exactly that: a marketer. So we transition from publicity into talent development, coordination, grooming, and realization."

"And it's profitable?"

"That's where the money is: back-end advertising, product placement. Lifestyle! Do you think Kara would like to be a blogger?"

"I think she'd rather be a celebrity. Have you told her about this plan?"

"I have not told her anything, I don't even know if she can read."

"That's racist."

"What are you talking about? Never presume that a celebrity can read."

"Kara can read," Nicola assured her. "She's really smart."

"Don't get carried away, Nicolita. Anyone who's smart should not be trying to be famous."

"Good point, but she's smart. Self-obsessed but smart."

"Okay, well, I had Patrick build a blog template for her. We tell her today and start posting Monday. I've lined up cosmetics and clothing for the first two weeks, freebies, but once the hits go up, the money will pour in."

"Patrick your son?" Nicola said, stuck on the first part of the sentence.

"Yes, of course, Patrick my son. He just built a website for my church; it's so clever, he has countdown clocks to the holy days and he built a 'find Jesus' thing into the site. You have to click all over and when you find Jesus you win eternal forgiveness. It's so cute. On Easter, he appears on the cross above the church roof. It's genius."

"Then he must be supremely qualified to generate a beauty blog for Kara," Nicola laughed, standing and grabbing her coffee. "I need to go and start narrowing down Kara's outfits for tomorrow. Are we listening to anything Amber said?"

Gaynor dropped her cigarette into the dregs of her coffee. She shook her head and waved Nicola out of her office.

"*Mija*," Gaynor called out. "If we launch three online brands, we can fire Amber. But until then, I need you to keep Seamus very happy."

Nicola popped her head back into the smoky room. "Speaking of your cash cow, he wants me to go to Mexico with him next week for some early press on the movie, stuff to come out closer to release."

"Yes, I know. He already called and asked if you could join him."

"We're too busy, right? You said no?"

"Mamacita, nobody says no to their cash cow. You'll have a great time."

✳ ✳ ✳

Nicola had just finished pulling Kara's wardrobe against Gaynor's wishes, when Kara, in workout clothes and massive Gucci sunglasses, pushed into the reception area.

"Oh shit," Kara said loudly. "You guys finally fired Alicia?"

"Hi, Kara," Alicia called from the conference room. "Today, I'm a model. You'll have to pick up your own shit."

"You're so impossible," Kara called out with false sweetness while gesturing in horror at the mess that littered the floor. "I'm glad you're not unemployed."

Kara looked at the various piles of clothes littering the floor. Her eyes lit up when they landed on the rolling rack with the clothes that were being sent to Amber.

"Come to Jonesy," she cooed, running her fingers across the thousands of dollars' worth of designer wear.

"That's Amber's wardrobe for the shoot," Nic explained.

"Hmmm. Where's my stuff?"

Nicola pointed to a second rolling rack with a handful of outfits hanging on it and a neighboring small stack of swimsuits.

"You're joking, right?"

"Sorry, no. Amber has spoken. You can only wear these colors, these clothes."

"Fuck her," Kara fumed. "When is she coming in here to pick this crap up?"

"She's not. She's sending Bobo."

"What a coward."

"She's only letting you wear orange, purple, and yellow. Everything in that pile."

"Nicola," Kara wailed. "I'm doing *Vanity Fair*, not a Hallmark Easter card shoot."

"Talk to your boss. I'm just following directions."

Kara shrugged and started angrily tossing clothing into a crumpled reject pile.

"Easy, tiger," Nicola said gently. "You need ten looks."

"The only look this shit would get me is pity. She did this on purpose."

"Of course she did." Gaynor waltzed down the hall, another cigarette waving. "And you're smarter than her, and you're a damn good stylist, so make it work. I've called in extra clothes in the approved colors. Don't freak out. You will look better than her. You always do."

Kara straightened, surprised to get a compliment from Gaynor, who kept coming toward them, bending suddenly and snatching clothes from the reject pile and tossing them at Kara.

"This can work. This is good. This pairs well."

"Gaynor, was that a compliment?" Kara asked as clothing was showered into her arms.

"Celebrities don't come to meetings in gym wear." Gaynor grimaced, waving her cigarette at Kara. "This is the last time you turn up at my office looking like a neon fetus."

"I wish I had some red paint to throw on you," Kara said with a laugh. "You're also wearing Lycra."

"And fur, *mija*. Learn to accessorize. So you look like the successful beauty blogger I need you to be."

"Wait, what?" she stammered.

"You're branching out. Hyphenating. We're making you a brand. Are you . . . down, as they say?"

Kara looked from Gaynor to Nicola and back again.

"You want me to do a blog? You haven't even asked me to write a sample."

"Nicola will write your copy."

Gaynor spun and walked away. "In my office, now, *mujeres*."

Nicola sighed. She was never going to get anything done. She followed Gaynor, with Kara at her heels.

Gaynor reached into her desk drawer and pulled out a folder. She opened it on the desktop and turned the papers inside it around so that Kara and Nicola could see them.

"This, *mis amigas*, is the template for your new lifestyle blog. We bought the domain. It's called *Jones In Style*. Dot com, net, biz, whatever you like. We got them all. We have clothing, makeup, and lifestyle companies ready to pay you to feature their caca. They pay us, we write about it *after* you've worn it on the Amber show. Do not tell Amber what you're doing. She'll shut you down so fast. She's definitely not going to help you become competition." Gaynor smiled. "I have contracts. My son Patrick is your webmaster. He will be paid directly from commissions that the site generates."

"You're telling me I'm going to have a twelve-year-old webmaster?"

"He is thirteen, and yes, children know the Internet the way you know how to blow rappers. He is better than some pot-smoking millennial and half the price. Once we get to a million hits a day, we'll be making so much money, it won't matter. I get twelve percent, Nicolita gets twelve percent, Patrick gets twelve percent. You get twenty-five percent."

Kara was shaking her head. "Shouldn't I get a hundred percent of my own revenue?"

"No, you're getting paid a lot to do nothing. The remaining cash pays for your expenses. It will pay for your new car lease, your business-class travel, and your new lifestyle."

"Amber's gonna shit," Nicola smiled.

"That's just a gift with purchase," Gaynor smiled. "Now, you two bitches go make the reception look like a celebrity publicity agency; Paul Stroud will be here in two hours."

※ ※ ※

Nicola surveyed the 9,873 unread e-mails in her inbox. No matter how she prioritized them, the number never seemed to get any smaller. She scrolled down, her heart sinking. Every subject line was a version of "Seamus & Bette? Official comment please." She selected a random block of nearly two thousand e-mails and deleted them. It didn't feel bad. She did it again. Gaynor was right. This was probably the only way. She was smiling absently and hitting the delete button when a voice distracted her.

"Nicola, you look good enough to eat."

Her head snapped up and she jumped. Paul Stroud leaned against her office doorframe, his famous abs hidden inside a thick cable-knit sweater, a knit cap jammed down over his golden locks. He looked like he was about to set sail to Antarctica. It was nearly seventy degrees out.

"Oh, hi, Paul," she said flatly.

"I can never keep track," he said, winking. "Are you single or not these days?"

"I'm dating someone," Nicola said brightly. "I'm seeing him tonight."

Paul's face fell.

"What brings you in here today?" Nicola said, making small talk to change the subject. She lost her composure when Paul drew his hands across his throat, then pointed at Gaynor's office. He *was* here to fire Gaynor!

"Wait," Nicola whispered. "Why?"

"Hey, it's no hard feelings, but at this stage in my career, I really need to be with a more powerful agency."

"Gaynor had your back all through the bad times after your TV show," Nicola said, still whispering.

"I heard a saying, and you should learn it, too," Paul said, coming inside her office and leaning across the desk. "If you run with the leopards, you catch the spots. Think about it, Nicola. It took me a while to understand it."

"I understand it, Paul," Nicola said drily.

"Right, then you'll know that for an actual movie superstar like myself, it doesn't look good if my publicist only represents the stars of the seventies and eighties and a couple reality TV whores."

"We have Seamus O'Riordan," Nicola said.

"For now," Paul replied. "And I'm about to eclipse him, one stolen role at a time."

"That's a funny way to look at a major franchise, but hey, what do I know."

Paul's eyes widened.

"Shhhhhh." Nicola put a finger to her lips. "The news doesn't break till next week."

"But contracts are signed?"

"Yes."

"Wow, and have they cast the rest of the movie?" Paul said hopefully.

"That's not something I'm at liberty to discuss with soon-to-be-former clients," Nicola said. "Unless you'd like to give us a few more months to see if we can be the agency of your dreams. Because it's three movies. And a lot of money."

Paul stood upright and rubbed his chin in a pathetically comical attempt to look smart.

"That depends," he began, leaning forward again, "on whether you'd like to give me another one of those awesome blow jobs."

Nicola sat back in shock. She shook her head and stood slowly. "Paul, like I said, I'm dating someone. And—" She paused. "I didn't do that because it was in my job description. And I can guarantee you, Meredith Cox won't blow you, either."

"Maybe not, but she'd line up twenty interns to do it."

He placed both hands on her desk, pushed back toward the door, and vanished, heading down the hallway in Gaynor's direction.

"Hey, Paul," Nicola called after him.

"What?" he called back. "You change your mind?"

"Hardly. Just some parting words, on the house. Everyone in this town knows that you fart when you come! You're a punch line at every party."

She heard his footsteps stop.

"Laugh while you can, loser. You're gonna be out of a job soon. We'll see how cocky you are then."

Nicola sat frozen, listening as he entered Gaynor's office without knocking, slamming the door behind him.

Her teeth clenched in anger, Nicola selected the remaining unread e-mails and deleted them. Then she emptied her trash.

"Fuck you all," she said angrily as she watched the messages vanish forever. Then she remembered she had forgotten her noon deadline for canceling her date with Timothy.

She decided to get very, very drunk.

CHAPTER 19

KARA INCHED ALONG MALIBU ROAD and looked at the parking signs with all their conflicting instructions. Mason had assured her that parking was easy if you read the signs carefully. After too many mistakes in the tow-away zone that is West Hollywood, avoiding being towed had become a new obsessive compulsion. Surprisingly, it looked like she could legally park here, on this sandy stretch of road, until tomorrow morning.

She pulled a large Fendi bag from the backseat. It contained five changes of clothes, including some fetish underwear that she'd called in from Trashy Lingerie. And a whip that she'd found at an adult store off the 101 on her way here.

She laughed at the ludicrousness of it: one of the world's most bankable stars being so submissive, and at the same time, how much she liked being able to boss a man around. It was sexy.

She got out of the car and locked it, and then looked at the line of houses that blocked her view of the beach. Mason had told her to take the coastal access path and then walk back along the beach since he was sure that Felicity had people watching the house. She spied a sand track disappearing between two fences and looked down at her strappy Hundreds sandals. Those four-inch heels were not going to work on soft sand. She crossed the road and slipped them off. After looking left and right to make sure nobody was trailing her, she started down the path, her hand pulling the 'fro in so that it didn't get caught in the branches of a low-hanging oak. Once she cleared the tree and looked up, she stopped dead. The sun was just about to slip over the horizon, but it wasn't going without a fight. Beams of orange and fuchsia were shooting across the Pacific, catching little clouds and turning them into neon cotton candy.

Kara ran the last fifteen yards and dropped her shoes and bag on the sand, expertly drawing her phone from her pocket, thumbing it open, and reversing the camera as she ran. She fired off several shots of the sunset itself, then started on some selfies. She pulled off almost fifty different looks, then set her phone to timer, resting it against some driftwood while she did a suite of full-length shots, all backlit by the dramatic sunset.

When she was sure she had enough stills, she opened Snap and began filming.

"Hey, Snappers," she said, pouting and using the sun's glow to silhouette her Afro, "It's yo girl K hurr at a little beach you might a' heard of. Havin' a *Baywatch* moment."

She stopped filming and typed "#baywatchmoment" and "#kara-jones" and uploaded it. As the sun dropped even farther, the sky alternated from pink to orange. It was like the air around her had become alive, visible.

"Girl, this is beautiful," she said aloud. The beach, if you could call it that with all the rock barriers and immaculate lawns covering most of the sand, was deserted. Anywhere else in the world this beach would be lined with people holding hands, photographers, and dog walkers. A sign told her that she wasn't allowed to walk within fifteen yards of property boundaries, and a post showed her where that line was—about three feet from the crashing waves.

Mason had told her to wait for dark to arrive, so she wasted some time doing more Snaps and selfies until, with a final burst of topaz light, the sun vanished. She picked up her shoes and bag and, not taking her eyes off the incoming surf for one second, made her way along the beach until she saw the landmark in Mason's front yard: a metal sculpture of the earth, with mirrors where the continents were, standing in the middle of an emerald lawn.

As promised, the gate was unlocked, and with one last furtive glance along the beach, Kara unlatched it and stepped onto the softest grass she had ever felt.

Before she crossed the pool area, Mason appeared behind the glass doors, dazzlingly handsome, a smile on his face. He was wearing

Sundek shorts and a threadbare white T-shirt and he'd done his hair. Dang, this was going to be a real date. Like he promised.

He slid the glass door open wide and stepped out onto the patio.

"There's my girl," he said, wrapping her in a hug. "I told you not to bring anything. You didn't need to lug that big bag all the way along the beach."

"Mason, it's like a hundred yards. And trust me, you'll be glad I did."

He pushed her back, his face like a five-year-old's.

"Really? Really? Tell me, tell me!"

"Goddamn, chill, baby." She reached up and tugged on his hair. "All will be revealed."

"I hate waiting," Mason said, whining slightly.

"Good things come to those who wait, Dwyer. Keep it in your pants. For now. Also, I just drove in LA traffic for you. Again. And I'm starving. Where's this home-cooked meal you promised me?"

Mason turned through a doorway on the left. Kara hadn't even had a chance to check out his house. She did a quick spin. *Glass. Metal. Marble. Modern art. Got it.*

She followed him into a stark dining room, all white walls, floor, and table. Twelve white chairs with royal blue cushions flanked the table in two rows. At the far end, the table had been set for two.

"You don't eat here when you're home alone," Kara said, half questioningly.

"Eh," Mason said simply. "Sometimes. It's still my dining table. I like to sit here and watch the dolphins. The glass is treated so nobody can shoot through it, so I can just sit here without worrying about being photographed. If I go out to the pool, I'll have a human or a drone waving a camera at me in two minutes. But what am I telling you for? You're in the biz. You know."

"You're kind. I'm a reality TV sidekick."

"With a *Vanity Fair* shoot tomorrow!"

Mason walked into the kitchen, off the end of the dining room, and opened the fridge. He returned with two pitchers. He set them on the table and gestured for Kara to sit.

"I made us mojitos," he said proudly. "My own special kind. They have cucumber juice and lots of mint, and they're so good."

He poured two tumblers full as Kara took a seat opposite him. He raised his glass and she raised hers.

"To booking your next project," he said.

"To my next project." She smiled, and touched her glass against his. After she sipped she set her glass down and shot him a glare. "Mason, how much rum is in this?"

"I make 'em strong, KJ. No point pussyfooting around."

"I guess not."

"So, tell me, do you want to always be in front of the camera, or would you be happy in production?"

"You're funny," Kara said, steeling herself for a second sip of the drink. "I have no experience behind the camera. Hell, I hardly have any experience in front of it."

"I love it—you're so naïve," Mason said. "You know that every leading man and lady in Hollywood hooks their affairs up with their first job, like an associate producer gig, not a lot of work. But if the relationship continues, the jobs get bigger. You'd just have to always work on my movies."

Kara set her drink back down and stared hard into Mason's violet, guileless eyes. Even though he'd been texting her constantly day and night, and they'd talked at least once daily, she hadn't thought that this would ever go beyond whatever it was right now.

"Well, that's something I hadn't thought of," Kara said, not breaking his gaze. "I . . . uh. Is that something you do?"

"It's something I *would* do." He paused and sipped. "For you."

"Why, Mason, helping me out is more of a big deal than going Facebook official."

"It's not that big of a deal," he said disdainfully. "Someone has to do that job; might as well be you."

"Well, when we get to that stage, we can talk about it."

"Kara, you're the first woman I've brought to my house. This is a big deal to me."

Kara looked into Mason's eyes and saw a new softness there.

"Mason, what's going on?"

"You make me happy."

"Thanks." Kara broke his gaze. This was getting uncomfortable.

"I like you, Kara; there's something about you that's kind of old-fashioned."

Mason reached across the table and took her hands.

"Did you hear me? I'm trying to tell you something. I have . . . you know . . . feelings for you."

"And I'm honored, really I am, but baby, this is our fifth date."

"Glass half full, glass half empty," Mason said, proud of his joke and unaware that it didn't really work. He refilled their drinks as if to underline the point of it.

Kara looked at his dumb, open face, framed by his perfectly cut long-on-top sandy-gray hair. It really was a million-dollar face, and it was giving her a look that was making her uneasy. The urge to check her phone was making her fingers dance on the tabletop. She broke the moment by chugging her newly filled mojito.

"Glass totally empty," she said, setting her glass down.

"Did I upset you?" Mason asked, his beautiful eyes narrowing.

"No, baby, not at all. But you wouldn't believe how horrible my week was. You just took me by surprise."

"Hey, nobody likes their first Hollywood gig," he said, assuming Amber was the problem. "But chin up, you've turned a slot on a reality show into a *Vanity Fair* shoot. Now move on. Probably best to keep it brief. Short and sweet. You can bounce back clean. Nobody will remember *Bank on This*. It'll be the *Filthy Rich: Cattle Drive* of your career."

"Huh? What's that?"

"My point exactly. At least you don't have the unholy alliance of your ex-wife and Meredith Cox trying to destroy your life and career."

Kara flinched at the mention of Meredith's name.

"You'd be surprised," she began, squeezing Mason's hand and glancing at her empty glass. As he refilled it Mason stared into her eyes. She couldn't meet his gaze, instead staring at the floor.

"Kara, I don't understand. What's going on?"

"I don't . . . I mean, I can't tell you, I can't say anything."

"About what?"

"I had a run-in with Meredith already," she said quietly.

"I've been around Meredith for years," Mason said, reaching across and rubbing his fingers along Kara's forearm. "I've watched her claw her way up from the little league. She's ruthless. If she ever figured out that I gave your friend Billy that awesome little story this week, she'd have me skinned alive."

"Mason, she attacked me."

"Huh? Oh, she shit-talks everyone; it's her job." Mason paused, lost in thought. "Weird you'd be on her radar," he said finally. "No offense, but she usually only goes after A-listers."

"I was collateral damage," Kara said bitterly.

"She probably didn't even know," Mason said. Kara snatched her hand back from his and glared at him.

"You're not listening," Kara said, exasperated. "She beat the shit out of me, Mason. She fucking smacked me to the floor and kept on hitting. And then she kicked. She knew who I was." Kara stood and pulled her shirt up, revealing the remnants of a dark maroon bruise on her side.

"I didn't bother covering this one up with makeup."

"Oh my God," Mason said slowly. "Baby, no. I'm sorry. I'm so sorry." He reached for the bruise and placed the flat of his palm gently against Kara's skin. "I've heard rumors that she does violence, but nobody has ever confirmed it. Did you tell your friends?"

Kara nodded, horrified to feel the sting of tears in her eyes.

"Just Nic. She's trying to figure out how to get back at her."

"You have to forget about it," Mason said angrily. "You won't win. She knows some bad hombres. Do you know why she did it?"

Kara nodded.

"And did she get her way?"

Kara stood and began to walk around the table.

"Yes," she said loudly. "It worked. And she came at me again, like a shark. She didn't let it go; she got what she wanted and she's still going to erase me."

Mason walked over to where Kara was and rested a hand gently on her shoulder.

"Was it because of me?" he said softly. "*Fuck*, does my wife know about this?"

"It wasn't because of you," Kara said, facing him. "I just hope I'm off her radar now. I'll settle for that."

"I know the feeling," Mason said, hugging her. "I'd do anything to just get on with making another movie and not seeing my face on *Access Hollywood* every night with another made-up story about me. She plants them all."

"I know. My best friend is a publicist, remember?"

"The girl with Seamus?" Mason said. "From what you say, she's too nice to be a publicist. Gaynor is, too. Even Crystal, she's yesterday. They're Old Hollywood. I wish we could go back to Old Hollywood. Secret affairs. Opium dens. Hearst Castle."

"Jesus, fool; you're forty-five, not eighty-five."

"I meant I'd just like an easy life."

"Well, who's your publicist?"

"I don't have one. . . . It was . . . I mean, it was Meredith for most of my marriage. When things went bad, she bounced me. I'm letting the studio handle it for now. I have two movies out this year, same studio. They'll hook me up."

"Mason, no wonder you're getting destroyed."

"There's nothing I can do," he said. "She Who Must Not Be Named will block anything I try. So I'll just suffer through it and sign the divorce papers and see what happens. I have enough money."

Kara kissed his nose and considered suggesting that he sign with Nicola until she realized that would throw Nicola in Meredith's path much, much more dangerously than she already was.

"I thought I was going to be your associate producer, baby."

"Yeah, I'll still make movies. You'll be fine."

He hugged her tightly.

"See? Another thing we have in common."

He reached up and touched her cheek. "I made us dinner. Are you hungry?"

"What did you make?"

"I made my secret-recipe barbecue ribs and sides."

"Because I'm black?"

"Because I'm southern. And it's the only thing I know how to cook."

Kara laughed and kissed him. He was being so charming.

"Yeah, my tummy's a-grumblin', so git yo ass in the kitchin and hook mama up." She tugged his hair. *"Now."*

⁂ ⁂ ⁂

A wreckage of bones and half-eaten bowls of beans and mashed potatoes littered the table.

"Shoot, I forgot to buy wet wipes," Mason said, wiping at some barbecue sauce at the side of his mouth. "You know, like at the end when they bring you that bowl of wet wipes?"

"We could take a shower," Kara said. "I'd like to wash today off, and your face is such a mess, it would take more than a wet wipe."

Mason stood and she could see that he was already hard. "A shower, huh? I like the sound of that."

He took her hand and led her through the darkened first floor and up a flight of stairs at the back of the main room. There was enough moonlight that Kara could see where they were going, but she couldn't make out much else about the house except that it was so empty it looked like a gallery, white walls and big art. No personal touches.

"Cover your eyes," Mason said when they reached the bathroom. He flicked on the light, and as Kara adjusted to it, she saw him shuck off his clothes and step into a shower that was as big as the bedroom she grew up in. He turned a series of controls on the wall, and water and steam began to spout into the center of the shower from every direction. He stepped back quickly and reached for her tank top.

"May I?" he asked.

"Mason, sometimes you just have to man up and rip my clothes off. You have permission."

His smile faltered, but he recovered, his hands moving up to the neck of her loaner Helmut Lang black tank. He gripped the seams and tore it in half, right down the front.

Fuck, I'll have to buy it now.

"Nice," she said.

"I don't think I can tear your jeans," he said apologetically.

"No, and that's fine." They were Marc Jacobs loaners and she didn't feel like paying for them too.

Kara unbuttoned her jeans and stood there. "You can pull them down, though. Slowly."

Mason, as usual, did as he was told, kneeling before Kara and maintaining some slightly creepy eye contact as he struggled to get her jeans down and over each of her feet.

"Would you like me to wash you, ma'am?"

Ugh. He's just saying ma'am *so that I punish him.*

Kara bit her lip to stop herself from laughing.

"I've told you before," she said sternly. "Ma'am is my mom. If you want to be my bitch, you can call me Miss Jones. And yes, you can wash me."

"I'm sorry, Miss Jones," Mason said, standing and walking into the clouds of steam in the shower area. He turned and beckoned Kara to follow. She stepped into the jets of water and Mason wrapped his arms around her, kissing her lips as he flattened her wet 'fro with his hands. As they kissed she felt him rub soap across her back, slowly, and then down her back, his fingers trailing just along her ass crack.

"Good boy," she murmured, moving her feet slightly apart and resting her shoulders against the back wall of the shower. He moved his hands around to her front and began lightly soaping her breasts, his kisses becoming more insistent.

"Would you like me to wash your feet?"

Kara shook her head. "Miss Jones would prefer it if you ate her pussy," she said, grabbing a fistful of the hair on the top of his head and pushing him down to his knees.

Mason was acceptably good in bed, but Kara had learned that if she was bossy, he was so much better. Within a minute, they were moving as one. *This could go on all night*, Kara thought. And she hoped it would.

Suddenly, he broke. "Miss Jones, I . . . I really want to fuck you."

"Did I tell you to stop?" Kara said, playing along.

"I'm sorry," Mason said, immediately returning to the job at hand.

"I'm kidding, fool, get up here," Kara laughed, slapping him lightly across the face.

With a grin, Mason stood, lifting her right leg with his hand. With his other hand, he slid inside her, groaning loudly. Kara raised an eyebrow. This was the first time they'd done it without any props. She wrapped her arms around his shoulders to stay upright as he began to fuck her with an urgency that was new to them. She pushed back and bit his neck, and he groaned even louder, and then, to her disappointment, he shuddered, gave three heaving thrusts, and held perfectly still.

"Miss Jones, I'm sorry, I couldn't hold back," he said into her neck. "Let me take you to the bedroom. I'll make it up to you, I'll do anything you ask."

Kara rolled her eyes. *I drove an hour in traffic for a forty-second fuck?*

Mason pushed back from her slightly, his eyes boring into hers. "You're so beautiful, you don't even know it," he said hoarsely. "That's why I couldn't hold back. You're the woman I've dreamed of my whole life; that was just an appetizer. I've got something special planned for us, for tonight. You're gonna love it."

He pulled away from her and killed the water, then dragged a thick, soft white bath sheet from a pile, draping it around her shoulders. He massaged her dry, from her feet to her hair, kissing each area as he dried it. As fetishy as he was, he also treated Kara better than any other lover she'd ever had.

"So what do you have planned for me?" she asked, her anger subsiding.

Mason, still covered in droplets of water and starting to get hard again, took her by the hand and led her out into the darkened hallway. They walked in darkness until Mason said, "This is the guest room," and turned the light on.

Kara gasped.

On a slate blue coverlet on a king-size bed, Mason had arranged two whips and leather panties with a black rubber dick in the front.

"What the hell, Mason?" Kara exclaimed. "You want me to peg you?"

"To what me, Miss Jones?"

"You want me to fuck you up the ass in them panties?" Kara said, trying to be funny.

Mason nodded, then looked down, ashamed.

"I'm sorry, Miss Jones. I went too far."

"Why do you want me to do that? What's in it for me?"

"I want you to make me yours," Mason said. "I've wanted this my whole life."

Kara looked at Mason standing naked in front of her, his erection growing by the second, his movie-star face looking at her with something between love, shame, and raw lust.

"Okay, baby," she purred. "Get on your fucking knees."

She reached for the strap-on. She prayed that she could get through this without laughing, and then prayed again that the fuck afterward would last more than a minute.

CHAPTER 20

THE HANGOVER THAT HAD BEEN lurking ominously behind her forehead exploded as Nicola bent over to pick up a feather that had fallen off Amber's boa. She drove a knuckle into her temple and winced in pain.

"Never had a hangover before?" Amber snarled. "The Oscars are in a few weeks. Let me see if it's not too late to get you nominated."

"Whatever," Nicola said, refusing to be drawn into a fight. Amber had been on fire all morning. Nicola wondered if she was sober. She didn't seem like her usual stoned self. "It might be a migraine."

"Either way, the best thing is another drink, or is that unprofessional? You know, like banging your client?"

"Which client am I banging?" Nicola tossed the feather back onto the floor, instantly regretting engaging with the snakeskin-pantsuit-clad reality bitch.

"Seamus really loves having his birthday parties at Disneyland, huh?" Amber said with an evil grin. "Let me guess. Club 33 and then you guys got high and rode Small World. . . . Oh wait . . . he's sober now, huh? That must have been fun. Was there some birthday head at the very least? He's a fan of that."

Nicola froze. The pain in her head was almost blinding her, and her brain was refusing to process Amber into something she understood. She pretended to take a call and walked out of the suite that they were using as a dressing room.

Taking the elevator to the Roosevelt lobby, she went to the bar, ordering a shot of tequila and a slice of lime. The bartender delivered it without making eye contact, and Nicola threw it back, chomped angrily on the lime, and waited for the pain to subside.

Despite drinking way too much tequila last night, she had valiantly fought off Timothy's advances at Soho House and had thrown herself into an Uber just after midnight. Kara had woken her up around two with wild eyes and promises of some big gossip, but Nicola had fended her off, pleading drunkenness.

She paused at the bar and reviewed last night. It hadn't exactly been the worst date of her life, but if Timothy had been expecting romance, he'd gotten the opposite—a somewhat messy pressure blowout. Nicola ordered shots before dinner and they'd ended the night dancing wildly on couches at SoHo House. It hadn't been fun, exactly, but it had been necessary.

Nicola had changed her mind about sleeping with Timothy almost hourly as the night progressed, and she did have a fuzzy memory of them finally making out while dancing to a Beyoncé remix. She also remembered swatting Timothy's hands away from her boobs, and that he was an aggressive but not terribly seductive kisser. It was the kissing that convinced her that sleeping with him would be neither a good idea nor a good experience. That, and it would hurt Seamus.

Nicola looked at her phone. New texts came in so regularly that her home screen scrolled them like a news ticker. She considered ordering another shot and answering some work calls. The shoot was scheduled to end at sundown. She didn't want to let work pile up all day. She flicked absently at the texts as she felt the tequila start to sink in, stopping at a series of texts from Seamus.

She groaned. Seamus was saying they needed to leave for Mexico tomorrow. The studio was sending a car to pick them up in the morning. He was excited.

Her eyes rolled back in their sockets. She had been looking forward to crawling into bed after this shoot and not getting up till Monday morning. Those dreams were now dashed. She turned to go back to the bar when her phone rang. It was Kara.

"Where the good gravy are you? Hurry! Poolside." The line went dead.

Nicola's shoulders slumped, her plans for a second shot of tequila derailed. She gathered her purse, threw ten bucks on the bar, and went back to the elevator.

The shoot was in full swing when she got to the pool deck. The blazing California winter sun would pass easily for the midsummer when the story ran in August as part of *Vanity Fair*'s "Guilty Pleasures" cover. The concept for the shoot was to have Amber and, to a lesser extent, Kara, model brightly colored fashions while surrounded by monochromatic models dressed in 1940s film noir swimsuits and leisurewear.

She scoured the crowd for Kara. The photographer was setting up a shot with Amber and four male models in perfectly fitted black or gray slacks and polos, so Nicola headed that way.

"Glad you could join us," Amber said antagonistically as she approached. "Where is Gaynor? I need an actual publicist. There's a conflict of interest at this shoot."

Nicola looked at Amber with dead eyes.

"Gaynor's on her way," Nicola lied. Gaynor was at a last-minute meeting with buyers for Torrid to pitch Alicia as a model. "So either I solve your problem, or your problem exists all day. Your call." She turned and began to walk away.

"Someone's gotten tough," Amber said. "Let's see how tough you are now. Come here." Amber began walking away from the shoot, the photographers' assistants glowering at her since they'd just gotten the light levels right. Nicola followed her to a cabana beside the pool.

"What's up?"

"You better drop that tone and you better take my fucking side in this," Amber said, kicking the heel of her Kate Spade boot against the leg of a sun lounger. "This is my shoot. This is *my* shoot. I agreed to have her here, so she could be in, like, one photo. And that was one photo *maybe*."

"The pitch was for both of you. The magazine decides content."

"The pitch was for my show. *My* show. And the star of my show is me. I've done one setup with her, and I'm not doing any more. So can you tell her to leave?"

Nicola felt anger surge in her throat and took a deep breath to derail it before it became a string of insults.

"I can talk to the photographer," she said as if talking to a toddler. "But this is *Vanity Fair*. They want two models: one white, one black."

"Don't make this a race issue," Amber mumbled.

"You got this shoot because you're the only reality show with mixed . . ." Nicola paused; she'd nearly said *leads*. ". . . casting."

"That's so boring. Who cares if she's black? I don't care; black bitches can be as basic as white ones. Chinks can be hungry tigers, like that whore you hitched Seamus to. Nobody fucking cares about race."

"A lot of white people say that," Nicola said, knowing it would go over Amber's head.

"That's right, they do," Amber said, not sure what she was even agreeing with.

Nicola could not tell Amber how much work it had taken for Gaynor and Nicola to convince the fashion department at *Vanity Fair* that Amber was classy enough to carry the shoot. The editors had not been worried about Kara at all.

Amber continued to kick the leg of the lounger.

"They told me you wouldn't take my side," she said angrily.

"Did *they*?" Nicola continued. "Well, this *is* your side. I am your side. And your side is a deal for a shoot with two people, and Kara is one of them. If you blow this, they'll never work with you again."

"Who even reads *Vanity Fair* anymore?" Amber said. "Old people like you, I guess."

"Yep, old people like me." Nicola couldn't even remember the last time she'd actually read *Vanity Fair*. And wasn't she the same age as Amber? The entire photography crew was staring at them. "Now, what can we do to make this work?"

"I need some weed. I'm out."

"I don't have any," Nicola said bluntly. "You can have a friend bring you some, but I can't go off-premises right now. We have a lot to get through, and it's already afternoon. We only have light for, like, three more hours."

"Do you think that Meredith Cox tells her clients to have a friend bring their weed?"

"I don't give a fuck what Cox does with her clients. You want weed, get weed. Don't ask me to keep wiping your ass. Now get out there and get this photo. We have four more setups to do today."

"And if I don't?"

"I'll have Bette Wu here in one hour and we'll give them so much mixed-race magic that they won't miss you for a minute."

Amber glared at Nicola as they walked back to the cameras.

"We good?" the photographer asked hesitantly, and Nicola nodded. Amber slouched into the center of the group of male models and began to pout and wave her arms slowly around her head as flashes bounced off the stone walls around the pool. Stylists rushed into the fray every minute to rearrange Amber's ensemble and straighten the edges of the men's clothing. In the distance, Nicola spied Kara emerging from the shadows by the elevators. She shook her head and motioned for her to wait there, out of Amber's sight. She turned to Amber and mouthed, "Is everything okay?" Amber gave her a short, steely nod and went back to pouting. Nicola tried to look calm as she walked over to Kara, dressed in a lime green Beach Bunny swimsuit and intricate, strappy Christian Louboutin wedges.

"Did you fix it?" she whispered as Nicola got close.

"I think so," Nicola said. "And we don't need to whisper. She can't hear you from here."

"Did she tell you she kicked me out of the last shot?"

"She did not. But don't worry." Nicola rubbed Kara's arm. There were goose bumps forming. "They'll use frames where you were both there. You both have one solo shoot—yours is next."

"Girl, I'm telling you, she's up to something."

"Well, let's just get through it, let's not engage, let's hope she gets high, and let's hope that at five p.m. we can go sit in the bar and I'll charge a bunch of drinks to Gaynor and we can laugh."

"How is Gaynor doing?"

"About the Paul thing? I think she's shaken," Nicola said. Gaynor had known that Paul was coming to fire her, so when he had entered her office, she beat him to it, telling him that she had terminated their contract due to his "lack of talent and surplus of gas." He had told her to fuck off, many times, as he strode out of HHPR.

"But she's Gaynor; she's focusing on you."

A commotion behind them made them both turn to see Amber being wrapped in a blanket and walked back up to the Monroe Suite to get started on her next look. She waited until Amber vanished before she wrapped an arm around Kara's waist and took her to the photographer.

"She's awful," the photographer moaned, cocking his head in Amber's direction. "I'm not getting what I need from her. This is *Vanity Fair*, not *Pussweek!* Miss Jones, we might need to shoot extra solos of you. New York is loving the test shots of you that I've sent them from earlier."

Kara squeezed Nicola's arm.

"*Vanity Fair* loves my test shots," she said excitedly, through chattering teeth.

"I know," Nicola said, wondering how Amber would take *that* news.

Kara's solo shoot was one of the most complex setups of the day: balanced on a floating platform in the middle of the pool, surrounded by eight female models in monochrome swimsuits and matching black rubber swim caps, all of them doing an Old Hollywood water ballet.

For someone without any real model training, Kara nailed it, her limbs trailing down toward the water as she pretended to rest her weight on the upstretched arms of the models below her. *This looks amazing*, Nicola marveled proudly. The photographer was shooting to the south, and as Nicola watched on the laptop, they could see Kara framed by a horizon of palm trees disappearing into the distance.

"This is the best shot we've set up today," the photographer said.

"Yeah, I'm just praying that Amber isn't looking out a window and seeing it," Nicola replied, looking in the direction of the Monroe Suite. The curtains were drawn.

For a minute, she felt peaceful and proud of her friend, who looked radiant and happy. It was crazy how a week that began so horribly could end so perfectly. Suddenly the silence was torn apart by Amber's voice screeching at them from the elevator lobby.

"You fucking whore," she yelled. Nicola looked around—in Amber's world, she could have been talking to anyone. Amber's gaze was locked on Kara, and she was headed straight for the edge of the pool nearest her. Nicola double-timed her steps to try to intercept her, curling her hand into a fist as she approached.

"Back off, you pathetic loser," Amber spat, "or I swear, I'll break every bone in your basic face." Without stopping, Amber rushed into the frame.

The photographer called out, "Hey, what's going on here, you guys?"

"You stay out of it, faggot," Amber said, not even turning to face him.

"Amber." Kara's shoulders slumped; her moment stolen. Her lip trembled, but Nicola could see her fighting to stay calm. "What's going on?"

"You absolute whore," Amber said again. "You tried to sell a sex tape? You tried to blackmail Tom Kendall? While you were starring on my show? You're so stupid. Basic Valley whore. You think you can come in here, stealing my fucking photo shoot?"

"Amber, let me get out of the pool and I'll come talk to you; we can work this out."

"No, we literally can't. There's nothing to work out. I tried to be nice to you. You said you weren't a hungry tiger, but you're worse. You're just some eight-one-eight ghetto bitch on the make. You're so disgusting. What was I even thinking?"

Kara struggled to keep her composure. The models had all

dropped their arms, huddling around the floating platform and looking anywhere but at the melting-down star.

"Amber." Kara's voice was breaking. "I don't know where you heard that, but it's not true. There's no tape. I would have told you."

"Oh, would you? Would you? Do you think I don't have sex tapes? I could make millions of dollars with the unreleased sex tapes I have. But I have too much pride, too much respect for my body. I don't need a whore on my show. You're fired. You're fired from the show, you're fired from this shoot, and you're fired from my *life!*"

Tears appeared in Kara's eyes briefly, then Nicola saw her take a deep breath.

"You can't do that. I have a contract."

"Which I can terminate at any time, without notice. I'm your boss and you're fired. Get out of that pool, and get out of my shoot."

Kara stood frozen on the platform. The photo assistants threw a rope to her and dragged the floating platform to the edge of the pool. As she stepped onto the concrete, Amber flew toward her, her fists flailing. Kara's eyes narrowed, and at the last second, before Amber's punch could land on her cheek, she ducked, and the momentum carried Amber out into the air, and then down into the pool with a loud splash.

"Everybody, please calm down," the photographer said nervously as the splash subsided. "Let's all take a moment and reset. We can break for lunch, and we'll reconvene when everyone has had a chance to cool off."

"There'll be no need for that," said a female voice at the rear of the photo crew. The people parted and Nicola saw Meredith Cox striding forward. "I've talked to the fashion department in New York, and we all agree that the shoot works better as a solo. Amber, go dry off. We will resume as soon as you can be ready."

A grip pulled Amber out of the pool and wrapped her in another blanket. She stumbled and then took three steps toward Nicola.

"Looks like I'm not waiting till the end of the shoot to tell you that your shitty agency is fired, too." She glanced at Meredith. "I'm going where they know how to treat a star."

As if on cue, Meredith reached into her purse and pulled out a pill bottle emblazoned with a green cross. She handed it to Amber, who snatched at it greedily. It vanished beneath the gray blanket, and two stylists led Amber away.

"Do you ever enter like a normal person?" Kara yelled, storming up to Meredith, who raised a palm like she was cautioning a dog.

"One more step, whore, and I'll split your lips so hard you won't be able to suck dick to make your next rent check. *And* I'll have your ass arrested."

Nicola stepped in. "Meredith, how lovely of you to join us. And thank you for taking an underperforming client off our hands. Now, if you don't mind leaving the shoot that I set up, we'd like to get on with our business. I have some calls to make."

"Check your phone," Meredith said coldly.

Nicola looked and saw a string of apologetic texts from the *Vanity Fair* office in New York advising her that Kara would no longer be a part of the shoot.

"I see," she said. "You do realize that this shoot is my idea, my concept, and my pitch?"

"This is like when a child shows you a finger painting. Well done, well done, you." Meredith waved a finger at Nicola. "I've alerted security," she continued. "You have five minutes to vacate the property."

"I paid for this; it's all on our company card."

"Was, darling. Was. If you're ever lucky enough to work for a real publicity agency you'll learn how things are done. Give my regards to that glittery dinosaur that you work for, and please ask her how she's coping with the loss of yet another client. I certainly hope that Miss Jones and Mr. O'Riordan are enough to pay for her lifestyle. The clock is ticking. You have approximately three minutes to clear the property. I've taken the liberty of having the stylists bring your clothing down, Jones. Keep the outfit. Sell it on eBay. It'll be the only money you earn this year. I'll make sure of that."

Nicola walked over to Kara and gently grasped her arm.

"Let's go," she said kindly, feeling Kara tremble with anger.

A stylist handed a sports bag filled with Kara's clothes to her.

"I'm really sorry, Kara, that was horrible."

"Thanks," Kara sniffed. "Nice working with ya."

They stood in silence as the elevator took them down one floor. When the door opened, Nicola pointed Kara to the ladies' room.

"Go change," she said softly.

Kara walked away, and as the door of the ladies' room closed behind her, Nicola saw her shoulders begin to shake.

She texted Billy, her fingers barely able to hit the letters.

Shit just got crazy at the shoot. Come to my place immediately. We need you.

Be right there sis. Can we bring anything? You OK?

Amber went crazy, fired K, fired HHPR, Meredith is here. We are headed home. Come!

Nicola fought down an urge to text Seamus. What exactly could he even do? She realized she was about to hyperventilate, and she pinched at her sides, hoping the pain would distract her. Kara wouldn't come back out of the bathroom until she'd stopped crying out of fear that she'd be photographed. Spying an uncomfortable-looking wooden carved bench against the wall, Nicola went and sat down. She knew she had to text Gaynor but didn't know what to say. Her phone buzzed. Gaynor always seemed to text when Nicola thought about her.

Don't worry, Nicolita. We are better off without that awful witch. Take an extra day in Mexico if you like. Te amo mucho. I'm sorry you had a shitty day. —G

She felt tears sting her eyes as she read the message. She hated it when Gaynor was nice to her. It was easier to deal with her as a raucous cartoon. Her phone dinged with Billy's response.

Just talked to Gaynor. Holy shit.

Hurry

Nicola stared at her phone, trying to get her breathing under control. She rose and went back to the bartender who'd served her earlier.

"Hi," she said brightly. "I'm with the *Vanity Fair* shoot out by the pool. We need two bottles of Johnnie Walker Blue. Can you charge that to Meredith Cox? She's with Amber Bank. Thanks."

CHAPTER 21

NICOLA BECAME AWARE OF THE motion of the car as she slowly woke up, not sure where she was. *You're in a car headed to Mexico,* her brain said. *With Seamus.* She kept her eyes closed and asked her brain if she'd quit drinking early enough to avoid a hangover. She didn't sense any of the telltale signs, no queasy stomach, no thudding behind her eyeballs, no creeping nausea. She didn't want to get her hopes up, but it felt like she might have gotten lucky for once.

By the time she had dragged herself to her room to pack around one a.m., Kara had finally stopped crying and drinking. She'd fallen asleep on the couch cuddling an empty whiskey bottle. Billy and Bluey had left earlier, around midnight, after ordering in Thai and doing their best to make the girls laugh.

Seamus had changed the car booking once he heard what had gone down at the shoot, making it come and get him first so that Nicola could sleep longer. She'd set her alarm for just a half hour before his ETA of nine a.m. She'd showered quickly, brushed on a light foundation and some mascara, and dragged on her comfiest Joe's Jeans and favorite Tory Burch cashmere sweater and was waiting on the curb when the SUV pulled up.

Seamus bounded out and tossed her bags into the trunk as if they weighed nothing before opening her door and helping her up into the car with one hand. Inside, she saw that he had already stopped at Starbucks and gotten her two Venti Americanos, one iced, one hot, as well as a bag that probably contained pastries.

As she locked her seat belt, he climbed into his seat and gave her a wide smile.

"If I was to judge by lookin'"—he reached out and moved a curl of brown hair away from her eye—"I'd not be guessing you had a rough night."

"Thanks, you smooth bastard," she said, matching his smile. "I had a good teacher."

"So you switched to water early on?"

"I switched to iced tea in a shot glass; they never knew."

"Not often enough, I'd venture, by the smell of whiskey on your breath."

"It was a rough day," she said, reaching for the iced coffee, mainly to mask the smell of booze.

Seamus took her hand, holding it loosely.

"Well, don't drink too much of that caffeine. It's gonna be a four-hour drive to Rosarito, so get some sleep. Silence your phone; it's Sunday and your problem client is right here. What could go wrong?"

She nodded, pulling her phone out and switching it to silent. The screen was already filled with texts from the UK press. Seamus and Bette had been out last night. She didn't feel like asking him how it went.

As the limo made its way to the 101 south, she laid her head back and drifted off to sleep before they hit downtown LA.

✳ ✳ ✳

Sensing no hangover, she opened one eye and looked out the window, spying rolling hills and houses and lots of trees, none of which gave her any indication of their location. She stretched and sat upright.

"Good morning again," Seamus said brightly. "You sleep okay?"

"Yeah," she said groggily. "How long was I out?"

"Well, we passed San Diego, and we'll be crossing the border in about ten minutes."

"Holy shit, I've been asleep for hours?"

"You must have needed it."

"Did you sleep, too?"

Seamus shook his head and reached for the coffee. She hoped he hadn't been staring at her the whole drive.

"Would you like formerly warm, or the mostly melted ice?"

She pointed at the plastic cup. "Melted ice, please."

236

"Listen, Nico," he said as he passed the cup to her. "I changed something else about this trip. We aren't staying in Rosarito tonight."

"Seamus! First it's Disneyland—now what? You have to ask."

"Hear me out, hear me out." He took her hand. "Rosarito is a business town. The movie is in preproduction, so anywhere we go, it'll be work. I've shot two other movies down here, and I found a place that I love. So I got to thinking, this whole thing with me and Bette and whatever, it's adding to your workload. A lot. I figure, let's go to my secret place. Our phones won't work. We can step out of our lives for a day."

"You're basically kidnapping me," Nicola said. He waited for her to smile. She didn't.

"I'm trying to do something nice for you," he said, crestfallen.

"People ask," she said. "You are doing that actor thing and not asking."

"People also throw surprise parties, Nico," he said. "We'll have separate cabins. Basically all I did was move the location of our hotel, and even then, only about sixty miles."

"Sixty miles in a country I've never been to."

"Stop being so uptight," Seamus smiled, pointing out the window. The car was pulling into a line of traffic that swirled in a circular drive around a set of low government buildings. "And right about now, you are leaving the United States."

The car emerged from the spiral and instantly America felt light-years away. As they sped toward a highway that promised to take them to *playas*, Nicola stared out the window. A tall arch in the distance had a video screen suspended from it. All the signage was in Spanish, and the buildings were a mishmash of vibrant colors and odd shapes.

"It looks immediately different," she said.

"What do you mean?"

"I kind of expected it to just look like an annex of America," she replied. "I went to Cologne once, a long time ago, and I went to see the big cathedral, and all around it was America—an Apple store, American fast food—and I remember thinking I was so far from home and at the same time, it was too familiar. This isn't like that."

"Nope, Mexico is instantly Mexico, and I fell in love with it the first time I came here. This was the first place I felt like I could retire to outside of Scotland. Bluey says that I should consider Australia, too."

"I'd love to go to Australia."

"I've been a couple times, just those lightning press visits. Private jet, two parties, fifty interviews, some photos in front of a landmark. The only thing that told me I was in Australia was that they made me hold a koala."

"Was it soft?"

"Yeah, it peed on me."

"Does anything ever go well for you?"

Seamus roared with laughter and took her hand as the car picked up speed and headed for the coast.

✳ ✳ ✳

Nicola had stared out her open window the whole drive down the coast as the *carretera* hugged the cliffside, the angry Pacific roiling below, a mess of blues, greens, and muddy browns. Small farms and houses dotted the dry fields on the inland side. After they crossed yet another road toll terminal, the car left the highway and began to climb a winding narrow road into the mountains, away from the sea. As they drove, a vineyard opened up around the car on all sides, grapevines trailing along runners in geometric patterns that crisscrossed the rolling red desert hills. Nicola was surprised to see two large wooden boats in the middle of a field in the distance, and she had an instant uncomfortable flashback to the spaceship on the set of Seamus's movie. The one they'd had sex in. The last time they had sex.

Seamus saw the look on her face change. "What's up?" he said, turning in his seat. "Is something wrong?"

Nicola shook her head. "No, I'm just being silly."

After half an hour, they arrived at their destination, which a sign informed Nicola was named Encuentro Guadalupe. The car pulled up at a low postindustrial wood and rusted-metal building. The driver got out of the car and walked inside to handle their check-in. A golf cart sped down a dirt road toward their SUV. Nicola reached to unfasten her seat belt and Seamus gently put one of his hands over hers, stopping her.

"Are we okay, Ohio?" he asked softly.

"Yeah," she said begrudgingly. "Just make sure this is the last thing you ambush me with on this trip."

He saluted with two fingers. "Scout's honor."

The cart drove her up to the most beautiful home she'd ever seen, a rustic modern wood, metal, and glass casita. Inside it was a sleek loft with a private balcony high above fields of grapevines, the strong winter sun heating the fields enough to send a warm earth-scented breeze up from the valley floor.

After taking a proper shower, she stood out on her balcony, letting the wind dry her hair naturally so its light curls came out. Since she'd only worn the Joe's Jeans and the cashmere sweater in the car, she slipped back into them, but that was already a little too warm. She was changing into a T-shirt when a knock sounded at her door. She pulled the sweater back down and went to answer it.

"Hello?"

"You decent, Ohio?"

She opened the door and there stood Seamus, in shorts that stopped mid-thigh and a faded red rugby jersey. He thrust a fistful of wildflowers at her.

"I got you flowers." He beamed. She kicked him gently in the shin and ushered him in. He went into her bathroom and came out with a glass of water, which he set the flowers in, then went and placed it on her bedside table.

"You know it's winter, right?"

"It's hot out, lass." He looked her up and down. "Why are you dressed like that?"

"I was just about to change into a T-shirt," Nicola said.

"Don't let me stop you." Seamus plopped onto the bed and put his hands over his eyes. "I promise not to peek."

Nicola rolled her eyes. He was clearly excited; he was acting like a ten-year-old boy. She whipped her sweater over her head and tossed it onto his head.

"Just a little insurance," she said as she pulled on the Clash shirt he'd bought her. "You can open them now."

"They were open the whole time."

"Figured. So what's the plan?"

"Wanna go for a hike?"

"I didn't bring any shorts," she said ruefully. "I thought this was a business trip."

Seamus bunched up his face and looked out the glass doors.

"Does that also mean you didn't bring a swimsuit?"

"It does."

"Okay, change of plans. You hungry? Let's go into town for lunch and we'll see what we can rustle up."

Seamus picked up the house phone and spoke Spanish that sounded almost fluent to Nicola.

"You speak Spanish?"

"*Sí, guapa*," he laughed. "Too many summers on Ibiza. And I took it in high school."

"You're a man of mystery, Casanova," she smiled, walking toward the door. "We going or not?"

"*Listo!*"

※ ※ ※

Nicola didn't even know the name of the tiny town that they were in, a small collection of stores and restaurants around a dusty town square with a statue in its center. Seamus had ventured into several stores and emerged with bags, assuring her that she now owned a swimsuit and several pairs of shorts as well as some souvenirs. He refused to show her what he had bought. Nobody bothered them at all as they shopped, but Nicola had noticed that their driver was trailing them on foot, always at a distance. She also noticed the outline of a rather large gun tucked into his jeans, underneath his shirt. It was the most poorly concealed weapon she'd ever seen.

240

Suddenly Nicola's nostrils filled with the smell of something delicious, and she realized she was very hungry.

"What the hell is that food I can smell?"

Seamus took her by the shoulder and guided her into a tiny corridor between two stores. It opened into a tiled courtyard ringed by roses blooming red and pink and filling the air with their scent. As they walked in, a tall, thin woman with a long black ponytail rushed up to them.

"Señor O'Riordan! *Es tan bueno verte de nuevo!*" She hugged him warmly and kissed him on both cheeks.

"*'Ola, Edith, como estás?*"

"*Bien, bien,*" she smiled, turning to Nicola. "*Bienvenidos, me llamo Edith. Habla español?*"

Nicola shook her head. "I'm sorry, no."

"Not a problem at all," Edith said, switching into American-accented English. "I'm Edith; welcome to Valle de Guadalupe. I hope you're hungry."

"My name is Nicola," she said, shaking Edith's hand. "And yes, we are both very hungry."

"Good, good," Edith said, walking them to a table that was still bathed in the afternoon sun. "We were busy at lunch, but now we are not busy—just how you like it, Mr. O'Riordan."

"Edith, I've told you, please call me Seamus."

Edith snapped her fingers theatrically, and a young man appeared from inside the kitchen with a pitcher of sangria. He brought it to the table with two ceramic goblets and filled them both.

"Can you join us for a drink, Edith?" Seamus asked.

"I can't fire myself," she laughed, signaling for another goblet. They all sat down.

"You look well, old friend," she said, raising her drink. "*Salud.*"

They clinked their cups together and Nicola tasted her drink, a floral, fruity wine filled with chunks of pineapple and orange.

"So what's been happening since I saw you last?" Seamus asked.

"I bought a little house, with your help. *Muchas gracias,*" Edith said warmly.

Nicola's face changed and Seamus saw it.

"I got photographed here a few years ago," Seamus explained. "Edith's cooking suddenly got a lot of notice."

"Anthony Bourdain came here because of you!"

"Figures," Seamus said with fake horror. "Edith, do you have any photos of your house?"

"*Sí, sí*," she said, pulling out her iPhone. "I decorated it in your honor; I say it's my movie-star casa. I put the Hollywood lights and some chairs from America in the yard. I can sit outside at night under the stars, and I am just so grateful to you."

Nicola leaned in and looked as Edith flicked through photos of a small brick house ringed by a field with a vegetable garden and a chicken coop. She got to the photos of her Hollywood yard, with string lights and Adirondack chairs, and Nicola's heart began to swell. In a corner of the yard, Edith had built an altar to the Virgin, and there was a framed photo of Seamus among the candles.

"Hey, Edith, you can take my ugly mug out of there," Seamus laughed. "You don't owe anything to me; it's your cooking that got you that house. How are the kids?"

"You're too kind, Señor," Edith said quietly. "My son is in college in Mexico City, and my daughter is still working in Rosarito for the movies. After the job you got her, she had experience. And thanks to you, she makes them pay her in American dollars!"

"Like I said." Seamus rubbed Edith's upper arm. "I didn't do anything special. I'm glad to see you so happy."

Edith stood up sharply. "Your food!" she said, her voice raspy. "*Por favor*, let me bring you something to eat. I have a tuna that was caught this morning just in Ensenada, and I have the *lengua y maíz* that Bourdain gave a lot of stars, so please, let me get out of the way."

"Edith! Please, stay and drink."

"No, *gracias*," she said, heading inside. She paused and smiled at Nicola. "He is a very good man, but he will never tell you this," she said. "You're a very lucky woman."

After they ate, they headed back to Nic's casita. The sun was setting over the valley, and with it, the warmth drained out of the day.

Nicola went out on her balcony again, to stand on the edge, watching the waves of orange bounce off olive trees and grapevines and cars driving along a dusty road in the distance. Seamus walked out onto the deck carrying a shopping bag and a bottle of mezcal. He put the mezcal on the small wooden table and presented the bag to her. Nicola took it, surprised by its weight.

"Open it," he instructed.

She untied the handles and peered inside, seeing what looked like a blanket patterned in black and white, a repeating Aztec motif.

"What is it?"

"Try it on."

Nicola took it out and shook it open, revealing a square poncho. She pulled her head through the opening and let it fall around her, feeling instantly warmer.

"That looks even better on you than I expected," Seamus said.

"Where's your stupid wolf whistle?"

"I thought it would be inappropriate," he laughed. "I don't want to get accused of ambushing you with a wolf whistle."

Nicola thought back over the time they dated, how Seamus had made it a thing to whistle at her when she did something clumsy. One time, he'd whistled after she farted.

"It wouldn't have been an ambush," she said. "Thank you for this; it's really comfortable."

Seamus turned and poured mezcal into two shot glasses. He passed one to her.

"Nico, I really want to thank you for coming with me on this trip," he began.

"This better not be another ambush," she cautioned.

"I can't promise that," he said, sipping his drink. She nervously took a sip, too, feeling the acrid liquor fill her mouth with its smoky goodness. "But I do want to talk about what I can promise."

"Seamus, I—"

"You need to just listen," he interrupted, gently placing a finger against her lips. "Nico, I messed up. But I watched you at lunch today, and I saw it in your face."

"What? What did you see?"

"I saw the only thing I needed; I saw the look you gave me at your flat, the night you cooked dinner for me. I saw through the walls and I saw that I have a chance."

Nicola looked out over the valley, watching as the sun slipped behind the mountains. She felt nervous.

"What you did for Edith," she began. "You didn't have to."

"Her husband died when the kids were young. She has run that restaurant for so long, before this region took off with this new hipster wine thing. And the first time I went in there, she recognized me, but she said nothing, and she protected me like a wolf. She lied to the photographers who came looking for me, she hid me in the kitchen, and she fed me. Ever since then, she's given me a sanctuary when I'm down here. You know how valuable that is to me."

"Yes, I do."

"But that's not what you are to me," he continued. "You're more than my sanctuary. *Tú eres mi otra mitad*." He paused, and she could see tears in his eyes.

Nicola fidgeted and took a too-big gulp of her drink, and it burned her throat. She coughed wetly and then sneezed.

"That sounds like a compliment, which means I've never heard it at work and don't know what it means."

Seamus wolf-whistled her. "Nico, that means you're my other half. That's how I feel when I'm with you. I feel like myself. I feel complete."

"Seamus, there's ambushes and then there's this," she said, wiping her mouth. "You knew you were bringing me here to do this."

"I didn't know. I hoped. I didn't know until this afternoon. I honestly just wanted to give you a break from the stress I've caused."

He set his glass on the edge of the railing and put his hands on her shoulders.

"I still don't know. I still hope." He leaned in and kissed her forehead lightly. "And I know that I hurt you."

"So much."

"I'll always have to carry that. That's my burden. But Nico, that guy, he wasn't the real me. You showed me how lost I'd gotten. I just wasn't able to grab the rudder fast enough before I hit the rocks."

"Seamus . . ."

"Shhhh," he whispered. "Hear me out. I insisted on drug tests for this movie. Weatherman got the studio to agree to no drug tests, but I said I wanted them. And I'm going to share them with you. You'll know that I'm sober."

"Seamus, I don't want to be a parent. I don't want to have to say 'good dog' every time you test sober."

"You don't have to. That's not what this is about. We have a good thing here. You can't deny our chemistry. If you let me, I will devote myself to you, and to earning your trust, and to being worthy of your love."

"Easy on the schmaltz, O'Riordan," Nicola said with a nervous laugh.

"I'm a corny old fool," he laughed. "And I'm going to say this, and please, Nico, know that I mean it. I love you. And you can trust me."

Nicola turned her face up to his, staring into his deep green eyes in the fading light.

"I . . . ," she stammered. "I . . . think I'm the stupidest person in the world for even coming here today."

His face fell.

"I knew you were going to do this. I knew one hundred percent. I knew that night at Runyon Canyon that you'd try eventually, and probably before I was ready."

His hands slid down from her shoulders to her elbows.

"But you still came," he said.

"Yeah, here I am. Acting like a stupid girl."

"It's not stupid." He kissed her forehead again, then raised his hands and cupped her cheeks. "Every relationship has bumps at the start. Ours was ugly and necessary and it helped me get my ship back on course. This isn't an ambush. It's a plea. The one thing I need and want and love is you. Nico, I love you, so, so much, and I promise here, now, and for as long as you'll tolerate my stupid Scottish arse, that I will make you happy and proud."

He stepped back, and for a minute she thought he was going to kneel.

"Don't you dare propose to me," she said nervously.

"I wouldn't dream of it," he laughed. He picked up the mezcal bottle and refilled their glasses. He took a deep swig of his. "Just working up me Dutch courage, lass."

Nicola remembered the phrase. Seamus had used it before they dived into the ocean. A lifetime ago.

"What do you need Dutch courage for, then?"

"For this."

Seamus wrapped his arms around her and placed his lips lightly on hers, tentatively, as if he was half thinking she'd reject him. She considered it, her arms folded against him inside her poncho.

"Just wait," she said, pushing him back gently. "A kiss won't solve this. I can't . . . I can't be like my mom, Seamus. She put up with way too much from my dad, always promising he'd stay clean. I put up with way too much with my ex."

"I would never do that to you, Wallace. I swear on us. Never again. Not a single drug shall pass these lips. You're my long game. A few more years of this big-buck bullshit, and we can retire, to Scotland, to right here, to anywhere that makes you happy. Because the only place I will ever be happy is by your side."

"I'm not afraid of getting hurt, Seamus," Nicola said, a tear in her voice. "I'm afraid of looking stupid. My dad made my mom's life a living hell. We never understood why she let him make her look like a fool."

"I didn't know your dad, but I see your bruised heart, and lass, please, if you let me back in, for one last time, I'll guard it and you till the end of me days."

"Was that from one of your movies, you jackass?" Nicola laughed and leaned her forehead against his chin. He kissed the top of her head.

"Can we try?" he whispered. She lifted her face until their lips met.

"You fuck this up, O'Riordan, and a broken heart will be the least of your worries."

"Wouldn't have it any other way," he whispered, then began to kiss her tentatively. As if no time had passed since their last kiss, they exchanged waves of slow, languid kisses, their eyes closed. Seamus's hands kept a respectful pace, gripping her tightly at the hips, until she grabbed them and lowered them to her ass. He pulled her tightly against him. She wasn't surprised at all to feel his erection through her poncho.

"Hello, old boy," she said with a laugh.

"Uh, yeah," he grinned in the moonlight. "He missed you, too."

Seamus stepped back and pulled his rugby shirt over his head, then bent and whipped his pants down to his ankles, stepping deftly out of them and standing naked in front of her, a sea of stars twinkling behind him.

"You got room for two in that thing?" he asked, ducking under her poncho. He undid her jeans and slid them down her legs, holding the hem while she stepped out of each leg.

"You're not ripping my Clash shirt off," she said seriously.

"I can get you another one," he said, his face near her belly button, his whiskers grazing her skin.

"No, this one is special." She slipped it off without ditching the poncho. Seamus reached around and undid her bra, tossing it onto the deck. His head popped out of the opening, next to hers, and they stood there, her nipples grazing his chest, his penis poking her stomach gently. He moved closer and kissed her again.

"Thank you, Nico," he whispered in her ear.

"We shoulda bought one of these ponchos ages ago," she said huskily, leaning back onto the railing of the balcony.

"Don't rush this," she said. "Lift me up."

He raised her by the armpits and she wrapped her legs around his waist.

"I want to feel you. I want you all over me. Hold me."

She felt him slide all the way in, and his rough hands cupped her butt. He made his penis pulse, and winked at her.

"Don't spoil it," she laughed. "Seamus, this is serious."

"I won't."

"Just hold me. Be together with me."

"I've missed this." He moved slightly and Nicola groaned loudly. "Fuck it, Nico, I gotta . . ."

"No," she whispered. She hugged him so tight he could barely breathe, and they stayed locked together, kissing, their faces inseparable.

He held her aloft for several minutes, then he carried her, still inside her, into the bedroom. He turned his back to the bed and carefully sat, then rolled her onto her back. He tried to reach for her face, but his hands were caught inside the poncho.

"Can we take this thing off now?" he asked. "I want to touch your face. This stupid blanket keeps getting in the way."

She kissed the tip of his nose. "I'm in no rush," she said with a smile. "The blanket stays on."

CHAPTER 22

BILLY LOOKED AT THE TIME on his phone. It was almost eight a.m., and Sandy had not arrived at the office yet. Everybody else had to be at work by seven on Mondays, but Sandy always had an excuse. Kara had snuck Mason into her apartment yesterday afternoon, and according to a text late last night, she'd somehow convinced him that Billy could be trusted. *Spyglass* was going to run the first ever anti–Felicity Storm story. Meredith Cox was going to lose her shit, which would make Nicola happy.

Via Kara, Mason assured him that "an earth-shattering exclusive" was destined to land in his e-mail around nine a.m. Sandy had spent the weekend checking out a new hotel in Laguna "for work" and had told him not to text her. The last he'd heard from her, on Saturday, was a text that informed him she was scheduled for a "full-bush Brazilian with small-batch wax." He'd been grateful not to hear from her for the rest of the day.

He'd been less grateful that none of his messages to Nicola had been marked "delivered," meaning that she had actually gone offline in Mexico. He'd even tried to have Bluey text Seamus to see if he could get a message through. Sandy had promised that she'd fire Billy if he didn't have a Seamus exclusive this week, and he was starting to believe her. "Let her fire you," was Bluey's response, which was easy for him to say—he'd just gotten a lucrative promotion back onto Seamus's team. But Billy had argued that he hadn't worked there long enough to qualify for unemployment and he wasn't going to let Bluey support him. Thirty seconds later, Bluey magically provided him with Bette's cell number. Billy cold-called her, explained that he was good friends with Seamus and he needed a setup story. Unsurprisingly, Bette had loved the idea.

"Okay, make sure you print that you guys had a reporter corner me in the bathroom at Laurel Hardware," she'd whispered conspiratorially. "Let me think, what can the quote be? How's this? You guys can say that I told your reporter, 'Seamus is a great guy. We've only just started dating, so it's early days yet. I don't want to curse it by saying anything more.' Is that okay? Just make sure you say that a reporter talked to me in the bathroom so I don't get in trouble. What photography are you going to use?"

Within ten minutes, Bette had e-mailed Billy a selection of her favorite WireImage photos of herself. She then texted that if *Spyglass* wanted to use that quote, they had to use one of her suggested photos. Billy had agreed, knowing that Sandy would balk at having to pay the more expensive WireImage rate instead of the cheaper paparazzi rate. It was worth it for a "Bette Tells All" cover inset.

The sound of chaotic bumbling from the hallway told him his boss had arrived. He stepped out to see Sandy, clad in her favorite vintage Cynthia Rowley dyed-beaver coat, jeggings, and leather slides, doing her usual juggling act—a too-large purse, her Venti half-caf sugar-free extra-hot upside-down caramel macchiato, the morning New York newspapers, and her pair of self-described "fuck me" boots in case she had a meeting with advertisers.

When he was sure she'd be settled at her desk, he picked up his pen, notepad, and thermos of coffee, which Bluey made for him every morning, and headed her way.

"Billeeeeeeeee," she whined as he came in. "They said that the artisanal wax would make it hurt less." She was wrestling a large embroidered cushion onto the seat of her Aeron office chair. "My ladygarden hurts so bad, and not in a good way."

Sidestepping that information completely, Billy pulled up a guest chair and crossed his legs, using them as a table for his notepad.

"So you had a good weekend in Laguna?"

"Does it look like I had a good weekend, you big silly?"

Billy shrugged, still refusing to get drawn into a discussion about Sandy's painful waxing.

"Actually," she continued, "I ran into Audrina Patridge and some of her friends. I don't remember their names because they weren't on *Laguna Beach* or *The Hills*, but anyway, they're going to tweet about my book and Pin it and Snap it."

"And what does Audrina get?"

"You're so cynical, Billy."

He sat silently.

"Fine." She rolled her eyes. "She is going to be our guest beauty blogger four times a year."

"Well, that's her free makeup taken care of for the foreseeable future."

"Like it's coming out of your pockets, Billy. Why you gotta hate?"

"I don't gotta hate, Sandy, but I do gotta talk to Mason Dwyer in twenty minutes. I am confident that by the morning meeting, I'll have a cover story that will blow the New York office out of the water."

"That's my protégé," she said proudly before dropping to a weird basso voice. "The current cover is another Zina Zandrian story, about her and her sister."

"Please tell me it doesn't say 'stabbed in the heart.'"

Sandy looked ruffled. "Well, it does at the moment, but it's early. It's probably just a placeholder."

"Unless she's actually been stabbed in the heart by Zora, we probably shouldn't use that cover line. And anyway, I have your story. I just need an hour."

"What else you got for me?"

"I got your cover chip. Exclusive quotes from Bette Wu on her relationship with Seamus."

"Get the eff out," Sandy said breathlessly.

"Yeah, I talked to her last night."

"But it's on record, not sources say?"

Billy nodded.

"I'd get up and hug you, but seriously, I just got my little missus settled." Sandy grimaced and pointed at her crotch.

Billy prayed that the pain in her groin would be enough to distract her from what he was about to tell her. He realized he was nervous.

"So, the last thing to discuss is Kara Jones. There was a huge scene on Saturday, and Amber fired her."

"She's going to be double unemployed, then," Sandy said without skipping a beat. "We can't have a nobody in *Spyglass*."

"She's the reason we got Bette. She's still the best inside reporter we have."

"Oh, I doubt it," Sandy said, wincing as she leaned forward to grab her coffee. "Can you get us a new celebrity, like, this week?"

"Okay, I'll let her know," he said flatly. "I have to go prepare to deal with Mason. Do you want me to let you know what he says before we go into the morning meeting?"

"So dramatic," Sandy said, flapping her hands at him. "Get out. Let's keep it a surprise."

Billy went to his desk and sat down, trying to get his breathing under control. He hated Sandy so much; he hated her lack of integrity, her lack of empathy, her self-absorption, her casual racism, and her fucking mom jeans.

"I'm glad her pussy is wrecked," he said out loud in his office. His phone rang from a blocked number. He picked it up immediately.

"Hello?"

"Billy? Hey, man, it's Mason."

"Hey, Dwyer, thanks for calling."

"Listen, man, you at your computer? I'm going to e-mail you something. It'll come through from a stripped e-mail, no subject, no nothing. Open it."

"Okay."

Billy looked at his e-mail for a second, and instantly, a blank line appeared at the top of his inbox. No subject, no sender info. He clicked on it and the e-mail opened to a completely blank page.

"There's nothing there, Mason."

"Click on the attachment, Billy, and dude, do not screw me on this."

Billy scrolled to the bottom of the e-mail and there was the attachment, also untitled. He clicked it and a Word document opened on his screen. It was headed PRIVATE AND CONFIDENTIAL. PSYCHIATRIC ASSESSMENT HISTORY: FELICITY STORM.

"Mason, did you just send me Felicity's psychiatric records?"

"I didn't send them. You got them by yourself. Nobody knows we talked, right? You just got these by being a great reporter."

"Yeah, that's right," Billy assured him.

"Good, thanks, man. Listen, I gotta get off the phone, but long story short, you're gonna see that she's the crazy one. She's bipolar, she's schizophrenic, delusional, and also she suffers from borderline. She's a monster."

"Is she treated for any of this?"

"No, man, unless you count coke and Oxy."

"I don't. I can't print that. I don't even know if I can print this."

"You can, man. You can."

"Oh, so you're a lawyer now, too?"

"No, but my lawyer is the one who gave this to me."

"Of course," Billy said, an angry edge creeping into his voice.

"Look, man, I know it's a low blow, but you also know the stories she's been planting on me. At least these are the facts. This story is true. I'm doing it as a favor for Kara. She says you always take care of her, and she needs a friend right now."

Billy gripped his phone. He wanted to beat Mason with a rusty pipe.

"Thanks, *man*," he said, and hung up.

He sat there, feeling sick to his stomach. There was no way he could pretend he did not have this story. Sandy would have told the head office that he was bringing in a strong cover story. The thought of printing the medical history of a legitimately mentally ill celebrity made him nauseous. And he got this story as a favor from Kara, whom he was about to let down big time. He texted Bluey.

I hate my job.

He answered immediately.

Is it worse than buying hooker nuns for Max?

Yeah. Exploiting the mentally ill for a cover story.

Kara got a cover? ☺

Billy laughed in spite of himself.

No, babe. It's bad. You at home tonight?

Yeah, do you know what time you're finishing?

No. It'll be late, but knowing that you'll be waiting for me will make it much better.

I'll be keeping the bed warm mate. Promise.

✳ ✳ ✳

The corner of Billy's laptop screen said it was four forty-five p.m., the dead zone in the production cycle of every issue. The Felicity Storm story had passed the lawyers and was definitely the cover story. The rest of the pages were laid out, and it was a waiting game to see if the stories were legally approved, or worse, if a big story broke at the last minute. Until either of those things happened, everyone sat at their computer and posted on social media or watched crap on Netflix.

The current cover line, pending lawyer approval, was "Crazy in Love: Felicity Storm's Mental Illness Battle," with a photo of the actress that staff artists had been working on all day, adding blotchy skin, bags under her eyes, and wrinkles. If this didn't push Felicity over the edge, nothing would. Billy had been forced to file several "insider" quotes about Storm's "crazy behavior on the set of her latest movie" as well as one that incorporated several distasteful morsels of information from Mason.

This wasn't the job he'd signed up for. He felt disgusted with himself and couldn't shake the feeling. He considered giving his notice and returning to the freelance party circuit. Hanging out in nightclubs and trawling the celebrity trash for leads didn't sound as good as a night on the couch with Bluey.

He was unemployable.

Nicola had popped up on Messenger, saying that all was well in Mexico and that she wanted to see him soon, and that Seamus had the flu or something, so they'd been able to leave Rosarito right after the interview with *Entertainment Tonight*.

His phone call with Kara had been a disaster. A brief, angry call that ended with her screaming, "Thanks for fucking nothing, ass-hole," and hanging up on him. All things considered, it could have gone worse.

He looked at the time again. It was now 4:51. He decided to start *Downton Abbey* for the sixth time.

"Oh, Grandmama, I couldn't possibly," he said in a posh English accent as he logged into his Netflix. *Downton* was the first thing he saw, in his "recently watched" section. He clicked it and then selected season one, episode one, slipped his Bluetooth earbuds in, and sat back, a happy smile on his face.

Lord Grantham hadn't even told the family that cousin Patrick had gone down with the *Titanic* when Billy's phone began to buzz on his desk. He jumped, startled, when the word BIOMOM appeared on the screen. He'd added it after the last call. He paused *Downton* and slid the answer button across without thinking.

"Hi, Mom," he said warily. Nobody replied. He waited and heard a muffled rustling. "Mom? Are you there?" The silence continued. He figured his mom had butt-dialed him, and he was about to hang up when she finally spoke.

"William." As soon as he heard her voice he knew something was wrong.

"Yes, Mom."

"William." She burst into tears. "We lost Poppa today. He's gone."

Billy sat there, and a dull numbness started in his toes and hands and spread inward.

"Mom, I . . . didn't know it was that bad . . ."

"Neither did we, William. This came out of nowhere. Doc says it must have been something else, something the tests didn't even pick up."

Billy looked around his office, searching for comfort in anything, something to take his mind away from the conversation.

"Mom, I'm so sorry," he said finally.

His mother cried into the phone. Billy blinked. His eyes remained dry. He looked left and right, as if the tears might be hiding somewhere. Nope.

"Mom, when's the funeral?"

"I don't know, William. Friday?"

"Do you want me to come home?"

"William, the whole family will be there. It's gonna be at the Christ Evangelical Lutheran."

"So that's a no," he said, anger rising in his chest.

"I just thought you should know, son. I'm gonna go now."

And she was gone. Billy took a deep breath and waited to feel something for his father, but his heart was just full of anger at his mother.

He was overcome by a wave of confusion. He didn't know what to do. He closed his laptop and slid it into his Jack Spade messenger bag, then shoved his car keys into his pocket. He walked stiffly along the corridor. He paused at Sandy's office to tell her he was leaving, but she was taking selfies, her back to the door, so he kept on moving. He made it to his car in a daze, tumbling into the front seat and just sitting there for a minute. He took out his phone and sent a text to Nicola.

Hey sis come to Bluey's as soon as you're back. I just joined the dead dad club.

And one to Bluey:

Babe. You home? I'm on my way. Waze says 49 minutes. My dad died. I'll need a hug and a drink. Not necessarily in that order.

He started the car and listened to the Waze lady tell him which turns to make. He could hear pings as texts came in, and four times calls came in that he ignored. He just needed to make it home.

CHAPTER 23

BLUEY GREETED BILLY AT THE door with a bunch of flowers and a martini. Billy's heart melted, and he closed the door behind him, leaving his satchel on the floor. He took the flowers and the drink and put them both on the old oak dining table.

"I didn't know how to wrap a hug," Bluey said, stepping forward and enveloping him, pulling Billy's head to his chest. Billy breathed in a mix of Bluey, his sweater, and the candles that were burning around the guesthouse. He wondered if the tears would finally come, but instead felt a wave of happiness.

"How you doing, sunshine?" Bluey asked.

"That's the thing." Billy pushed out of the hug slightly so he could talk. "It's like someone just told me that the actor from a sitcom I watched when I was twelve died."

"You've been in Hollywood too long, mate."

"No, it's not that. It's not a fame thing; it's just the same level of detachment, like, oh, that happened, but it's not really going to impact my life in any real way."

"You're probably in shock," Bluey said, running his hand over Billy's tousled hair.

"I guess I could be," Billy said, hoping that it was true. His lack of response was starting to trouble him.

"And also, mate, you don't have to be. These people checked out of your life a long time ago, so maybe you did your grieving then."

"Back then grieving would have made more sense." Billy straightened and gave Bluey a kiss. "I was a teenager; they wanted me out. I went to Nicola's, and Mom2 just treated me so nice. I'd never known that. It didn't hurt so much at the time because I went somewhere better. So I didn't really grieve then, either."

"I talked to Seamus. I can get some time off to go home with you for the funeral."

Billy tensed up and immediately Bluey picked up on it. "What?"

"So, uh . . . they kind of don't want me to go home for it."

"Ah fuck, Billy. Baby, still because of the gay thing?"

"Yeah, that good old religious rejection of family."

"They're not your family."

"I know, they're not. But you know what? As soon as she said it, even as the words were coming out of her mouth, I expected it. And the worst part is, all of a sudden, I was thirteen again. I was as vulnerable to being rejected by my parents as I was then. But there's a difference now. I'm older. I know more than she does. And so I got angry. I'm angry now. At them both, even though he's dead. Why even bother telling me? They stopped having a son fifteen years ago. How come I didn't get to stop having a father?"

And then the tears came, long, angry, shuddering sobs that felt like they were being torn from the bottom of his stomach. Tojo the cat began to rub around Billy's legs as Bluey clutched him and they stood there, holding tight, until the tears subsided.

"I think I got snot on your sweater," Billy mumbled into Bluey's chest.

Bluey kissed the top of his head and rubbed his strong hands up and down Billy's back. Billy heard footsteps on the stairs outside.

"It's not locked," Bluey called out, and the door opened. Billy turned slightly to see Nicola, her face frozen in worry, spill into the room holding a huge bouquet of flowers. Seamus followed close behind, carrying a handle of gin.

"Welcome to the dead dad club," she said, dropping the flowers on the love seat and rushing toward him, her arms open.

"I'm not crying because I'm sad," Billy said, turning from Bluey's arms to his best friend's. "I'm crying because I'm angry."

"So be angry," Nicola said, pulling Billy into a hug. With her heels on, she was slightly taller than him, and Billy had always loved her hugs. "Who you angry at?"

Billy heard Bluey and Seamus leave the room.

"Where'd they go?"

"They had to bring our bags in," she said. "So who you angry at?"

"Guess who didn't make the invite list for his own father's funeral?"

"Fuck that bitch," Nicola said. "Your biomom is still such a reptile."

Billy laughed. That had been one of the first things Nicola had said to him after they'd moved in—that his mom was like an alligator who laid her eggs and then never saw her offspring again.

"Shit," Billy said suddenly. He'd forgotten to text Sandy. He pulled out his phone, and sure enough, the screen was a jumble of all-caps demands from his boss.

Hey Sandy my dad died. Sorry had to leave.

He hit send just as Bluey and Seamus returned, hauling all the luggage from the Mexico trip.

"How you doing, Bill?" Seamus came over and hugged him.

"I'm all right, actually," Billy said, realizing it was true. "It feels like Valentine's Day in here with all these flowers." He went to the table and picked up the martini that Bluey had made for him. "You aren't gonna make a semi-orphan drink alone, are you?"

Seamus picked up the bottle of gin he'd brought in and went into the kitchen.

Bluey walked over to Nicola. "You guys got back in okay, I see?"

"Yeah, thanks to you." She punched Bluey in the arm.

Billy shook his head. "What's going on?"

Nicola pointed into the kitchen. "I guess no matter how famous you are, you're not going to get across the US border without your passport."

"I forgot it, big deal. Like, the guy could literally look out the window and see a billboard with my face on it."

"A movie that you apparently also forgot that you even made," Nicola said, laughing.

"I didn't forget I made it, lass. I made it so long ago that I forgot it hadn't been released yet." Seamus wrapped his arms around Nic.

"Whatever," Nicola said, nuzzling her face into his arm. "It's just more work for me. My first Seamus junket. Yay."

"What the Ross-and-Rachel is going on here?" Billy said, a smile spreading across his face.

"Oh yeah," Seamus grinned. "I guess Nico forgot to tell you—she begged me to take her back."

Nicola turned and slugged Seamus in the stomach, then turned back to Billy.

"Who are you gonna believe?"

"You, always, but I don't care. You happy?"

"Getting there," Nicola said as Seamus wrapped his arms around her again.

"Well, it's lovely to have some good news." Bluey walked out of the kitchen with four martinis on a tray.

"Put that one down, mate," he said to Billy, pointing at his drink with his chin. "I made you a fresh one. Or you can tip it onto the floor for your old dad."

"Oh, shit, I forgot about him for a minute. Nah, he ain't worth the mop-up." Billy brought his martini to his lips and drank the whole thing. "Waste not, want not."

They each took a drink, and Bluey put the tray on the table. They raised their glasses.

"Who are we gonna toast?" Bluey asked Billy.

"Let's toast to trust. And to Seamus making Nicola as happy as Bluey makes me."

Billy saw tears in Nicola's eyes as their glasses all met.

"Can we sit down now?" he said nervously. Seamus and Nicola took the love seat, her on his lap, so Bluey and Billy took the big couch. Billy sat back and kicked his Sperry boat shoes off and leaned against his boyfriend.

"I have two questions," he said. "One, how did you get back to-gether, and then how the hell did you smuggle him back into the US?"

"I'll take this one," Seamus said, nuzzling Nicola's neck with his nose.

"You two are sickening," Bluey said with a smile.

"Have you seen yourselves?" Nicola laughed.

"Fair point," Bluey said, ruffling Billy's hair again.

"Simple answers, Bill," Seamus said. "I owned up to my mess and I promised never to lie again."

Billy's eyes widened, and Seamus caught him out.

"I also agreed to drug testing."

"So romantic, right?" said Nicola.

"Every month I'll put the results in a Hallmark card if it helps," Seamus joked.

"So let me get this straight," Billy said, waving his martini theatrically in the air. "Seamus, you are now secretly dating the woman who's orchestrating your fake relationship?"

"More than dating, I'd say."

"And Nicola, you're now dating your biggest client, all the while deceiving his fans with a media-lightning-rod relationship that's not even real."

"The capacity for lying and duplicity does suggest that I'm finally a real publicist," she said chirpily. "Deception is the name of my game."

Billy shot Nicola a vaguely disparaging look.

"I know, I know," she said quickly. "It sucks and it's fake, but what the hell are we going to do?"

"I really don't see a problem," Seamus said. "I'll tell Bette about it. I mean, for fuck's sake, she's engaged to someone else."

"She IS?" squealed Billy.

"You can't print it," Nicola said.

"Wasn't gonna," Billy said. "After today, I don't want to print anything ever again."

Seamus raised an eyebrow. "Should I be nervous?"

"Seamus, there are other actors in the world. Just be grateful that you're not Felicity Storm, who's gonna see her psych records on the *Spyglass* cover on Wednesday."

"You didn't," Nicola said. "I wanted to kick Meredith Cox's ass. That's gonna do a little more than kick it."

"I had to, and I feel disgusted about it. The best thing my dad did was die at the right time so that I didn't have to make that phone call."

"Which one?" Seamus asked, oblivious.

"The phone call to her representative," Nicola said. "Every publicist sits in fear of getting one on a Monday evening. It usually goes, 'Oh, hey, we got photos of your client doing something shitty, can you comment?'"

"That really happens?" Seamus asked. "People actually bother to call to see if a story's true?"

"Legally, you have to," Billy explained. "And how the hell can you not know this?"

"It's not my job," Seamus said innocently.

"No, it's mine," Nicola said. "For you."

"That's stupid. As your client, I instruct you to either ignore them or tell them to fuck off."

"I can't do that."

"Yes, you can. There's no such thing as bad press."

"Ojai would have been bad press, boss," Bluey joined in.

Seamus went quiet. Nicola scrambled to fill the silence.

"And Bluey got us back into the US with a very expensive courier delivery of Seamus's passport."

"You sent a messenger from here to the Mexican border?"

Bluey nodded.

"And what did you guys do for the three hours it took for him to get there?"

"Oh, it was great," Nicola enthused. "We went back into Tijuana and explored the tourist area. Billy, you'd love it. All the kids are taking it over; there's fashion and art and like this whole renaissance happening."

"Yeah," Seamus said. "It was exciting. Nicola ate crickets."

"I don't want to hear about your weird sex life," Billy said.

Nicola screwed up her face. "They're tasty and crunchy, for bugs," she said. "Our security guy was flipping out that we were gonna get into trouble just walking all over the place, shopping and eating. Oh yeah, we bought you guys a present."

She got up and went to their luggage, tearing into a large, brightly colored shopping bag. She pulled out a massive, thick blue-and-white poncho. She draped it over Billy, his head popping through the hole in the center.

"A poncho? Just what I always wanted."

"It's for both of you," Nicola said with a sly grin. "You'll figure it out."

✳ ✳ ✳

Several hours later, after making sure that Kara was spending the night with Mason at a hotel, Seamus and Nicola called a car and left the boys alone. As he closed the door behind them, Bluey dimmed the lights and came over and kissed Billy lightly on the lips. He'd stopped drinking a while back, but Billy had had a few more martinis and he was curled up with Tojo on his lap.

Bluey went into the bathroom and started the water in the bath, bringing some candles in from the living room as the water filled the tub. He returned to the living room.

"Arms up," he said, and Billy raised his arms obediently. Bluey pulled his shirt up over his head.

"Sorry, Tojo, you're gonna have to move." The cat made a long, low snarling sound as Bluey grabbed Billy's arms and lifted him to his feet.

"Hold on to my shoulders," he instructed as he unbuckled Billy's jeans and slipped them down. He held Billy's hips as he shucked off the jeans, and led him to the bathroom. Bluey tested the water and then held Billy's hands as he stepped into the tub and sat down.

"Bluey, you take such good care of me," Billy said, surprised at the lump in his throat.

"I think we're a pretty good match, mate." Bluey stood behind Billy and started massaging his shoulders.

"Bluey, I don't care that my dad died. I tried to care, and I am just gonna come out and say it: I don't care. Like, it doesn't even suck. It doesn't even anything."

"Babe, I know we haven't been dating that long, but you've

changed my life. This is my family. You, me, and the cat equals home. This is where we belong."

"Don't make me cry again," Billy said, drunkenly splashing his hands in the bathwater. "I don't know what I did to deserve this."

"Let's make it official," Bluey said, and Billy's hands froze. He wondered if Bluey was going to propose to him.

"Huh?"

"I want you to move in here. I want this to be your actual home. I want us to live together."

"Sure," Billy said, relieved and disappointed at the same time. "We just need to get that pesky superstar to move out first."

CHAPTER 24

THE LOBBY OF THE PANTAGES was a blur of chatter and people, crowded and too bright. The sold-out *Hamilton* crowd spilled from the theater doors in search of booze, merchandise, or somewhere to smoke.

Crystal, clad in her usual tailored men's Gucci suit, wrapped her arm around Gaynor's waist and led her through the lobby and its press of people to the bar area.

"My god," she hissed. "The bar line is already a mile long."

"*Juepucha*, that can't be. I need a drink after that."

"It's not over," Crystal seethed. "This is intermission."

"Listen, *coño*," Gaynor said, squeezing her arm, "if I can't get three drinks inside me in two minutes, I can't go back in there. This isn't the future of Broadway. It's *Bye Bye Birdie* mixed with *Straight Outta Compton*."

Crystal chuckled and craned her neck to see if she could even locate the end of the alcohol line. Two young women appeared in the crowd, blocking their way.

"Excuse me, ladies," said one, a pretty post-teen in jeans and a *Hamilton* shirt. "Could I please take your photo?"

Crystal made to push past them, but Gaynor stopped her.

"But of course," she purred, fluffing out her pink, white, and purple Pucci cape and making sure her diamond choker was showing.

The girl pulled out her phone and snapped a photo.

"Thanks, ladies," she said, and her girlfriend pulled her away into the crowd. Before they vanished, Gaynor and Crystal both overheard the girlfriend say, "Oh my God, old dykes are the best; I hope we can be like that one day."

Crystal laughed, a dry, humorless sound like the creaking of an old house. "She thinks we're together," she said.

"I don't care what she thinks, as long as it inspires her to stop dressing like a construction worker at the theater," Gaynor said. "Where's my Negroni?"

Crystal reached up under Gaynor's cape and gripped her arm, dragging her in the direction of the booze queue. As they approached, an usher raised her palms at them.

"Sorry, we're cutting off the line," she informed them. "No drinks inside the theater, and there's only ten minutes of intermission left."

Gaynor took a deep breath, and before she let the poor girl have it, Crystal deftly redirected them toward the doors that led to Hollywood Boulevard.

"Forget about this crap," Crystal said. "I have a better idea."

"It better be Musso and Frank," Gaynor said as she was hauled out onto the street.

Crystal didn't reply. She wove through the cluster of smokers, and Gaynor smiled broadly when she realized that Crystal was taking her to the Frolic Room, the dive bar next door to the theater. Over their many years of friendship, whenever they'd been on good terms, the Frolic Room was their place. They'd ended up there after one particularly romantic date in 1988, and it had remained a destination when they didn't want to fight. Crystal called it their demilitarized zone.

A line of booze-hungry *Hamilton* hopefuls crowded the door. Crystal shoved them aside.

"Move it; we are the owners," she barked to the startled crowd, and in seconds they were inside. The tiny bar was crammed to the rafters, and the sole bartender was frantically taking orders and making drinks.

Gaynor leaned across the bar and snatched up a bottle of tequila and a metal mixing spoon. She loudly chimed the spoon against the bottle.

"Ladies, gentlemen, the curtain for act two will rise in sixty seconds," she called out above the din, and the place erupted as patrons threw back full drinks and pushed to the exit.

The bartender, a solid woman in her fifties, glared at Gaynor and walked over.

"You just cost me a fortune, you crazy bitch," she said, snatching the bottle back from Gaynor, who produced a purse from inside the folds of her cape, flipped it open, and pulled out a roll of hundreds. She peeled off one bill and handed it to the woman.

"This is for three Long Island Iced Teas," she said with a smile. Before the woman had a chance to respond, Gaynor pulled another note from the roll and slid it alongside the one still resting in the woman's palm.

"And this is for your troubles. My name is Gaynor, what's yours?"

"Elliott," she said.

"Shake my damn hand, Elliott, and then get on with making the drinks, please. One of them is for you. Please join us."

A gruff laugh emerged from Elliott, but it didn't touch her eyes. She crumpled the bills in her fist and then pushed them into the pocket of her black jeans. She gave Gaynor's outstretched hand a quick one-two pump and moved down the bar to start making their drinks.

"Do you always have to be so theatrical?" Crystal sighed, her eyes rolling.

"You sound like my sons," Gaynor said, digging in her purse for something. "Do we have to go back inside that theater?"

"We don't have to do anything, you old fool," Crystal said, struggling to find a comfortable perch on her barstool, her chunky heels slipping on the bar floor.

"*Magnifico*," Gaynor smiled, producing a yellow pill bottle from her purse and setting it on the bar with a flourish. Crystal's eyes widened slightly as she read the label.

"Quaaludes? You still have Quaaludes?"

"You know I stocked up when they went off the market."

"That was in 1984."

"A good year. I invested in Quaaludes and a vacuum safe. These little beauties are fresh as a daisy."

Gaynor popped the cap off the bottle, then delicately placed three pills on a bar napkin.

"You're giving one to the bartender?"

Gaynor cast her eyes around the dive bar.

"Look where the poor bitch has to work every night. She deserves it."

Crystal shrugged absently as Elliott returned with two balloon glasses full of brown liquid. She set them in front of the women, and then returned with the third glass.

"I would never be so rude as to ask your age," Gaynor said. "But I wonder if you remember Quaaludes."

Elliott's eyes glazed over in memory and she smiled.

"Honey, I had some wild times on those puppies when I was a teenager. Haven't thought about them in years."

Gaynor dropped her eyes to the napkin and back to Elliott.

"Shut up," the bartender said loudly, her voice still gruff.

Gaynor picked up one of the pills, using her long burgundy nails like chopsticks. She held it aloft, waiting for the other women to follow suit. When all three pills were raised, she nodded.

"To fun," Gaynor said. "And to being the last generation who knows how to have it."

She dropped the pill into her mouth and took a flamboyant sip of her cocktail. Crystal and Elliott locked eyes and did the same.

"I probably shouldn't have done that," Elliott said. "This place gets crazy busy when the play gets out."

"By that time you'll be ready for them," Gaynor laughed.

In the darkness at the end of the bar, a guy raised his empty glass at Elliott.

"My people await," she said ruefully. "I'll come check in on you two in a minute. And thanks, I think."

"*De nada*," Gaynor said, leaning in close to Crystal's ear. "We need to talk," she said.

"So talk."

"Meredith is gunning for my agency," Gaynor said with a sudden seriousness that caught Crystal by surprise. There was no trace of a

Colombian accent. She sounded like a New Yorker. Crystal recognized that as a sign that Gaynor was being honest.

"You told me already," Crystal drawled, finishing half her cocktail in a single drag.

"And you're next."

Crystal set her drink down slowly. "Are you sure?"

Gaynor nodded, her cloud of blue-black hair bouncing around her face. "I asked my psychic."

"Oh good." Crystal snatched her drink back up and polished it off. "I'm glad we have concrete proof."

"She signed Amber. And Nicola just texted me that Meredith has requested a meeting with her."

"Nicola told you that Meredith's after us?"

"No. God bless her, that girl is trying to solve this mess on her own. This is a benefit of having Bluey on my payroll now."

Crystal waved two skeletal fingers at Elliott. "More drinks, stat," she called. "Why are you in Meredith's crosshairs?"

"I don't really know. That bitch is a big-game hunter; she wants to have all of the A-list trophies mounted on her wall."

"Seamus is the only A-lister on your roster. Shouldn't she have come after me first?"

"Don't flatter yourself," Gaynor cackled. "It's Kara's fault. She made a sex tape with Tom Kendall."

Crystal spat her cocktail. "That thing would make a fortune." She felt the pill working. "They could have called it *The Devil in Miss Jones*."

"Remember we saw that movie?" Gaynor said with a hoot.

"Vaguely," Crystal said dismissively. "I'm surprised Jones survived."

"Well, so far, she's alive, but her career is *verkakte*. Do not resuscitate. Finished."

"She got off lightly," Crystal said. "Were you ever able to find out what happened to that one girl who went missing, the one who got pregnant by Cory Fisher?"

"Do you think I have the cartel on speed dial?"

Crystal shrugged. "She'll never get Seamus," she said eventually.

"Not without Nicola." Gaynor shook her head. "So she asks for a meeting and offers her the world."

"Have you talked to Wallace about this?"

"Indirectly. She is loyal like nobody else of her generation."

"But everybody has a price."

"Normally I would agree with you, but that one, I want to meet the mother, because whatever she did, that's how I want my boys to turn out. She cares. Young people don't care about anything but being the first person to make a meme, pizza, and *The Simpsons*. She's not like that."

They paused as Elliott returned with two drinks.

"Nothing for you this time?" Gaynor said, plying her with another hundred-dollar bill.

Elliott inhaled deeply and blinked twice.

"I think the pill is coming on," she said with a wink. "I need to keep my shit together."

"Don't we all?" Crystal said darkly, snatching up her drink.

"So what's your plan of defense?" she asked when they were alone again. "Give Nicola a pay raise?"

"Oh no, your dementia's worsening," Gaynor said angrily. "I don't save myself on the back of one person. It's bad enough that I'm surviving on my retainer from O'Riordan. The answer is to be smarter."

"Okay. I'll bite. How does the old dog outsmart a wolf?"

Gaynor's eyes closed and reopened slowly as the first tingle of the Quaalude hit her system.

"The old fame is dead," she said grandly. "The kids don't need it anymore. They don't need rock 'n' roll, they don't need illusion, and they don't need magic."

Crystal saw a fiery sadness enter Gaynor's eyes as she spoke.

"Our business is changing. The world doesn't want to believe that celebrities are special anymore. They want their stars to be boring and average and just like them. What we do, taking money from people in exchange for getting them press, that's dying, too. They don't need us. They can go on Instagram and put up a photo and the *Washington Post* will message them directly for a quote."

"Yes, dear," Crystal said, her voice throaty. "We've discussed this. But that's not all we do. We guide, we nurture, we keep the flame burning, often for years after it should be extinguished."

"Do your clients do what you tell them to do anymore?"

Crystal paused and then shook her head.

"Right. So we diversify. We look at where fame is now, on the Internet, on YouTube channels and vlogs and blogs and whatever the hell they'll call it next week."

"Those people don't need publicists."

"Wrong. They need our taste. Our exquisite, refined taste. Otherwise, it's all shit they copy off *Drag Race*. Alicia got over a half million likes this week. She will be as big as Beyoncé in a year. And she has no talent. So we find the right people, the right markets, and we pour ourselves in, and we stay rich."

"So you're saying we become managers?"

"Star makers. We are the new studio system. We are a production line of today's fame. Do you have any idea how much those kids can make? Twenty percent of that is a lot more than any of our clients pay us."

"I knew you were up to something," Crystal said, a note of admiration in her voice.

"I had Kara ready to launch this week. I went with Alicia instead."

"I saw. When are you going to finally launch Kara?"

"You can't save everybody," Gaynor said sadly. "Crystalita, how many girls like her have we known?"

Crystal chuckled.

"Too many, and before you say it, yes, I know there's a million more of them headed our way, in their dusty Honda Civics, crawling across the desert, posting Instagram stories from every truck stop."

Crystal smiled lazily. She had always loved Gaynor's boastful nature when she was loaded.

"It's too bad for Kara; she's a nice kid. I'm gonna have her help out in the office, see what pans out. She's boning Mason Dwyer. I told her that the only things that can save her career are him proposing or knocking her up. If either of those things happen, she can be a judge on *America's Got Talent* by Christmas."

"Even when you're high, you're ruthless."

"I had a good teacher." Gaynor rested her hand on top of Crystal's. "I still do."

"No need to get maudlin," Crystal said, snatching her hand away. "Why do I feel like I am getting hijacked here?"

"Because you're smart and you know me. I'm saving your own ass. We need to pull together."

"Keep your enemies closer?"

"Please stop that act." Gaynor put her hand back on top of Crystal's. "We've never been enemies, but now is the time to drop the old routines. I want to combine forces and figure out how to come through this bigger, badder, and richer than before. Do you think that a bitch like Meredith could have threatened us ten years ago?"

Crystal shook her head. "Gaynor, did you spend all this money on *Hamilton* tickets just to get me alone, to ambush me with this? Because I'm too high to care about this shit right now. And I kind of want to go back in and see the second act."

"Here. Let me save you the time. He dies. Everybody raps. The end."

"I thought you loved musicals."

"Loved, *mija*. Past tense." Gaynor stretched her arms over her head, her patterned cape opening like a superhero's. "In our day they had musicals. Did I ever tell you I was in the Colombian production of *Hair*? Now, that was a musical. That's what brought me to New York City."

"I thought you floated into the city in a barrel."

"Both of those stories can be true at the same time, you bitch," Gaynor laughed. "I hate it that you remember everything."

Their fuzzy reverie was broken by the return of Elliott.

"Ladies, this shit is amazing," she said, licking her lips and looking around the bar wildly.

"And you know what will make it better?" Gaynor said, pulling another hundred off the roll. "Disco music on the jukebox, and you locking the doors so that we don't have to hear about the future of Broadway."

CHAPTER 25

LOST IN THOUGHT, SEAMUS WONDERED how long he'd been sitting on Bluey's couch. An Uber had returned him from Nicola's place around eleven. Bluey had greeted him with fresh juice and a box of pastries before taking off to do their laundry. Seamus's croissant sat untouched on the coffee table. Bluey always stayed to do the laundry in person. Seamus had told him to leave it with the lady, but the last time he'd tried that, Seamus's underwear had appeared on eBay.

"That was Beverly Hills," Seamus had argued. "That won't happen here, right?"

"Can't be too careful, mate," Bluey had replied. "Highland Park is Beverly Hills East these days."

The mailman had just delivered Bluey's first check from the studio. He was officially working for Seamus again. Crystal hadn't even tried to keep him. "I don't blame you," she'd said. "I'm sorry I made you do such appalling things for Max." Bluey had made Crystal laugh for the first time ever by joking that at least he hadn't had to dress like a nun and watch Max jerk off, unlike Gaynor.

Seamus drew his knees up to his chest and wrapped his arms around them. It felt like he'd brought a cold back from Mexico. He considered asking Bluey to bring him some wheatgrass juice. He pulled out his phone and texted him.

Seamus coughed painfully. He ached, his head pounded, and he looked lousy.

"Just fucking have me, then," he said to the cold. Tojo looked up from his perch among some succulents by the window, then gave his paw a good lick. Seamus groaned as he leaned over and picked his phone off the coffee table. He stared at the blank screen, willing Nicola to text him, but the screen stayed blank.

He was due to go to dinner with Bette at Madeo, but he was

leaning toward canceling, even though he knew she'd be angry and Weatherman would be furious.

He'd received an e-mail from Tobin this morning, outlining his various production dates for the movie in Mexico and saying that they'd asked him to present an Oscar. He had angrily replied that he didn't want to go to the Oscars.

You do recall that the gifting suites are tax free? Tobin had replied.

I think Bette is doing well enough out of this without thousands of dollars' worth of free crap.

Seamus, don't make me beg. It's the Oscars.

I'm never gonna win one, so handing them out isn't terribly rewarding, Tobin. It's a hard pass.

Nicola will talk to you about it later. You can let her down if you want.

That's dirty pool, Tobin. Also, I have the flu. Going back to bed.

He'd been sulking ever since. He'd been to the Oscars twice and presented once. It was a boring clusterfuck; too much hassle for not enough spark. The time he presented, he'd been so high on Oxy he didn't actually remember giving the award. The next day, *People* magazine had praised his "effortlessly sexy demeanor" as one of the night's highlights. He'd been mortified. That was in the early days of his drug use, when he hadn't known what he was doing. As his mind wandered, something inside him flashed warmly to that feeling when the Oxy kicked in, reminding him of those peaceful, comfortable times, that warm numbness, and he felt himself salivate.

"Fucking heck," he yelled, jumping to his feet. He'd caught himself slipping into a craving. "Fuck. Fuck. Fuck." He paced around the living room, wringing his hands together until he realized that he was doing something his mother used to do when she was upset, so he willed his hands to drop to his sides. They were shaking. The craving washed over him like a pang of homesickness and he walked to the window, looking out through the curtains at the pointy roofs of Highland Park, his twitchy fingers absently trailing through Tojo's fur.

He held a deep breath until his lungs were bursting. Releasing it, he walked to the kitchen, got himself a large glass of water, and chugged it. Shaking, he picked up his phone and called Bluey.

"What's up, mate?" he said, answering before Seamus heard it ring.

"Hey, uh, hi," Seamus began. "Listen, I just had a craving."

"Okay, calm down," Bluey said, his voice softening. "You did the right thing, you called me instead of acting on it. I want you to breathe. I want you to think about all the things you learned in treatment. I'm coming home."

"No, just talk to me for a minute," Seamus said. "The craving is subsiding. I think I just daydreamed my way into it. That doesn't even make sense. I'm sorry. I freaked myself out."

"Too late, boss, I'll be home in two shakes of a lamb's tail." Bluey hung up.

Seams angrily stripped off his clothes and ran the shower, dancing nervously from foot to foot as he waited for the water to warm up. He hoped that taking a hot shower was going to work as well as they said it would in rehab.

When Bluey got home ten minutes later, Seamus was still in the shower, with the water as hot as his skin could take it.

"I'm in here," he yelled.

"It's a small apartment, mate; I'll just follow the trail of steam. Where's the fire?"

Seamus pulled the shower curtain back and saw his friend, a worried look on his face, leaning in the doorway.

"I had a craving, Don, a bad one."

Bluey made a face.

"You called me Don—it must be serious."

Seamus killed the water, and Bluey handed him a fresh towel. He took it and roughly toweled his head. As soon as his face was dry, he paused.

"It wasn't even just a craving, it was like a physical pang, like something crashed inside me."

"That shit takes a while to leave your system, huh?"

"It's got to be gone by now. I haven't had anything at all since Ojai. We're getting on close to four months now."

"Has it passed? Do you feel it now?"

Seamus paused, standing in the shower with his head cocked to one side, conducting a mental check.

"Yeah, it's gone. At least I hope it is."

"Dry off and get out here." Bluey turned and left the bathroom. Seamus quickly toweled off the rest of his body and legs, wrapped the towel loosely around his waist, and walked into the living room.

Bluey jumped off the couch and pulled the heavy drapes across the window, plunging the apartment into near darkness and sending Tojo darting for the bedroom.

"I've told you, O'Riordan. Fully clothed at all times."

"Nobody knows I'm living here," Seamus said, flopping onto the couch that faced the window, with his legs open, deliberately flashing Bluey.

"And they'd need a damn good lens to make much of that, mate," he laughed. "Just listen to me. Make it easy on us for once. Let's save the drama for the real battles. Not another shitty nude-photos payoff."

"Wanna get us a couple whiskeys?"

"I'd like nothing more."

Bluey vanished into the kitchen. Seamus picked up his phone. Nicola had been quiet for a couple of hours. There was a text from Bette.

I'll pick you up at 6. I'm coming in from Arcadia so you're on the way. :P

He sighed and sat back on the couch, tossing his phone down beside him. He really didn't want to go anywhere, much less with Bette.

Bluey handed him a heavy shot glass. "For God's sake, Seamus, cover yourself up."

"What's gotten into you? The two of us have been in more locker rooms and nude beaches than any two friends I've ever . . . . oh wait. Billy?"

"Yeah, it's weird, huh? I don't think he'd like it if I was sitting here with ya, balls out and all."

Seamus spread his legs even farther.

"He'll just have to get used to it," Seamus laughed. "How's he doing with the dad thing?"

"Seems right as rain," Bluey said. "He's a resilient little bastard. I don't even think it's gonna catch up with him down the way."

Seamus shook his head. "Kids these days, huh?" He took a sip of his whiskey.

"You feeling better?"

"Yeah, mate, I am. Maybe it was a panic attack?"

"They don't make it easy, these drugs," Bluey laughed.

"They sure don't," Seamus smiled. "Remember that time we figured out that Hot and Spicy Cheez-Its smell like cocaine?"

"Because they do."

"I'm gonna go out with Bette in a couple hours."

"I thought you were gonna cancel?"

"I just canceled the Oscars with Tobin. I figure she's a fair price to pay."

"I'll drive you there and wait."

"She wants to drive."

"Where you going?"

"Madeo."

"Excellent choice." Bluey fished his phone out of his pocket and punched some numbers.

"Hey, Marie, it's Donald Matson. Yeah, good to talk to you, too. Been too long. I need a table for one. Tonight? Yeah. Seven p.m. Not too close to the Wu table, but you know the usual deal. Clear eye line. Thanks, love. See you soon."

✳   ✳   ✳

Bette talked the entire slow drive from Highland Park to Beverly Hills while Seamus sat in silence. By the time they pulled into the valet line at Madeo, Seamus had heard every detail about the costume fittings and martial arts training that she was doing for a movie role she didn't even have yet.

He could not remember ever being that excited about a job, not even in the early days. He tuned her out for most of the drive, grunting his approval when she paused or saying "Cool, huh?" whenever he thought it worked. It didn't matter. Bette wasn't looking for his input anyway. He debated telling Nicola about the craving but decided against it. After flipping his phone over in his hands for several minutes he texted her that he would come to her place by nine.

As Madeo appeared in the distance on Beverly, he could see flashbulbs popping against its glass windows. He flipped down the sun visor to block any photos being taken through the windshield.

"We are gonna get hit hard," Bette said, an edge of excitement in her voice.

"You get out first, let the valet in, then as you walk around, I will get out and take your hand. Then we turn and walk straight in. Please don't pause or stop this time."

"You're such a spoilsport," Bette said as they pulled up and a group of photographers swarmed the car. A valet opened Bette's door and she got out and straightened her asymmetrical gray Tom Ford wool sable dress. She paused so that the photogs could get a full-length before she came around. Seamus timed it perfectly, emerging from the car head down, grabbing Bette's arm with fake angriness and practically dragging her inside. It made for better photos, Nicola had assured him.

Once inside the tiny restaurant, the maître d' greeted them both warmly and walked them to their table in the back. Bluey flashed a quick grin at Seamus as they walked by his table, and Seamus sat with his back to the street, so that only Bette would be in any long-range shots.

"I need to pee," he said as soon as they sat.

"You are like a little kid," Bette teased him. "If I didn't know better I'd say you were going in there to do blow."

"Well, you know better," Seamus said, more angrily than he'd planned to. He pushed away from the table and went to the bathroom. After he peed he texted Nicola again.

If I'm not at your place by 930, I'll be in jail for justifiable homicide.

Returning to the table, he saw that, once again, Bette had ordered cocktails for them.

"That doesn't look like Laphroaig neat," he said as he sat down.

"And you don't look like my sad uncle Chen and his boring whiskey drinks," she laughed, raising her glass in the air. He followed her lead and took a sip of his drink.

"What is this?"

"It's a whole new thing, whiskey with sarsaparilla root, some honey, some cloves. It's called the Cocaine Cowgirl."

Seamus took another sip. "I guess that's better than calling it a cocksucker or whatnot." He smiled.

"Have you talked to Weatherman at all?" Bette said, switching from starlet to businesswoman without warning.

"Not really; haven't had any need to. The deals are done for now. I'm getting all my instructions from Tobin. Why?"

"I don't know. I'm getting this weird feeling that they're kind of not managing this situation to its maximum potential."

"What do you mean?" Seamus relaxed back into his chair. This was gonna be good.

"Have you seen the response to us as a couple? It's only been a few weeks and our Q rating is sky-high. We have massive viewer appeal. I think that now is the time for us to sign up to do a movie together."

"I'm locked down to this movie for a year; they're shooting all three back to back."

"And I read the script, and there's a part for me."

"Then you need to be talking to the casting agent."

"Have you even read the script?"

"Why spoil the surprise?" He took another swig of his drink. It was very floral but better than he expected.

"Are you telling me you never read your scripts?"

"Are you telling me you do?"

"Of course I do." Bette got flustered. "Seamus, I dream of getting a shot at a good script."

"So the movie in Mexico has a good script?"

"It's formulaic, but it's decent. And you have a love interest."

"And you'd be perfect for it?"

"It's a small role, of course. Girlfriends always are. But if you told Weatherman, I bet he could make it happen."

"And how does that impact our deal?"

"I'm talking about strengthening it. I promise, you get me this, and we can become a once-in-a-while public couple; nobody will care."

"I'll ask him tomorrow."

"Or you could text him now."

"Or I could text him now."

Seamus picked up his phone and shot a quick text to Weatherman and Tobin.

I want Bette as love interest in Parallax.

"Done."

"Okay, so I was doing some research and there are a lot of ways we can go about being a fake couple."

Seamus looked into Bette's eyes. It made him sad to see an intelligent woman like her so desperate for fame.

"I'm all ears."

"Well, it depends on how frequently you want this. Do you want us out every week or other week, or do you want one month on, one month off? That works for some couples."

"I'd heard it was six months on, six months off for the big ones," he said, realizing he'd drained his drink.

"Right, but we're only doing this for a year, so we don't have that kind of leeway."

"What about one month on, two months off. We do that four times and the year is up."

"Well, your movie is going to take care of most of it. That's okay, I guess."

"You guess?"

"I want a trip to Scotland. I want the trip home."

"This isn't *The Bachelor*."

"No, but it's an excellent press op," she sniffed. "Imagine the photos! We could probably get the cover of *People*. Do you want another drink?"

"Not yet," Seamus grinned. He was feeling lightheaded and wanted to be sober for Nicola later.

"I have another suggestion," she said quietly.

"Yes?"

"What if I fake a pregnancy?"

Seamus screwed up his face.

"It's crazy, but other people have done it," she said. "So here's the deal. We get fake pregnant soon. I wear a fake tummy for like the second trimester. And then I lose it. We do a final round of press."

"Bette, no."

"Hear me out, Seamus. After the heartbreak of miscarriage is too much, we separate."

"Bette, you seem nice for long stretches of time, and then you sound absolutely insane."

"Hey, I'm just telling you what's worked for other people."

"And I'm telling you what won't work for us."

"Fiiiiiiiiiine," she said, signaling their waiter that they were ready for their menus.

After they'd ordered, a text came in on Seamus's phone. He read it, then leaned forward and took Bette's hand.

"Bette, I got you the gig in Mexico. Can I ask a favor in return?"

"Sure, my love," she said with an eager grin.

"I need to know if I can trust you."

"Yes, of course you can," she said without hesitating. "We're business partners, at least."

"Okay, well . . ." He paused. "I'm dating someone."

"Well, I hope she's fine with being in the background," Bette said sharply.

"She's much happier in the background. It won't be a problem."

"That's what you say now, but just you wait, in nine months when we are still doing this, I bet it's a problem."

"I could say the same thing about your fiancé."

"No, he knows the deal. He knows that this is the price we have to pay to have a good future. White girls don't know how to wait."

"How do you know she's white?"

"Isn't she?"

"Yeah, she's white. But she's different."

"Tell me who it is."

"If you tell anyone, I will end this deal."

"Don't be so dramatic, Seamus. What's her name?"

"It's Nicola, my publicist."

"What? She's dating Timothy Thompson, you idiot."

"You're not the only person fake dating someone."

"Oh shit, he's gonna be so pissed; he thinks he has this in the bag."

"And that's why he'll die an assistant agent," Seamus laughed. "Wait, you talk to Timothy?"

"Literally everyone will be so pissed," Bette said, ignoring the question. "Literally."

"I'm so used to that part. It's not a problem."

"And she's okay with this?"

"She understands it," Seamus said. "Look, Bette, it's really recent, and I didn't expect that she'd ever take me back."

"I *knew* she was your girlfriend," Bette said, as if she'd solved a murder.

"She was, you're right. And I fucked her over. So we'll be taking things very slowly. I'm not telling anyone. I'm only telling you because we're going to be working closely together for the next year, and I'd rather not be keeping secrets from you."

Bette gave Seamus a look that he didn't understand.

"What?"

"They said you're a really nice guy," she said quietly. "I didn't believe them. It sucks."

"What? That I'm a nice guy?"

"No, that you're the only one."

CHAPTER 26

THE NOISE OF GAYNOR'S TWINS arguing in the reception area overrode the music coming from Nicola's desk speakers. Grimacing, she turned it up. Again. She could still hear Patrick screaming at Sylvester, something about their upcoming fashion line. In the days since Gaynor had arranged for *Women's Wear Daily* to cover "the world's youngest fashion team," the twins had been working from a hastily arranged office next to the conference room, which they shared with Alicia.

Clicking open her iTunes, she scrolled down until she found her Ramones folder. She selected *Leave Home* and turned the volume up again, and immediately, her office filled with enough thick guitars to drown out a pair of screeching thirteen-year-olds.

She looked at her e-mail inbox and sighed. It was like a zombie swarm, and she felt overrun. *Smart mailboxes are bullshit*, she thought. *They're just harder to delete.*

Her meeting with Meredith Cox was an hour away. Since Meredith had summoned her to this meeting on Monday night, she had prepared thoroughly to discuss the fallout from Saturday. Gaynor had been focused on launching Alicia on her new plus-size beauty blog, *CholaBear*, all week. There was no point telling Gaynor about the meeting until she knew just how bad it was going to be. She sighed and looked at her calendar.

After the Cox meeting, she had to spend the afternoon with her sadistic client Brian Gregory at a premiere for yet another stoner buddy movie. The worse her mood, the easier it was to deal with Gregory. If she was a bitch, he was well-behaved. It was gross, but he was her most obedient client. And the premiere was at the Egyptian, so she could get takeout Chinese and walk home afterward.

An e-mail arrived in her VIP mailbox. It was Tobin. Someone at AMPAS had leaked to the press that Seamus had declined to be a presenter at the Oscars, so the wolves were at her door. He had heard rumors that people were suspicious about Bette. She rolled her eyes. She'd already dealt with this. She called Tobin.

"Hey, it's me. I can't talk long, but check your e-mail," she began.

"Nicola, always a pleasure."

"I've been giving on-record statements saying that it's a simple production conflict."

"Yeah, the studios have talked. They know that's not true."

"It's kind of true. And it's on record."

"So there's no chance he'll do it?"

"He's not into it, Tobin."

"Weatherman says he'll pay you a hundred thousand dollars if you can change his mind."

"Weatherman says a lot of shit."

"Not this time."

Nicola chewed her pen. Her mom earned forty-five thousand dollars a year. She scrunched her eyes closed.

"He ain't gonna do it. I think we've pushed him hard enough," she said through clenched teeth.

"Thanks, but keep on him, huh? The offer is real," Tobin said, clicking off. Nicola laid her head on her desk. Sometimes her job felt like a game show, and she had just lost again.

✳ ✳ ✳

The interior of the elevator that was speeding Nicola skyward was entirely brushed metal, reflecting blurry Nicolas in every direction she looked. When the doors opened, the reflective theme continued inversely: a black marble floor and dark smoked glass bounced Nicola's reflection back at her from everywhere she looked. In front of her, a logo was etched into the glass, and a young black woman in a classic charcoal wool suit sat at a desk that had nothing on it but a computer monitor.

"Why are you here?" the young woman asked abruptly. *She sounds like Siri, if Siri could get bored*, Nicola thought.

"I have an appointment with Meredith Cox."

The woman looked at her computer screen, then clicked a button on a mouse that was out of Nicola's sight.

"I have Nicola Wallace for you," she said into the air. Her eyes gazed left and Nicola spied a Bluetooth earpiece in her left ear.

"Yes, Miss Cox." The receptionist looked at Nicola. "Wait there."

Nicola stood, trying not to look nervous, for several minutes. Eventually a painfully thin young woman in a bland black jacket and skirt emerged from an invisible doorway within the black glass.

"Miss Wallace, follow me." She turned and walked back through the door without waiting. Nicola had to dart to catch the door before it closed. The woman did not turn around or slow down, and Nicola struggled to catch up to her as they passed an endless stream of assistants sitting at neat, bare desks outside walls of black glass that concealed the publicists working behind them. The place was eerily silent, and Nicola could hear her footsteps echoing back like gunfire.

The dark corridor stopped at a dead end, until the assistant opened a handle-less door in the black glass by pressing it inward. It clicked and swung open.

"Go in," the assistant said. Nicola walked through the door into an office that was as large as her living room, with glass walls that looked down over all of Hollywood and north to the Hills. She could see Yamashiro, the 101, and the Hollywood sign hovering in the haze. Couches ringed the walls, and through a smoky glass doorway she saw Meredith at her desk, a phone pressed to her ear.

Meredith gave her an unfriendly wave, ushering her in. Nicola stepped into Meredith's office, slate-gray carpet and walls. Meredith sat behind her desk, a vast, messy space with three laptops open. The area around the desk was a jumble of opened shipping boxes. Clothing, shoes, and makeup peeked out of packing peanuts and airpaks. Meredith was nodding furiously as the other person chattered. Nicola could make out that it was a woman speaking, but she could not understand what she was saying. Suddenly Meredith's thin lips drew even tauter and she reached down and took off one of her shoes, a peacock blue Jimmy Choo with a needle spike heel, and held it by her head.

"I'm going to stop you right there," she said into her phone. She stood up and inhaled deeply before speaking again. "None of that is going to happen. None of what you told me is true." She began hitting the heel of her shoe on the top of her desk, the rhythm keeping time with her words. "This is not a denial. This is not a 'no fucking comment.' This is an if. You. Run. This. Story. I. Will. Destroy. You." Her shoe smashed against her desk with the final word. "Are we clear, you pathetic little liar? Or do I get my lawyers onto you, and that cute new apartment you bought? Because you'll lose it to pay for your legal costs. Got it?"

The voice on the other end of the phone talked for another ten seconds, and then Meredith punched the disconnect button. She threw her phone down onto her desk and turned to the wall behind her and began slamming the heel of her shoe into the gray drywall, which was already pockmarked from previous heel-shaped impacts.

"RAT'S ASS VAGINA," Meredith screamed. "RAT'S ASS VAGINA."

She turned and looked at Nicola, her eyes red from the force of her screams. She bent and put her shoe back on.

"Take a seat, Wallace," she said, sitting down.

Nicola pulled a hard leather chair in front of Meredith's desk and sat, placing her purse on the floor beside her.

"You have such a great view," she said.

"Can it, for fuck's sake. I don't do small talk."

"Then let's get this over and done with. I assume I'm here to talk about what happened between Kara and Amber last weekend?"

"Who?" Meredith said, sucking on a vape box and exhaling a cloud of thick white gas. "I'm unfocused. You wouldn't believe the fucking shit I get from *Us Weekly* since they got sold. Oh, you have photos of my client doing coke? Congratu-fucking-lations. I have photos of your mom sucking the devil's dick. When will they learn that they will never win? These tabloid losers. I don't have this kind of shit from the *New York Times*. Whatever happened to journalism school? At least bloggers can be trained."

"To do what?"

"Anything I want, if I send them shoes." Meredith laughed bitterly. "Wait. What do you think you're here to talk about?"

"Kara Jones. My client."

"Nope. Not ringing a bell. She in movies?"

"You beat her up last week, then had Amber fire her on Saturday."

"Oh, is that what that was?" Meredith said, her mind still clearly elsewhere. "You mean the sex tape slut? Whores never learn. I didn't want to use violence, but she asked for it. Amber wanted her off the show, it was basic synergy. I love mixing business and revenge."

Nicola was confused. Meredith's agency counted most of Hollywood's hugest celebrities among its clients. Amber was both too low-brow and too low-income to be of much importance.

"I'm surprised you would go to so much trouble for a reality star."

"It wasn't that much trouble. The Roosevelt is just down the street."

"That's not my point."

"And it's not mine. Your whore client is not why you're here. I'm giving you a free lesson that most people would kill for. If you pass, I'll give you the job of your dreams."

"I'm too busy for this," Nicola said, standing to leave. Something flew past her ear and smashed into the wall behind her. A quick glance told her it was Meredith's shoe.

"Sit your ass down now; this won't take long."

"I don't work for you." Nicola stood. "And trust me, you won't beat me in a fight."

"Take one more step and I will destroy you, your whore client, and your junkie boyfriend."

"Lady," Nicola said, proud of the steel in her voice. "You say 'destroy' more often than I say 'hello.' I don't respond to threats. I don't respond to bullshit. And I don't respond to rude, disgusting people."

She turned and began to walk out of the office.

"Do you respond to the news that I monitored every step of Seamus

O'Riordan's little vacation in rehab? Seattle, Malibu, and even his little trip to Portland. I have it all. Photos, video, medical records."

Nicola froze in her tracks. Seamus went to Portland? She turned slowly.

"And what do you plan to do with that information? Release it to *Entertainment Weekly*?"

Meredith laughed, a sound like a lion eating a baby.

"Gimme a fuckin' break," she coughed. "Less than a thousand people read *Entertainment Weekly*. I use information to get what I want."

Nicola's mind raced. She decided to play neutral. "And what, precisely, do you want?"

Meredith made the same laughing sound, but her eyes narrowed. "Sit your ass down."

Nicola returned to the chair with deliberate slowness.

"If that shoe had hit me, I would have beaten the shit out of you," she said, locking eyes with Meredith.

"And I would have sued you back to Dayton. You'd be lucky to get a job as a car-wash checkout bitch when I was done with you. But luckily, it didn't come to that."

"Yet."

"I get it. You're feisty. Calm down." Meredith did a lopsided walk over to retrieve her shoe, then stood there by the window sucking on her vape box.

"I want you. Come and work here."

"No. Thanks," Nicola said steadily. A job interview was the last thing she'd expected this meeting to be.

"I repeat. Come and work here. Here's your little lesson: the business that supported your agency has stage-four cancer. You work for the way things used to be, a relic of another time. Gaynor Huerta doesn't just dress like it's 1974; she lives like it is. That's not how Hollywood works anymore."

"Cool lesson. Got it. New world order, you're the queen. I'm not looking for a job. Thanks."

Meredith stalked across the room and shook her vape box in Nicola's face.

"I am the meteor that killed the dinosaurs," she said, a vein appearing in her left temple. "I am the judge and the executioner and, honey, NOBODY FUCKS WITH ME."

"I didn't come here to *fuck* with you," Nicola said coldly, pushing the vape box away from her face. "I also didn't come here to listen to your delusional rants."

"What does she pay you? I will pay you three times that amount. Plus bonuses. Plus commissions. Your assistant will answer or ignore all your e-mail. You will receive more freebies than you ever dreamed possible. A hard day's work will involve screaming at someone from *People* for two minutes and then accompanying a megastar to a charity lunch. I'm offering you the fucking life."

"You know I'm not really a publicist, right? I fell into this job three months ago. Why me?"

"Why *not* you? You're tough. Your clients like you. One of them more than likes you, from what I hear. You'd fit in well here."

"There are hundreds of girls like me out there."

"No, there aren't. I'm not going to make this offer again. Do you want to end up like Gaynor, jerking off Max Zetta in a desperate attempt to keep him as a client? Or do you want to be the boss? That's right. We tell our clients what to do, and they listen. Come with me. Get rich. Leave that shitty rental behind and get a house in the Hills. Literally move in next month."

"I don't get it," Nicola said. "You're doing all this to get Seamus as a client?"

"The time of these boutique agencies is at an end. You're too young to remember. I'm a corporate raider. Remember when there were bookstores and toy stores and pet stores? Now there's Amazon. We are headed that way, and I'm at the tip of the iceberg. This is fun for me. We are talking exclusive studio deals, agency deals, synergy out the ass, and there's absolutely no room for this old-school bullshit. Come on, nobody wants to fucking jerk off their client for ten thousand a month."

"Crystal's getting nearly thirty."

"And she's not jerking him off. She's gonna be harder to destroy." Nicola saw a flutter of admiration cross Meredith's face.

"But you'll still destroy her?"

"Yeah, it's the name of the game. Those old broads are too stuck in their ways to adapt to this new world. They have to go."

"Those old broads gave me my start," Nicola said, standing. "And now I have to take a client to a red carpet, so I really must leave. Do NOT throw another shoe at me."

"I'll give you some time to consider my offer," Meredith said with an incongruously friendly smile. "You'd be happy here. My assistant will take you to my personal gifting suite. Please choose a couple outfits and some pairs of shoes. We'll deliver them to your office tomorrow."

"That won't be necessary," Nicola said. "But thank you." She got up and turned for the door.

"Tell your roommate that we're even now," Meredith said behind her, and Nicola froze again. "She messed with my client. No hard feelings."

Nicola walked out of Meredith's office without looking back, deciding on her way that she would choose clothing from the gifting suite and give it to Kara as payback.

She paused and smiled, turning back to Meredith.

"Hey, what about that *Spyglass* cover, huh? Karma and you aren't the only bitches in this town."

Nicola hurried out of the office before Meredith could respond, or throw a shoe.

CHAPTER 27

FOR THE SECOND DAY IN a row, Gaynor had called out of work. The mountains of deliveries in the reception area were approaching chest height. When Alicia heard Nicola swearing as she threaded her way through the piles of deliveries, she yelled from her office that she was tired of waiting for Gaynor to hire a new receptionist and she'd be asking some friends "at church this Sunday."

Instead of setting up her laptop like she did every morning, Nicola pulled out her phone and searched for the name and number of the publicist from the Peninsula Hotel. She'd met her at an event a month ago and the woman had told her to call if she ever needed a spa day.

Ten minutes later, she had arranged a complimentary spa day for three. She caught Billy en route to *Spyglass* and successfully rerouted him to her place to gather up Kara, with instructions to meet in the Club Bar of the Peninsula. She left the office without telling Alicia where she was going.

A quick zip along Little Santa Monica later, she was settled into a comfortable chair, a mojito sitting on the table in front of her.

Nic took out her phone and texted a photo of the drink to Seamus with the caption *11am mojito & 0 fucks given*

He texted back immediately. *Attagirl. Love you.*

She resisted the urge to pull out her new work phone and look at the e-mail situation. Some of what Meredith had said yesterday had stuck with her, most notably that she shouldn't be drowning under e-mails. She also shouldn't be working harder than Gaynor, who always managed to make her weekly hair, nail, therapy, and Thermage appointments. She tossed the work phone back into her purse and started on the mojito.

As she drank she glanced around the club lounge, unoccupied except for her and the bartender. She closed her eyes and leaned against the high back of the chair, relishing the quiet. Since Seamus returned to LA, she hadn't had any time to herself, not a single night alone at home with some TV, some records, and some booze. She made a mental note to arrange something like that in the future, with an added long bubble bath.

Her mind flashed an image of Seamus in a bubble bath, and Nicola screwed up her face. *Nope. It's just you and me, brain.* She saw imaginary Seamus in the bath again, and felt that stupid tug at her heart.

Okay, maybe he can come. But that doesn't count as your night to yourself.

"It's a deal," she said out loud, cheersing her strong decision-making skills with herself.

"Are you talking to yourself?" Billy said, waving to her from the bar.

"Kinda sorta," Nicola laughed. "It's Beverly Hills, *innit?* My options for intelligent conversation are limited."

"Want another?" Kara said, materializing beside Billy in a cloud of hair.

"Yes, I'll join you guys," Nicola said amiably. "We aren't due in the spa until noon anyways. We have massages first, and then facials and mani-pedis."

Billy placed their drink order, and he and Kara came to join Nicola at her little table.

"Thanks for coming, you guys," she said as they sat down. "I really needed this today."

"Are you having a bad week?" Billy said, suddenly concerned.

"Not as bad as either of you," Nicola said, rubbing his leg with her hand, then rubbing Kara's too so she wouldn't feel left out. "Too much Hollywood, not enough real life."

"If this was a Lifetime movie, you'd be about to tell us you have cancer," Billy said with a raised eyebrow.

"If this was a Lifetime movie, I'd be white," Kara said, snapping her fingers.

They all laughed as the bartender brought them their drinks. Nicola smiled admiringly when she saw that Billy had added three shots to their order.

Billy followed her gaze.

"I hate having my feet touched," he said. "I figure the pedi will be less squirrelly if I'm tipsy."

"Who's doing the toast?" asked Kara, lifting her shot.

"I'll do it," Billy volunteered.

"Okay," the girls said.

Billy raised his shot glass and looked right into Nicola's eyes.

"This shot is for Nicola, my sister from another mister. Nic, knowing that you have our back in life makes the crappy parts so much less crappy. I love you."

He threw his drink back and put the shot glass on the table. Nicola and Kara followed suit.

"I love you too, Nic," Kara said. "Real talk, you're the best friend I have. And you forgave me. And you're willing to work for me for free."

"Let's not get carried away, you two." Nicola picked up her drink. "This has turned into something outside my comfort zone."

"Is Seamus still at our apartment?" Kara said, and Nicola was grateful for the change of subject.

"Yeah, how'd you know?"

"You guys are loud," Kara said, giving a thumbs-up. "And I went into your room this morning to use your big mirror to check out the free shit you jacked me from Meredith's and he was snoring like a truck."

"Was he naked? He was always naked at our place," Billy said.

"Yeah, but he was facing the window," Kara said.

Nicola groaned and pulled out her phone.

"No phones when we are together," Billy said.

"I'm texting Bluey. He's going to have to get reflective film installed on our apartment."

"Who knew dating a movie star could be so romantic," Billy laughed. "What's next? Blackout shower curtains?"

✳ ✳ ✳

Two hours later, they reconvened in the spa's quiet room, wrapped in thick white robes.

"Look at my toes," Billy said, sliding off his spa scuffs. "I never knew my feet could be like this."

"Bluey won't recognize you tonight."

"Yeah, he's really gonna miss having my rough old hooves scratching against his legs all night."

"Is he a foot taller than you?" Kara asked, posting a selfie to Snapchat.

"Have you even paid attention?" Billy swatted at her with the belt of his robe. "It's like seven inches max."

"Baby boy, seven inches always makes me pay attention," Kara purred.

"I'm five-seven; he's six-two."

"Yes, shorty," Kara said, grabbing his belt.

"Well," Billy said, ignoring her, "are we starting the show-and-tell portion of today? Is there a prize?"

"You're being gifted a thousand dollars in free spa treatments and a day away from Sandy."

"Bluey asked me to move in."

Both girls smiled broadly.

"That was fast," Kara said.

"That's wonderful, B," Nicola said. "Oh, wait. You guys want Seamus to move out so you can have a love nest you can lay around naked in."

Billy nodded.

"We do. Bluey's going to talk to Seamus today. He's got a call in to Tobin to see if the new studio will spring for another penthouse."

"I hated visiting that penthouse so much," Nicola said, remembering the West Elm blandness of Seamus's old rental. "It was like he lived at Soho House."

"From what I hear, that's where he did live before he met you."

"I don't want to think about it," Nicola said with a wave of her hand. "I choose to focus on the future."

"Nicola, do you really think you should do this?" Kara set her phone on the little table. "I mean, he just fucked you over big time."

"So did you, *mi amiga*," Nicola said with a smile. "It's a gamble. Getting hurt isn't the worst thing, and we have some stupid chemistry. We got so derailed."

"Ugh, another fan of getting hurt. You sound like Gaynor." Kara waved a finger. "And don't be fooled by good fuckin'."

"I'm not," Nicola said. "Though it is certainly good. It's something else. We fit together. He's easy. No guy I've ever dated has been easy before. Effortless."

"You're a sweatpants couple," Billy said.

"Yeah, but like from that first date on the boat."

"Do you fart in front of him?" Kara said. "Because that's where I think this is going, and that's disgusting."

"Yeah, if I need to," Nicola laughed. "He loves it. He doesn't care. He loves me for me."

"Well, remember, you're also dating an actor who was a junkie," Kara continued. "Billy, help me out here."

"I'm actually on Seamus's side," Billy said, and Nicola turned to him.

"You are?" she said.

"Yeah, I talked it over long and hard with Bluey."

"Seven inches long, from what I hear," Kara cut in.

"How is someone with your comic timing currently unemployed?" Billy smiled. "Seamus is the only actor that Bluey's ever worked for that he actually cared about. He swears he's a good guy."

"All I know," Kara continued, doing the closed-fist prayer thing that she usually did when she impersonated her mother, "if it was me dating some actor who just got out of rehab and was doing a showmance with some martial arts chick, y'alls would be ripping me a new one."

"Kara, you're secretly dating Mason Dwyer," Nicola said. "And he's developing feelings for you."

"Yeah, yeah, but it's a secret love, so it ain't a real love. I'm on my way to being Hollywood's best-kept secret, for real. And I haven't even had a chance to tell you guys just how freaky he likes it in bed. He's a superfreak."

Billy and Nicola looked at each other, then laughed and stuck their tongues out and made gagging noises.

"Oh, come on," Kara protested. "I'm super vanilla, but he's pushing my envelope, and I like it."

"Lalalalalala," Nicola laughed, sticking her fingers in her ears. "Kara, stop. My mom and I watch his Christmas movie together every year. I don't need to picture weird sex while I'm watching it."

"God, I finally have some good news and you two are too chicken to hear it. Fine."

"Speaking of good news," Nicola began. "Since I didn't see you last night, I can tell you that Meredith is done messing with you."

"Does that explain the weird text about getting me clothes to sell, and the boxes outside my room this morning?"

"Yeah, those clothes were meant for me," Nicola said. "You're hurtin' for money, so sell them."

"She just had shit like that lying around?"

"Her poor assistant took me to a room—imagine Amber's wardrobe rooms, but now imagine them with every piece in most sizes, every pair of shoes available in most sizes, racks of makeup and perfume, boxes of jewelry and phones and sunglasses. The assistant was shivering as she walked me through it."

"Was she cold?"

"No, I think she had PTSD from Meredith. She told me that she was Meredith's fourth assistant in five months. I'd hire her for HHPR, but I'm giving Alicia's old job to you, Kara."

"Girl, what makes you think I'm looking for a desk job?"

"I can pay you eight hundred dollars a week, you can audition whenever you want, and you can keep as many clothes as you can safely steal."

"Well, if you put it that way." Kara smiled. "Thanks, boss."

"When are you going to tell Gaynor about Meredith?" Kara asked.

"I thought you told her," Billy said. "She called me last night to talk about it."

"What?" Nicola threw her phone onto the table. "What are you talking about?"

"She asked me if you were going to take the job. I told her to ask you."

"She's terrifying," Nicola said with a smile. "How the hell did she find out?"

Billy shrugged. Kara shook her head.

"Dammit," Nicola said. "I'm gonna have to go talk to her. This is why she's not in the office."

She fired off an angry, brief text.

"Kara? Can you start work today?"

Kara nodded without looking up from her phone. Nicola sent another text, this one to Alicia, telling her not to hire an assistant from church or anywhere else.

"So," Billy began. "When can Seamus move out?"

"He's not moving into our apartment," Kara said. "Sorry."

"Of course he's not, *idiota*," Nicola said, hating that she'd adopted all of Gaynor's Spanish insults. "We'd have an army of paparazzi parked in Runyon Canyon and shooting through your bedroom windows."

"Does this mean you're moving out?" Kara panicked.

"No. Why does everyone assume we're going to live together? He just needs something until he leaves for Mexico. He's about to start shooting, and he says he just wants to come back on weekends, so Kara, he'll be with us, probably."

Billy smiled, and it made Nicola feel good to see her old friend so content and so settled.

"Holy shit," Billy said suddenly. "I think my dad's funeral is happening like right now."

"Der," Nicola said, reaching over and ruffling his short hair. "Why do you think we're here? I need to welcome you to the dead dad club in style."

CHAPTER 28

SEAMUS FLICKED HIS PHONE OFF and on, off and on. He was in the Beverly Hills office of Dr. Adnan Kessorian, nervously pacing. His first scheduled drug testing was happening in seven days, and after yesterday's cravings, he'd been unable to sleep a wink. Nicola slept in his arms all night, but he had lain awake, visualizing having to tell her that he had started using again.

Nobody can make you put it in your mouth, you idiot.

That pang could.

After two consecutive nightmares in which he tested positive in front of Nicola, he had decided to get tested immediately, if only so he could sleep better. He considered asking Bluey to help but didn't want to make him suspicious. Since his best friend was also dating his girlfriend's best friend, things were murky and he couldn't risk freaking Nicola out. The Internet had been frustratingly noncommittal about how long the effects of opiates remained in the system. It was either total panic or stoner acceptance, with most websites focusing more on how to beat the tests so you could get a job at Best Buy.

The only doctor he'd ever been to in Hollywood was the same guy who wrote prescriptions like he was writing thank-you cards. The same guy who'd helped him whenever Amber was out of Oxy.

Still, desperate times and all that. He'd called Dr. Kessorian's cell, not surprised that the doctor answered on the first ring.

"Seamus, it's so nice to hear from you," he'd said in his thickly accented deep voice.

"Hey, doc, how you doing?"

Seamus had quickly explained that he needed an urgent pee test. Kessorian was on the seventh hole at some golf course but could be at the office in ninety minutes. *Of course he's golfing,* Seamus had thought. Seamus had an unreasonable hatred for golf.

You have nothing to worry about, Seamus reassured himself. He knew he hadn't taken any pills since Ojai; he simply wanted the peace of mind that he was going to pass his upcoming test. He flipped his phone back and forth in his hand like a Magic 8-Ball. *Poor choice of words,* his brain said.

Dr. Kessorian came into the room with a printout.

"Well, it's as we expected," he said bluntly. "Positive."

Seamus felt his knees shake. "You mean negative."

"No, I mean it came back positive for opioids, but that could mean Vicodin, Oxy, whatever. Look, I'll just write you a prescription and then it doesn't matter. It doesn't say heroin; don't panic."

"But it can't be right," Seamus said, his voice breaking. "It's been months. How far back does a pee test go?"

"It depends," Kessorian said, scratching at his beard. "The quality of the stuff you had was probably much better than what everyone else had. It makes it harder to be certain."

"I googled it," Seamus said. "They say that it's, like, a week max."

"WebMD makes everyone a doctor," Kessorian said dismissively. "It's Hollywood. Everyone's on some sort of pharmaceutical. You just need an insurance certificate, right?"

"Is there any chance it can be wrong?"

Kessorian shrugged. "Everything is possible, I suppose. Do you want me to run another test?"

Seamus shook his head. His first studio pee test was in a week, and he'd promised Nico that he'd show her the results.

"What can I do to help clear out my system?" Seamus asked, his voice cracking.

"Lots of water, steer clear of booze, and quit taking pills," Kessorian said, pulling out his prescription pad. "From anyone. You ask someone for an Advil in this town, they give you Opana."

"The only pills I've taken have been cold pills," he protested.

"Just a warning," Dr. Kessorian said, his eyes boring into Seamus's, "be careful in this town. Now, can we write you a prescription for anything today?"

Seamus shook his head.

"Look, it's not a big deal; everyone tests positive. It's just a pee test. Get clean pee. You'll be fine."

"No," Seamus said, getting slowly to his feet. "I won't."

✳ ✳ ✳

Pulling his black hoodie over his head and yanking the cords tight so that most of his face was hidden, Seamus stepped out onto Rodeo Drive. He glanced nervously left and right for any marauding photographers but didn't see any. He knew that Nicola was at the Peninsula, half a mile away, but the way his luck was going today, he expected to bump into her at any second.

He paced up the block, toward Santa Monica, then turned and walked south, his mind racing. It was a mistake. It had to be a mistake. With Bluey off-limits, he racked his mind for anyone else who could help him. Bette would tell Crystal. He briefly considered calling Timothy, then realized that he was thinking about trusting an agent. Even Amber was more trustworthy than an agent. He pulled out his phone and searched his contacts for her number. He'd given her a code name in case he got hacked. There it was: "Bank of America." His tapped the phone number and almost immediately, Amber's baby-girl voice was talking down the line.

"I wondered how long it would take you to call me, Daddy," she said. His gut clenched at the sound of her voice.

"Hi, Amber," he said drily.

"I'm just glad you came to your senses," she continued. "We had a good thing. I don't know why you ever had to try to pretend with that basic ratchet—"

He cut her off. "Amber, I need your help."

"Of course you do, Daddy."

Seamus started to get angry. She'd never called him "Daddy" before. She was with someone and didn't want them to know who she was talking to.

"Can you meet me? I'm in Beverly Hills."

"I thought Daddy hated Beverly Hills," she cooed. "I'm in the middle of a scene at my house. For my show. I mean, you know, a scene for my show, not like a dirty scene, Daddy." She giggled.

He heard her moving through her house, and then a door closed.

"Hey," she said in her regular voice. "Sorry, we have new cast members; I can't trust anyone."

"I know the feeling," Seamus replied.

"Seamus, it's really good to hear from you," Amber continued. "You have no idea, I'm just getting betrayed by everyone, all these hungry tigers. You're one of the good ones, you know? You're one of my best friends."

"Thanks, Amber," he said hurriedly. "I'm in a bit of a bind. I tested positive and I haven't used. I need your help."

"Seamus, that means so much to me." She took a dramatic breath. "I think I'm gonna cry."

"Don't cry, Amber," Seamus said. "How long are you shooting the scene for?"

"It's my show, silly. You remember that, right? I'm the boss. I've been dragging it out because I'm bored. I can go in there and nail it and be done in ten minutes. Come here. I'll send everyone home."

"No cameras?"

"Not unless you want them, Daddy."

Seamus used his newfound rideshare skills to call a car and spent the entire ride focusing on the screen of his phone even though he knew it would make him carsick. The driver had recognized him, despite using Bluey's account. She was staring at him in the rearview mirror every time he looked up. As the black Prius wove its way along the backstreets north of Santa Monica Boulevard, Seamus began to panic and considered changing his destination, except he still didn't know how to alter a rideshare destination, or even if he could. Amber's it was.

His screen lit up with several texts from Tobin and then a barrage from Weatherman and some from Bette. Seamus quickly silenced his phone after the machine-gun dings filled the car.

"Somebody's popular, hey, Donald?" the driver said, since the rideshare account was in Bluey's real name. Seamus nodded without looking up. When these text avalanches happened, Seamus's favorite trick was to stuff his phone into his pocket and ignore it for a couple of hours, but right now, reading them was better than talking with the driver. Same old shit. Everybody wanted him to do things he had no interest in. He felt a wave of carsickness wash over him, and he shut his eyes. When he opened them again, they were on Sunset Boulevard, about to turn onto Amber's street.

"Just up here on the left," he said with a friendly smile. He knew he was going to have to turn on the charm to make sure her next call wasn't to TMZ. "You got us here really fast," Seamus said, giving the rearview mirror a full-wattage smile and winking. "Thanks so much."

"Is this your place?"

"No, no, just visiting a friend." Seamus started to open his door.

"I bring a lot of people here when I drive at night," the driver said, an edge of sarcasm in her voice.

"Yeah, lot of parties here," Seamus said, beginning to get out of the car.

"I'm just trying to figure out why a big star like you—"

"Amber's a friend, all right?"

"Huh? I was just wondering why a big star like you uses a fake name to call cars. Don't you have like an army of drivers?"

"Oh, heh heh," Seamus laughed nervously. "No, love. No army of nothing. Just another arsehole Ubering around Hollywood on someone else's dime."

"Well, okay, *Donald*. Here's my card in case you ever need a driver who can keep her mouth shut."

The woman picked up a card from a stack near her gearstick and passed it to him. Seamus read it.

"Thanks, Kat," he said, reaching forward to shake her hand. "I'm Seamus."

"I know."

As Kat drove off, Seamus glanced nervously at Amber's medieval wooden gate, realizing he didn't know how to get inside unless there was an intern handing out wristbands. The wooden door had no bell.

He stepped forward and rapped his knuckles twice against the wood, the knocks echoing back but not getting any other response. Several cars cruised past behind him and Seamus was too scared to turn around in case they were photographers. He shouldn't have come here. His panic levels had been rising all day, and they were approaching fever pitch. He texted Amber that he was going to leave, then pulled Kat's card out of his pocket to arrange his ride home.

A door opened farther along the ivy-covered wall and a shock of platinum curls popped out. Amber ran up to him and leapt into the air, landing in his arms and kissing him.

"Amber, what the hell are you doing?" Seamus said angrily, pushing her off him as his nose filled with sickly perfume, probably her latest scent she sold at Target. Amber stumbled backward against the wall.

"Oooh, Daddy," she cooed. "I heard you like it rough."

"Do you ever stop?" Seamus stormed past her into the house. He'd never seen it so empty. Amber had sent her staff home. He groaned. She obviously presumed that he wanted to party.

As he turned back to the living room, decorated with a series of knockoff Warhols of Amber, he watched as Amber slowly opened her legs.

"So you still haven't learned to wear underwear?" he scoffed.

"Oh, so I see rehab hasn't made you any less boring." Amber snapped her legs closed. "I thought you'd be happier to see me."

Seamus shook his head. He barely remembered the last time he'd seen Amber, on that disastrous night in Ojai, when she had tied him off and shot him up high enough that he nearly died.

"I shouldn't have come here," he said, pulling out his phone. "I'll go. I'm sorry I bothered you."

Amber sprang to her feet. She wasn't going to let him escape so easily.

"Look, what's going on?" she said, using her serious deeper voice instead of the baby-girl voice. "You tested positive, big deal."

"It *is* a big deal, Amber." Seamus walked away from her, back into the kitchen. It felt less dangerous in the kitchen. "I just need to pass the test until it finally clears out of my system. I am about to do a movie, and insurance is requesting that I pass or my insurance goes through the roof. And I pay for it."

"You can afford it, superstar," Amber said, back in the baby voice. "You act like the poorest multimillionaire I've ever met."

"I don't want to afford it; I want to test negative."

"Well, quit taking drugs, you idiot," Amber said, anger setting in.

"I did. And I have promised Nicola that I'll test privately for her, too."

"Oh, come the fuck on." Amber's voice started to rise. "Do not for one split second tell me that you are trying to climb back onto that basic bumpkin."

"Jealousy isn't pretty on you, Amber."

"It makes me gorgeous, O'Riordan." Amber poured herself a glass of vodka and turned to face him.

"I see that our reunion isn't going to be the homecoming I'd been hoping for," she said. "And I'm tempted to kick you out, but who can resist a face like that? Especially when I'm the only one who can help you."

"Yeah, Amber, baby steps and all that," Seamus said, trying to control his panic. "Just tell me what I need to do."

"I got you covered. Pee tests are easy. We'll go buy some pee in a minute."

"Oh, you have a guy?"

"I have a girl," Amber said. "You're not going to love this, but it's Courtney Hauser."

"Courtney Hauser does not have any fluid in her body that does not contain every drug known to man."

"Exactly, but she passes all her drug tests. She's dealing, too, if you want some Oxy or just some Vicodin; she's got it all."

"So she's given up on acting, then?"

"Hardly. She's on a Freeform show right now. Three whole episodes." Amber paused for a snide smile. "Where have you been? Oh wait, you didn't have TV in rehab?"

"I had a TV. And I completed rehab, and I haven't had anything since that day in Ojai. I don't know how I failed the test. I thought it was like a month or something till it was out of your system."

"Nobody knows," Amber said airily. "Everyone's got a different theory. Best way is just to always use someone else's pee. Takes the pressure off. Ready to go over to Courtney's?"

✳ ✳ ✳

A short while later, Amber pulled her red Bentley into a driveway almost at the top of the hills above Hollywood. Seamus took it in. The house was a faded mid-century in need of some TLC. The patio was dotted by dead plants in expensive pots, the glaze covered in the black freeway soot that rained down on all of LA. Several overfull ashtrays helped set the tone, aided by empty beer bottles in the dying succulent garden that separated the patio from the street.

Seamus caught Amber staring at him.

"It's nice, huh?" she said sarcastically.

"She's managed to give the Hollywood Hills a definite East LA crack-house feel."

"That's the last shitty thing you can say till we get back in the car," Amber cautioned. "You know how touchy Courtney is. Just pretend you like her."

Amber strode forward and rapped once on the door. A busted blind over the large glass windows shuddered and Seamus saw an eye and some matted hair appear briefly at its edge.

"O'Riordan, remember your etiquette. How long does one stay at a dealer's house?"

Seamus rolled his eyes. "A minimum of half an hour," he said as if Amber were a school teacher and this were a test.

"Good boy."

"But we have to leave after that. I need to get home."

"You're welcome," Amber said icily as the door swung inward, revealing Courtney Hauser in shredded denim cutoffs and a baggy T-shirt with a cat and a devil on the front. Her dirty chestnut wig didn't quite match the real strands of hair beneath it. Her left forearm was bandaged.

"Seamus O'Motherfuckin' Riordan," Hauser said in her husky voice. "I'd like to call this a pleasant surprise, except I'm not surprised. Let's stick with pleasant. Get your asses inside."

Hauser slammed the door behind them, plunging the room into dusty near dark. All of the windows were shielded from the daylight by thick mismatched blackout curtains and blinds, shafts of weak light peeking through random gaps, casting blades of illumination through the thick air. Seamus could see cigarettes burning in several different ashtrays.

"Who else is here?" he asked sharply.

"It's nice to see you, too," Courtney said, circling him. "Relax. We're alone."

Seamus looked for a clean space to sit down. Plates of moldy, half-eaten, and long-forgotten food littered almost every table surface, and the two couches were strewn with copies of *Us Weekly* and pillows that said PEREZHILTON.COM, which Courtney had probably stolen from one of his events. Seamus decided to stand.

"Why you so quiet, superstar?" Amber breezed around Courtney and planted herself alongside Seamus.

"Just didn't see the day going this way," he said honestly.

"We never do, do we?" Courtney scratched absently at the bandage on her arm. Seamus could see that the edges of the bandage were black with dirt. "Can I get either of you a drink? I have beer. Bottle or can?"

"I'm good, thanks," Seamus said, attempting to sound friendly.

"Do not be that post-rehab guy," Courtney said, striding into the small kitchen to their left.

"Who says I was in rehab?" he said.

Amber raised her hand and shrugged. "What? It's a good story," she said with a smile. "Calm down."

Seamus heard her rummaging in the fridge, and she returned slinging three cans of Keystone Light. She tossed one to him. He caught it and examined the can.

"What's this?"

"All the hipsters are drinking it nonironically," Courtney drawled. "They send it to me free. Or someone does."

Seamus popped his can, then wiped around the hole with his finger-tip. He faked a sip and smacked his lips together. He could taste it on his lips. Like most American beers, it tasted like the can and little more.

"So how does this work?" he asked, turning to Courtney, who was lighting a fresh cigarette despite the fact that Seamus could still see at least three burning down in ashtrays around the room. He was going to have to shower and take everything he was wearing to the laundromat as soon as he got home.

"It's easy. You come here. You buy piss. You smuggle the piss into the doctor's with you. Easiest is inside a condom inside your under-pants. They don't pat you down, but they're not going to let you take a backpack in the bathroom either. You need to give them half a cup, so make sure you have at least that much with you."

"How long does it keep?"

"A couple days, a week. I always have it in stock, baby."

"Thanks, Court," Seamus said, smiling at her. "Hopefully this will be the only time I need it."

Courtney's eyes glanced quickly at Amber's, and they both burst out laughing.

"What's so fucking funny?"

"Oh, nothing," Courtney said, still trying to stop laughing.

"Yeah, uh . . . ," Amber began. "It's just . . ."

"That's what everyone says the first time I sell them piss," Courtney said.

Seamus stood there awkwardly, taking fake sips of his beer. Courtney crumpled to the couch and started poring over an issue of *Closer*.

"Aren't you a little young to be reading *Closer*?" Amber said haughtily.

"A girl can dream, can't she?" Courtney said, and Seamus did a double take. She suddenly looked her age, twenty-two. Most days she could pass for forty.

Seamus pulled out his phone and was unhappy to see that he had screens full of texts and notifications of missed calls and unheard voice mails. The most recent were from Nicola.

"I need to make a call," he said. "Can you two keep it quiet for a minute?"

Courtney jumped up from the couch and took Amber by the hand, leading her off along a hallway. They disappeared quickly into the darkness at the end.

Seamus called Nicola. She answered immediately.

"Hey, you," she said perkily, and Seamus felt a pang in his stomach.

"Hey, lassie," he said, hating himself. "Sorry, had me phone on silent, just saw this whole Oscars shitstorm. What do you need me to say? We're not doing it, right?"

She didn't respond.

"Right?" he repeated.

"That's why I wanted to get you before Tobin or Weatherman. Or even Bette."

"Well, you got me. What is your vision for this mess?"

"It's easy. I've talked to Gaynor. We can get you in and out of the Oscars without a single interview. You don't have to do any parties."

"Good," Seamus growled. "They're so fooking boring. But Nico, I fucked up bad last time."

"And you'll fuck up good this time," she said. "I would like to go back to your team today and tell them that you'll do it on one condition. The Oscars and the first production phase of the Mexico movie will signal the end of your contract with Bette. After Parallax, she can land her Marvel gig on her own. By the end of the principal photography, you guys will have been together six months. We sell the breakup story, then at the junket in a year, you guys get to pretend to not want to talk about your difficult breakup that happened on set. The studio will love it. It's win-win, and baby, I know you don't want to do it, but I don't feel good about starting our revamp while I'm orchestrating your fake girlfriend."

Seamus felt his breath quicken with every word. Nicola was working for him, to let them be together as a couple. And here he was buying piss off a junkie Nicola hated, in order to deceive her.

"I'll do anything you want, ladyboss. As long as you're by my side, I'll do whatever you say."

Nicola went silent.

"Nico . . ."

"Seamus, there's something else I need to tell you; I can't lie to you."

"You're scaring me."

"Seamus, Weatherman said he'd pay me a hundred grand if you said yes to the Oscars," Nicola blurted. "That's not why it's a good idea; I just want to get rid of Bette and get on with some sort of normal life. I don't have to take the money."

Seamus gulped, feeling like even more of a liar. "Nico, keep the money, I don't give a fuck. Think of it as cunt tax."

"Cunt tax?"

"It's an Australian saying. If someone's really awful, they should pay cunt tax. Bluey taught me it. This is Weatherman paying it. I'd call it deserved. Keep it."

"Okay, Groundskeeper Willie," Nicola said with a laugh. "Where you at right now?"

"I just went out for a walk," Seamus lied. "Not sure where I am. Gonna have to use me GPS to get home. You working late?"

"I need to make an eight p.m. client dinner."

"Oh, you're busy tonight?" Seamus said, unable to hide his disappointment.

"You're my client, stupid," she said breezily. "Where do you wanna eat?"

He chuckled. "Surprise me. I'm getting good at this whole car-calling thing. I can meet you anywhere. Just tell me where and when and I'm all yours."

"Okay, O'Riordan, I have to go call your oh-so-pleasant team. My place at eight. Thanks for being awesome."

"Bye, Nico. Love you."

He hung up and saw Amber and Courtney staring at him from the darkness of the hallway.

"I told you," Courtney said. "He's totally into that invisibly bor-ing publicist of his."

"For now," Amber said, sashaying out and knocking her beer against Seamus's.

"I met her," Courtney said. "I get it. I'd fuck her. If I felt like, you know, a farmer's daughter fantasy."

"Knock it off, you two," Seamus said angrily. "So, how do I go about buying this clean urine?"

"You call me." Courtney fished beneath the bandage at her wrist and pulled out a business card. "Only use this number. Then come by and pick up."

"And how much is it?"

"It's five hundred dollars for a pint bag."

"I don't have five hundred dollars on me." Seamus patted his pock-ets for emphasis.

"You silly foreigner," Courtney laughed. "You know the routine. The first one is always free."

CHAPTER 29

NICOLA TURNED THE OVEN UP to 250 and slid the foil containers inside. She wondered what her mother would say about someone taking a delivery of a three-hundred-dollar steak dinner from Musso and Frank, and then having to warm it in the oven because their movie-star boyfriend was caught in traffic. It probably would be something similar to what she was thinking herself.

Surveying the living room, Nicola did a quick check for cleanliness and went and gave the couch cushions a final plump, then a karate chop in the top seam, just like she'd seen on HGTV. After she'd chopped six cushions, she admitted to herself that she was nervous.

Before she'd accepted her banishment for the evening, Kara had given Nicola some unsolicited advice: Don't trust Seamus. Don't trust anyone. "I'm ten steps ahead of you on that one," Nicola had laughed nervously. Kara had called bullshit and then asked Nicola to pay for her car to the Nice Guy, where she'd reserved a bar space.

She pulled her phone out of her Rag & Bone jeans back pocket. It was eight forty-five. She'd been tidying and checking her phone for an hour. Something about today was bugging her. She texted Billy.

I'm really antsy. Tell me why!

Because you're always antsy came the reply almost instantly.

No this is different

My dear, you're scared and that's fine. But I've been around him for weeks and he's serious about you. About this. Just relax.

I don't do relax.

You know what I don't do? I don't get nights alone with my boyfriend, and I have one. I'm gonna switch off my phone. Your special friend will be there soon. RELAX.

Nicola went out onto the balcony. Her downstairs neighbor was outside smoking weed. The smell made her nauseous. She made several loud tutting sounds that she hoped he heard, then stepped back inside her silent apartment.

The silence was broken by the buzzer. She sprung up and saw Seamus's lower beard extending from a dark hood on the video monitor. She pressed the intercom button.

"You know the code," she said.

"I forgot the code," he replied.

"It's one-eight-zero-three."

"Or you could buzz me in."

"And then you'd never learn."

She clicked off and walked to the door, unlocking it. While she waited for Seamus to make his way up to her door, she nervously checked the oven, turning it up to 450 to help the heating. She was starving. She heard the door open and peered around the corner to see Seamus, the hood of his jacket now pushed back, a grin from ear to ear. He held out a large canvas shopping bag printed with the logo of a food co-op on the east side.

"What's that?"

"I'll tell you after you kiss me." He stepped forward and wrapped his arms around her, planting his soft, pillowy lips against hers. She felt his shoulders relax as the kiss drew on, and she inhaled a long draft of him as he nibbled on her lower lip like he always did. Against her will, she felt her own shoulders drop, and she leaned against his chest.

"I missed you," he said, breaking the kiss but keeping their faces touching.

"You smell clean," she said.

"I showered," he chuckled. "Just for you, my queen of deflection."

"And you are wearing cologne."

"I got a box of Tom Ford colognes today, be a shame to waste it."

Nicola rolled her eyes. As soon as she'd confirmed to the Academy that he would be a presenter at next week's ceremony, the office had been deluged with phone calls from designers and publicists, all desperate for their products to be on Seamus when he walked the carpet.

"That was quick," she said. "They only called this afternoon. Wait—how did they send it to Bluey's?"

"I didn't say it was free. I said I got it. I bought it."

"You bought a box of them, or you bought one?"

"I couldn't decide," he laughed. "I had to have Billy guide me on which one you'd like the most."

"They're two hundred and fifty dollars a bottle." Nicola pushed him back. "How many did you buy?"

"Don't be silly," he laughed. "I had Tobin put my entire advance for this movie into my savings account. We can send one to Biscuit."

Nicola laughed. The Tom Ford would definitely be a step up from the Axe that her brother wore when he went on dates.

"Baby," she said, nuzzling back into his chest. "Money is still money; that thousand dollars could have been sent to a dog shelter or something."

"It was closer to three thousand," Seamus said, raising his arms in mock defense.

"Seamus!" She swatted a hand at the top of his head. "You're ridiculous. Why would you even tell me that?"

"Because we're doing honesty, and I didn't think. I mean, when five million dollars appears in your account overnight, it's kind of a waste of time to spend an hour in a Sephora buying man perfume. I'll return some of it."

"No, you won't," she said. "I know you."

"What's that burning smell?"

"Oh shit, the Musso and Frank." Nicola spun and yanked the oven door open, releasing a cloud of dark smoke up to the ceiling.

"Let me, love." Seamus blocked her with his arm and grabbed a dish towel from the sink. "You put cardboard into the oven?"

"I forgot to take the lids off," Nicola said as Seamus hoisted the blackened, smoking box onto the countertop. "Here, take it out to the balcony."

She ran across the thick gray carpet and slid the balcony door open, and Seamus followed, a theatrical curl of smoke billowing behind him. He set the containers on the tiled floor.

"Shall we eat out here?" he asked with a grin.

"I set the table, jerkface."

"But it smells like a campfire." Seamus lifted Nico's face with a gentle finger under her chin. He began kissing her cheeks, first one, then the other.

"Listen, Casanova, I didn't nearly set fire to this food only to have you freeze it up again."

She bent and tried to pick up the foil container, but it was too hot for her to lift.

"We need to figure this one out," she laughed. Seamus ducked inside, returning with two large plates from the table. He slid one under two foil containers and walked them to the table as if he were a waiter.

"Madam, your dinner is served," he said in a truly terrible French accent. He removed the singed white paper lids from the foil dishes and waved his arm. Nicola used her fingertips to carry the remaining smaller containers to the table. She set them down and then returned to close the oven door. When she turned back, Seamus had removed all of his clothes except his underpants.

"What's going on?" she asked with a growing smile.

"It's been a while since we had a nice night at home." He grinned. "Do you still have that apron?"

Even though she had just caught a whiff of the steak and it smelled amazing and her stomach was growling, Nicola scampered back to her bedroom. She pulled open her bottom drawer and rummaged until she found the apron she'd worn the first time she cooked for Seamus, a purple gingham thing that had originally been Kara's. Finding it, she quickly shucked off her jeans and pulled her sweater over her head, then deliberated for a second before ditching her bra and panties, too. She deftly tied the apron and walked back to the living room.

"Oh my flippin' God," Seamus sighed. "Yes. Everything is yes."

"Oh, stop, you old goat," she laughed, sitting across from him at the small dining table that Kara had dragged in from the street soon after they moved in.

"Do we have to eat first? I'd rather have you for my first course."

Nicola sliced into her steak and inhaled deeply.

"That's going to have to wait," she said, lifting a chunk of steak to her mouth and biting into it. The burning lids had given it a BBQ twist. It was delicious. After she had helped herself to some sides and demolished half of her steak, Nicola looked up to see Seamus staring at her.

"What?" she said. "Are you going to eat?"

"Nope, m'lass. Watching you tuck into that steak is more than enough for me."

She leaned across the table and cut a chunk of his steak and lifted it to his mouth.

"Trust me," she said, pressing the steak against his lips. "It's like breaking glass windows; once you start, you can't stop."

"I can't wait to hear that story," Seamus said, accepting the steak. "Holy shit," he said, chewing. "Yep. You're going to be the second thing I eat tonight. You just got bumped."

They ate in silence for a while, sipping on glasses of red wine.

"You're not playing any records tonight?" Seamus asked.

"Oh, I forgot to put another one on."

Seamus got up and went over to the bag he'd left in the kitchen. He handed it to her.

"What's in here?" She laughed. "Ten bottles of Tom Ford?"

"I only brought you one," he laughed. "It'll make you smell like a summer vacation to Ibiza."

"Is that a good thing?"

Seamus pointed to the growing bulge in his underpants.

"Even the mere thought of you, in that apron, spraying that perfume on, is intoxicating enough."

"Well, before I unwrap whatever's happening in your undies, what else do you have in here?"

Nicola reached in and pulled out a stack of vinyl LPs.

"You really did go shopping, didn't you?"

Seamus walked over and started kissing her neck. "Yeah, but let's get to that later. I need to hold you. I need you against me."

"But we still have more dinner."

"I'll reheat it later while you listen to your new records. Now spray some of that shit behind your ears and get into your bedroom."

When they were done, after he had held her for a very long time, Seamus went out to the kitchen to "save dinner." Nicola could hear him clattering pots and pans and doing whatever it took to reheat the food.

She lay on her side, looking out her window at the moon in the clear sky. She wished that there could be just one star, but tonight, like every night, the moon sailed solo through the light pollution. She couldn't shake the wistful feeling that was tugging at her.

A coughing sound at her bedroom door made her roll onto her back, and she saw Seamus, clad in her apron and nothing else, holding a tray with one large bowl and two very full glasses of red wine. He set the tray carefully on the bed and began to untie the apron.

"No," Nicola exclaimed. "Leave it on."

He spun around, giving her a good look at his fuzzy ass, before facing her and doing a small curtsy.

"Does m'lady have a thing for a servant who cross-dresses?"

"An apron is not cross-dressing; it's just cute."

"Hang on." Seamus spun, giving her another chance to check out his butt, and trotted out of the room, returning with the bundle of records he'd brought for her. "Here, check out what I got you. I kind of bought everything the dude in the record store told me to buy."

"Oh great," Nicola said with an exaggerated scowl. "You probably bought me a bunch of girly crap like The 1975 or Radiohead?"

"Nicola, I know you don't like fake machine music," Seamus said. "I told the guy I wanted the real deal. But romantic."

"Well, okay, then." Nicola opened the flap on a bag from a store called Permanent Records, pulling out the albums. "Glen Campbell? Nice. Ike and Tina Turner? That's not exactly romantic."

"No, ma'am. That's mood music."

Nicola kept pulling the records out. "Mazzy Star, lovely . . ." Nicola didn't have the heart to tell him she already had that one. She flipped through the last few, stopping on one. "Margo Price?"

"The guy played me this one. I really want to put it on for you." Seamus took the record and went back into the living room, and soon the air was filled with country music.

"Oh, dang," Nicola laughed. "This is totally something my dad would have played me."

"Then we have a winner." Seamus clambered onto the bed. "Now let's finish our dinner. I've taken the liberty of cutting it all up into bite-size chunks. Nobody wants knives in bed. We can talk."

"We have to talk?" Nicola said, searching for the fork and not making eye contact.

"I want to talk," Seamus said, reaching for her hand. "This time around, I want to talk all the time, about everything, and I want you to be able to just chat my ear off."

"I am not a chat-your-ear-off kind of girl, and you know it."

"It's good to have a goal." Seamus speared a chunk of steak with the fork and fed it to her. "Nico, thank you for giving me a second chance."

"I didn't," she said with her mouth full. "This is still your first and only chance. Don't let it become another shitshow of lies and crazy bitches."

"That could be the title of my autobiography till I met you," Seamus laughed, feeding himself some spinach. "*A Shitshow of Lies and Crazy Bitches: The Seamus O'Riordan Story.*"

"That's encouraging," Nicola said, rubbing her hand along his inner thigh, up under the apron.

"I exaggerate, but only for effect."

"So what do you want to talk about?"

"Well, you know, the usual things that a guy who likes a girl wants to talk about with her, you know, before he goes to the Oscars with his fake girlfriend and then takes off to Mexico for two months with said fake girlfriend to make a two-hundred-million-dollar movie series that will most likely suck."

"Yeah, I figured it would be a standard situation just like that. So what does a guy say in such a conventional scenario?"

"What's the timeline for adding a real girlfriend to my menagerie? I already have a fake one in there."

Nicola gave him a puzzled look. "I'm not seeing anyone else; we're monogamous. Not sure what you're getting at."

"I want us to be official."

"Like Facebook official?"

"Is that a thing? I've never had a Facebook."

"Yeah, that's what my mom calls it."

"Okay, yeah, I want to be able to call you by a word that links us."

"You can call me your girlfriend, if that's what you're asking."

"Sweet. Thanks. Now sign me up for some anger management."

"Why?"

"Every time I have to go somewhere with Bette or talk about how great she is to a reporter, I want to punch myself in the nuts."

"Want me to do it for you? I'm perfectly situated."

"No, that's fine, but lass, if you'd like to raise your hand a little farther, you'll encounter someone who's very happy to see you again."

"We just did it, you old perv."

"And we'll do it again. As soon as this talk is over."

"What else is there to discuss?"

"You know Timothy is gay, right?"

"He so isn't," she protested. "Billy would have told me."

"Oh, so Billy knows all of the gays?"

"In this town, yes."

"Apparently not. And my thinking is, Weatherman set you guys up to keep you away from me."

"So now you're a conspiracy theorist?" Nicola desperately wanted to change the subject; she felt stupid. "Maybe he's bi? Anyway, there won't be any more dates with him, or anyone but you."

"I need to figure out what to do about my whole team. Something's different with them this time around."

"Yeah, it's been an eye-opener for me, too. They treat you so Hollywood."

"You think you're becoming Hollywood?"

"When did I ever say *I* was?" She gently flicked his nuts. "Hollywood is just a city; my job is just a job."

"Do you still really believe that?"

"In what ways is it not true? Los Angeles is just houses, malls, and cars. And I turn up and work a job that I get paid for and wouldn't do if I didn't."

"And today you made a hundred K for nothing."

"I'm gonna give it to my mom. As soon as I told Tobin you'd do it, Weatherman's assistant called and asked for my account details. Do I pay taxes on it?"

"I'll call him tomorrow and tell him to give it to you in cash."

"I'll never get used to this."

"And you've lived here how long now? Nearly two years?"

"Yeah, it's coming up," she paused, marveling at the milestone. How the hell had that happened? "It's still not my home. I'm here because I love being around Billy. Everything else has been moving too fast for me to notice if I actually like it here or not."

"It took me two years to realize I like Los Angeles."

Nicola shook her fist at the window. "LA, you have a couple months to prove your case, or I'm out."

"Do you really want to stay here?"

"What's with you tonight?"

"Just been doing some thinking," Seamus said, flopping back against the pillows. "My life is all about jumping through hoops for other people. These days, the hoops are a lot harder to jump through."

"You don't have to jump through them if you don't want to."

"Tell that to Weatherman."

"Gladly," she said, crawling around the LPs and the bowl of food that she wished she were still picking at. She lay down alongside Seamus and slid her hand back up under his apron. She bypassed his boys and rested her hand on his stomach and kissed his shoulder.

"You've settled right into this."

"Seamus, we could be living in Omaha, we could be just hanging out anywhere. I want to admit something, I didn't even try to stop loving you. I expected it would just happen, like it did with Antony. But it didn't. We're comfortable. Two weirdos who fell in love and are trying to make it work. Billy says we're good together. I think we are, too."

"See?" He ruffled her hair. "Sometimes you do just talk and talk."

She leaned her head onto his chest.

"Yeah, sometimes I do."

CHAPTER 30

THE SOUND OF SANDY'S VOICE from down the hall froze Billy's blood. He turned the music up on his computer and pressed his thumbs into his temples. Sandy's inability to have a thought that didn't come out of her mouth was driving him crazy. He couldn't hear what she was talking about, but she sounded friendly, which meant she was out in the general area, trying to solicit compliments on something—her outfit, a new purse, her makeup. Billy messaged the office manager, Christine, a spry, zaftig matron in her forties who despised Sandy specifically and working at *Spyglass* in general.

What's she crapping on about now?

Oh honey, Christine responded immediately, *today it's all about how someone on Bravo wore a top that she wore a year ago.*

Probably Jax.

Or Giggi.

Billy smiled. If he could ever get out of this place, he'd take Christine, too. He and Bluey had started to work on his exit strategy. Billy knew he couldn't resume trawling the party circuit, since a lot of his work involved flirting with people to get into the private parties. Monogamy came easily to him, and with it, he'd lost his desire to use his looks to get behind the velvet rope.

Bluey was talking with Robert Flanger, the legendary gay director who'd orchestrated the takedown of Max Zetta last year. The two of them had been cooking up an idea of an openly gay talent management agency. Bluey had also told Billy to just quit, if things got that bad. Billy had said he wasn't at the breaking point yet, but that was yesterday, when he couldn't hear Sandy's strident voice echoing down the hall. Today, being a kept man sounded like a great option.

He looked at the time, realizing that he only had twenty minutes before the morning meeting. He was still waiting for Mason Dwyer to call with a "much juicier story" on Felicity Storm. Last week's cover story had been their best-selling issue of the year. Mason was so grateful someone had printed a favorable story on him that he wanted to source another, even dirtier story. Billy texted him.

Hey man, can you call real quick? Meeting in 20. Need to know what you're going to say.

His phone rang immediately. It was Mason. "Hey, man, what's up?"

"Not much," Billy said. "How are you?"

"Your story really helped me," the star said enthusiastically. "Felicity lost her shit—she's fired half her staff already, thinking that there was a mole inside her house. If we do a good job this week, she'll have to fire everyone. Maybe even Meredith."

"And she doesn't suspect you?"

"Not one bit," Mason laughed. "No offense, Billy, but she knows I hate magazines like yours."

"Dude, I hate magazines like mine."

"Yeah, but now I see how it works; it's kind of awesome."

"What? You like that you can work out a grudge match in public?"

"How stupid was I? To not know how to play this game?"

"Arguably, you're super successful and you already were before this whole scandal. You don't need *Spyglass*."

"Ah, but young Bill, I do. After your story hit, I started getting calls. My agent said it's like the old days. I might land a blockbuster. It's time to hit the gym!"

"Well, I'm glad to have helped. What do you have for me today?"

"Take your pick, man. I can give you sex stuff, personal stuff, or really dark stuff. What sells best?"

Billy rolled his eyes. "We can't really do sex stuff. How personal is the personal stuff?"

"She beat our nanny," he said.

"Can you get the nanny on record?"

"Do you think I have our ex-nanny's phone number?"

"What else do you have?"

"She likes being choked out during sex with strangers. She's a cutter. She had constant affairs while we were together. If I had to kiss a woman for a movie, she'd send that actress shit in the mail; like one time she sent Paula Pristana a rotten cow's heart in a Tiffany's box. She's full-on crazy, man."

Billy found himself getting suddenly angry with Mason. "Dude, it's not a witch hunt to print whatever you make up," he said, an edge in his voice.

"Does it really matter?"

"To me it does," Billy said. "So, what do you want to give me?"

"I can send you screen grabs of texts between her and her last affair."

"Now you're talking," Billy said. "Who's her last affair?"

"Xaviera Bolt, her trainer."

"Timeline?"

"Before we separated."

Billy smiled. This was a good, simple story. And it would be a killer cover.

"Thanks, man," he said. "I'll pitch it in a few and call you back."

"Hey, Billy, before you go, a little bird told me that you're close with Seamus O'Riordan."

"A little bird named Kara," Billy said.

"You got me there."

"So what do you need from Seamus?"

"I was thinking a boy's night out with him and me might be paparazzi gold."

"He'd never go for it."

"He's such a sanctimonious asshole."

"He's actually not, but he's not gonna go around setting up press photos. He hates the press."

"So did I."

"Well, maybe in a few years, I can set you guys up for a drink."

A few minutes after hanging up, Billy glanced around the conference room. Sandy was late to the meeting and everybody in the room was on their phone. One of the new interns was Snapchatting a photo of herself, no doubt bragging about her entry into the glamorous world of publishing. Billy pulled out his phone and texted Bluey.

How's your day babe?

Just Seamus stuff, last minute fittings and his drug test. I'll be done in an hour.

Oh crap—tell me how he tests?

Sure. How's work?

Billy replied with the green toy-gun emoji as Sandy entered in a maelstrom of flying papers, a long winter scarf, and the train of her floor-length peacock blue North Face puffer. It was nearly eighty out, and she was dressed for a polar vortex.

"You all are so not going to believe what just happened to me," she announced to the room before continuing without waiting. "Felicity Storm just tweeted at me that she loved my latest novel, and she's going to tweet the cover."

Billy felt his stomach drop. "But I just talked to our source inside Mason's camp," he began.

"Interrupt me again, Billy, and you'll be on red carpets for the next month," she cooed. "So, you guys, just think about it. We now have a direct line to Felicity."

"We already had one," Billy said. "And I have a great pitch for next week's cover."

"Billleeeeeeeee," Sandy whined. "Why can't you see what's happening here? We were wrong to take Mason's side; that's not what our readers want."

Billy's eyes met Christine's. She was shaking her head.

"What do our readers want, Sandy?" Billy snapped condescendingly.

"They need Felicity to be the victim, the sweetheart, the innocent bystander."

"Two things," Billy said, careful to keep his voice light. "One, that's what all the other weeklies are printing, so we'd just be crowded at the newsstand. Two, it's not the truth. Actually, three, last week was our biggest-selling issue of the year."

"Whatever, Billy," Sandy said. "We're going to go with Felicity's response. She says that Mason slept with the nanny and the kid saw it."

"She's feeding you lies."

"Jealousy really doesn't suit you," Sandy crowed. "Just because my sourcing on this is better than yours."

"Can we discuss this in private after the meeting?" Billy asked, not wanting to reveal to the entire staff that he was talking directly to Mason.

"Nope," Sandy said. "I've made up my mind. *Spyglass* is a pro–Felicity Storm magazine."

"Excuse me, then." Billy pushed away from the table. "I have some calls to make. Urgently."

"Billy, don't you dare walk out on me," Sandy yelled. "If you walk out of this meeting, you'll—you'll—"

"I'll what?"

"Oh, nothing, silly; it's just fun to boss you around. Go make your calls."

Mason picked up on the first ring. "How'd we do?"

"Not good, Mason. Your ex-wife is a genius."

"An evil one," he laughed. "Wait—what do you mean not good?"

"She got to my editor," Billy said. "The bitch got to my boss, and she's promised to help her sell her self-published novels."

"Who fucking reads self-published novels?"

"That's beside the point," Billy said. "Felicity discovered the one Achilles' heel in this whole situation. And she's exploiting it."

"So what can we do?"

"I'm sorry, man, there's nothing we can do. She wants us to do a story saying you slept with the nanny."

"I didn't sleep with the nanny. Any of the nannies. She slept with quite a few of them, mainly the female ones. She hit one of them."

"And she's apparently convinced one of them to say she slept with you."

"Fuck this. Fuck this whole business. I'm sunk if you can't help me here."

Billy actually felt sorry for Mason. "I'm really sorry, man. I'll continue to try to kill these stories."

"Yeah, I bet you will. Hollywood's a helpful town." He hung up.

Billy let out a long, slow breath and stared at his phone, half expecting Mason to call back. After a while, he laid his phone on his desk and checked his e-mail. Nicola had sent him various Oscars e-mails, parties to try to get into, saying she'd walk him in as part of Seamus's entourage, as long as they could convince Seamus to go to them at all. He winced, knowing that Sandy planned to be glued to his side on Oscars night.

His phone vibrated on his desk with an incoming call. It was Bluey.

"Hey, babe, what's up?"

"Um . . ." Bluey trailed off. "So I just got home to a letter from ICE."

Billy felt his mouth dry up instantly. "Yeah?"

"Looks like Gaynor didn't file the paperwork for my sponsorship since I left Crystal's payroll."

"Oh, phew," Billy said. "Well, let's just get her to send it in, then."

"Too late," Bluey said. "The letter is my official notice that I have to leave the country. Within sixty days."

Billy sat in silence.

"You there, babe?"

"I'm going to go see Gaynor. She'll fix this."

✳ ✳ ✳

The door to Huerta Hernandez was locked. Neither Nicola nor Gaynor had picked up her phone while Billy had driven the couple of miles across Hollywood. He bashed his fist against the door. How the fuck could a publicity agency be closed and unoccupied on a weekday?

He heard shuffling behind the door and was surprised to see Kara, in sweats and a dirty apron, her hair pulled back behind a do-rag.

"Don't say anything," she said, motioning him inside. "Apparently there's no such thing as free publicity. This is my job. I'm a shipping and receiving clerk who answers phones."

"And you look gorgeous doing it," he said without a smile. "Is Gaynor here?"

"What's wrong with you? She's in her office with Nic. Some big meeting."

Billy stormed down the hallway, kicking boxes aside. He pushed open the door to Gaynor's office and stopped dead. Gaynor had a half-empty bottle of mezcal on her desk, and she and Nicola were both about to do shots.

"What the fuck is going on in here?" he demanded.

"We are toasting loyalty. My Nicolita just sent a delightful note to Meredith Cox, declining her job offer," Gaynor said, throwing back her mane of black hair and tipping the mezcal down her throat, making sure that her shot glass didn't touch her bloodred lips.

Nicola ignored her drink. She was staring at Billy. "What's up, B?" she asked, alert to his expression.

"Gaynor," Billy said, his voice shaking. "Did you remember to file Bluey's new paperwork for sponsorship?"

Gaynor looked at him, her eyes still watering from the booze.
She gave a shrug. "I think so," she began.

"Don't *think* so," Billy said, his voice rising. "I need you to know so."

"I told Alicia to handle it with my lawyer."

"So that's a no," Billy said, turning to Nicola. "Bluey got served papers today. Crystal filed papers ending his sponsorship, so since you didn't do a new sponsorship, he's been working illegally, and now they're kicking him out."

"Of what?"

"America," Billy said, grabbing for Nicola's drink. He poured it into his mouth, barely wincing. "He has to go back to Australia within sixty days. All because Gaynor thinks it's funny to hire useless people and expect her business to run."

"What do you expect for two hundred dollars a week?" Gaynor said, stepping forward and putting her hands on Billy's shoulders. "Don't panic. I'll call my lawyer; it will all be settled. Bureaucracy is so boring. A good lawyer can fix anything."

She pulled Billy into a hug, then reached under her desk and found a third shot glass. She released him and poured three more shots.

"Welcome to the new Huerta Hernandez, home of influencers, YouTubers, and social media giants."

"Isn't Alicia your only influencer?"

"We need a gay influencer. Say yes right now, and I'll have Patrick build you a blog platform by lunchtime."

"Have you forgotten that my boyfriend is being deported? And also, my boyfriend makes your only A-list client happy?"

Gaynor pushed some buttons on her desk phone, and the sound of ringing filled the room. A man answered in Spanish and he and Gaynor got into a heated argument almost immediately. Nicola squeezed Billy's hand as they waited.

"*En inglés, en inglés,*" Gaynor eventually shouted. "Tell my friends what you're telling me."

"I'm sorry," said the lawyer. "It doesn't matter what I do at this point; it's too late. The size of the check that Bluey received from the studio must have flagged something with ICE. The letter is a judgment. Donald Matson will have to leave the country, and it's unlikely they'll let him back in. He worked illegally, yes, just for a week or two, but Crystal ended her sponsorship, and the immigration guys are fast these days."

"So there's nothing we can do to keep him here?" Billy interrupted.

"He could marry someone—that will help—but before that . . ."

Billy pulled Nicola by the hand, hauling her to her feet.

"What's going on?"

"You're coming with me. I need to propose to someone."

✳ ✳ ✳

The only sound in the car on the tense drive up Laurel Canyon to the 134 East was Waze. Billy hated it when the Waze lady made him drive a long way to take the shortest time, and today, his jaw was clenching so hard he thought his teeth might crack. Still, in a traffic miracle, they were racing up the stairs to Bluey's guesthouse less than twenty-five minutes after leaving HHPR.

Billy pulled his key ring out of his satchel and nervously dropped the keys twice before simply bashing on the door with his closed fist.

"Are you sure he's home?" Nicola said, breaking her silence.

Before Billy could respond, a series of latches clicked and the door opened, revealing a frazzled-looking Bluey, shirtless and holding a beer.

"What's gone wrong now, babe?" he said, ushering them inside.

Billy dropped his satchel and threw his arms around his boyfriend and burst into tears. Bluey set his beer on top of a speaker and hugged him back. Nicola slipped past them, scooped up Tojo and curled up on the couch.

"Hey, hey, Billy," Bluey said softly. "We'll work this out, we will be okay."

Billy pushed himself out of the hug and did a poor job of wiping his tears away with his bare hands.

"I worked it out," he said shakily, his breath rattling in and out. "Just give me a minute."

Bluey and Nicola exchanged glances. Bluey pointed at the kitchen and mouthed "Make drinks." Nicola shook her head and stayed where she was.

"Necessity is the mother of invention," Billy said, "so, I, uh—No, that's the wrong quote."

"Baby, let's just sit down. I know people; I'm on this."

"Bluey—Donald—I'm only doing this right now because we have to, but I'm also doing it because I really, really want to." Billy dropped to one knee.

"Oh, mate," Bluey said, tears springing along the bottoms of his green eyes.

"Bluey, for the first time since I moved in with Nic when I was a teenager, you've given me a home," Billy said, his voice growing steadier with each word. "And you've shown me truth in a town where the word doesn't mean a damn thing. I am young and I don't know as much as you, but family and truth are the two things I'll die defending. So I want to offer you my heart, and I want to ask you to let me take care of yours. Baby, will you marry me?"

And then he burst into tears again.

Bluey's lip shook and then his whole body followed. He nodded. "Yes, mate, you bloody idiot, I'd be proud to."

He started crying. Nicola felt herself crumble, too. And the silence stretched out, broken by sniffles, Bluey standing, Billy kneeling, for nearly a minute.

"Oh no," Nicola blurted. "We forgot a ring."

Bluey let out a throaty laugh.

"No worries, Billy. Let's go downtown; we can go to the jewelry market."

"No, no," Billy said, grabbing for his satchel. "I'm on my damn knees, I need to seal the deal before you change your mind. This didn't happen in *Green Card*." Billy pulled his keys out of the satchel and flicked through them. He slid two keys off a silver ring, then slid that ring off the mother cluster, triumphantly holding it up to Bluey's teary face.

He gently took Bluey's hand, and Bluey extended his ring finger.

"Oh no," Billy laughed. "You have big fingers. I hope this works."

He slid the key ring along Bluey's finger. It stopped at the last knuckle.

"Oh well," Billy said, standing. "That's near enough for now. I put a ring on it. You're locked down."

Bluey pulled Billy into a hug, burying his face in his shirt.

"Thank you, Billy, thank you. I love you," he said, over and over. On the couch, Nicola let out a loud sob, and Tojo sprang from her lap, heading for the bedroom.

"Hey, sis," Billy said, "get up here; I need to hug my family."

CHAPTER 31

SEAMUS ROLLED OVER IN NICOLA'S bed and looked out the window. Every night, since their reunion in Mexico, he'd watched as Nico drifted off to sleep staring at the moon out her window. And each time, he'd stayed awake, watching as her breathing deepened, her face awash with moonlight.

Last night, he had watched her sleep for an hour, maybe more; he wasn't sure. He lay next to her, propped up on one elbow until his shoulder screamed in agony, his stomach in knots. Their sex had been tender and passionate, and Seamus was noticing that each time they did it, Nicola's inhibitions relaxed slightly more. If anything, he felt that last night, she had finally fully relaxed; she trusted him.

And he was lying to her.

"You're gonna ruin this again," he said aloud. He had come close to confiding in Bluey every time he saw him, but his mind always argued that this problem was temporary. His liver would clean itself up soon, and he wouldn't need to buy the pee anymore. He wasn't using. Hell, he told himself, he would probably test clean now, if he could just muster the courage to use his own pee. But the timing was beginning to work against him. Preproduction for *Parallax* was about to grind into action, most of the time on the Disney lot, but there'd be more and more private jet trips to Mexico. The studio had scheduled a surprise pee test for this afternoon for the insurers, and that necessitated a visit to Courtney's, since he couldn't exactly keep the pee in Nicola's fridge. He suddenly wanted to talk to someone, anyone. He felt alone.

"You really don't have any friends, mate," he said to the air.

In Scotland, before the fame, there'd always been a group of friends. He didn't need a cell phone. He could just wander down to one of the four pubs near his flat and find someone to hang out with. Even these days when he went home, it wasn't impossible, though the conversation had changed. After a few beers, everyone wanted to know what this actress was like, or if he'd banged that actress. He sighed. Maybe that friend circle *was* gone. Being nostalgic for friendship made him feel even lonelier.

Padding naked out to the kitchen, Seamus poured himself fresh orange juice from a glass bottle in the fridge. Nicola juiced two bottles every morning, saying that it was the one thing that she remembered from her parents being married that made her happy. Another wave of guilt swept over him, and he had to steady himself on the kitchen counter. When the fuck would the shit leave his system? For the millionth time, he considered just telling Nicola everything. She deserved nothing less.

"You need to grow the fuck up," Seamus said angrily, to no one. "You're not doing anything wrong."

He put the lid back on the bottle and put it in the fridge. He went to Nicola's bathroom and started the water, running his hands under the shower, waiting patiently for it to heat.

He thought back to his earliest days in LA, how it had all been so new and exciting. He'd gone from a small role in a guns-and-gangsters indie in Edinburgh to a small role in a Spielberg war movie that also shot in London. Somehow, Tobin, whom he'd met years earlier in Ibiza on vacation, had been able to parlay those roles into seven years of back-to-back movies. It had been a heady blur, and the shoots had taken him around the world at least a dozen times. But in the downtimes between movies, he'd found himself alone in Los Angeles for a month or two, living in a long-term rental apartment, isolated from his past and the outside world. Dating was impossible after several betrayals, and Amber had filled the void that followed. She'd given him company, free rides to constant parties, and his first Oxy. His anger flared up. If he'd never met her . . .

He wouldn't have met Nicola. They met at Amber's birthday party.

He stepped into the shower, feeling the warm water wash over his goose bumps. *This is the last time,* he promised himself, *the last time I will go to Courtney's. Yeah, right,* his mind shot back. *How many last times have there already been?*

He waited for the car to drive off before he knocked on Courtney's door. The blinds gave their customary flutter as she checked out who was knocking, and then the door opened. Courtney stood there, in clean jeans and a simple white T-shirt. She'd taken her ratty extensions out and ditched the wig, and her hair was clean and cut into a nice auburn bob. She wasn't wearing the bandages on her arm.

"You look great," Seamus said honestly as she gestured for him to come inside.

He stepped into the smoky darkness, and she closed the door behind him.

"Don't sound so fuckin' surprised," Courtney said, as a hacking cough bent her double. She recovered and went to the kitchen, grabbing a pack of cigarettes off the counter on her way. She flipped one into her mouth and held the pack out to Seamus. He shook his head.

"Actually, Courtney, would you mind not smoking till after I've left? I don't want to leave here smelling like smokes."

"Another favor," Courtney said, plucking the cigarette from her lips and shoving it back inside the packet. "Everybody wants favors, don't they?"

"Sorry, Courtney, I just can't go from here to a meeting stinking like I've been in a bar."

"Oh, but you can go carrying a bag of someone else's piss?"

"Hey, I didn't come here to fight. Do you have a date today? You look nice."

"Yeah, right. I'm shooting the sitcom. Wouldn't you like to be doing a guest slot on a kid's network after fifteen years in the business?"

Seamus looked around nervously. He didn't have an answer.

"Exactly," she continued. "I'm an insurance nightmare, and I'm a tabloid joke. I provide half the drugs in this town, but will anyone give me a fucking break? No. I made half a billion dollars for Disney before I was eighteen, and do you think they'll put me in a movie? The studio guards have my photo on the 'never let this bitch in' list."

"You did set fire to that director's car on the lot."

"How many abortions can one guy force you to have? He told me he loved me and that he'd leave his bitch wife, and every time I got knocked up, it was too soon. I was *seventeen*, dude. I was sick of being pushed around by him."

Seamus looked at the girl in front of him. At certain angles he could still see the kid from the movies that had made her famous, but then she'd move and he'd see the deep lines in her cheeks and around her mouth. Her teeth were gray, and in this dim light, so was her skin.

"Look, Courtney, I don't know your story, but if you're asking why you're not getting jobs, you're not gonna like what I have to say."

"I've heard it all before, asshole," Courtney said, going back to the kitchen and lighting the cigarette defiantly. "I'm an addict, I'm high-maintenance, I'm a cunt, I'm a man-eater, I'll fuck anything, I'm unreliable, I'm unstable, I'm bipolar, I'm not worth the trouble."

"I wasn't going to say any of those things," Seamus said bluntly, glaring at the cigarette.

"What?"

"You're an actress in Hollywood. All of those things are standard-issue."

"Okay, so lemme have it."

"You have no self-respect."

"That's rich coming from a dude who's still using and lying to his stupid girlfriend."

"I'm not using; it's just still in my system."

"You're so stupid, you just . . ." Courtney trailed off. She lit a cig-arette and sucked at it angrily.

"I just what?"

"You just don't get it," Courtney said, walking to the other couch and sitting down like a collapsing house of cards. "You're golden. You can do all the drugs, get sold out by every bitch you stick it in, get fired from a blockbuster because of a tiny overdose, and the second you're out of rehab you're shooting a new blockbuster and you even get your fake TV-actress girlfriend a role in it."

"How do you know Bette got a role in it? That's not announced yet."

Courtney paused and nervously smoked her cigarette down to the butt. "Lucky guess, man," she laughed humorlessly. "Or maybe Amber told me. I can't believe your team even chose her. Why couldn't they pick me?"

"I don't think you're at the top of anyone's list when it comes to sober companion searches."

"Fuck you, you Scottish retard." Courtney scowled. "I can't make up my mind whether you're really stupid or entitled or the fucking queen of denial. You really believe your system was polluted by high grade . . ." She paused, smoking. "Fuck it. You're a coward. Why do you even come here? Are you too scared to ask Bluey to buy it for you? Of course I know that guy. His hands aren't as clean as you'd like to think."

"I know what his job is, Courtney. I know I'm not the only addict he's ever worked for. Quit trying to shock me."

"I'm not trying to shock you, believe me. If I was, I got ammunition, and dude, you're on ice that's so thin. You live in a bubble of your own imagination."

"We all do, kid." Seamus walked to the door and opened it, flooding the room with light. "You think that anywhere else in the world you could live in a house like this and deal drugs to celebrities? You're not exactly working at Walmart and collecting food stamps."

"You're not my father." Courtney waved her cigarette dismissively at Seamus. "You're just another pretty hypocrite who's using me."

"You invite the world to use you, Courtney. You're smart—every time I see you on TV they talk about how smart you are—and here you are, an addict selling drugs. And human piss. Not the smartest of career choices."

"You can't save the world, Scotland." Courtney defiantly lit another cigarette. "And you're hardly in a position to give me advice."

"Do you talk to all your customers this way? Business must be booming."

"Nobody is more sanctimonious than a recovering junkie."

Seamus reached into his pants pocket and pulled out a wad of notes. He peeled off five hundred-dollar bills and placed them on the kitchen counter among empty beer bottles and full ashtrays.

"If I can just get my bag of piss, I'll be out of your way."

"I don't want your money. I want you to put me in a movie, or I'm going to go to the fucking tabloids and tell them everything."

Seamus froze.

"Courtney," he said, hoping his voice wouldn't break, "there's no need to do that."

"So you'll tell your team to put me in your next movie. Like you did for Bette."

"Do you realize how impossible you've made it?" Seamus walked nervously around the living room, unable to sit on any of the stinky couches. "Until you quit this, quit using, quit being a disaster, nobody can hire you. But your comeback could be easy. I'll make a deal with you. You quit all this, and I'll hook you up."

"Yeah, I've got a counteroffer, junkie. You get me a contract by the Oscars on Sunday and your secret is safe. If you don't, I'll be talking to every blog, magazine, and TV show on the party circuit. They'll hear about Ojai and Bette and a bunch of shit I'll make up. The press doesn't care if you lie anymore."

She pulled out her phone and quickly took some photos of Seamus. He stepped toward her, and she raised the palm of her hand.

"I'm filming now. Be very careful of what you do next."

"Hey, Courtney," Seamus said, his voice full of venom. "How about we open the blinds and let some light into this place?"

Seamus walked to the windows and tore the curtains apart. One of them pulled loose of its rod and fell to the floor. As Courtney's eyes blinked in the bright light, Seamus darted to her and snatched the phone from her hand. He stopped the camera from filming, dropped the phone to the floor, and stomped on it as hard as he could.

"Fuck. You," he growled as his heel stomped down a third time, and he felt the phone finally come apart beneath his foot.

"You stupid Brexit asshole," Courtney snarled. "You're so fucked now. So fucked. How dare you?"

Seamus looked around the squalid room, then at the red-faced young woman.

"I've paid you for what I came for. Now hand it over."

Courtney turned slowly and stalked into the kitchen. She opened the fridge and retrieved a Ziploc bag full of yellow liquid. She faced Seamus, and before he could react, she hurled the bag at him. It hit him squarely in the chest and burst open, splashing his face with cold urine. Seamus felt nausea and anger rise. His vision went red, and then his stomach contracted as he realized his face was covered in piss.

He ripped his jacket off and used the back of it to wipe himself clean.

"You can leave now," Courtney said. "And remember, if I don't have a contract in my hands before the Oscars, I'm going to finish you off so bad, you'll wish you'd died in Ojai."

Seamus slammed the door on his way out and stood on her front stoop, shaking, the chilly winter breeze highlighting some spots of piss he'd missed on his cheek.

CHAPTER 32

BILLY DROVE AROUND THE DARK, circuitous streets of Park La Brea, searching for Sandy, who texted him that she was standing in front of the tower she lived in, Tower 2. He'd driven back to the guard building twice, but nobody was there. As he crept along, looking for building names, another text came in. From Sandy.

How hard is it to find Tower 2?

He gritted his teeth and surveyed the dark night sky for any building that could conceivably be called a tower in this awful antiseptic housing development in the middle of West Hollywood. He ignored the rapid-fire dinging of texts coming in to his phone and continued to crawl along the winding roads. Shadowy figures walked dogs in the cold night air. He pulled up alongside one of them and rolled down his window.

"Hey, do you know where Tower Two is?" he asked.

An older woman spun suddenly toward him, a small spray can in her hand.

"This is Mace, asshole. Keep driving."

Billy rolled up his window and did as he was told. After a while, he spied Sandy, standing by a building that was at most five stories high. In the frosty glow of the security lamp by her head, Billy could see that the outfit she'd been bragging about at work was indeed a bright yellow feather jacket and faux leather pants. She looked like slutty Big Bird. The fashion department must have been laughing their asses off when she agreed to wear what was clearly an awesome practical joke at her expense.

Her lank brown hair had been tortured into matted curls and her equine face hung lifelessly among them. Her hands clutched the Marc Jacobs baguette purse she had forced the fashion department head to order in, promising to return it without a scratch.

He pulled alongside the curb in front of her and waited. She was taking a selfie.

"Oh, there you are, you big silly," she cawed as she teetered toward him. "I thought you'd never find it."

"I bet you say that to all the boys," Billy said under his breath, deliberately not opening her door for her. He sat patiently while her new gel nails scrabbled with the Audi's handle.

"Billeeeeeeee," she whined.

"What?" he said innocently as she finally managed to open the door and slide into the passenger seat. "This place is like a rat's maze."

"It's perfect security," she said perkily.

"Because nobody can find where you live?"

"Billy, you're so dumb all the time."

"A tower is usually taller than that."

"You're such a size queen," she said. "How do you like my outfit?"

"Well, I said dress inconspicuously, so of course you have chosen to dress like a heavy metal Muppet."

"It's a pre-Oscars party."

"Technically, it's just a house party on the Tuesday before the Oscars. That outfit would be perfect for the Nickelodeon Kids' Choice Awards."

Sandy sat in silence as she often did when Billy made a joke she didn't like.

"So," he continued, "before we arrive tonight, there are some ground rules."

"Billy, do not act like this is my first celebrity event."

"Sandy, this isn't an event. This is a private party, in someone's house. If anyone figures out that you're the editor of *Spyglass*, you'll either get beaten up or lynched."

"So dramatic," she said, flipping down the sun visor and checking her makeup in the mirror, her lips pursing in and out.

"I mean it, Sandy. I had to pull strings to get a plus-one."

It was true. Billy had promised his friend Solstice two product mentions in this week's issue in exchange for it. Even private parties needed publicity to get free booze.

Sandy didn't answer for a while, continuing to pout in the mirror.

"No photos. No sourcing stories. No telling anyone where we work," Billy said firmly.

"Okaaaaay," she said with a huff. "But let's make that the last time you tell your boss what to do tonight."

Billy pulled into the valet line in front of a classic Hollywood chateau on the last street below the Hollywood sign. A man took their car without a word, handing Billy a valet ticket. He guided Sandy toward a metal gate and rapped on it. Solstice's head appeared from behind the bushes, making him laugh out loud.

"What's so funny?" Sandy piped up behind him.

"Hi, Solstice," Billy said. "Why are you hiding in the bushes?"

"Neighbor problems," she laughed. "Stranger danger. I dunno. I'm not gonna stand out on Ledgewood like some random-ass hooker." Billy saw Solstice look over his shoulder and watched her eyebrows rise as she surveyed Sandy's outfit. "Speaking of random-ass hookers," she whispered. Billy laughed again.

"Hi, I'm Sandy." A feather-wrapped arm snaked in between them, and Solstice shook Sandy's hand.

"Hi, Sandy, I'm Solstice. Here, let me open the gate."

Solstice turned the lock and swung the gate inward. When they were in, she quickly closed it and locked it again.

"Sandy," she said with drag-queen enthusiasm. "What is up with your outfit?"

"I know," Sandy said. "It's everything."

"Girl, you're giving some serious *Fraggle Rock* realness."

Sandy laughed, then looked at Billy nervously to see if that was a good compliment. Billy nodded agreeably, and he saw Sandy's shoulders relax and she did a strange pose.

"It's a new designer; the fashion department assured me I'd be perfectly cutting-edge for tonight. They told me it's post-Björk."

"And they're right," Solstice said, gesturing for them to come in close to her. "So post. Her bird phase was so long ago, it's vintage. But listen, Sandy, that's the last time you can mention the magazine tonight."

"I didn't."

"Fashion department. Most people don't have one. Remember it, or you'll be kicked out and I'll be asking you for a job tomorrow."

"Oh, send me your resume."

"No, Sandy, I don't want to work for you. I don't want to lose my job. But I will if they find out I'm letting the editor of *Spyglass* into this party. Now, are we on the same page? Get your Muppet ass inside."

The inside of the house was completely black. All of the light switches were covered in duct tape. Glowing orbs scattered around the floor of the living room gave off a murky radiance but didn't illuminate the shoulder-to-shoulder crowd. Billy could hardly make out anybody's face. A DJ deck took up almost a third of the room. Billy took Sandy's wrist and led her through a doorway, hopefully to where the bar was.

It wasn't. It was just another crowded room. Billy stood on his tiptoes and searched for a door that led outside. He saw a door that looked promising and dragged Sandy in its direction.

"Hey, stranger," said a male voice way too close to his ear. Billy let go of Sandy's hand and spun around, finding himself face-to-face with Ethan Carpenter, the closeted actor he'd dated last year.

"Oh, hi, Ethan," Billy deadpanned.

Ethan glanced at Sandy and made a strange face.

"Oh, so you brought a date, too. I mean a girl date. Are you switching teams on me?"

"Ethan, this is my *friend* Sandy. Sandy, this is Ethan."

"Oh, I get it, you two used to date," Sandy said before she caught herself.

"Did we?" Ethan said stridently. "Is that what Billy told you?"

Sandy stood there, nodding. Ethan shot Billy a death glare.

"I'm straight, remember?"

"How could I forget," Billy quipped, turning away from Ethan and dragging Sandy through the door that led to the backyard, which was decorated in apocalyptic moderne: flame heaters shot fire tornadoes inside glass spires, smoke billowed from every direction, and fragmented lasers threw blue and red dots all over the plants, people, and sculptures.

"Welcome to the end of the world," Billy said.

"I can't tell who a single person is," Sandy complained, shaking her hand free of his.

"Whoever designed the lights for this party has done a good job."

"But what's the point?"

"Sandy, remember how you get angry because I don't see all the people that are rumored to have been at a party? This is why."

"Did you bring any weed?" she asked.

"I'm your date, not your drug mule."

Billy felt someone tap him on the shoulder, and he turned, face-to-face with Mason Dwyer. He flinched, half expecting to get punched in the stomach. He hadn't seen him since he'd told him that Sandy had torpedoed his story.

"Hello, traitor," Mason said, waving an almost empty glass in Billy's face.

"Uh, yeah, hi, Mason," Billy said, shaking his hand. "It's good to see you. And I'd like to introduce you to someone. This is Sandy. Sandy Sandstein."

Mason's eyes widened slightly as he realized this was the person who'd killed his plans for tabloid revenge on his ex-wife. Billy watched as Mason fixed his movie-star smile on his face and took her hand.

"Sandy, it's a pleasure to meet you. Billy's such a lucky guy."

"Oh, what?" Sandy blushed. "We're not together. I mean, he's gay."

"Oh, that's right, I forgot," Mason said. "Well, it's very nice to meet you. I hope we get to hang out tonight."

"Oh my God," Sandy said, fanning her face with her other hand. "Billy, why didn't you tell me your friend was so charming?"

"Sorry, it must have slipped my mind," he replied. "Hey, would you mind going and getting us some drinks? There's something I need to discuss with Mason."

"But Billeeee," she began.

"Thanks, Sandy," Mason said, turning her shoulders around and patting her on the ass. "Two triple vodka sodas, and something for yourself."

She vanished into the darkness.

"So that's the fucking bitch that sold me out," he hissed into Billy's ear.

"Yeah." Billy nodded. "Felicity retweeted her, and now they're all best friends. Your wife played her perfectly. I'm so sorry, man. I really did have your back. She's just the worst."

"Oh, it's okay," Mason said. "She was just the frosting on a really shitty year. I'm outnumbered. Hey, is Kara here?"

Billy shook his head. "Did she say she was going to be here?"

"I invited her, but she said it would be too hard to keep her hands off me."

"You're gonna hurt her," Billy said bluntly.

"Naw, man," Mason said. "She's great."

"Can I announce you as a new couple in the magazine?"

"What? Are you crazy?" Mason's eyes struggled to focus, but he was angry again. "She's great, but she's not worth an extra hundred million in my divorce settlement."

"Well, as long as she knows her place," Billy said. "And her dollar value."

Mason shot his hand into the darkness behind Billy, pulling a passing person into their circle. Billy's heart did a flip when he realized it was Kurt Masters, bad-boy actor and legendary party boy. Billy had only ever seen him on red carpets. Masters was usually at parties so exclusive that even Billy could only dream of getting in.

"Hey, Mason," Kurt said in his deep voice. "Good to see you, man."

"Hey, Kurt. This is my friend Billy."

"Hey, Billy, you holdin'?"

Billy shook his head.

Mason shook his, too. "Last thing my divorce needs is a drug bust, dude," he said.

"I hear ya," Kurt said, wiping his nose and surveying the crowd.

"I know who's carrying," Mason said. "But she tried it with me; she's kinky."

Kurt's eyes widened. "What do you mean, mate?"

"This girl, she's wearing, like, a yellow feather jacket, she's disgusting, she just wants to get fucked all the time. And afterward, she always breaks out the best coke you've ever had."

"And how's the fuck?"

"The coke is better," Mason laughed. "I saw her at the bar." He raised his chin in the direction that Sandy had gone in.

"She sounds like my kind of girl, gents. Unless either of you have seen Courtney Hauser?"

"Not so far," Mason said. "I saw Amber over by the pool. They're usually not too far apart."

"This party is dark as a mine shaft," Kurt said. "I can't find the gear room. I can't find anything in there."

"No kidding, man. Nice chatting," Mason said, clearly dismissing him. "If I find Courtney I'll tell her you're looking for her. But I'm telling you, the bitch in the feathers will hook you up."

"Thanks, dude," Kurt laughed, pushing himself into the crowd without saying good-bye to Billy.

"What was that about?" Billy laughed.

"Oh, Billy, she's the enemy, right? Just a little light revenge."

"I'm not sure I follow. He'll go hit on her and she'll think she's hot shit."

"Let's not spoil the surprise," Mason laughed. "We're gonna have to get our own drinks now."

Mason gently pushed Billy ahead of him through the throng. When the bartender saw Mason approaching he began pouring drinks beneath the bar. Mason held up two fingers. The guy nodded back, and a second later he handed them both very full tumblers.

They clinked glasses, and Mason drained half of his in one sip. Billy took one ginger sip. Hardly any soda.

"What's the matter, you don't like it?"

"I drove," Billy said.

"Well, that was stupid." Mason wrapped an arm around his shoulder and led him back into the dark crowd. "So, before I get any drunker, I want to ask you a favor. And don't make me remind you that you owe me one."

"I do owe you."

"So I heard today that Seamus is *thisclose* to signing on to a new Star Wars franchise, and I want to be a part of it. I want it so bad, and my wife has pretty much killed my chances with Disney. I need someone strong in my corner. And it's Seamus."

Billy furrowed his brow. He'd talked to Seamus briefly today, a weird phone call that hadn't really gone anywhere. He'd been looking for Nicola. Billy was sure that if he'd signed on to a Star Wars movie he would have mentioned it.

"I talked to him today," Billy said. "He's doing the Parallax trilogy. He didn't mention Star Wars."

"Oh, I don't think he knows yet," Mason said. "This is super-inside-track stuff."

"So the inside track knows before the actor?"

"You wouldn't understand because you're not a star, but we are always the last to find out," Mason said, his arm getting too warm around Billy's neck.

"So how did you find out?"

"Meredith Cox told my wife, who texted me congratulations on losing another role I could have walked into a year ago."

Billy rolled his eyes. Hollywood was just a big, ugly high school playground where everyone's allowance was millions of dollars.

"Your wife is a charmer."

"My wife should have been a spy. She can cover tracks better than anyone. I had to get a DNA test on my kid; she looks nothing like me. She probably had the results faked so I keep on paying alimony."

"So you don't even look like your kid?"

"Not a whole lot," Mason said, finishing off his whiskey. "I'll tell you one thing, you gays got it right. No bitches and no kids."

"Gays have kids."

"Why? For the love of god, why?"

"You really need to stop drinking, Mason. You can't be sloppy drunk every time you leave the house; you're just playing into her hands."

"I'm a prisoner, man," Mason said, pulling Billy close. "You don't understand. She's set up a meeting for tomorrow. Me, her, and Meredith. Fuck knows what it's about."

"Don't go."

"I have to. They pull the strings."

"Oh, that's right. Meredith and her hobby of destroying. Well, it sucks to be you, but you don't want to turn up with a hangover. It's time you left this party that you shouldn't even be at."

"I don't get why you're so nice, I really don't."

"Call Kara, then call a ride."

"You're right, man, and yeah, if things were different, I'd be serious about her."

"Like I said, as long as she knows."

Mason made a quizzical face and glanced at his phone again. "I'm gonna treat her right."

"Okay, it's been great talking to you."

Billy left Mason and did a lap of the backyard, carefully stepping around and over people getting high and making out. *This party was Dante's celebrity ninth circle of hell*, he thought. There was nothing special about tonight. Rounding a group of boy-banders, he spied Sandy and Courtney Hauser deep in conversation. Courtney was speaking urgently, her brow furrowing angrily. Sandy was waving her arms in excitement. The fog cleared slightly and he saw that Kurt Masters was with them. As Billy watched, Courtney pulled a baggie of coke from her pocket and popped open the top. Kurt dragged a set of keys from his pocket and scooped a bump up to his nose, then did the same to Courtney and to Sandy.

Billy's eyes widened in shock. Then Kurt pulled Sandy by the shoulder and started kissing her angrily, his hand squeezing at her leather-clad ass. He watched as Kurt pulled Sandy inside a tool shed at the back of the yard, slamming the door closed behind them. Billy bolted back to where he had left Mason.

"Hey, man, I'm gonna split. If you're going to meet Kara someplace I can give you a ride."

CHAPTER 33

NICOLA JUGGLED TWO ARMFULS OF packages as she unlocked her front door and then pushed it open with her left shoulder. She barely made it to the sofa before the load of freebies tumbled. Some of it landed on the sofa and the rest scattered across the carpet.

"Dammit," she said as the front door swung closed and the apartment fell into darkness. Nicola felt her way cautiously to the door of her room using her left toes as guidance until she felt the wall. She needed to pee, so she inched through the darkness of her room till she found the light switch, flooding the room with light. She quickly pushed down her jeans and sat on the toilet.

As she peed she took out her phone and surveyed the screenful of notifications. She'd worked until ten p.m. after a phone call from Weatherman had alerted her that Seamus was going to be announced in a new Star Wars franchise movie tomorrow, "a huge payday for all of us," Weatherman had assured her. "And he can film during breaks in Mexico. The joys of working for the Mouse!"

It wasn't until several hours later, after a string of Skype meetings with Weatherman, Tobin, Timothy, and a succession of similar-looking men and women from Disney that she asked if anybody had told Seamus yet. According to Tobin and Bluey, her boyfriend was MIA. She presumed that he was at the Grove indulging in his new love for shopping. She'd texted him, but he hadn't answered.

As she finished peeing, she arched her back. She was bone-tired. Maybe a shower could wash some of the stress away. She shucked off her jeans and pulled her sweater over her head. She started the water, then sighed when she noticed that there weren't any towels. She made her way into her dark bedroom to get one, absently flicking the light switch as she went. Light filled the room, revealing a man crouched on her bed.

She screamed sharply, then fell into the defensive fight pose her father had taught her when she was little, ready to kick ass. Her muscles tensed and she brought her fists in tight to protect her face. By the time she realized that it was Seamus, she was humming with adrenaline.

"Seamus," she screamed. "What the fuck? Do you think it's okay to scare me like that?"

He was sitting cross-legged on the bed, a hoodie over his head, his face down. He slowly raised his face, and she could see that he had been crying.

The adrenaline drained from her system, leaving her clammy and cold.

"I'm sorry, Nico," he said, his voice breaking with emotion.

"Were you asleep like that?" Nicola said.

"No, no, I was awake."

"Then why didn't you say something?"

"I didn't hear you come in."

"I made a lot of noise," Nicola said, studying his face. She hated herself for her first response, which was to wonder if he was high. "I literally dropped a ton of shit on the living room floor."

"Sorry, I was wrapped up in me thoughts."

"Well, alrighty then," Nicola said. "This doesn't make sense, but I'm standing here naked, so I'm just gonna get in the shower. If you'd like to join me."

"Nah, I'll just wait here," Seamus said, patting the top of the comforter with his hand.

Nicola took a towel from the wardrobe and wrapped it around herself, feeling suddenly vulnerable.

"Is everything okay?" she asked.

"We need to talk," Seamus said, very softly. "Or at least, I need to talk."

The shower could wait. Nicola dashed to her bathroom and killed the water.

"Here, sit by me," Seamus said as she walked back into the room.

"No, I prefer to stand for bad news," Nicola said drily. "You know, the old firing-squad mentality."

"So we're off to a good start, then," Seamus said with a wry smile.

"Go on."

"I have something to tell you. I've been struggling with how to tell you. So here's what I've arrived at. There are two fundamental pieces to this. Please listen to both of them before you react."

"Okaaaaay." Nicola felt slightly ridiculous, standing there in her towel, waiting for bad news and simultaneously grateful that she had only peed.

"Nico, before I start, can you promise not to leave me over this?"

She shook her head, her lips tight. "No way, no how."

"Well, here goes. Now, remember, listen to both facts before you respond."

"Get on with it, O'Riordan."

"I tested positive for opiate use," Seamus said, his eyes boring into hers, his voice strong. He raised a hand to remind her to wait before speaking. "I have not taken a single drug since that night in Ojai."

Nicola stood perfectly still. She stared into his eyes and saw tears starting to pool along his lower lashes.

"Seamus," she began, "those two things don't make sense."

"I know, Nico. I know. I just don't understand it."

"But you've been testing negative."

"Well, here's the part you might not like. But again, let's do it in two parts."

"Seamus, please stop this."

"First fact: I've been buying clean pee so that I pass." Nicola felt her anger start to burn. "But I did it because Dr. Kessorian told me that I still had residual crap in my system. It was just a temporary measure, since I knew that I wasn't taking anything."

"Seamus, why didn't you tell me?"

"Because drugs. Not the easiest thing to discuss with you."

"I'm not a shutdown machine, Seamus," Nicola said, anger and emotion making each word louder than the one before it. "We agreed to full disclosure."

"We did, and I'm disclosing. I'm disclosing because I tried to fucking fix this, and it's not working. Dr. Kessorian says it depends on how much you took before."

"Wait, what?" Nicola said. "I googled the crap out of this whole thing, and opiates vanish after, I don't know, a month? From pee, at any rate."

"I didn't think I'd taken so much, but I guess my system is just full of it. You wouldn't believe some of the stories online, people losing their jobs and shit."

"Someone's getting bullshitted here," she said slowly. "And it better not be—"

"It's not you."

"Seamus, you could have called your rehab."

"Why? I didn't relapse. Who's gonna believe an ex-junkie who's testing positive? Nobody. I didn't have anywhere to turn."

Nicola paced around the room in angry silence, her mind awash in competing, flickering emotions. She hated Seamus and herself; she felt stupid and she felt used.

"I think you should go to Bluey's," she said finally.

"If I walk out of here now, you'll never let me back in."

"Yeah, likely." Nicola put both hands to her temples and pressed her knuckles hard into her skull until she saw white spots in front of her closed eyes. "It was never going to work, was it?"

"It's been working," Seamus said, raising his hands and then dropping them limply. "Nicola. On everything and anything that I hold dear, I have not taken a single drug since that night. That's it. It's been nearly five months. Why do you act like something couldn't be in my system for five months? You're acting like I'm stupid or something. I'm not. I went to a doctor; he says it's normal."

"Justifying your actions isn't my job, Seamus. At the very least, you should have told me as soon as you knew. You went right back to sneaking around as if that's the best way."

"Nicola, the worst thing I've ever done, the very worst thing, is letting you down. I can't expect Bluey to do everything. I tried to fix something by myself for the first time in years."

Nicola stopped pacing and turned, her eyes burning a hole through Seamus.

"Seamus, did Bluey know? Did he?"

Seamus shook his head. "I didn't want to let him down, either."

Nicola started pacing again. Her bedroom was nearly as big as her old apartment in West Hollywood, but suddenly she felt claustrophobic.

"Stay there," she barked, stumbling from the room. She let herself out onto the balcony, a sobering gust of frigid air striking her face. She stopped and gasped as a sob rocketed up from her gut, nearly choking her.

"No," she commanded herself. "Do not cry. Not now."

She stood still, breathing in the night air, begging her heart to stop hurting. She considered dragging the couch out there and sleeping under the moon. She thought about going to Billy's; it was empty and she had a key. She gazed at the tree on the hill, as if it were a talisman that could tell her what to do. She couldn't even call Billy; her phone was still on the bathroom counter.

She returned to the bedroom. Seamus hadn't moved.

"I'll leave if you want me to, lass," he said softly. "I fucked up again. I should have told you straightaway, and I always planned to tell you. I got in over my head."

"The bottom line here, O'Riordan, is very simple. You're asking me to trust you at the same time that you're telling me you lied to me again. I don't think I can do pick-and-choose honesty."

Seamus kicked off the covers, clambered to the edge of her bed, and stood up. He wasn't wearing any pants.

"You're Donald Ducking?" she said incredulously.

"Yeah, my jeans are in the wash. Long story."

Nicola looked at the ceiling. Would this day ever end?

"Nico, look at me." Seamus stepped toward her and put his hands on her bare shoulders. "I love you. I love you with my entire heart and my stupid brain and with everything I have. And I swear to you, on the love I have for you, the only pills I've taken since Ojai were cold pills. I did hard-core cold turkey, and then I did behavioral work. I don't want drugs. I don't take drugs. I haven't touched a single fucking thing."

"Then how is this possible that you're testing positive?"

"Now, that I can't tell you," he said. "But I'd like to ask if I could hug you? I've been sitting here shitting my pants all afternoon."

"Is that why they're in the wash?"

"No, I'm speaking metaphorically. Why don't Americans understand metaphor?"

"Can the hug wait just a bit longer?"

"It can," Seamus smiled. "Not sure I can, but it can."

Nicola gently removed Seamus's hands from her shoulders and slowly paced around her room. She switched on her bedside lamp and killed the ceiling light. It was beginning to feel too much like an interrogation in there.

She sat on the corner of the bed. "Seamus, you know what's happening inside me right now."

"I do. You want to cut and run. I can see it."

"Well, that's what is different this time. I do and I don't."

"Is that good news?"

"Maybe? I guess so. Because I know one thing about you—you don't lie. You can be an evasive bastard when you don't want to say something, but you've never actually lied to me. My dad lied. All the time. This is insane and stupid, but this time, I'm going to believe you."

Seamus stepped forward, and a tear spilled down his cheek.

"Can you please not cry, just this once?" she asked.

"I've been terrified of this," he began.

"And I haven't?"

"Fair point," he said, running the sleeve of his hoodie across his eyes.

"You do realize that this is exactly where my mom was with my dad? The second chances, the third chances, the lies."

"Nico, with respect, your dad continued to use. I haven't. I swear."

"I don't know what to say," she said softly. "Can we call Bluey?"

$*$ $*$ $*$

"Mate, we had a fucking deal," Bluey thundered angrily. He snatched a pillow from the couch, held it against the wall, and punched it as hard as he could.

Nicola had never seen him this angry. She was bemused that Bluey was much more offended than she had been.

"You come to me with anything, and we sort it out together."

"I'm not a child, Bluey," Seamus said.

"You're worse, you're a fucking actor," Bluey said, punching the pillow again. "You don't know how to do anything."

"That's harsh, and not entirely true."

"Okay, then explain to me how Dr. Feelgood manages to be your number one choice here?"

"I didn't know any other doctor. It's not like I can just rock up to the urgent care down the street and see someone."

"And that's why you have me."

"I didn't want to disappoint either of you," Seamus said. "I love you both so much. I wanted to show you that I could handle this."

"So what are you gonna do, Nicola?" Bluey asked, still too angry to sit down.

Seamus nodded and looked at Nicola with pleading eyes. He wanted to hold her more than anything.

Nicola met his gaze and felt her heart melt and her anger thaw. He wasn't lying to her. Then it hit her. He still didn't know about the Star Wars job.

"Seamus, have you talked to anyone on your team today?"

"No. I turned my phone off when I got home and forgot to turn it back on."

Bluey shook his head and went into Nic's bedroom to look for it.

"Well, bad timing, et cetera, but hey, congratulations, you're going to be in the new Star Wars franchise."

Seamus went pale.

"You're fucking kidding me," he laughed. "Let's get some

champagne. . . . Oh, wait. Right. Let's sort this drug thing out first. But really? Star Wars?"

Bluey came out of the bedroom and threw a phone into Seamus's lap.

"Can you believe it, Blue?"

"Billy texted me about it an hour ago."

"Who told him?"

"Mason Dwyer," Bluey said. "Billy is on his way here; he just dropped Mason and Kara off at a hotel."

"Let's be grateful she's tied up for the night," Seamus said, laughing like a schoolboy. "Or is that the other way around?"

"Can we focus, please?" Nicola, said raising her voice. "And while you're coming clean about all this stuff, how come you went to Portland during rehab?"

"Huh?" said Seamus and Bluey at once.

"Meredith told me you went to Portland during your stay in Seattle."

"Yeah," Seamus said, exasperated. "It wasn't prison. I was doing okay, so my sponsor and I went to Portland to see a show and hang out. We were away one night. It rained. Jesus, she is terrifying."

"What's terrifying is that we are just now hearing about it," Nicola said. "From now on, no secrets. That's my deal, and it's not negotiable."

"No secrets." Seamus walked over to her, holding up his little finger. "Pinky swear."

Nicola wrapped her finger around his.

"Can I hug you now?" he asked. She nodded and he pulled her close, her head resting on his chest.

"We'll have to call Weatherman," Bluey said. "We'll need to delay the Star Wars announcement."

"It's pegged to the Oscars on Sunday. Turns out it's why it was so important for him to present. I'll see if they can't wait until Friday to announce."

"Well," Bluey said. "They can't announce until Seamus signs the contract. I'll take Seamus to my doctor. Find out the real story."

Nicola nodded. "Let's try that."

Seamus kissed her on the top of her head. "She didn't run," he said proudly.

"It nearly killed me," Nicola said ruefully. "This doesn't feel good."

"Growing pains are never fun," Bluey said. "I'm proud of you, lass. I don't think our boy here is taking drugs or lying. We just need to get things back on track."

The front door opened and Billy, dressed in jeans and a Ted Baker blazer from the party, walked straight over to Nicola, nudged her away from Seamus, and wrapped his arms around her shoulders. He glared at Seamus.

"You're okay, sis?"

"I'm not sure that's the word for it. This isn't ideal."

"What do you think is happening?"

"We don't even know if anything is happening," Bluey said. "Our diagnosis comes from Dr. Kessorian."

"Oh, that's great," Billy said. "I've been pitching a story on him all year; I have two sources who say he's not even a real doctor, his certifications are fake."

"Unsurprising," Bluey said. "What else have you heard?"

"I don't know anything. There hasn't been any gossip about Seamus at all. Everyone seems to have bought the Bette story hook, line, and sinker. Nobody has any sourcing on Seamus this year."

Nicola tilted her head against his chin.

"Hey, wait a minute." Bluey turned suddenly. "Seamus, where have you been buying the clean piss from, mate?"

Seamus looked at the floor and rubbed his foot back and forth nervously.

"I got it from Courtney Hauser."

"Oh, for fuck's sake!" Bluey said angrily. "Seamus! How could you be so stupid?"

"I don't know," he said. "She lost her shit at me today; she's a mess."

"What do you mean?" Bluey said urgently.

"She thinks I can get her a movie role," Seamus said. "I can't. Nobody will hire her."

"And?" Nicola said.

"She threatened to sell me out. She says she has something on me, but it's just that she's been selling me clean pee. She can't tell that story; she's the one who's dealing drugs out of her home."

"Seamus," Billy said slowly. "Courtney was talking to Sandy at the party tonight."

CHAPTER 34

"*MIJA, NOBODY WILL TAKE COURTNEY* Hauser seriously." Gaynor huffed at her vape box and a fog of strawberry-scented vapor reached from her lips to the ceiling. "She's like a junkyard dog, covered in fleas and barking at shadows."

"She is threatening to undo all of the work we've done," Nicola said, turning and opening the door to let fresh air into the office. "Seamus could lose Star Wars—hell, it's not too late for them to kick him off *Parallax*."

"Publicity is all cover-ups," Gaynor said matter-of-factly. "If they'd had publicists in the White House, Nixon would have been fine. Trump would have looked competent. Some clapped-out whore threatening to unseat a beloved movie star? Happens every day. Nobody will listen. She probably tries to sell these stories every week."

"Gaynor, we built a house of cards," Nicola said, as if she were talking to a child. "All she needs is for someone to offer Amber money to talk."

"Eh." Gaynor waved at the air with a bejeweled hand. "Let them talk. We just deny. Nobody has photos."

"I'm not sure," Nicola said slowly, horror dawning in her voice. "When I went to Meredith's office, she knew about Ojai. She hinted that she had proof."

Gaynor paused. "I wonder if that's why she hasn't made a stronger effort to sign Seamus," she pondered aloud. "If he wasn't keeping us afloat while we launch our new . . . venture . . . it might be time to get rid of him."

"Gaynor!" Nicola rapped her knuckles on the table. "Our job is to outfox Courtney, not abandon Seamus."

"Don't worry, Nicolita, there'll be another client for you to date.

Today, you must be a publicist; tonight, if you want, you can be a girlfriend. You know I'm not in favor of this reunion."

"Fine, if you won't even try to help him, I need to get on with my day."

"Me too," Gaynor said. "Alicia got two million hits yesterday; I need to revise her ad prices, and the boys are having a meeting with a buyer from the Gap this afternoon."

Nicola rolled her eyes. "I don't want to talk about Alicia. I want to talk about Seamus. He's at the doctor's now, undergoing tests. Someone must have paid this doctor to mess with him, and we need to figure out why."

"It could be Bank," Gaynor said, blowing vapor toward the open office door.

"That's what I'm thinking. But we have the Star Wars announcement tomorrow, and we have the Oscars in three days. Courtney will be at every party and on every red carpet this weekend. We need to contain this. Drug addicts just aren't Disney."

"Does Courtney have a publicist these days?"

"Rosa Barbero in the Valley is her agent, her publicist, her manager."

Gaynor cackled. "How convenient that Courtney is dealing; she can pay her manager in heroin! Rosa is almost homeless. I will call her."

"We're on thin ice. If Amber joins forces with Courtney, they can destroy Seamus."

"We'll come up with something," Gaynor said, pushing back in her chair. "Go announce your boyfriend's lightsaber or whatever. When you get back, I'll have a plan."

"Great," said Nicola, heading for the door. "Can you also plan to not be vaping? Your Chanel No. 5 is clashing with the fake fruit, and it's the worst smell on earth!"

"Wrong again, Nicolita," Gaynor purred. "The worst smell on earth is desperation."

✳ ✳ ✳

The drive to Global Talent was once again slowed by late-season rain. Nicola wondered if it was a sign that every time she came here, it rained. It always felt like she was entering Mordor. In many ways, this was the Hollywood equivalent.

Nicola strode purposefully from her car to the elevator. She smiled warmly at the receptionist and asked which room the meeting was in, getting directed to the biggest conference room on the top floor, still without eye contact.

"They're already in there," the receptionist informed her.

"Am I late?" Nicola looked at the clock behind the reception desk. It was 11:55 a.m. "The meeting isn't due to start till noon."

"Yep, that's right. They just had some business to deal with earlier, so some of them got an early start."

Nicola clutched her purse and laptop to her chest and rode the elevator up to the top floor. She paused outside the conference room, knowing that whoever was inside could see her through the frosted glass.

Steeling herself, Nicola took a deep breath, fixed her best poker face, and pushed the door open.

Weatherman, Tobin, Timothy, and their assistants were arranged around the table and barely looked up when she walked in. Nicola fought to maintain her composure when she saw Meredith Cox sitting at the table. Meredith was the only one who smiled at her, a dead-eyed grin that made Nicola's hair stand on end.

"Gentlemen, where should I sit?" Nicola pointedly ignored Meredith.

"Hello, Miss Wallace," Weatherman said. "Sit wherever you like."

Nicola stood for a few seconds, weighing up the options. She chose a seat at the far end of the table, several seats from Timothy on one side, Meredith on the other.

"Thanks for waiting, guys," she said as she sat down.

"Hi, Nicola," Tobin said affably. "Sorry, it was just contract stuff; we needed to get our ducks in a row for the Star Wars contract. It's pretty complex."

"Which doesn't explain why she's here?" Nicola flipped a thumb in Meredith's direction.

Weatherman ignored her. "Do you have a press plan for the announcement? We've guaranteed Disney that the releases will go out tomorrow morning, so that Seamus can talk about the movie on the carpet at the Oscars."

"Before we get to that," Nicola began, "I have something to discuss, and it's not appropriate for Miss Cox to be here."

"Since I invited her," Weatherman said with quiet force, "I decide what's appropriate."

Nicola looked from Weatherman to Cox and then at Timothy, who suddenly found something to look at in his lap.

"All right then," she said. "Please just give me a minute to get my notes."

Nicola opened her purse and took out a binder of the press plans she had worked on last night with Gaynor. Placing her phone inside her purse, she set it to silent and called Seamus's number, quickly hitting the mute button. She watched until she saw that Seamus had answered before speaking.

"So the matter I have to discuss is something that may jeopardize the Star Wars deal."

"I doubt it," Weatherman snapped.

"Please, Jon." Tobin reached a hand across the table. "Nicola, what is it?"

"It's come to my knowledge that Seamus is currently testing positive for opiates," she stated. Nobody at the table reacted. "In light of his drug-testing requirements and also his continued health, it seems like this is going to be a problem at the studio level and beyond."

"Let's move on," Weatherman said dismissively. "This is not a problem."

"It is for Seamus," Nicola replied. "He swears he's not using, he swears he's sober. He's freaked out, and he's not sure what's going on."

Weatherman looked at Tobin. "Has your client told you any of this?"

Tobin shook his head. Weatherman stood up.

"Miss Wallace, this is the last straw," he said, placing both hands on the tabletop. "You do not have the power to keep Seamus in line. That is why Miss Cox is here. You have one choice, today: if you wish to be in the Seamus O'Riordan business, you must transfer to Miss Cox's company. That is the only condition that we will accept for your continued employment as our client's co-publicist."

"Welcome to the team, or your endgame. Your choice," Meredith said with a broad grin. "Just this morning, I met with Bette Wu, and I'm happy to report that she is also now under my care. We can be a full-service agency to you, Jon."

"Respectfully," Nicola said, ignoring Meredith, "the bigger issue here is that your *client* is still testing positive for the opiates that cost him, and you all, a lot of money when he lost the last movie."

"With equal respect," Weatherman began, "let me spell things out for you. O'Riordan may have you fooled, but he's a veteran junkie. Everything was under control until you came along. He was perfectly happy to show up and shoot whatever shit we signed him up for as long as he had a bottle of OxyContin in his luggage. In under a decade we have made him into one of the most bankable stars in the world."

"So you guys don't care if he keeps using, just that he keeps working?"

"His drug use is actually of no concern to us," Weatherman said bluntly. "His ability to work is."

"That's a little harsh," Tobin said, trying to be diplomatic. "Seamus is a paradox, Nicola. I'm sure you're seeing this. He says he doesn't love being a movie star. But he does. He loves the money and he loves the attention."

"I thought you were his friend," she said bitterly.

"I was his friend," Tobin said frankly. "Now I'm his manager, and he does what I say. And if I say he's going to do this blockbuster movie series and pitch it at the Oscars, then that's what he'll do. Trust me."

"Well, how do you feel about this?" Nicola's voice grew stronger. "He's getting blackmailed by Courtney Hauser, and she's going to tell everyone that he's been buying clean piss from her to pass his drug tests."

"I'll shut that down five minutes ago," Meredith said, dramatically unlocking her phone and beginning to punch out a furious text.

"Before you hit send," Nicola said, splaying her palm in Cox's direction, "I'd like to clear something up with you, Miss Cox. I did not say that I would work for *or with* you. So please do not interfere in *my* client's business."

Meredith held her finger above the send button.

"Don't fucking do it," Nicola said.

"Miss Wallace," Weatherman said, trying to sound friendly. "Can you please tell us how you've planned to deal with this attempted sabotage?"

"I have already worked out a response. Bette will announce that their relationship is over on Twitter on Friday night. Seamus and Bette will both talk about it on the red carpet. It will overwhelm any desperate attempt by Courtney."

"Did you get them onto *60 Minutes*?" Cox snarled.

"I don't think a two-month relationship needs to discuss its dissolution on national TV in a sit-down interview," Nicola said evenly. "Everybody knows that only fake relationships break up on *60 Minutes*."

"Once again, Wallace, you and Miss Huerta are screwing up. This time, the price tag is higher than we are prepared to risk," Weatherman cautioned. "Your services are no longer required. We've prepared an NDA for you to sign as part of your exit from this team. Nothing you've heard or learned in this room can be shared with anyone, least of all Mr. O'Riordan, our junkie cash cow. We like him just the way he is. Passive and lucrative. Now sign the damn paper and get the fuck out."

Nicola glared at Tobin as she waited for him to stand up for her, or Seamus.

"Tobin, Seamus would be devastated to hear this."

"Nicola, let me break this down for you," Tobin said with his usual smile. "This is your first year in the Seamus business. You've gone from around forty thousand a year to around a hundred thousand a year. That's nothing. That's what I waste on a car when I'm having a bad day. We are on the verge of earning hundreds of millions of dollars." He paused for effect. "Each. We paid you one hundred thousand dollars for getting Seamus to attend the Oscars. Imagine the money you'll see when he's really earning. All we have to do is keep our precious idiot happy in his little bubble. If you join forces with Cox, you'll be very, very rich. We all will."

Nicola felt nauseous, and she wished that she hadn't called Seamus. She watched as Tobin glanced nervously at Weatherman, then back at her.

"Nicola," he resumed slowly. "All of us are in the 'keep Seamus happy at any cost' business. And he is happiest when he is high. We've been keeping him happy."

Hot anger rose in Nicola's chest as the penny dropped. They were somehow slipping drugs to Seamus.

"You guys are drugging him? How? He's only seen Amber one time."

"Can we stop this?" Meredith said, yawning. "It's embarrassing to watch you be so clueless."

Nicola froze.

"Oh no," she said slowly. "Bette. You guys are paying Bette to dose Seamus."

"Paying, blackmailing, forcing," Weatherman said, standing as tall as he could. "This is Hollywood, you dumb redneck. Everyone's a fucking puppet; if you tell them they're the lead puppet in a puppet show, they'll let you pull the strings."

"Wait," Nicola said angrily. "Was Crystal doping him, too?"

"As if she is that clever," Meredith crowed. "She still thinks it's the golden age of talkies."

"Amber has done our job very nicely for many years," Tobin said coldly. "Until you came along. Now please, agree to work with Meredith, or sign the NDA and get out of here. We have a lot to accomplish."

"Seamus will never go along with you," Nicola said.

"You'd be surprised what a billion dollars and an increased opioid intake can do to a man's decision-making process, Wallace," sneered Weatherman. "Now, for the last time, sign this frickin' NDA and get your hayseed ass out of this office. You don't belong here. You never belonged here. And so help me, if I have to drag you out of here by the hair, I'll fucking do it."

Timothy pulled a sheet of paper out of his binder and slid it toward Nicola without meeting her eyes.

She took it, folded it in half, and put it in her purse, then took her phone and set it on the table.

"I won't be signing your form," Nicola said, smiling broadly at all of them. "And I'd like to turn the meeting over to Seamus O'Riordan, who has been listening the whole time." Looks of shock met her gaze as she unmuted the phone. "Seamus, honey, what would you like to say to your team?"

"Hey, everybody," Seamus said, his voice steely. "Weatherman, you're fired. I'm not doing Star Wars. I haven't signed a damn thing, so it'll be your breach of promise, not mine. I hope you have to write a huge check. Meredith, you're disgusting. Tobin, wow, man. Money sure does change everything. You're fired, too. Timothy, keep your fucking gay hands off my girlfriend. Nic? Call me from the car."

He hung up.

"I believe that is a wrap," Nicola said, closing her binder and putting it back into her purse. "Now, if you losers have nothing else to threaten me with, I'm going to go have lunch with my boyfriend. Meredith? Did I just destroy you? And the rest of you and the billions of dollars you just lost? Sorry." She paused, and flipped them all off. "Not sorry."

CHAPTER 35

"WELL, HELLO, SAILOR," KARA SMILED at the handsome, muscly UPS guy who pushed the door open. "What do you have for me today?"

"You're new," the guy said, lugging a large brown box into the tiny square of free space left in the Huerta Hernandez reception area. "I don't know what is in here, but it feels like a sack of sand."

"I'm Kara," she said, wiping some sweat off her brow and extending her hand.

The UPS guy stood up and grinned. "I'm Steve."

They shook hands.

"Can I get you a bottle of water?" she said.

"Thanks, but no. And you're gonna hate me. I have two more boxes out in the hallway. Not sure you have anywhere to put them."

"Leave them there," she said, glancing into the hallway with a grimace.

"What the hell is going on?" Steve asked, gesturing at the stacks of brown and white boxes, one of which nearly reached the ceiling.

"Oscar fashions," Kara said. "Even though we've said we've already made our selections, nobody takes no for an answer."

Steve paused on his way to the door.

"Hey, wait a minute, don't I know you from somewhere?"

Kara's chin dropped to her chest. She didn't feel like being recognized while she was in leggings and a sweaty T-shirt and the 'fro was tamped down in a bandanna.

"I don't know," she sighed. "Do you?"

"You're from *Bank on This*; you're the funny girl on the show."

"Thanks, baby. I was. Past tense."

"Oh shoot, you quit? Are you filming a new show?" Steve abruptly started looking around the lobby area. "Are there cameras on us now? Do you need me to sign a release?"

Kara rolled her eyes. Even UPS drivers in Hollywood knew the drill.

"No, honey. I needed a sanity break, and I'm here dressing some clients for the big one."

"Well, you should get your own show, Kara. You were the best thing on that show. My boyfriend made me start watching when you came on. That time you had to go to trampoline school and they didn't know what to do with your hair, that was hysterical."

Kara felt herself smiling. "Why, thank you, sugar—" she began, only to be interrupted by Alicia stomping down the hallway in nothing but a Spanx one-piece.

"Hey, *puta*, why you no answer your texts?" she barked. "I need you to order us some food, and I want a macchiato, and we don't have time for you to stand around flirting with . . ." She looked at Steve. *"Buenos días, guapo!* What's your name?"

Kara's shoulders slumped as Steve mumbled something and hurriedly left, pulling the door closed behind him.

"Now order my food, *chunty*," Alicia said. "I texted you what we want. I have to photograph my food for the blog, so can you go pick it up? It has to look amazing."

"No can do," Kara said. "Gaynor wants me to clear out all the returns so that we can fit into this office, and then I have a date."

Alicia's nostrils flared, and she stepped so close to Kara that their toes touched.

"Listen, *puta*, I don't know if you got the memo, but things have changed. You're the secretary. I'm the talent. Secretaries don't shit-talk the talent. Now get my food. Send that shit back next week. I wanna look through it."

"Girl, you're a celebrity in the way that Shamu was a celebrity. Right place, right time. And there ain't no plus size in these boxes."

Alicia started laughing in Kara's face.

"You can't really fat shame someone whose figure is their fortune," she said slowly. "Did you hear? Patrick and Sylvester are gonna sign a deal to do plus-size at the Gap, and guess who's going to do the campaign?"

"Hmmmm," Kara said, pushing Alicia back. "Chrissy Metz? I dunno. But probably an actual star."

"Yeah right. They're using me. We're a team. And we're gonna get a reality show, and if you learn to do as you're told, maybe we'll let you be my secretary on TV."

Alicia took two steps backward and waved a hot-pink talon up and down at Kara.

"You'd have to dress a little better, but you're definitely a . . . well, a maybe. You're definitely a maybe. Now order my food."

She stomped off.

Kara surveyed the mountains of boxes. "Fuck this," she said. "You can't talk to me like that."

She texted Mason.

Hey! Are you at the Bel Air yet? I can get off work early if you are.

Mason replied that he was already in the room. Kara pulled the bandanna off her 'fro, which immediately puffed to full height. Alicia could feed herself. She had a movie star to tie up.

✳   ✳   ✳

Mason had either been collecting bondage gear for a long time, or he'd gone on a huge online shopping spree, because the scene that greeted Kara when she arrived at the suite at the Hotel Bel-Air looked like a porno shoot.

The bed was strewn with black nylon ropes, handcuffs, dildos, several varieties of whips, and objects Kara couldn't even identify.

Mason, dressed as usual in Nike workout shorts and a shirt promoting one of his movies, had been smoking a cigarette when she arrived, and even though she hated the taste of cigarettes, Kara threw him against the wall and kissed him hungrily.

Without a word, Kara ripped off his clothes and forced him onto the bed, tying his hands and feet at each corner. She let her anger at Alicia drive her as she picked up a whip with multiple soft strands of leather and began to wail it across his exposed six-pack, watching as his dick became increasingly solid. The first few times they'd hooked up, she'd questioned it, wondering how someone could enjoy pain so much, but she was used to it now, and she knew that if she blew his mind, he'd more than make it up to her when she untied him.

She kicked off her pants and mounted him, guiding him inside her with one hand and going for the old failsafe hair-pulling with her other hand. Mason began fucking her frantically, his eyes glazed over. *Damn, these abs are good for something*, she thought. *He's moving like a fuckin' snake.* She let go of his hair; she wanted this to last a while, and if she kept up the pain, he'd finish too quickly.

He was too tall for her to kiss in this position, so she focused on grinding herself into him, but that tensed him up, too, so she had to slow it down. After dealing with Alicia all day, she needed him to screw the tension out of her shoulders, and that was going to take longer than forty-five seconds.

She slowed her roll and closed her eyes, focusing on herself and starting to enjoy the ride.

"Hey, can you pull my hair again?" Mason said, a rasp in his voice.

"Can you just shut up and let me do my thing?" Kara replied angrily. She lost her rhythm. She paused and sighed.

"Listen," she said, sounding like a schoolteacher and hating herself for it. "There are two people here, and two people need to be getting off, not just one."

Mason looked at her with unguarded innocence. "Are you okay, baby?" he asked, genuinely concerned.

"I'm so tense," she said. "Just once, can you drive the bus?"

"Is that code?" Mason asked playfully, thrusting his hips with comedic exaggeration. "Is it like *Speed*? You want the bus to go over fifty?" He made a stupid face as his hips began to jackhammer painfully beneath her, hurting her.

Kara, realizing she wasn't going to get anywhere with this spoiled fool, slapped him on the chest.

"Stop, Mason, this hurts."

He paused, a twinkle in his eye. "In a good way?"

"Would I have asked you to stop if it was in a good way?"

His face fell.

"Look, dude, I get it, you need all this to get off, but if your hands are always gonna be tied up and useless, you have to use what's left to get my job done."

"Sorry, Kara," Mason said, motionless beneath but still inside her. "I got a lot on my mind."

"And now we're talking," Kara said as the mood turned suddenly awkward. "Should we . . . uh . . . take a breather?"

They stayed like that for several breaths until Kara felt Mason begin to shrink inside her and she noticed that he couldn't look her in the eyes. She attempted a graceful dismount and snatched her T-shirt from the floor. Without looking at Mason's face, she untied his wrists and ankles and sat beside him on the bed.

"What's up, golden boy?"

Mason pulled himself upright and sat beside her, rubbing absently at his wrists.

"They got me," he said at last, in a dull voice. "I can't win."

"Who got you? The paparazzi?"

"Nah, my ex-wife. We had a meeting: me, her, Meredith, our manager. This divorce is killing my reputation, and her career is in a tailspin."

"Mason, you're still one of the world's top five movie stars."

"And I don't want to be bottom five," he snapped. "She lost out on a couple of jobs, and you know that my phone hasn't exactly been ringing."

Kara felt anger build in her throat, and as Mason continued mansplaining, a roaring like a beehive inside her ears started to drown him out.

"Stop," she said, putting her hand to his lips. "Are you getting back together with your wife?"

"We weren't together to begin with, but yeah, the business deal is back on the table."

Kara's stomach flip-flopped. Just three days ago, Mason had been telling her what kind of money she would be earning as his assistant producer. . . .

"Mason, but what about us? I thought we were gonna be a team, that I was gonna be your producer and your eventual public girlfriend . . . like Facebook official and everything." She attempted a wan laugh.

She heard him sigh, and he continued. "Kara, I'm sorry, this has to happen; it's easier for me, and my kid."

"But not me?"

"I didn't say we had to break up."

"Are you going to say that next?"

"No . . ."

"So, you just decided all of a sudden that reuniting with Felicity would solve all your problems?"

"No, they offered me—"

"Who they?" Kara said, struggling to stay calm. "They offered what?"

"Please don't be angry," Mason said, trying to hold one of Kara's hands. She snatched it away and sat on it. "Looks like Seamus O'Riordan didn't get the Star Wars job after all, and if I, you know, if Felicity and I can play happy families, I'm in the running for it all of a sudden. Felicity called my agent last night."

Kara swallowed hard, remembering that the pathetic man next to her was an idol to millions, which only made the searing pain in her chest both more surreal and more acute. She cursed Gaynor, because this was what getting hurt felt like and it wasn't anywhere near as enjoyable as shopping or cunnilingus. It fucking sucked and she didn't feel alive. She felt burned and wounded. She counted to ten in her head, crushed all her hurt deep down, and decided to salvage as much of her dignity as she could.

"So what about us?" she asked, her voice steady.

"We can keep on doing this," he said enthusiastically. "And we stay secret, but who knows? When I'm done with Star Wars, if things are going well, who knows?"

"So, a year?"

"Oh no, it's three movies over five years, so it would be in five years."

"And what about my assistant producer? Do I get to make some of that Star Wars money?"

"It wouldn't work that way," he said condescendingly. "Not on a franchise like this. So, not this time, but soon, baby."

Kara fought back tears. "Have you already told Felicity yes?"

Mason dropped his head and stayed silent.

Kara closed her eyes again. She'd gambled big on Mason, and after the Amber fiasco, this had felt like a potential path of least resistance to reclaiming something of a career in Hollywood. She felt like she'd been kicked in the stomach.

She bit her bottom lip and thought hard. "How can you promise me that Felicity won't force you to stop seeing me?"

"She doesn't care. I told her I need my freedom."

"So how much freedom do you have?"

"Well . . ."

"Well what?"

"We'd need to take a short break at first," Mason said. "She and I are attending the Oscars together. On Sunday."

Kara felt her anger turn to fire and fought to remain calm. "Jesus, you move fast."

"That Star Wars job won't wait for anyone."

Kara turned and kissed Mason on the cheek. "I get it," she said, her voice cracking a little. "Dude, it's your career, it's your life. I had just hoped that you—"

"I knew you'd be cool," Mason said, jumping to his feet and pulling her up with him. He kissed her nose. "That's why I waited to tell you. I knew that you'd get it, and we could be okay."

Forcing herself to hug him back, Kara bristled as he kissed her neck.

"Shall we get back to business?" she said, patting his ass.

"You really are the best . . ." He paused. "I nearly said 'girlfriend.'"

Kara put her hand back to his mouth, then dropped it to his chest and pushed him back onto the bed. She picked up a pair of handcuffs from the floor and rattled them at him.

"This time, really show me what you can do with no hands."

A slimy grin spread across his face. "Oh, Miss Jones, I promise."

He held his hands out to her and she shook her head, taking one wrist in her free hand and moving it behind his back. He brought his other arm back around and she gripped it, pushing his wrists together. She leaned across his broad, tanned shoulders and smiled as the handcuffs ratcheted around one wrist and then the other. She pulled the key from the lock and stood in front of him.

"You ready to show me what you can do without using your hands?" she asked.

He nodded down at his growing erection. "Yes, mistress," he smiled.

"Good, you weak-ass fucked-up pussy-whipped adult baby," she said, finally unleashing her anger. "You can start by figuring out how to Houdini your way out of those cuffs without the key."

She picked up her booty shorts and dropped the key into a pocket, then, as she slid the shorts on, she kept on talking.

"If you manage to get out of the cuffs, I'll see you at the Oscars on Sunday."

She dragged her top on, then picked up her shoes and ran barefoot to the door.

"Kara, what the fuck? You can't leave me like this. Come back, we can work it out."

As she pulled the hotel room door closed behind her, she doubled over as wave after wave of wracking sobs pushed out of her. She fought to control her breathing as she slid her feet inside her Prada wedges and pulled a pair of mirrored aviators out of her purse.

Walking slowly along the deserted corridor, listening to Mason's angry shouting fade in the distance, she dropped the key onto a plate of half-eaten scrambled eggs on a tray on the carpet.

CHAPTER 36

EVERY MORNING SINCE HE'D TAKEN Sandy to the party, Sandy had been the first person to arrive at the *Spyglass* meetings. By the time Billy got there, a solid gossip circle had been taking place. Sandy had been holding court about all the famous people she had met at the party, hinting that she'd hooked up with Kurt Masters, and dishing about all the celebrity contacts she had harvested.

"You better watch your back, Billy," she'd said yesterday, in front of everyone. "I'm our star reporter these days."

"Any of it on record?" Billy had quipped, satisfied by Sandy's droopy facial response.

Thank Beyoncé it's Friday, Billy thought as he walked the hallway to the *Spyglass* conference room. He could already hear Sandy's voice, both throaty and nasal, boasting that Courtney Hauser had just texted her.

"Sssshhh, here he comes," Sandy whispered as Billy walked in.

"Huh?" he said, taking his seat.

"Oh, nothing," she brayed. "Just joking."

Nobody laughed.

Sandy continued. "So, let's just start this meeting by saying that I've met with the lawyers and I have locked in the biggest cover of the year." She paused, as if waiting for applause.

"What is it?" Billy asked.

"It's a need-to-know only, Billy," Sandy said. "You know what that means."

Billy didn't but nodded, knowing that Sandy would explain it to everyone regardless.

"This one is going to be a secret. I've handpicked a small team to work on the story as it develops. It'll just be me, Johannes from the photo department, and the lawyers."

Billy gave her a quizzical look.

"Sorry, Bill," she said. "Looks like you got outscooped for once."

"Looks like I did," Billy said neutrally. "So you're saying that what you have is better than the inside story on Seamus O'Riordan and Bette Wu's breakup?"

Heads all around the table jerked toward Billy.

"Oh no, they broke up?" asked a new intern.

"Nice try, Billy," Sandy whined. "All of a sudden you can get Seamus stories? That's convenient."

"Everyone's going to be talking about it," he argued. "We can have on-record quotes from both sides, as well as some unseen photography. We can hold your Felicity and Mason propaganda for next week."

Sandy leaned forward, her low-cut Missguided top showing off her pendulous breasts.

"We are sticking to the plan," she said. "This is my big story. This is my issue. We'll cover the breakup as a half page in the front of the magazine."

"A half page? Then you can forget about quotes and exclusive photography," Billy said tersely. "Anyway, let's move on. We need to organize the party coverage."

"Meredith says she can get me into some of the after-parties," Sandy crowed, before pointing at Debra, the fashion editor. "What's the ETA on my gown selection?"

"We have some stuff," the harried woman replied. "Everything should be here by lunchtime."

"And I will have forty gowns to choose from?"

"Yes."

"You need how many gowns?" Billy said incredulously. "Did you get a ticket for inside the awards?"

"No, Billy. Those tickets are impossible. AMPAS told me that they don't give them to any members of the press."

"I've had mine for weeks," he reminded her.

"And who's your plus-one?"

"That's a secret," he said.

"Please see me in my office after the meeting, Billy."

When the meeting ended, Sandy stayed behind, regaling the interns with more tales from the house party. After three days of this, their enthusiasm had waned. Sandy's had not. Billy went into her office and sat down.

"Oh, did I keep you waiting?" Sandy said as she swept in.

"Sandy, what's going on with the cover?"

"It's so explosive," she gushed. "And we have to guard it."

"From who?"

"From you, basically," she said. "Remember how pissy you got when I sold out Mason? That was just so unprofessional. I'd hate for you to get in the way of this one."

Billy relaxed. Meredith must have decided to give Sandy the exclusive about Mason and Felicity's reunion.

"So you're still getting sourcing from Felicity Storm?"

"Billy, I'm not playing a guessing game with you."

"I just want to say congratulations, Sandy. She's a great source."

"Oh, you," she said, licking her lips. "You'll literally die. And that's all I can tell you."

"So why am I here?"

"Because I want you to give me your ticket to the Oscars. I want to sit inside and see it all happen."

"Jeez, Sandy, I wish I could, but I'm going as Kara's guest, and I don't think she'd really want to sit next to the woman who fired her."

"How the honeybucket did that nobody get two tickets? I can't even get one!"

"You really should think about what you just said," Billy said. "Anyway, why don't you ask your crazy pal Storm to get you in?"

✳ ✳ ✳

The afternoon was dragging on. Sandy was holding most of the pages for awards coverage, so nobody had anything to do. Billy looked at his Facebook Messenger and saw that everyone in the office was "active right now."

He was trying to come up with an excuse to leave early. Bluey had texted that Seamus had unsurprisingly tested positive at the real doctor's and he wanted to go for a beer. *Poor Seamus*, Billy thought. *Famous people problems are really messed up.*

Bluey added that he had tracked down Bette at her studio in West Hollywood and had talked to her through the door. She wanted to make a deal to save her role in *Parallax*.

Suddenly, a long, low animal howl split the muffled silence of the *Spyglass* office.

"Burning hell, what's that?" Billy exclaimed, jumping up and rushing to the hallway. The low wail turned into an earsplitting screech that morphed into words.

"Jesus fucking Christ, somebody help meeeeee."

It was Sandy.

Billy saw her assistant and some of the junior reporters rushing to Sandy's office. He hurried along the hallway. By the time he got there it was crowded with staff all trying to see what was going on. Sandy's screams were earsplitting and getting worse.

"Somebody call 911, I'm dying!" she screamed.

Billy pushed through the cluster of reporters and stopped dead at the sight of Sandy, writhing on the floor of her office, both hands clutching her crotch.

"Billeeeee, something's wrong," she screamed. "Call 911."

Billy pulled out his phone.

"Already calling," Christine the office manager said, tapping him on the shoulder and pointing to the phone at her ear.

"We'll get an ambulance," Billy said, kneeling by Sandy's head. "Stop screaming and tell me what's going on."

"You stupid faggot," she screamed. "If I knew what was happening, I'd be a doctor and not running this shithole magazine. FUUUUUUUUUUUCK!"

"Okay, everyone, back to your desks," Billy said, waving his hand at the gathered throng, some of whom were crying, an equal number looking like they were about to laugh. Nobody moved.

"Is she having a miscarriage?" asked a young reporter named Tara, bursting into tears.

"Come on, you guys, get back to your desks," he yelled. Christine swept them all out the door with her arm. Once they were dispersed she returned.

"Sandy, where does it hurt?" she asked. "The dispatcher needs some facts."

"My pussy is on fire," she screamed. "I think I'm hemorrhaging."

"I think we have a miscarriage on our hands," Christine said into her phone.

"I'm not pregnant, you stupid old bitch," Sandy yelled, then she clutched at her crotch again. "I think something is biting me. Ouuuuuch, this sucks. It hurts so baaaad."

Christine stepped out into the hallway so she could hear the dispatcher.

"I think I'm having a reaction to the artisanal wax," Sandy bellowed.

Billy considered rubbing Sandy's shoulder, his hand hovering in the air near her, but he pulled it back.

"Sandy, you need to breathe and calm down; the ambulance is on its way."

"I need you to quit telling me what to do," she screamed at him. One of her hands released her crotch and swung up to Billy's chest, grabbing his sweater.

Great, he thought. *I'll have to burn this sweater now.*

"Don't let them take me," she yelled. "I have to get this cover story to the lawyers as soon as the files arrive."

"Don't worry, I'll take care of it."

"No, you fucking won't," she screamed. "Christine, don't let anyone go in my office until I get back."

Christine popped her head around the corner.

"No worries, Sandy," she said. "Billy, why don't you go wait out on the street for the ambulance guys? I'll wait here with Sandy."

Grateful for the excuse to leave, Billy stood rapidly, but Sandy didn't release her grip on his sweater, grimacing as another wave of agony rolled across her midsection. As Billy stood, he raised her with him until her hand lost its grip and she dropped to the floor, her head whacking the carpet with a muffled thud.

"Ouch, my head," she wailed. "Fuck you, Billy. Just wait till Monday, let's see how smart you think you are then."

"Sorry, Sandy," he said, looking at where her hand had stretched out his sweater. "Christine, I'll be right back."

He took an elevator down to Hollywood Boulevard to wait for the ambulance, starting a group text as soon as he hit the sidewalk.

Sandy has collapsed with some mystery ailment, he texted Bluey, Nicola, and Kara. I'm on Hwood Blvd waiting for ambulance.

I hope she's in pain—Kara

Probably demonic possession—Bluey

Some people will do anything for attention—Nicola

Billy stood there in the weak sunshine, waiting to hear sirens. He texted Nicola privately.

She swears she has a huge story that will piss me off. Has frozen me out of editorial. Maybe Mason and Kara?

Do you know her laptop password?

Get out of my brain. You bet I do.

The sound of sirens filled the air and Billy watched as a CHP officer on a motorcycle, two ambulances, a fire rescue van, and a full-sized fire truck came up La Brea, all turning right and heading to where he was standing. He waved his arms to signal them over.

The CHP officer drove his bike up onto the sidewalk and screeched to a halt beside Billy. The officer stepped off his bike and removed his helmet.

"Oh, hai, girl," said Harrison, the swarthy, tattooed officer Billy had met at Robert Flanger's place months earlier. He kissed him on the lips. "What is going on in there?"

Billy burst out laughing.

"Oh, so nobody's dying?"

"Harrison, I have no idea. There's a lot of screaming and pussy-grabbing."

"Sounds like a Trump rally." Harrison turned to the first ambulance truck. "We'll need a gurney," he yelled. As soon as it was unpacked, he turned back to Billy. "Lead the way."

When Billy opened the doors to the *Spyglass* office for the EMTs, he immediately saw that things had gotten out of control. Sandy's guttural screaming drowned out any other sound, and every single member of staff was holding up a camera, either taking photos or filming it. People were laughing. He hoped for Sandy's sake that nobody had gone live and broadcast this, then he reconsidered. It wouldn't be the worst thing.

The EMTs pushed the cart down the hallway and into Sandy's office. They closed the door, and Billy could hear them telling Sandy they were going to lift her onto the gurney and do an inspection. *Poor Christine*, he thought.

There were a few seconds of silence, and then they heard the EMTs count down "Three, two, one," and lift Sandy onto the gurney.

"Help meeee," she screamed.

"We're with you, miss," said an EMT.

The door crashed open, revealing Sandy, now covered by a blue sheet, thrashing violently from side to side, her brown hair a messy tangle.

"Excuse me, everyone," the lead EMT said, and they swung the cart out through the crowd and down the hallway.

"I'm dying," Sandy screamed. "Get me out of here!"

Silence fell as the EMTs rolled her through into the reception area, and the door swung shut behind her.

Christine came out of Sandy's office, her face pale. She looked at everyone standing around, their phones pointed at her.

"If one single frame from this makes it onto social media, you are fired," she said severely. "I mean it. Now get back to work."

As people slowly returned to their desks, Christine motioned for Billy to come into Sandy's office, where Sandy's jeans and thong were lying on the floor.

"What was it?" he asked.

"I don't know." Christine shook her head. "I didn't want to look."

A knock sounded at the door, and Harrison popped his head in. "That was wild, Billy," he said. Billy pulled him into the office and closed the door, introducing Christine.

"So what's wrong with her?"

"Dude, the EMT said it's the most explosive outbreak of herpes he's ever seen."

Christine's face lit up like a kid at Christmas, and she burst out laughing.

"That's funny?" Harrison said.

"Couldn't have happened to a nicer person," Christine said through her laughter.

"Oh my God," Billy said.

"What?" asked Harrison.

"She fucked Kurt Masters at a party the other night."

"Well, that'll do it," Christine said. "Everyone knows that guy is like an STD petri dish."

Billy nodded as he figured it out. Mason Dwyer had set her up knowing the consequences. Revenge *was* sweet.

After the office returned to normal, Billy texted Christine and asked her to sneak Sandy's laptop to him. Two minutes later, Christine dropped a pile of magazines on his desk, Sandy's laptop sandwiched between them.

Billy blew her a kiss and opened the laptop, punching in Sandy's password: 1234.

He clicked on Mail and waited for the application to launch. As the window filled, Billy saw a string of incoming e-mails from Courtney Hauser, and his stomach dropped. The story that Sandy was so excited about wasn't Mason. It was Seamus. Courtney had apparently decided not to wait for the Sunday deadline to see if Seamus would get her a job. He forwarded every e-mail to himself, then deleted the originals from the *Spyglass* server. Then he called Nicola.

"I need a summit meeting. Now. Call Bluey and Crystal. Bring Gaynor. Your place. I'm leaving right now. This is bad."

CHAPTER 37

"A PERFECT MANHATTAN IS BETTER than all the coke in Bolivia," Gaynor whispered, waving her magenta talons over her cocktail and summoning the aroma to her nostrils like a scientist.

"Gaynor, six months ago, I was saving your ass just like this," Billy said. "I feel like we're stuck in Groundwhore Day."

"Manhattans are perfect for drama," she said, flipping him the bird.

"Thank you, holy mother," Billy laughed, crossing himself.

"Just give us a hint," Nicola pleaded. Billy shook his head. He'd been sitting at her dining table since he got there, poring over the e-mails he'd forwarded from Sandy's laptop.

"This is really fucked up," he said every few minutes.

"Billy, either give us a clue or shut up," Nicola said nervously.

"Nicolita is right, Billy. Please stop being a drama queen. We're trying to make cocktails here."

Gaynor poured a full tumbler for herself and a half one for Nicola.

The front door opened and Bluey and Seamus stumbled in.

"*Madre mía*, they've been day drinking," Gaynor said, taking a swig of her drink. "*Mamacita* has some catching up to do."

"Where's the fire?" Seamus said, walking over to Nicola and kissing her on the lips.

"Up Billy's butt," Gaynor said, finishing her drink. Nicola's eyes widened as she watched Gaynor pour herself another drink from the pitcher.

"I hope not," Bluey said, walking over and mussing Billy's hair. He bent over and kissed Billy's head, and Billy threw his arms over the laptop screen.

"Hey, keep your eyes on your own paper," he laughed. "Hi, baby." They kissed.

Billy picked up his laptop and went and stood in front of the couch.

"I'll take a Manhattan," he said to Gaynor. "And then, if you'd all be so kind as to take your seats on the couch, the presentation can begin."

Gaynor handed Billy a Manhattan in a beer glass. He set it next to Nicola's turntable and faced his friends.

"I don't even know where to begin, so I'll just start by saying that I love you all very much."

"Is someone dying? I would have worn black," Gaynor laughed.

"Not quite," Billy said. "This is more of a near-death experience. Also, Seamus, can you text Bette and have her come here, now?"

Seamus's face fell. "Oh shit. We haven't talked since yesterday."

"Just do it."

Seamus sent a text and put his arm around Nicola, squeezing her tight.

"Billy," Nicola said. "This is too dramatic. Even for you. Spill it."

"So, it seems that Miss Hauser is looking to add 'celebrity source' to her resume."

Gaynor shook her head and drained her drink. "What a multitasker."

Bluey cuffed Seamus across the back of the head.

"So Courtney *is* making good on her threat to blackmail you," Billy continued. "But you're not the only person who she's selling out."

Seamus slumped back against the couch.

"Just spill it, Billy," Seamus said.

"You're being cruel," Nicola said.

"I love it," Gaynor laughed, getting started on a third drink.

"Courtney was doing double business on this," Billy said. "She was selling Roxi to Bette so she could drug you, and then she was selling the piss to you to cover up. She was double dipping."

"I don't even know what Roxi is," Seamus said. "I've never heard of it."

"It's liquid OxyContin," said Billy, Bluey, and Gaynor all at once.

Seamus shook his head. "You guys, it wasn't like I was a career junkie," he said firmly. "I knew about OxyContin, and I got it from Amber. That and the occasional Adderall, and that was it."

Nervous glances and silence filled the room.

"Sorry, right, that's heroin and speed. That's a lot," Seamus said with a weak smile. Nicola sat next to him and took his hand.

"Somehow, Courtney figured out the fake relationship deal, too. We have to ask Bette who she talked about it with. Probably Amber. But you guys, she was selling the entire massive scoop to Sandy: Ojai, Oxy, and Bette. It's a triple-headed scandal, and it would be nearly impossible to bounce back from."

"Such drama," Gaynor said, standing and sloshing her drink to emphasize each syllable. "Celebrities can get away with murder, literally. A little bit of painkiller abuse and the word of Courtney Hauser is a scandal I can defuse without breaking a sweat."

"No, Gaynor, there's more. The final e-mails are about Nicola."

Nicola spun to face Billy, then she looked back to Seamus, expecting to see him crumble. Instead, she saw a fire blazing that she hadn't seen since before Ojai. He stood suddenly, his cheeks red.

"That's it," he said loudly. "That's fucking it. She's crossed the line. Nobody hurts the woman I love."

"Okay, Prince Charming," Gaynor cackled. "*Ay Dios mío*, who doesn't love a grand gesture? But Nicola is a publicist. She could set herself on fire at the Oscars and it would only make the news if it upset Sandra Bullock."

"Wrong. This stuff is pure gold," Billy argued. "Courtney tells all about dating Paul Stroud, she says that Gaynor runs a whorehouse, and honey, she knew about the Max Zetta stuff, too. It's all here."

"And as of right now, *mi amor*, Sandy does not have these e-mails. We have time."

The buzzer rang.

Nicola got up to answer it and saw Bette's face on the monitor.

"Apartment four-oh-nine," she said drily before buzzing her in.

"Did anyone talk to her after the meeting at Global?" Nicola asked.

"I talked to her this morning; she wants to save the deal," Bluey said.

Silence descended as they waited for Bette to arrive. Gaynor moved with surprising speed to the kitchen, where she whipped up another pitcher of drinks in under twenty seconds, returning to the living room just as a knock sounded at the door.

Nicola got up to open the door and gasped aloud when Crystal stepped in ahead of Bette. "What are you doing here?" she said. "I thought she defected to Meredith's camp."

Crystal leaned in and placed an air-kiss about a foot from each of Nicola's cheeks.

"It's lovely to see you, too," she sneered, sniffing at the air. "Gaynor, is that fresh Manhattans I smell?"

Gaynor rose in slow motion and approached Crystal with a cocktail. Nicola expected them to air-kiss like they always did and was shocked when they actually touched cheeks. What the hell was going on?

Crystal took her drink and then raised her other hand.

"Greetings, O'Riordan. Bluey, it's always a pleasure. Billy, well done, you've missed your calling, you should be with the FBI. Before you all start yelling at my client—" She paused. "Yes, she's still my client—I'd like you to allow her to speak. She wanted to come to you yesterday, but things were so . . . raw. . . . Anyway, Bette, over to you."

Bette, dressed in a navy Gucci minidress with a red bow at the collar and pitch-black sunglasses, stepped out from behind Crystal, her face ashen.

"First, I want to apologize, to all of you," she said, making eye contact with each person individually over the rim of her glasses as she spoke. "I am not here to make excuses. I was offered a job, an opportunity, and I took it. The facts of that job were misrepresented to me. If I had known at the time that Seamus honestly wanted to be sober, I would never have agreed to it. This is not who I am."

Nicola glanced at Seamus and saw the telltale muscles bunching as he clenched his jaw angrily.

"You guys, you know who recruited me for this? Tobin. That guy told me he was Seamus's oldest friend. He told me he knew what

Seamus really wanted, and that I was just the latest in a long line of . . . I don't even know what you'd call them."

"How about dirty, lying bitches?" Seamus spat.

"Okay," Bette said without skipping a beat. "I deserve that. He swore that deep down you knew, that this was how things were. He made me promise to keep it secret."

"Well, you told someone," Billy said. "Courtney Hauser is trying to sell your entire story to *Spyglass*."

"I know. Crystal told me."

"Meredith was pretty adament," Nicola said, holding Seamus's hand again. "She told me you'd signed with her."

"I met with her, in the morning. And she did something so disgusting that I couldn't believe it. I know you guys think I'm, like, just the worst, but I have limits. Standards. If they'd said, hey, drug this guy against his will and fuck up his life, I would have said byebye. I'm a gold-medal martial artist; I would have found another way to get onto the A-list. So when Meredith was telling me about how much she hated all you guys, I got intrigued. As weird as this has been, you've all been nice to me. Well"—she pointed at Gaynor—"not you, but everybody else. So when she started telling me that she had beaten Kara up, I couldn't believe it."

Gaynor spat her drink onto Bluey's arm.

"She did *what*?"

Nicola nodded slowly. "You were under enough stress," she explained. "She beat her up over the sex tape."

"You guys, she filmed it," Bette interrupted. "And she's like totally trying to sell me on coming to her agency and she's bragging about beating up Kara, who was really nice to me a couple times, and then she shows it to me on her phone."

Gaynor groaned loudly. "If only we had that footage, we could bury her."

Crystal reached into her pants pocket and pulled out a thumb drive.

"The goods," she said, smiling.

Seamus's eyes went wide. "How the hell did you get that?"

Bette pointed at the glasses she was wearing. "I filmed it on my Snap Spectacles. She is so ancient, she didn't even know what I was doing."

Billy snapped his fingers, and Crystal tossed the drive to his waiting hand. He inserted it into the side of his laptop. A few clicks later, he turned the screen to face them all, and the video began to play.

Even though Kara had told Nicola about what happened, seeing it was so much worse than she'd imagined. The only sounds in the apartment were Kara's painful screams and plaintive begging, and Meredith's rain of fists and boots and her hateful tirade.

"I've seen enough," Nicola said, waving at Billy to stop it. "Please."

Billy hit the space bar, and silence rang out.

"Kara said she'd been beat up. I imagined some slaps, a kick. That's disgusting enough," Nicola said softly. Seamus wrapped his arms around her shoulders. "I feel sick; that was so much worse than I imagined. That was a beatdown."

"Why didn't you tell me?" Billy said angrily.

"Kara was humiliated, and intimidated," Nicola said. "Now I can see why. She didn't want anyone to know."

"That's assault," Billy said, his jaw set. "We have evidence of assault. Are you guys okay if I show this to a cop?"

✳ ✳ ✳

"Meredith?" Bette said into her cell phone on speaker, half an hour later. "Yeah, it's Bette. Listen, I'm totally sorry I flipped out yesterday, I dunno, you triggered something—"

"And you can lose this number, you stupid whore," Meredith's tinny voice interrupted her. "In case you weren't paying attention, the Seamus deal is over, and so is my interest in representing a dumb bitch like you."

"I'm here with Seamus O'Riordan," Bette continued. "We'd like to talk to you about representation."

"Yeah right, and I'm here with Michael fucking Jackson," Meredith began. Bette handed the phone to Seamus.

"Hey, Cox," he said, and her tone changed instantly.

"Seamus, old friend, how the hell are you?"

Nicola stuck a finger down her throat. Billy and Bluey fought to stifle giggles, and Harrison the cop shushed them.

"Good, love, good. Now, listen. Do you want to represent us or not? I'm not too happy about losing Star Wars. Think you can help me save the deal?"

"Can you come here right now? I'm still in the office."

"Nah, Hollywood Boulevard on a Friday night? We're just around the corner at Bette's apartment; can you come here? We're on Fuller."

"Oh shit, give me the address, I can be there in five minutes," she said.

Bette read the address on Fuller from a piece of paper on the table.

"See you soon," Seamus said, and they hung up.

"Should we have invited Kara?" Billy said.

"The Oscars are on Sunday; she's still at the office," Gaynor said. "She is dressing nearly everybody in this room. At least she will receive some good news when she gets home."

"I do need her to come and press charges tonight," Harrison said.

"I'm sure she'll be happy to," Nicola said. "She told me she'd be home around nine."

"Perfect," Harrison said. "That gives us an hour and a half."

Gaynor and Crystal exchanged mysterious glances.

"Everybody, into my bedroom now," Nicola said, gesturing at her door. "Take your drinks. Billy and I will clean up real quick and join you."

Ten minutes later, Meredith was knocking at the door.

Seamus and Bette, standing side by side, called out "Come in" in unison.

The door opened slowly and Meredith was preceded by an enormous bunch of roses and a cloud of silver foil balloons with CONGRATULATIONS and WELCOME printed on the sides.

"You guys," she said. "This is such a pleasant surprise, on so many levels." She handed the roses to Seamus. "Sorry, this was the best I could do on such short notice."

"Yeah, this week has been full of surprises," Seamus said, taking the flowers and setting them on the coffee table. She let go of the balloons and they clustered on the ceiling, their curled strings hanging down around her hawkish face. "Bette and I got to talking today, when the dust settled, and she told me some things that really opened my eyes."

"Oh yeah?" Meredith dug inside her chunky purse and pulled out a bottle of Veuve Clicquot, which she handed to Seamus. "Like what?"

"I hear you beat up that bitch who was trying to sell my pal Tom Kendall's sex tape."

Meredith puffed up with pride, failing to notice Bette pressing the side of her Snap Spectacles, the little ring of lights sparkling.

"That was nothing," Meredith crowed. "I take my clients' careers very seriously. If I have to knock some sense into a hungry bottom-feeder every now and then, it's no skin off my ass. I protect my own."

In her bedroom, Nicola flinched, glad that they hadn't made Kara come home for this.

"You wouldn't believe some of the shit I've had to do to protect my clients. I have people—I mean, I don't normally do that shit myself. I have guys."

"What do you mean?" Bette asked with fake innocence.

"I'd rather not say," Meredith said, twisting the foil off the champagne. "Let's just say that a few people have gone missing, a few houses have burned, and some people's beloved pets met untimely ends. That little whore got off lightly."

"Girl, you showed me the video," Bette said admiringly. "You got some martial arts skills."

"I grew up in Jersey," Meredith said. "I got some Mafia in me. You wanna see the video, Seamus?" She pulled out her phone. "That black bitch got off lightly. I had to hold myself back. I wanted to kill her. She was so uppity, she kept on talking back to me . . . to ME!"

"She sounds awful," Bette said, the little spiral of lights still spinning on her glasses.

"She's the worst; that's why I had to destroy her. I hope she's turning tricks in West Covina. No, scratch that—I hope she's dead. That would be the literal best outcome here."

Nicola's bedroom door swung open, and Nicola strode into the living room. Meredith's eyes narrowed.

"Oh, what the hell are you playing at, O'Riordan?" she hissed. "Don't make another mistake that you're going to regret forever."

"Hey, Meredith," Nicola said, linking arms with Seamus. "Looks like it *is* possible to beat you at your own game, huh?"

As Meredith drew in her breath to reply, a flash of panic crossed her eyes as Gaynor and Crystal, followed by Harrison, Bluey, and Billy filed out of the bedroom.

"Stop right there," she screamed, brandishing her phone at them. "I'm going to go Facebook Live!"

She stabbed at her phone and started yelling. "This is Meredith, I'm being threatened by these bitches—"

She spun to point the phone at her nemeses, but at the same time, Bette dropped to a low crouch, and then in one long, fast, fluid move, she swung a rock-hard leg in Meredith's direction. Her bright pink Choo connected with Meredith's phone, smashing the screen and sending it rocketing into the ceiling, dropping shards of glass into Gaynor's blue-black cloud of hair.

Before Cox could say another word, Harrison stepped forward, a pair of handcuffs in his hand.

"Miss Cox, you are hereby charged with assault and battery occasioning grievous bodily harm. You have the right to remain silent. Anything you say can and will . . ." He paused. "Bette, why aren't you filming this?"

"Oh, sorry, dude, my bad," Bette laughed. She flipped the finger at Meredith and then let the finger continue to the button at the side of her glasses.

"Miss Meredith Cox, you are hereby under arrest for the assault and battery of one Kara Jones . . ."

As the handcuffs clicked around her wrists, Meredith began to scream.

"You faggots have fucked with the wrong bitch this time, and you, you stupid chink, are you filming me? I'll cut your fucking face off, you dog-eating bitch."

"Keep it up, honey, I'm broadcasting this shit live," Bette smiled. "And I have four million followers. Lots of Asians. How do you like this crazy bitch, my Asians? Did you hear her call me chink?"

"You have the right to remain silent," Harrison tried again, and Meredith lunged for him, kicking him in the shins. He pulled her arms up behind her and she howled in agony as he drove her to the floor.

When he had her subdued, he pressed his chest walkie and requested backup from his partner, Randy, who was parked outside, then he radioed for a paddy wagon, while Meredith screamed muffled threats into the carpet.

Bette stepped in close to Meredith, and delivered a short chop with the side of her palm just below her ear. She sprawled into unconsciousness.

"Thanks," Seamus said.

"It takes a lot to ruffle me," Crystal said, pointing at the still form on the floor. "That came close."

"That was like watching a Cartagena cockfight," Gaynor laughed. "What a stupid *puta*."

She picked up the bottle of champagne from the coffee table and prepared to pop the cork when the door opened and Kara stepped inside, a look of shock on her face.

"What the actual fuck?" she stammered, staring at Meredith crumpled and drooling on the floor.

"Champagne?" Billy asked as Gaynor popped the cork, sending it flying into the silver balloons, making them dance across the ceiling.

CHAPTER 38

THE SILENCE WAS DEAFENING AS Kara fumbled with her keys to unlock Huerta Hernandez for the last time. Oscar Sunday morning in Hollywood was preternaturally quiet. She'd driven from her place to the office in under five minutes. The streets had been deserted apart from cops setting up road closures and traffic restrictions.

After the madness of Friday night, giving statements and pressing charges, she'd lain awake in her bed, listening to the sirens, the coyotes, and the owls. She didn't feel victorious, she felt hollow. Just before dawn, she had opened her bedroom windows, filling her room with freezing air that still reeked of dog piss. Pulling her comforter tight around her, she decided to quit. Leave. Stop. She had to get out of Los Angeles. Hollywood was killing her.

Saturday, in a sleep-deprived haze, she had dressed Nic, Gaynor, Bette, and Seamus for some big party. She didn't even register where they said they were going, she'd just been grateful for the time alone in the apartment.

As soon as they departed, she felt lonely. Music didn't work. She ate a chocolate bar and didn't feel guilty or happy. A hundred-milligram weed cookie calmed her down.

"If you're gonna do it, just do it," she said angrily to the air.

And something in her heart answered. She'd leave. She'd move home. Instantly, the thought of her parents, and their house in Van Nuys, made her feel something close to peace. Tears had followed, and she'd let them have her, crying until her pillow was soaked. Occasionally, she'd picked up her phone, thinking maybe she'd call Billy but secretly hoping that someone was checking in on her, but her screen had remained stoically blank. By the time she'd smoked a little weed and fallen asleep around nine, her mind was made up, and she was okay with it.

She lethargically stepped inside the dark office and let the door close behind her. Mountains of cardboard boxes were still piled up in every corner of the reception area. She had to make her final decision on outfits for Nicola, Alicia, Seamus, and herself, and mark everything else for returns.

"This wasn't what I signed up for," she said to the stacks of dirty boxes.

She looked at the labeling on all the boxes, trying to remember which publicists had sent clothes for which person. She gave up and, taking a Stanley knife from her desk drawer, started opening each box. She made little stacks of clothing for everyone, until she needed to assemble a rolling rack because the mess was getting to be too much.

After an hour, during which time her phone did not ding once, she sat at her desk and cried again. The morning of the Oscars, and here she was, covered in dirt, pulling clothes and packing boxes like a junior assistant. She should have been waking up at home, hungover after a string of fabulous parties, texting Amber and God knows who else with tales of debauchery and fabulousness.

She checked her phone again and called her dad.

"Hey, sweetheart," he said, answering on the first ring. "This is a nice surprise. What are you up to?"

"Hey, Papa," she said quietly. "I just wanted to ask you something."

"Sure, Kara," he said nervously. "What's up?"

"Can I move back home with you and Mom?" She barely got the sentence out before bursting into tears.

"Hey, hey, of course you can, darling," her dad said. "Is everything okay?"

"No, Papa, I've wrecked everything, I'm done. I need to get out of Hollywood."

"Do you want me to come get you right now, darling?"

"No, Papa, I have to work today, but then I'm done, I'm out."

"Have you told your roommate?"

"Not yet, Dad," Kara said through her tears. "It doesn't matter.

She doesn't want me around anyway; she can afford the place by herself. She'll be happier when I'm gone."

"Well, it sounds like a good time to come home and let me and your mom take care of you for a while until you get on TV again."

"I'm done with TV, Dad," she said. "Or it's done with me. I'm gonna go back to school, I think."

"You gonna be a nurse like your mom?"

"Maybe, Dad. Probably. I don't know."

"Don't rush yourself; it'll come to you in time. I'm gonna tell your mom. She's gonna be so excited, she'll be fixing your old room up as soon as she hears."

"Oh, Papa," Kara said, her sobs taking over her body, "thank you, thank you so much. I can't do this anymore."

"Kara, are you sure you don't want me to come get you?"

"No." She wiped her nose on a T-shirt from the send-back pile. "All the roads are blocked and weird for the Oscars. I'm okay. I'll come tomorrow. Things just got on top of me, but now that we've talked, I feel a lot better."

"Well, why can't you come home today?"

"I got one last awards show to go to."

"Of course you do, sweetheart," her dad laughed. "I still can't believe you're going to the Oscars. Your mom will have your old room ready right away. We'll be waiting for you. We love you, Kara, and we're real proud. Your mom has all your clippings up on the fridge. You'll see."

"Papa, don't make me cry again. I'll see you tomorrow."

Kara wiped her eyes and then looked through the clothes on the rack. She had four outfits apiece for herself, Nicola, and Seamus. She'd pulled enough for the awards themselves, and then they could change twice or three times if the party circuit demanded it. She knew that whatever she put Seamus in, he'd wear all night.

Grabbing a thick Sharpie, she addressed all the boxes that were to go back on Tuesday. She got out her tape gun and sealed them shut.

When she was done, she went and sat at her desk. She hadn't

decorated it at all. No photos, nothing personal, the drawers empty. She considered taking a box of clothes for herself but didn't want to let Gaynor down again. With all the blinds drawn the way they were, the office was a depressing space. She looked around in the dim light and nodded.

"If this is Hollywood," she said, "I'm done."

She wheeled the rolling rack out the door and felt the tears start anew as she locked the door to HHPR, a small agency in a big town. It was the last connection to her failed shot at fame.

✳ ✳ ✳

When she got home, she reassembled the rolling rack in her parking space under the apartments. She looked at her dusty Jetta parked in a field of shiny Priuses and Audis.

"It was never gonna work, was it, girl?" she asked herself, feeling the tears come on again, wishing she didn't always have to be so dramatic.

She hung all the clothes back on the rack, locked her car, and pushed the rack to the elevators.

Inside the apartment, she could hear the shower running in Nicola's bathroom, then laughter. She couldn't remember the last time Seamus hadn't been there, and even though he'd been paying her share of the rent, he was still that always-there interloper. She couldn't believe that the paparazzi hadn't figured out that he lived there yet.

She looked at her phone. Still no messages. It was two and the red carpet for the awards started at four. Well, it started at four for stars like Seamus. If she'd been going to do the carpet, she would have been expected at three. As it was, she and Billy, in his rented tux, could just take their seats at four thirty. She wouldn't be doing the carpet.

Nicola's door opened and Seamus came out wearing a towel.

"Oh, hey, Kara," he said cheerfully. "How you doing?"

"I been better, boy," she said, busying herself with the clothes on the rack.

Seamus walked up to her and touched her shoulder. "What's wrong?" he asked gently. It was enough to start the waterworks again.

Kara slumped onto the couch, crying her eyes out. She heard Nicola come out of her room and then she felt the couch dip as she sat down next to her.

"Hey, girl, what's wrong?" Nicola asked. "You can't be crying about that asshole Mason on Oscars day. You need to start your makeup."

Kara sat upright and threw her head back, sniffing deep to stop the sobs.

"I have something to tell you guys," she began. "Well, it's really you, Nic, I have to tell you. I'm gonna move out. I'm done here."

"Is it me?" Seamus asked. "Is this one of those 'the boyfriend is here too much' things? I'm so sorry."

Kara laughed through her tears. "No, you big lug, it's not you, I'm just done."

"No," Nicola said. "We can do this; you can't let this shit get you down."

"I'm beyond down," Kara said. "This ain't a pity party—we have an awards show to go to—but really, what was I thinking? I was every black-girl stereotype that I could be. I was girl in rap video. I was colorful club kid. I was stylist. I was black girl in reality show whose name couldn't be any lower in the credits. Fuck, I was nearly the stupid slut with a sex tape. I literally considered it; I didn't think about my parents, my sister, nothing. I got my ass handed to me, and you know what? I deserved it. It's time to bail out."

Nicola just sat there, stunned. Seamus pointed at his towel.

"I'm gonna leave you two to talk about this while I get dressed," he said, walking into Nicola's room.

"Just take a break," Nic said, rubbing Kara's shoulders. "Go home, get centered. Come back when you're ready."

"Don't be so damned nice to me. I also very nearly sold you out, and now you're just continuing to be so nice to me."

"We all make bad choices," Nicola said. "You've had a brutal year; it's probably the right time for you to go clear your head, eat a bunch of your mom's amazing cooking, and come back for ding ding round two."

"Thanks for being you, Nic. I mean it. But I'm a twenty-five-year-old never-was. I can't do what it would take to make it happen. I've seen too much; I'm not that hard."

"Well, like I said, I'll just live alone for a little while, and my door is always going to be open to you."

Kara leaned in and hugged her tightly.

"Let me lay out the clothes so you two can get started on choosing what you're gonna wear since you guys need to get there soon."

"You don't have to rush. We have a car coming in an hour; I figure if he gets onto the carpet by four forty-five and talks to two outlets, that's plenty."

"Are you gonna go into the show?"

"The Academy are expecting Bette Wu in the seat next to him, but Seamus says he wants me there," Nicola said. "It might be fun."

"You'll be in the headlines again, mystery girl."

"This time, I'm ready."

"Where is Gaynor?"

"She and Crystal have some meeting about Alicia, who is actually going to sit next to Gaynor."

"I can't even." Kara sniffed. "How the hell did she manage to out-fame me?"

"The world is ending, I guess," Nicola said. "So what do you have for me to wear?"

Kara got up and pulled everything off the rolling rack, laying out four full-length dresses.

"I got Balenciaga, Armani, Balmain, and Versace," she said, pointing to each one as she said the name.

"They're all gorgeous," Nicola said. "I'm gonna let you decide. Actually, where are the shoes? That might sway me."

Kara looked behind the couch, and then at the rolling rack, her eyes widening.

"The shoes. I forgot the stupid shoes at the office."

"Don't worry about it. I have some Louboutins here, let me go pull them out."

"But Seamus, I promised my friend that he'd be wearing their shoes."

"Tell them the movie star threw a fit," Nicola said. "Baby—what shoes do you have here?"

Seamus appeared in the doorway holding up a grimy pair of old black Chucks.

"I'm seriously happy if you let me wear these."

"No, I pulled incredible shoes for all of us," Kara said. "*No*. Your car comes in an hour? Nic, pick a suit for him, start dressing him, you try the Balmain. I'll be back with shoes for all of us in twenty minutes."

"You cannot get to the office and back in twenty minutes. Every street around us is closed."

"I got this," Kara said, grabbing her keys. "I'll take Outpost up and over the backside. Wait for me. Thirty minutes tops."

She leaned over and kissed Nic on the cheek.

"Thank you. You're a better friend than I deserved. I'll be better, I promise," she said. "See you in a minute."

Kara ran out the door and along the hallway. She hammered on the elevator call button, but it was stuck on P3. Somebody was probably moving in. Dammit. She threw herself into the fire stairs, descending two steps at a time in platform heels, until she got to P2.

She revved the Jetta as she waited for the automatic gates to open. The clock on her dash said two fifteen. She burned rubber as she turned out onto Fuller and then blew the stop sign at Orange. Franklin was a parking lot headed east, but there was nothing in the oncoming lane, so she floored it and drove the wrong way, then left up Outpost. She'd avoided the worst of it. She smiled. She kept her foot down as her trusty old Jetta began the crawl up to Mulholland, where she could just jump down on Laurel and be at work in no time.

She breathed a sigh of relief as she neared a sharp bend in the road. Today was going to work out.

As she entered the corner, she screamed. A bright red Maserati was speeding toward her on her side of the road. *This isn't a one-way street*, she thought, her mind confused, then panic filled her and everything slowed down except the Maserati. It sped up.

Holy no oh no. She registered that Courtney Hauser was driving, and Amber was in the passenger seat. Courtney had her phone up and was showing something to Amber, completely unaware that they were in the wrong lane and heading straight for Kara.

She swerved up onto the sidewalk, feeling a tire blow out, but it wasn't enough, and she felt before she heard the impact as the Maserati slammed head-on into the Jetta. Kara's airbag blew up in her face. Her nose cracked, then she felt herself, weightless, flying sideways. *This isn't going to end well*, she thought with surprising serenity as her car finally encountered something solid. She felt her arm snap and blinding agony filled her left side, then the car spun again, in another direction, Kara's head whipping back and forth.

Finally the noise and the spinning stopped and Kara sat there, breathing deeply, waiting for another impact. She tried to move her left arm, and it was a dead pulse of blinding pain. She peered cautiously down to make sure that it hadn't been torn off. Phew. It was still there. She tried to move her right hand and was pleased that she could. She slowly reached up and started patting down the airbag that was blocking her vision. Shattered pieces of the windshield clicked as they fell to the floor of the car, breaking the eerie silence. She felt warm blood spill over her lips as another wave of pain shot from her shoulder and across her chest.

Smoke and steam were billowing from her engine. She could make out the red of the other car, embedded in her hood, steam pouring upward. She squinted and fought for consciousness as darkness clouded her vision.

A breeze carried some of the steam away, and she cried out in horror. Courtney Hauser's head and part of one of her shoulders protruded through the smashed windshield of the Maserati. Blood was pumping from a gash in her throat, spraying onto the road. As Kara watched in horror, the jets of blood grew less powerful, giving way to a sickening river that ran down the glass and into the engine.

Amber began moving in the passenger seat. Kara watched as she undid her seat belt and opened her door, moving like a zombie.

"Amber, help me," Kara called out through her broken windshield.

Amber looked at her, then looked at Courtney's lifeless body. She stepped away from the car, blood pouring from a gash across her forehead.

"Amber, please, please, open my door. My arm is broken, I can smell gasoline."

"Shut the fuck up," Amber growled.

A man came out of a house a ways up the street. He pulled out his phone and began to dial. She took a deep breath. He was calling 911. He had to be.

"Amber, please, I'm really hurt, I think my car's gonna explode, will you—"

"I told you, shut the fuck up."

Amber bent over and Kara watched, horrified again, as she rummaged in the car's tiny backseat, retrieving a brown leather satchel, which she threw over her shoulder. She walked unsteadily to Kara's car.

"I wasn't here, all right," she hissed.

"You need to come to the hospital."

"I just did so much fucking MDA that I'll die if they sedate me," Amber said. "I need to get the fuck out of here. Don't tell anyone I was in the car."

To Kara's shock, Amber loped across the street and into Chelan Drive, vanishing behind a hedge.

Kara looked back up the street to see the old man walking toward her, a look of horror on his face. Another younger guy appeared, and the last thing that Kara saw before she blacked out was that he pulled out his phone and started filming.

CHAPTER 39

NICOLA PRESSED ON THE BUTTON in the Cedars-Sinai elevator for the fourth time.

"Won't make it go any faster, honey," said an old black lady in nurse scrubs. "I see it all the time. You'll get there in time; bangin' on the button won't help."

The woman looked at Nicola and offered a warm smile, then her eyes saw Seamus standing next to her, and they widened in recognition.

"Only in Hollywood," she chuckled, nodding at him. The doors opened.

"This is your floor, kids," the lady said.

Nicola grabbed Seamus's hand and pulled him down the hallway, following signs that said RECEPTION. Entering a waiting area, Nicola spied Mr. and Mrs. Jones sitting in the uncomfortable plastic chairs. Their faces were drawn, their eyes were closed, and they were holding hands tightly.

"Mr. Jones, Mrs. Jones," Nicola said quietly. Mrs. Jones opened her eyes slowly and smiled as she rose to hug Nicola.

"How is she?"

"Well, she's gonna be okay, eventually," Mrs. Jones said, bursting into tears.

Mr. Jones stood and introduced himself to Seamus.

"Yessir," Mr. Jones said. "All things considered, it's a miracle. She's got a broken nose, her arm is done snapped in two places, collarbone is busted, and she got a bunch of cracked ribs and she's gonna have one hell of a whiplash, but our girl is gonna be all right."

"That's great news," Nicola said, stepping back but still holding Mrs. Jones's hand. "Have you talked to her?"

"Yeah, she's on a bunch of painkillers. They reset her arm; they're just finishing the cast now. We just came out of the room because it was getting crowded. You can go in."

"I'll wait till they're done. I wouldn't like being interrupted if that was my job."

"Well, don't you two look nice," Mrs. Jones said, pointing a finger up and down at Seamus and Nicola.

"Thanks. We were on our way to the Oscars when you called. We were so worried; we didn't know where Kara was but we had to leave," Nicola explained. "We just had the nice limo guy bring us here instead."

"Kara chose these clothes for us," Seamus said. "She did a great job, huh?"

"I feel so guilty," Nicola said, her voice shaking. "She was rushing back out to get the shoes for our outfits. Such a stupid thing."

"How could you know, Nicola?" Mr. Jones rubbed her shoulder. "This is life; we got to go about our lives, and if that happens to be the end of the run, then that's how it ends."

"Well, come on, Larry," Mrs. Jones said. "No need to be so blunt; a young girl is dead."

Nicola had been able to piece together some of the details of the accident from TMZ, and she knew that Courtney Hauser had been killed in the accident. She'd even seen gory photos of her lifeless body half in, half out of her loaner Maserati.

"Did Kara tell you what happened?"

"Yeah, she said that that girl was texting and driving on the wrong side of the road, ran straight into her," Mrs. Jones said. "Just awful."

"Where the hell did Courtney Hauser get a Maserati?" Seamus asked.

"They're giving them to anybody these days," Nicola replied. "Everyone wants a Tesla."

"Except Bette," Seamus said with a wry laugh. Nicola gave him a puzzled look.

Several nurses came out of Kara's room, pushing a cart with plaster cast supplies on it.

"Looks like the room is free if you guys wanna go in," Mr. Jones said. "We'll come in in a minute. Give you a chance to talk."

"I'll wait out here," Seamus said. "See you in a second."

Nicola nodded and walked slowly to the door. She'd hated hospitals ever since she was little, since the first time her father had overdosed and her mother had driven them to the hospital like a crazy person, convinced that her dad would be dead by the time they got there. The last time she'd been in a hospital had been when she had to identify his body. Nothing good ever happened in hospitals.

She gingerly pushed the door open, steeling herself not to gasp and then gasping anyway. Kara's eyes were closed, and she lay in front of a wall of beeping, flashing monitors. A plastered bandage covered her nose, her arm was bent in its new cast, and one of her legs was raised in an air splint. Kara's eyes fluttered open.

"Hey, Nic," she said. "Sorry about the shoes."

Nicola started to cry and rushed to the side of the bed. "Kara, I don't even know how to hug you right now."

"It's probably best if you don't—I don't know where half these tubes go. You can go hold that hand." She glanced at her right hand, then noticed the drip needle going into the back of it. "Nope," she laughed groggily. "That's no good, too."

"You're okay, Kara. I'm so glad you're alive. I wish I'd never let you go out for those stupid shoes."

"She's dead," Kara said. "I watched Hauser die, Nic. It was the worst thing. Every time I close my eyes I see her face, I see the blood just shooting everywhere, and then it just like stopped, like slowly. And then Amber . . ."

"Wait," Nicola said, and froze. "She wasn't alone in the car?"

"No way, José," Kara said. "Amber was with her—they were laughing and looking at something on Courtney's phone and they drove right into me. They didn't even see me; they were speeding up."

Nicola could tell that Kara was pretty high and wasn't sure if she was making it up.

"I read on TMZ that Courtney was alone in the car."

"No," Kara said emphatically. "Amber was in the passenger seat.

She told me to keep my mouth shut and then she got her bag out of the car and she took off on foot. She was bleeding."

Nicola shook her head. She couldn't believe what she was hearing.

"She just left you there?"

"Yeah, she didn't call 911, she was just yelling at me and shit, and I was just trying to not black out because I thought if I did I would be dead, you know; they say you should fight it, so I tried, but then I woke up here."

"At least you woke up." Nicola leaned over and kissed Kara on the cheek. "You're going to be fine. We'll have you home in a few days."

"My folks want me to go to their place."

Nicola nodded. "Your room will be there when you're ready to come back."

A tear slipped out of the corner of Kara's eye.

"You look amazing," she said. "I wasn't sure about that Balmain dress on you, but I had a hunch it would be dynamite."

"You should see Seamus, he looks insanely good."

"Did he go to the awards?"

"No, we had just gotten into the limo when your dad called. We waited for you as long as we could. Kara, we didn't know. Seamus is outside talking to your folks."

Kara smiled. "That's gonna make my little sister so jealous. She's driving from San Diego to see me. Don't leave till she gets to meet him."

"We aren't going anywhere."

There was a knock at the door.

"Come in," Kara called.

Gaynor swanned into the room in a short white fur coat, white leather pants, and a too-large strawberry-colored felt hat, its brim adorned with crystals.

"You look like a nurse in a brothel," Kara croaked.

"You're well enough to be a smartass? Good. We need to work."

"What the hell are you talking about?" Nicola said.

Gaynor pointed an immaculate, bloodred claw at Kara.

"This is our client. She has been in an accident. The news is all over every channel. They broke the news during the Oscars—they talked about it when Seamus didn't show up—so eighty million people around the world heard about this. We need to craft our response."

"Gaynor, someone is dead, and Kara needs to rest."

But Gaynor had her eyes fixed on Kara's.

"You have to grab fame when it happens," she said. "I've been on the phone with Parents Against Distracted Driving; they want you as a spokesperson. And the NAACP thinks that this attention will be enough to launch a campaign against racist assholes like Meredith Cox. Jail isn't going to be fun for her."

"You've been making *deals*?" Nicola said, unable to hide her disgust.

"Watch and learn, Nicolita," Gaynor said, fanning her hands at Nicola as if she were a skunk.

"Kara, you don't have to do this," Nicola said.

"I'll do it," she said. "Do either of you have any makeup for African skin?"

"No makeup," Gaynor barked. "Not this time." She paused. "Actually, I'm changing my mind." She opened her white Givenchy leather purse, pulled out an eyeliner pencil, and deftly, using both hands, applied heavy smudges along the insides of Kara's lower lids.

"In case you cry," Gaynor said. "This will look better."

Nicola started to feel sick at what she was witnessing.

"I'm sorry, you two, but I'm struggling with the fact that even though Courtney was a pretty horrible human being, we're going to use her death to relaunch Kara."

"We're not just relaunching Kara, we're going to announce something that I've been working on for the past three months."

Gaynor looked incongruously happy. Nicola felt like she was losing her mind.

"Crystal and I are going to merge our companies into a boutique super-agency, and we're going to do management, press, and development. We will be the leading social media development platform in the world."

Nicola walked over and fake-punched Gaynor in the arm. "You

could have told me," she said. "I thought we were going down the tubes."

"We almost did. Meredith Cox nearly wiped us out. But me and Crystal, we've survived worse, and we can work less if we combine. I've been on the phone all day finalizing everything. I had planned to tell you all tonight after the awards."

"So when is the TV crew coming?" Nicola asked.

"They're outside."

"With Seamus?" Nicola panicked.

"He's charming the pants off them, of course. Don't worry."

"Okay," Kara said, her voice strong. "But I want to say a couple things."

"You're gonna keep it short and sweet," Gaynor said.

"Before you bring them in," Nicola said, "there's something you should know."

Gaynor turned toward her and made the face that Nicola recognized as Gaynor thinking she was raising her eyebrow, something the Botox made impossible.

"Courtney wasn't alone in the car," Kara said.

Gaynor's eyebrows actually moved. "You're kidding me?"

"Amber was with her," Nicola said. "She left the scene of the accident; she grabbed her purse and she took off."

"I bet it wasn't her purse," Gaynor said. "It was an awards show day. I bet it was their stash that they were going to sell at all the parties. No wonder she left."

"She said she was high," Kara said.

"Wait, that disgusting creature *talked* to you?" Gaynor spat. "*Madre mía*, I'm actually surprised. I thought those days had vanished forever."

"She yelled at me, she told me to keep my mouth shut, and then she just ran away. Some guy filmed it, I don't know if he filmed her."

"Have you told the police?"

Kara shook her head. "Nicola was the first person I told."

"And you didn't call me?"

"You walked in the door just after she told me."

"Oh, good." Gaynor actually smiled. "That's a crime, you know, leaving the scene of an accident."

"What should I do?"

"Have Billy call Harrison. We need her arrested before this press conference goes live. Have him call TMZ to see if anyone is shopping footage."

"I thought I was just giving a statement," Kara protested. "Now it's a full press conference?"

"Please listen to your manager, Jones," Gaynor said, fluffing the pillows around her head. "Do you want me to try to work on your 'fro? It's been years, but back in my day, I could add at least six inches to any sister's height."

Kara laughed. "You've been holding out on me, mama."

"If only you knew," Gaynor said, pulling a comb from her purse and beginning to tease Kara's hair into a cloud.

✳ ✳ ✳

Nicola called a car when the news crew went into Kara's room. She had to get Seamus out of the building before the rest of the media heard he was here. They sat quietly, holding hands, on the drive across West Hollywood. When they finally stepped back into the mess of her living room, she burst into tears.

Seamus held her quietly till the tears subsided, then he sat on her on the couch, made her a whiskey ginger, and tidied up the clothing that was strewn about the living and dining rooms, hanging everything back on the rolling rack.

"Put the TV on," he said, handing her the remote.

"Don't tell me you don't know how to work the remote," she smiled.

"They're all different," he protested.

She snatched the remote from him and turned the TV on.

The awards were on. Nicola looked at the time. They must be about to end. She lowered the volume and patted the sofa next to her.

"Get over here and kiss me before Billy turns up."

Seamus, still in his suit, bounded over to her and kissed her gently on the tip of the nose and between her eyebrows.

"Hold that thought. I need to make meself a drink, too." He bounced back to the kitchen just as a knock sounded at the door and Billy let himself in, with Bluey right behind him, both of them wearing black tuxes.

"You look stunning," he said. "Is the funeral tonight? We're all dressed for it."

"Billy, not yet," Nicola said, waving at both of them. She was too tired to get up.

"We'd love a drink," Bluey called out to Seamus, then plopped on the couch opposite Nicola.

"You okay, love?" he asked.

"Yeah, I wasn't in a car accident today," she said. "You?"

"Well, it was supposed to be a big day for all of us, with the new agency and everything."

"Oh, you already know about that?" Nicola asked.

"Seamus, didn't you tell her?"

"Not yet, mate; that's your news."

Nicola felt herself getting exasperated. Bluey saw it and raised his hand.

"Guess who's managing old Seamus these days?"

"What?" Nicola smiled.

Bluey nodded, and Seamus came out of the kitchen with three drinks in his hands. He passed one to each of the boys and kept one for himself.

"Cheers to my new team," he said, raising his glass.

"Hang on," Nicola said. "Billy, what's going on?"

"You're looking at your new Director of Queer PR," he smiled. "Or whatever the final title is. I'm going to be handling the comings-out of stars, and then managing their socials and sponsorships. It's lucrative AF."

"This is nuts," Nicola said. "I don't know what to say."

"Just don't cry again," Seamus said, sitting beside her and pulling her head onto his shoulder.

Billy's phone dinged. He looked at it, a smile spreading across his face.

"You guys, it's Harrison. They just arrested Amber at her house. She was unconscious on her couch, with a bag containing a ton of drugs beside her. He's confident they'll be able to DNA match her with blood on the passenger console and door. She's going to jail. After the hospital."

"Maybe she can share a cell with Meredith," Seamus laughed.

"Hey, you guys," Bluey interrupted, pointing at the TV.

Nicola fumbled for the remote, turning the volume way up.

"An Oscar tragedy as a teen superstar dies in a horror car crash," said the newscaster, before launching into a lurid description of the accident that killed "troubled former child star Courtney Hauser." The news then cut to a live press conference with the survivor of the car crash, "star of Amber Bank's reality show Kara Jones."

The image of Kara in her hospital bed filled the screen. A reporter held a microphone in front of her.

"Kara, we're live around the world right now, and we want you to tell the fans how you're doing."

"I'm hurtin'," Kara said. "I got some broken bones and some cracked bones, but I'm gonna . . ." She paused, taking a deep, shuddering breath. "I'm gonna be all right, my body's gonna heal."

She began to cry. Her lip trembled and then a fat tear ran down her cheek, leaving a charcoal line across her skin.

"But I don't know," she sobbed. "I don't know how I'm ever gonna forget what I saw, it was so awful, and . . . and . . . I don't want to talk about it, I'm sorry."

"That's okay, Kara," said the interviewer. "Take your time."

"It's just so stupid," Kara said. "She was texting, she was texting and driving, and she just ran straight into me, she didn't even see me before they hit me. I just want to say, everybody watching this, please, I used to do it, too, but please, just stop texting and driving." She broke down, crying for real. The camera cut to the interviewer, who made a sad face at the camera.

"I'm sorry, everybody," Kara continued. "I know we all gotta be on the socials all the time, and you know, I'm just as bad as everyone, but never again. I watched Courtney die, I watched that beautiful young woman die, because she was on her phone. I just want you all to promise me, promise your folks, your friends, that your phone, it stays in your damn pocket or your purse if you're driving. Please."

She broke down again.

"Miss Jones," the interviewer said. "Did you just say before *they* hit you? Wasn't Miss Hauser in the car alone?" Nicola saw the setup a mile off.

"Oh no, nuh-uh," Kara said. "Amber was in the car, too. Amber Bank, she was in the car. I don't know what happened, she didn't help—she left—I blacked out. I hope she's okay."

"Well, thank you, Miss Jones, we wish you a speedy recovery. And now we return to the Oscars on this tragic day. We have full coverage of the winners, the losers, and the best . . . *and worst* . . . fashions from the red carpet."

Nicola turned the volume back down.

"She did it," Billy said. "She really did it. That was a star turn."

Nicola looked at her phone. Gaynor had texted her.

"Apparently so," she said. "Gaynor just texted me that she has signed a deal with the company behind Amber's show to do Kara's own show that tracks her recovery and the launching of her new anti–text and drive charity initiative."

"When do they start shooting that?" Seamus asked.

"Cameras are on their way now. Let's face it. Amber's show just canceled itself. There's an entire crew looking for a job."

"Oh . . . ," Seamus said, sitting down.

"Why are you upset?"

"Well, that means they'll be filming here, right? I won't be able to be around you."

"Oh no, I just texted Gaynor that I wouldn't have a show film at my apartment. They can rent something for her when she gets out of the hospital."

"Oh, cool. Listen, you looking for a roommate? I have great references." Seamus jerked a thumb at Bluey and Billy. "These guys loved living with me—right, guys?"

"Yeah, it's all right, but it's hard to get him to wear pants."

"I already know that," Nicola smiled. "It's one of the things I love about him."

CHAPTER 40

NICOLA FIXED SEAMUS'S BOW TIE for the fourth time.

"How'd you learn to tie one of these things, anyway?" he said, kissing the top of her head.

"There's a YouTube for everything, O'Riordan."

"Aye, that there is, lass, that there is."

"Are you ready to go out there?" She glanced out the window, to the rolling cliffs of Robert Flanger's Malibu colony lawn, a lawn that ended at the Pacific.

"Nearly," Seamus said, pulling her to him. "I just need my girl right now."

She relaxed into his hug. "What's gotten into you? You got wedding jitters?"

"No, Nico. Somewhere out there, that was our first date, a year ago."

"You didn't want to jump off that boat, did you?"

"Nope, I was terrified."

"So why did you do it?"

"I wanted the kiss."

"I would have kissed you regardless."

"Yeah, but you would have thought I was a chicken."

"You *are* a chicken."

"Not when you're holding my hand, Wallace. When you're holding my hand, I'm good to do anything."

She wriggled out of the hug and took his hand.

"Then let's get this wedding started."

She pulled him to the door and out onto the sun-drenched balcony of Flanger's mid-century beachside "shack," as the director called it. At the far edge of the lawn, she saw the small half circle of white wooden chairs. She saw her mother and her brother talking to Harrison the cop and Kara, her arm in a bejeweled sling. She spied Gaynor in what appeared to be a satin cape, talking to Alicia, resplendent in a Huerta Squared burgundy sheath dress, and the twins, who'd designed it, were next to her with Bette. Bette was teaching karate to Patrick while Sylvester filmed them. Crystal was regaling Kara's parents with a story, but Nicola couldn't even dare to imagine what it could be. Flanger, his butler, and a few men who Nicola had met but whose names she'd forgotten milled around Christine, formerly of *Spyglass*, now making their new company, Cinco Reinas Management, run smoothly. The small crowd turned and applauded as they caught sight of her and Seamus.

They walked hand in hand up to Flanger, who kissed them both on each cheek, then sent them down the aisle.

"Nicola Wallace, you look so beautiful," her mom said, rushing to her and giving her a hug. Her brother, Robert, came up and slugged Seamus in the arm.

"So you're doing the ceremony?" he said.

"Yessir," Seamus beamed. "I got me diploma or whatever you call it. I'm a legal marrying machine. Why? You got a girl in mind?"

"Did you tell them, Biscuit? Nicola, did Robert tell you about his new girlfriend?"

"Mom!" Robert yelled, cutting her off.

"Sorry, Nic, I'll tell you everything later."

"Here, you guys. Billy wants you two to sit in the front row with me."

Seamus walked up to Gaynor and hugged her while Nicola moved her mom and brother to the three seats in the front row. Gaynor and her crew filled in the second row.

Seamus stood underneath an arbor dripping with wisteria, the deep silver-blue of the Pacific behind him. The noon sun was overhead, and the day was starting to gain some heat.

Nicola took out her phone and snapped photos of Seamus as he surveyed the house, waiting for a sign that Billy and Bluey were ready. He was so goddamn handsome sometimes she couldn't stand it.

"Mr. Flanger, gentlemen," he bellowed. "If you could take your seats, I have a wedding to perform."

The men sat down. Seamus took out his phone and sent a quick text to Bluey. He stared at his phone for a second, then smiled and slid it into his suit pocket.

"Will everyone please stand?" Seamus began, opening his hands like a preacher. Nicola felt her heart bursting with pride.

"Nicola, he's so handsome," her mother whispered into her ear.

"Yes, Mom, I know," she whispered back.

"May I introduce you to our grooms?" Seamus nodded, and everyone turned to see Billy and Bluey step out of the shadows by the house, and, hand in hand, they began to walk.

Nicola started crying immediately, and Gaynor passed a velvet pocket square into her hands. Gaynor wouldn't need it; she had her tear ducts Botoxed so that she wouldn't "look like *basura*" at the wedding.

Billy and Bluey were whispering to each other the whole time they walked, laughing quietly and beaming with happiness. As they reached the circle of their friends, Flanger started applauding wildly, and everyone followed suit. They kept walking until they were standing in front of Seamus.

"We are here today because my oldest friend has fallen in love with one of my newest friends," Seamus began, his voice already throaty. "I'm gonna make this quick, so please, take your seats, and I'll get on with it."

"So far so good," Bluey said, cuffing Seamus with the back of his hand. Everyone sat down.

"I don't get to talk honestly very often, or speak in public saying my own words, so this is a bit weird for me," Seamus said. "But I'd like to share with you how much I love this dirty Aussie you see before you. Never Donald, always Bluey. In the years that I've known this guy, he has taught me daily how to protect, how to be decent, and how to love. It wasn't until I lost sight of him and his kindness that I learned how truly, deeply I depended on his love.

"When I started falling in love with my girlfriend, I had Bluey check out her friends. I know that doesn't sound great, and hearing it come out of my own mouth, I think I sound like a wanker. But that's a different story, innit? This story involves how I sent Bluey to meet with Nicola's best friend, Billy. From their first meeting at the Montage—which I believe was technically their first kiss, right, lads?"

They both blushed and nodded.

"—to their subsequent, unexpected relationship, I've been by Bluey's side every step of the way. At first I was protective. I couldn't believe that this newcomer, this crazy Hollywood kid, could be the right person for the most important person in my life."

"I'm from Ohio," Billy laughed.

"Well, whatever, I won't hold that against you."

"Hey, watch it," Mauve called out, making everyone laugh. She squeezed Nicola's hand.

"It makes me very happy to tell you that I was wrong. Billy is everything I could want for my friend: he's loyal, he's honest, and he's kind. It has been one of the most beautiful things I've ever witnessed, watching these two fall in love, and then, in the hallmark of any good relationship"—he winked at Nicola—"they've become an instant old couple. They went from dating to sweatpants and Netflix in the space of a week."

"Like you're any better," Bluey laughed.

"I never said I was. So, instead of me talking any more, and because it's starting to get hot, I'm going to go for it.

"Bluey, my best friend, would you like to be married to Billy here?"

Bluey nodded. "Yes, mate. I would. I really would."

"And Billy, are you sure you want to marry this salty old bastard?"

"More than you'll ever know."

"Well, that settles it. Mauve, the rings, please."

Nicola was surprised. She didn't know they'd involved her mom.

Mauve stood up and held out her hand, and as soon as Billy saw the two gold rings sparkling in the sun, he trembled, fighting back tears. Bluey leaned forward and kissed Mauve on the cheek, taking both rings. He looked at them and handed the larger one to Billy.

"Billy," he began, his accent thick and throaty. "Everyone at home warned me that I'd never meet a single decent person in Hollywood, and until I met you, I believed them. Please, do me the honor of accepting this ring as a symbol that you are mine, to protect, to love, and to love some more, for the rest of my days."

He slid the ring onto Billy's finger. Trembling, Billy held the other ring between his fingers and took Bluey's hand.

"I was an idiot until I met you," he said. "From the minute I fell for you, you got my compass back on track. Your love showed me that I'm worth more than anyone's opinion of me, you expanded my family, and I love you so much. I can't believe you're mine."

He slid the ring onto Bluey's finger.

"Well, me lads, you two are married. We've averted a deportation! Kiss each other, for fook's sake."

They kissed, and Seamus looked past them at Nicola. He pointed at the boys, then at her, then at himself and nodded.

"I saw that," Mauve said, nudging her daughter.

✳ ✳ ✳

The wedding photos went on forever, with Kara, Alicia, Bette, Crystal, and Gaynor taking full advantage of the opportunity to get new headshots taken. Seamus whispered to Nicola that he wanted to go for a walk.

He took her hand and led her away from the wedding party. They walked across the emerald lawn until they were stopped by ragged cliffs that dropped down to the small beach that Flanger called "semi-private" since he'd bulldozed the only public path in.

"Are you taking me to the beach? Because these shoes are not exactly mine."

"No," Seamus said, encircling her in his arms. "Look out there," he said, pointing up the coast. "See the sun reflecting off that kelp forest? I figure that's pretty much where we were moored on our first date."

Nicola gave him a funny look. "You're acting weird today."

"It's a wedding. I'm allowed to be mushy, aren't I?"

She nodded.

"Nico, I want to thank you for giving me a second chance," he said. "You mean the world to me, and I want to spend the rest of my life trying my best to be worthy of you."

"Why? What have you done?" she said cheekily.

"Stop it; I haven't done anything. But I want to see if you'd *like* to do something."

Nicola's stomach froze uncomfortably. Was he going to propose?

"You're scaring me, Seamus."

"I'm not proposing to you," he said. "Relax. Not yet."

"You know me too well," she laughed.

"That's my goal. But I have something else, and I want to see what you think."

"Okay, go."

"So, Bluey's been shifting all my business away from my old team, right? And you're not going to believe this, but I found out how much money I have in the bank."

"That's not exactly where I thought this was going."

"I know, but Nico, it's stupid, there's money in accounts all over the world; Bluey's been consolidating it. There are hundreds of millions of dollars."

"That just makes me feel weird."

"Me too! But I got to thinking . . . that's enough money, right? That's enough for anyone, several times over."

"It surely is."

"So I talked to your mum," he said. "She doesn't want to leave Dayton, and I understand that. And she likes the hotel business. So I told Bluey to buy the hotel for her. We're gonna fix it up and she's gonna run it with Biscuit."

"Seamus, what are you doing?"

"I'm telling you my plan, which is to do everything I can to make you worry less."

"Okay." Nic felt tears sting her eyes. "What next?"

"Since they gave Star Wars to Mason, I just have to close out this *Parallax* shoot, and then I have a movie every summer for three years. I don't have to rush into another blockbuster just because it's there."

"That's not exactly an awful career; it's what you've done."

"Exactly. It's time to reconfigure that aspect. But that's Bluey's hassle. Not yours."

"So what's *my* hassle?"

"I want you to run away with me. I want a vacation. You need a vacation. I have a month off until they need me back in Mexico. Let's go."

Nicola stood there, unsure of what to say. "Seamus, I'm a partner in the new agency."

"I know."

"So I can't just run away right now," she said. "Kara's show is premiering next week, Bette's Marvel movie is about to announce, and you have a movie coming out at the end of summer, and . . . wait, you really bought a hotel for my mother?!"

"That's not all I bought." Seamus pulled her close and pointed to the ocean. A familiar white yacht was headed their way.

"Recognize her?" he asked.

"Is that the *Spicy Tuna*?"

"Aye, lass. It is. And she's ours now. And I've cleared it with Gaynor. In a week, she'll be in Hawaii, and so will we. It's gonna be a few weeks of just us."

Nicola didn't know what to say. "Whatever happened to, I don't know, a weekend in Palm Springs? I feel like I'm being kidnapped," she said, sighing. "*Again.*"

"You're not," he laughed. "I just want to get you away from this town so we can be ourselves, so we can have some sort of normalcy and be together. I'm asking."

"Buying a boat and cruising around Hawaii isn't normalcy."

"It's the closest I can get. So how's about it?"

Nicola looked out over the small gathering of her friends, still taking photos, drinking champagne, and laughing. Billy caught her gaze and walked their way, snatching a bunch of flowers from the table next to the wedding cake.

"Did you ask her?" he asked as he drew near.

"Yeah," Seamus said, crestfallen.

"I told you she'd say no," Billy said.

"I didn't say no," Nicola said, and Billy smiled. Without warning, he tossed the bunch of flowers at Nicola, and she caught them.

"Good catch, sis," he said, wrapping his arms around both of them. "Here's to not saying no to good things. Seamus, she caught the bouquet."

"She'll probably use it as a weapon!"

Nicola smacked Seamus on the head with the flowers, then stood on her tiptoes and kissed him on the lips.

"So," she said softly, "when do we leave?"

acknowledgments

We have been floored by the kind, generous support that surrounded us after *Blind Item* came out. Writing this sequel was made much easier by the love and kindness shown to us by so many wonderful people. We'd like to thank them here.

Firstly, our love and respect go to our publisher, boss, editor, and friend, Erin Stein. Her tireless passion and spot-on guidance for this project helped us infinitely.

There are no words to express just how awesome Lindsey Kelk has been to us and to this project, which she has guided and championed every step of the way. She really is our magical unicorn. Read her books. They're what you need.

We've been so grateful for the hard work done by our little team at Imprint and Macmillan—Molly Ellis, Ashley Woodfolk, Nicole Otto, Natalie Sousa, Mariel Dawson, Amanda Mustafic—*muchas gracias*.

We love our fabulous street team—Chad Schubert, Alex Amela, Ben Russo—you guys made us look so good, all the time.

We also love our secret squirrel team of friends in high and low places, helping us to get the word out about our books: Beth Sobol, Matt Sullivan, Terri White, Brandi Glanville, Madeleine Davies, Jenny McCarthy, Cynthia Wang, Perez Hilton, Dan Wakeford, Kristin Cavallari, Matthew McLaughlin. Thank you all, so much. Mai tais on us, when we next meet.

We want to thank each other. It's been nearly a decade since we hatched the plan for this story. We still can't believe we did it.

Lastly, we really want to thank everyone who read this pair of silly, scandalous books. We worked real hard to make you laugh and hopefully cry. Thanks for your time, your messages, and your support. Wait till you see what's coming up next.

Kevin Dickson:

Kevin would like to thank:

Lindsey Kelk, again. She upped the stakes this year, adding heaping helpings of otters, male strippers, drunken nights, astute advice (book and personal), and so much hilarity. Having a shared deadline on our latest books was super fun, and excessively procrastinational. Cheers, Kelk. And cheers some more.

Massive props to my righthand man, Steve Gidlow, for everything from photography to design to listening to my cranky ramblings about knotty plot points.

My mum, Vonnie Dickson, is so awesome. She dealt with another first draft being written at her kitchen table in North Avoca, plying me with stories, laughs, and our favorite red wine. I already started my next book at that table. As a proud Aussie, I love it that these crazy American stories all have their roots in the house where I grew up.

We were so lucky to have wonderful guides to Tijuana and Valle de Guadalupe—Edith Sanay, Karla Sanay, and Kat Sanay—*muchas, muchas gracias.* Thank you for showing us your beautiful world. I hope we did it justice. Same goes for our lovely Malibu hosts, Charlie Datin and Aaron Melendres; thanks for sharing the secrets of your beachside paradise.

A massive thank-you, once again, goes to the First Draft Club—Emily Thompson, Heather Taylor, Skye Pyman, Christine Beidel, Kristina Knight, Eric Williams, that Kelk woman again—your feedback was truly invaluable and so much appreciated. You guys helped shape *Guilty Pleasure* into the behemoth it is today.

Thanks to Giselle and Theron Trowbridge for an astonishing (yet normal for them) amount of generosity, love, encouragement, and cocktails. Thanks to Liz Tooley for on-call pep talks, hugs, and advice when things got craziest, and to my American mom Marta Knight for her endless supply of encouragement and love.

Every page in this book was written with my dogs Jack and Tuna either at my side or inside my shirt. Jack will be fifteen before this book hits the stands, and I hope that I get to write many more books with them both keeping me company.

I'm deeply indebted to the bands that soundtracked the writing of this book and gave me the headspace to let my brain run free—White Stripes, Siouxsie and the Banshees, the Breeders, Margo Price, X, Fuzz, the Resonars, Michael Nyman, Mazzy Star, Lamps, Leadbelly, Glen Campbell, Mind Meld, REM, and R. Ring—I had you all on repeat for the year of writing that went into this.

And, last but not least, I owe so much to my husband, George Castro. For dragging me out on hikes and smiling patiently until my brain returned to normal after tough days of writing, for spontaneous trips to beautiful places, all those date nights, and the endless laughter and hand-holding. I'm a lucky guy. I love you so much.

Jack Ketsoyan:

I want to start off by saying *Wow!* It's been a whirlwind since *Blind Item* came out. I am so excited for everyone to read *Guilty Pleasure*. I want to THANK all the fans who supported us; without you this would have never happened. Without all your support we would have never made the *Los Angeles Times* bestseller list. A special thanks to everyone who came out to our book signing in LA, and especially to Erika Jayne for hosting the event for us. My EMC BOWERY team: Ben, Pia, Dianne, and Shae, thanks for all your hard work on this book. I love you guys. Alex, thanks for organizing my life; without you I will be lost. Chad, you know how I feel about you—I can write pages but will keep to this for now. Also to all my clients and celebs: Kristin, Kim, Jenny, Joanna, Gretchen, Carmen, Cheryl, Teya, Jean, and Lauren, thanks for your support on getting the word out on the book. To my besties Daniel, Diana, Gio, Jonathan, Joey, Lucky, Mikey, and Nicole, thanks for always being there for me no matter what. Without all of you I would not survive. . . . Oh yes, I did put you guys in alphabetical order, bitches, so no favoritism. Also, a special thanks to the following people: Jeannie, Marigo, Sydney, Ruchel, Jamie, Scott, Michele, Allison, Jordan, Matt, Sammi, Anthony, Dane,

Ashley, Javier, Beth, Silva, Ani, Vartui, Takhui, Madeline, Amanda, Nicole, Taj, Eli, Chad H, JP, Brian, Justin, Kasey, and if I left anyone out, I love you all. Thanks to the amazing team at Imprint, especially Erin. Last but not least, I want to acknowledge my amazing family. My niece, Mariam, thanks for inspiring me everyday. I love you so much and you will always be my little princess. Zaven, my nephew, you teach me something new every day. I love you. My brother, Sam, thanks for keeping me in check and always having my back. Finally, Mom, I love you so much and thanks for accepting me for who I am.

KEVIN DICKSON is an author, musician, and animal lover who resides with his husband and Chihuahuas on the fringes of Los Angeles. A former journalist, Kevin spent most of this century in the tabloid trenches, dealing with the darker, more desperate side of fame. After leaving that world he set to work capturing it in the novels *Blind Item* and *Guilty Pleasure*, while touring and recording with his band, the Chew Toys. He is currently working on several new books and plotting new music. Kevin is sporadically available for a chat on his website, kevinjamesdickson.com, but is more often found hiking or watching the river otters at the Los Angeles Zoo. Those playful mammals are both entertaining and a reliable cure for writer's block. Their help on this novel was greatly appreciated.

JACK KETSOYAN is widely known as one of LA's most sought-after publicists and has earned his place as an elite businessman in the entertainment industry. With over ten years of experience, he has worked with some of the largest agencies, including Huvane Baum Halls and PMK-HBH, and molded the careers of many A-list celebrities such as Helen Mirren, Paris Hilton, Rachel Weisz, the Pussycat Dolls, and Erika Jayne, among others. After gaining a long list of loyal clients, Jack opened his own boutique agency called EMC BOWERY, where he focuses on building careers and crisis management. Jack cowrote the *LA Times* bestseller *Blind Item* with veteran journalist Kevin Dickson. *Guilty Pleasure* is its sequel. Currently, Jack continues to expand his firm EMC BOWERY, spends time with clients, and creates content for his novels.